Close Quarters

"Where are we?" Trinity's whisper was strained, and her cheeks burned with the intimacy of their position. She quickly laid both her palms against William's chest as a barrier between their bodies, though it be a frail one.

"Shhh. It is Father's secret cupboard. Stephen and I played here as boys."

She relaxed a bit, but her heart thundered anew as the clomp of heavy boots filtered to them from the distance. Squeezed very tight against Will's long, hard body, Trinity stood still. They were so close she could feel his heartbeat. "I've got to get out of here, Will, please!"

"Quiet." He lifted her up, until her cheek rested against the side of his face. "Not now. They'll search the outer room, too."

For a long time they stood entwined, the sounds growing distant now. She could feel his breath fanning the hair at her temple as he moved his head just enough to nudge hers aside. She felt his lips on the side of her throat, and her body reacted with a thrill she could not control.

His lips brushed hers, moved on, but then as she gasped first in shock, then outrage, he came back to her mouth, and kissed her deeply. Trinity could not move, could not free herself.

How long had she dreamed of such a kiss . . . ?

OTHER BOOKS BY LINDA LADD

A Love
So Splendid

Linda Ladd

A TOPAZ BOOK

TOPAZ
Published by the Penguin Group
Penguin Putnam Inc., 375 Hudson Street,
New York, New York 10014, U.S.A.
Penguin Books Ltd, 27 Wrights Lane,
London W8 5TZ, England
Penguin Books Australia Ltd,
Ringwood, Victoria, Australia
Penguin Books Canada Ltd, 10 Alcorn Avenue,
Toronto, Ontario, Canada M4V 3B2
Penguin Books (N.Z.) Ltd, 182–190 Wairau Road,
Auckland 10, New Zealand

Penguin Books Ltd, Registered Offices:
Harmondsworth, Middlesex, England

First published by Topaz, an imprint of Dutton Signet,
a member of Penguin Putnam Inc.

First Printing, December, 1997
10 9 8 7 6 5 4 3 2 1

 REGISTERED TRADEMARK—MARCA REGISTRADA

Printed in the United States of America

Prologue

Palmetto Point Plantation
1764

With his elegant, silver-buckled shoes dangling well above the plush crimson and navy blue Chinese carpet, Lord William Remington sat in the massive depths of a burgundy-colored leather wing chair. Spine stiff, hands folded respectfully in the fashion required by his exceedingly proper, disciplined father, he waited as patiently as any active young boy could.

It was, however, an immense personal struggle not to squirm forward so that he could catch a glimpse of his friends through the open French doors just behind the desk where his father sat writing with a quill pen. The whisper of a summer breeze invaded the curtains, billowing the thin panels of soft white lawn. The air smelled good, laden with a mingling of perfumes—the cloying sweetness from the pink blossoms on the spreading mimosa tree that shaded the pillared gallery, the spicy aroma of scarlet geraniums in the pots outside the door and the purple bougainvillea that entwined the marble stairs, and now and then, and most fragrant of all, a faint whiff of yellow tea roses.

Far across the lawn where a towering row of ancient magnolia trees formed a natural barrier between the grassy lawn and the cobbled stableyard, William could hear his little brother yelling. Stephen's cry was excited, and William squirmed restlessly, craning his neck to peer past his father's broad shoulder.

All the boys who'd come in their parents' carriages to attend William's wedding were out in the yard with Stephen. Probably planning strategies for tonight's acorn battle. They'd be choosing a new captain of the guard about now, he figured, since he was no longer available to lead them. Maybe they'd chosen Stephen, maybe that's why he'd given that glad shout. Frowning, mad as fire, William balled up his fists. It wasn't fair! He was the oldest, after all, and yesterday they'd voted him as the best one for leader.

Twisting impatiently in the confines of the big chair, he gritted his teeth until he felt a sharp pain in his temple. Why'd he have to be the one inside sitting so still? Listening forever as his father droned on about duty and honor? Sometimes he wished he hadn't been the firstborn male. It was fine, of course, that he'd be the Duke of Thorpe someday when he grew up, but sometimes he wished Stephen had been the eldest. His brother was barely three years younger than he, and Stephen was never called upon to closet himself with their father, or worry about getting some rich, suitable heiress for a bride.

The truth was William didn't care whether he ended up the duke or not, and he didn't even know what a member of Parliament did. He wanted to be a soldier! With a long musket that had a glossy, oil-polished stock of carved wood and a sharp bayonet affixed at the end. Or even more exciting, he could be a blood-crazed pirate like the infamous Blackbeard Teach, who'd sailed the seas and plundered ships in William's grandfather's time. Back then, the planters around Charleston had pooled their gold and put a price on his head. And they'd got it, too, cut it off and put it up on a pole to warn off other pirates. But William'd be too good a pirate to get executed.

But now, here he sat as if he were already a prisoner, bored and uncomfortable in the grandest crimson frock coat he'd ever owned, and a white neckcloth edged with fine Nottingham lace, waiting and waiting so he could repeat the dumb wedding vows. It didn't seem fair, not at all, that not one of his other friends had to be a husband so young! He'd just turned eleven, hadn't he, was still a lad, not even sent off to school yet? But worst of all was that his father was making him marry up with Geoffrey Kingston's little cousin, Trinity. And she was just four years old!

He sniffed at the idea, pure disgust puckering his mouth. Trinity Kingston acted like a spoiled little baby, wailing and blubbering and pestering him and Geoffrey until they had to sneak off and hide so she couldn't find them. Yesterday the brat even grabbed his wooden sword and stabbed him in the leg. What kind of wife was she going to grow up to be?

Outside, a loud yell drifted from the magnolias. Geoffrey, this time. William braced his wrists and raised himself up an inch or two off the arms of his chair so he could see better. His father didn't pay him any mind; his dark head bent in concentration as he put a few finishing flourishes on the wedding document. The scratching of the quill plume was the only sound as Geoffrey shouted out something about Blackbeard Teach and the way he stuck burning matches in his beard.

William's mind floated away from the boring study, and formed that frightful image. A thrill went through him when he imagined himself grown up with a long scraggly black beard that reached to his knees. He'd set lots of flames in his beard someday, so many that the ladies would swoon and the governor would quake in his fine high-heeled shoes. Maybe he'd even have a peg leg, if he got injured somehow in a battle. Smiling, enthralled with fantasies of derring-do, he sobered instantly at the sound of his father's deeply resonant voice.

"I'll remind you, William, that this day is most momentous, an occasion that will shape your destiny from this moment forward. There's no place for levity. I do trust you'll retain a dignified demeanor throughout the entire ceremony?"

Lord Adrian paused, his piercing eyes fastened upon his son and heir. His stern features softened a bit as he continued. "Your bride is hardly more than a toddler, and you a bit younger than is usual for a husband to pledge his troth. I'm certainly aware of that. I'm afraid, however, I've little choice since I'll be living in England while you and Stephen attend school. 'Tis a wise course of action to get this affair finished and done with, so Eldon Kingston and I can begin the task of consolidating Trinity's future inheritance with your own holdings. Do you have any questions you wish to ask me, son?"

William avoided his father's inquisitive gaze but there was something that had been plaguing him a good deal. "Does Trinity have to tag along with us? I mean, live at our house in London, and all that?"

A rare smile softened Adrian Remington's taciturn face. "No, William. In fact, you'll have little opportunity to see the child again until she reaches the age of sixteen. At that time you'll commence a normal courtship and become acquainted, before a second, more formal wedding is held in Charleston. I daresay our voyages back to the Carolinas will be few and far between until you come of age. Your mother will stay in the colonies for a portion of the year at Trenton Hill, but she'll be at Thorpe Hall in England the rest of the time."

"I understand, sir." Inside, William thanked the saints that Trinity wasn't going with them. The truth was that William couldn't bear the sight of her. She was such a bother.

"Anything else that concerns you, boy? The ceremony itself, perhaps? Do you understand what exactly will be required of you?"

"Yes, sir. I'm ready to do my duty as the future Duke of Thorpe."

"Most commendable, William." Adrian Remington nodded approvingly as he waved the parchment back and forth, allowing the freshly inked notations to dry. "This union will nearly double our land holdings here in the colonies, and since Trinity's the only child, she'll own this great plantation house and the thousands of acres of rice and indigo harvested annually here at Palmetto Point."

William nodded, smiled brightly, as if any of that actually concerned him, but he really wished everything was over so he could play soldiers with his friends.

"Now, William," his father said, rising, taking a moment to adjust the lace-edged sleeves that foamed from the wide, dark blue, turned-back cuffs of his gray silk brocade frock coat. "I suspect it's time for us to join Trinity and her father in the chapel. Our guests will be waiting. Straighten your stock, son, stand straight and proud, and remember to comport yourself as a gentleman and lord of the British realm. Someday you'll inherit a dukedom and you must never, ever forget your duty to your family and to your King. Do you understand how important you will someday become?"

"Yes, sir."

"Then come along. I daresay dear little Trinity's becoming a tad restless. It'll soon be time for her nap, I understand."

Dear little Trinity was more than restless, she was screaming her head off. William could hear her awful yelling all the way down the corridor. He hazarded a wary glance at his father, alarmed by the muffled din filtering out from the sanctity of the chapel. Adrian's stern mouth had thinned even more, now a stitched line of disapproval. As William well knew, Adrian Remington would never allow one of his children to behave in so shameful a fashion.

As they opened the double doors leading into the long, narrow chapel, they were immediately confronted with the full effect of his bride's eardrum-piercing shrieks. At least fifty pairs of relieved eyes turned to watch them make their way down the center aisle toward the raised altar. His mother was there at the front, holding his baby sister, Adrianna, in her arms. She smiled at him, and made him feel all warm and calm inside. He wished she'd be in England with them all the year through.

His arrival did not lessen Trinity's angry cries or even modify the shrillness of their pitch, and William's green eyes widened in disbelief at the sight of her. She was all dressed up like a pint-sized angel in rows and rows of white ruffles and had on a little lace bonnet that had fallen from her head and hung off one shoulder by its pink ribbons because she was in the middle of throwing the worst hissy fit that William had ever beheld.

Eldon Kingston, the child's unfortunate father—imagine having to be around the awful little girl all the time!—had her by the hand but she would have none of his soothing. Why, she looked like a fighting rooster caught by the feet, the way she was twisting and turning, and falling down on her back and kicking her white slippers at the priest's long black robe.

William considered it the funniest thing he had ever witnessed and wished Geoff and Stephen could watch her roll around and screech like a piglet caught in the handle of a slop bucket. But he dared not betray even the hint of a smile. No one else seemed to think Trinity's behavior was amusing, not in the least. All the guests watched from the pews, openly aghast and mightily concerned. William couldn't fathom why they were so shocked at the spectacle. Everybody in Charleston, and even out in the surrounding plantations, knew Mr. Kingston spoiled his only child rotten and had given the little girl everything she had ever wanted since her mother had succumbed to yellow fever two summers ago. She threw similar tantrums almost daily, did she not? And wherever she happened to be, too.

By the time William and his father reached the foot of the high mahogany altar, Mr. Kingston had managed to get his daughter up off the floor, at least, and had her under his arm, her feet off the ground. She was kicking and flailing her arms, and his round face had turned the color of a ripe cherry, and his loose jowls were flopping all over the place with exertion, but all William could see was how Trinity's curly red hair was flying all around in a big wild tangle, like a drawing he'd seen of Medusa's head with all the snakes writhing on it when Perseus held it up after he'd chopped it off with his sword. That was William's favorite Greek myth.

"There, there, Trinity, dearest, don't take on so. Young Will's here at last. Don't you want to be a good girl and hold his hand? You like the boy, now, don't you? You said you did, after all."

To everyone's surprise, not to mention relief, especially William's, Trinity stopped her struggling, yowling tantrum long enough to raise her freckly face and latch her weird eyes on him. They were the color of gold coins, old ones that were burnished and not as shiny as freshly minted ones, and seemed absolutely enormous in her tiny heart-shaped face, sort of glowing and peculiar against cheeks as flushed as fire and mottled from her hysterics. Then, to his shock, she outstretched her arms in his direction as if she wanted him to hold her.

A surge of hot blood crept up William's neck, making him burn all over and so horribly embarrassing him that he couldn't move. He tried to swallow, had to force it down with a gulping sound that even he could hear. He refused to look directly at her, attempting to remain where he was instead of fleeing back down the aisle, but it was difficult with so many people staring at them.

Boy, was he ever glad his father was taking him off to an English boarding school. At least he wouldn't have to put up with being around Trinity and watching her throw maniacal fits and knowing he was stuck with her as a wife until he died. He wished he were far away somewhere—on the levee that overlooked the sea would be good, searching the ocean swells with a sea captain's brass spyglass for skulls and crossbones.

"Now that's a good girl, dearie." Trinity's father set the wild child on her feet, gingerly, as if any sudden movement might set her off again like a cocked and loaded flintlock. He was crooning now in some strange voice, hopeful and gruff and sort of scared almost. William had heard other grown men resort to that queer tone when coddling recalcitrant children. William had never heard such conciliatory appeasement from his father. He'd have got a caning instead.

The moment Trinity's little slippers clicked down atop the shiny marble floor, she lit out for William like a field mouse fleeing a hungry tabby. William took a step backward, flushing crimson and gazing helplessly at his father as the frizzy-haired tot barreled at him with the energy of a whirling dust devil. No help was to be had and a second later she hurtled herself up against his chest so hard that the impact staggered him backward.

Somewhere in the audience he heard some lady's voice say "oooh" and another woman breathe out "aaah," as if Trinity's jumping on him and nearly knocking him on his back was a real cute thing. William groaned out loud in utter humiliation as the little girl clutched thin arms around his neck in a stranglehold that cut off his breath, then to his horror clamped ruffled pantalet-clad legs around his waist.

Above the heads of all the gawking, whispering onlookers, he caught a glimpse of Stephen and Geoffrey, their faces visible through the diamond-shaped panes of the arched chapel window. They were out there laughing at him, he realized with a rushing wave of shame, and then he got mad, and even more mortified, and tried to unpry the awful little urchin from his torso.

His efforts were in vain; she was stuck as tight as a bolted door, and holding on so hard that she was wrinkling up the smooth silk of his white waistcoat and pulling loose all the neat folds in his neckcloth that he had worked so hard to get just right. She smelled like she'd been eating strawberries all day long, and she was making him look as silly and babyish as she was.

"Quit acting like a ninny, Trin," he whispered close to her ear, making his tone vicious and harsh enough to make her shudder in her beribboned little pumps. "Or else Geoff and I will sell you off to the pirates and you'll never get to see your papa again!"

The threat settled her down quick enough, he thought with smug triumph as he untangled her and got her off him and on the floor again. She grabbed his hand, though, and then he found out why she smelled so fruity. Her fingers were so sticky with syrup that she must've eaten out of the jam pot with her hand!

But at the moment at least she was holding relatively quiet as they listened to the priest mumble lots of Latin words William couldn't understand. Unfortunately, her calm didn't last very long. When she began to balance on one foot and tug on his hand so that he had to hold her up to keep himself from stumbling into the front pew, he gave her a hard pinch on the arm. She yelped shrilly just as the priest got to the end of the marriage ceremony and smiled benignly at the two children before him.

"Now, William and Trinity, I declare the two of you to be joined together as husband and wife, forevermore, under the eyes of these good witnesses and with the sacred blessing of God Almighty."

The ensuing applause and cheers of congratulations were loud and enthusiastic, and fortunately so, because they drowned out poor William's groan of pain as his baby bride sank sharp little white teeth deep into the side of his hand.

Chapter One

"Truly, William, I'm surprised Trinity hasn't come yet to greet you. I suppose she misunderstood when I told her you were arriving from Charleston before the noon hour."

Lord William Remington, peer of the realm and heir to the fourteenth Duke of Thorpe, turned a skeptical glance upon Victoria Ballantine Remington where she sat on a high-backed, gold-and-white-striped silk settee facing the open doors of the rear gallery. He had not laid eyes upon his mother since he had last visited the Carolinas, a journey that had occurred nearly eight years ago, and in far better times, a good four years before the Americans had declared their independence.

With faint surprise, it dawned upon him that he hardly knew Victoria anymore. He'd remembered her as a younger version of herself with the rich chestnut hair he'd inherited from her, not as she was now, an aging woman with wings of gray fanning out from her temples and a fine etching of lines at the corners of her eyes. And he knew even less about Adrianna, his raven-haired little sister who was seated beside their mother.

Little wonder, since his father had insisted that both he and his younger brother, Stephen, obtain their education at English boarding schools. His mother had flatly refused to spend much time in London, and they'd returned to the Carolinas so infrequently that they'd veritably missed Adrianna's entire childhood. He swiveled his regard to Adrianna, a serenely pretty, pleasant young woman who'd had precious little to say to him since he'd arrived earlier that day.

After open hostilities had commenced between British regulars and American rebels, further visits had been forestalled for half a decade due to the fact that Charleston had been held by patriot troops until recently when the English had finally managed to reoccupy the city. Now that the town was filled with enough soldiers to maintain order, William had come home, his safety on the war-ravaged continent relatively assured. Sometimes, however, he couldn't bring himself to believe the Americans' political grievances against King George had deteriorated into such fierce fighting and bloodshed.

Good God, the colonists were Englishmen, after all, shared mutual ancestors, were distant cousins, and in his case bore even closer familial ties than that. He was used to fighting the French, England's nemesis in war, trade, and conquest, but to destroy other Englishmen was a harder task to stomach, be they rebellious or not.

When minutes ticked by without his offer of a suitable response to his mother's lame excuses for Trinity Kingston's deplorable behavior, Victoria fixed him with a disapproving, expectant stare, one elegant eyebrow arched in censure. A look he well remembered from his childhood and which finally spurred him to reply.

"I can't pretend I'm surprised by Trinity's display of ill manners, if that's what you wish to hear," he remarked, not really bothering to hide his dislike for the damned girl. "As I'm sure you'll remember, Mother, the last time I visited here at Palmetto Point, she foolishly forced her mare up the portico staircase like some bloody Mongol horseman."

William dropped into the cushioned depths of a peach and green floral armchair, crossed his legs, and tried without success to disguise a grimace full of distaste. He was thoroughly disgusted at the girl's outlandish lack of propriety, and had been for a long time. True, Trinity had only been twelve or so when she'd shown her recklessness on the stairs, but not so young she shouldn't have known the curved marble steps were slick and treacherous and no place to endanger expensive horseflesh. The image of the way she'd looked then was exceptionally vivid, even now, eight years later. She'd sat astride one of the most beautiful white mares he'd ever seen, her frizzy reddish hair flying all around and her freckled face flushed.

Lord Almighty, what an undisciplined hoyden she'd been! But she'd always had a wicked, troublesome streak, and apparently hadn't learned a blasted thing about being a proper lady. If she had, she wouldn't be out gallivanting around the countryside while he, the next Duke of Thorpe, sat waiting for her. But worst of all, and the most galling part to be sure, was that he'd been married to the little chit then.

William grimaced, clamping his jaw with frustration, as he did every time he thought of the ridiculous marital alliance. Scowling, he tossed back the remainder of his brandy, then looked up sharply when his heretofore silent sister suddenly came alive and raged a quick, impassioned defense against his assessment of Trinity's character.

Surprised, he stared at her. How the hell old was Adrianna, anyway? Seventeen? Eighteen? Her future was another less-than-coveted task facing William on this trip. His father had made all the appropriate decisions; all William had to do was tell her what was expected of her. Until now he had assumed her well trained enough to cause him no unnecessary problems. But as he listened to what she was saying, he wasn't quite so sure.

"I daresay, brother . . ." Adrianna paused dramatically for effect, slanting him a haughty stare before continuing. "That poor Trinity is hardly eager to meet up with the cad who jilted her so heartlessly before the whole of Charleston society, and not so long ago, I might remind you."

A jolt of shock coursed through William that the girl dared criticize him aloud, and in front of their mother. He was in a black enough mood already without having to dress down his sister. He remained calm, deceptively so, lifting one shoulder in a casual, dismissive shrug.

"I had little recourse, sister, as well you should know. Father reneged on the marriage contract when Trinity's father openly declared allegiance to the Continental Congress. Blatant defiance of the Crown is not looked kindly upon by the King, especially from the in-laws of the Duke of Thorpe."

"But you were such a coward about it! Canceling the wedding by courier was an appalling thing to do, even you must realize that. Trinity told me she felt like one of those thoroughbred fillies you and Father are always acquiring, one you didn't want anymore because she'd gone lame or something, and so you cast her off with impunity like you would any other unwanted trinket. Trinity was most indignant, being treated so shabbily by you."

"Adrianna, dear, I believe that's quite enough on this subject." Victoria's reproof, though steely under her soft voice, did little to eradicate his sister's open hostility toward him. Adrianna was not finished voicing her opinion, it seemed.

"Well, really, Mother, 'twas just abominable the way it all happened, seeking an annulment out of the blue in such a way. Thank goodness Trin loathes you so much, William, or she might've been utterly devastated by the awful insult."

William tented his fingers and calmly eyed his little sister over them, annoyed with her, to be sure, but his interest was piqued by her last revelation. "Trinity loathes me?"

"Why, of course she does, and has ever since that last time you visited us when you were so cruel and critical of every little thing she did. Don't you remember how mean you were to her when she showed you how she'd taught Moonbeam to ride up the gallery steps? You compared her to a stableboy and humiliated her in front of her father and everyone there. After that I'm sure she was secretly quite pleased to escape the horrible fate of having you for a husband."

Oh, yes, a horrible fate indeed, William mocked inwardly, resisting a contemptuous laugh. Trinity Kingston would do well indeed if she found another husband who would make her a duchess. Especially now that her family wore the brand of rebel.

Still, Adrianna's outspoken, defiant attitude rankled William, and made him worry that his sister had been exposed to Trinity Kingston's unsavory habits too long for her own good. Or were all American women willful, disobedient harridans?

"You'd be wise, Adrianna, to support the actions of your family and your King instead of pleading the case of known rebel sympathizers."

Adrianna bristled. "Trinity's my dearest friend, and will always be so, despite her father's politics. Besides, no one can prove she's guilty of any crime. The British command has no shred of evidence to support their accusations against her."

"Almighty God," William said, sitting up

straighter and staring at her in dismay. He turned
an incredulous gaze onto their mother. "Do I understand Adrianna? Is she intimating that Trinity's an accused criminal?"

His mother evaded his gaze, suddenly inordinately fascinated with the view outside the open
door. Completely uncharacteristic for her to evade
a subject, she'd always been one to meet obstacles
head-on. He dropped back against the pillows
with sinking heart, already knowing full well that
Trinity was indeed involved in something that
could bring disgrace upon the entire family.

"Well, madame? What pit of mire has Trinity
Kingston dragged our good name through this
time?"

Under the sting of his open sarcasm, his
mother's eyes found his face without the hesitation of the moment before. He was slightly subdued by the forlorn expression in their soft
nutmeg depths, a deep, abiding sadness that startled him. She was disappointed in him, he knew it
as well as if she had said the words out loud. Uncomfortable with that knowledge, he fought the
urge to shift in his chair like a schoolboy who'd
skipped lessons to go fishing.

"As Adrianna mentioned, there have been no
charges proven against Trinity."

"What kind of charges, Mother?" he persisted,
scandalized that a young woman her age was
even under suspicion, though in truth nothing
Trinity did should shock him. Her father had been
a widower for years, had adored his only child,
had spoiled her incessantly and unconscionably

since the day she was born. No wonder she'd grown up feeling free to comport herself in any fashion she desired. Hell, the last time he'd seen her she'd paraded around in male breeches and had looked just as he had described her that day—like a low-born, scrawny stable hand.

Victoria's sigh was a deep, chest-heaving inhalation that intensified the following silence. She took her time smoothing out a wrinkle in her shiny black bombazine skirt. "Cornwallis believes she might be riding courier for the rebel Will Washington. You've heard of him, I'm sure, he's the brother of General George Washington who commands the Continental Army."

William certainly did not need an explanation about the hierarchy of the patriot leaders. He'd heard enough of them throughout the halls of Parliament. He tried to school his incredulity. "Heaven help us, are you telling me she's actually riding with the enemy?"

Anger soon pushed the amazement from William's mind. Distress, annoyance, embarrassment, all came together like wind-driven streams surging into the sea. What could possibly happen next, for God's sake? London was still buzzing about Trinity's father, Eldon Kingston, formerly a wealthy man of class and stature smiled upon by His Majesty, now imprisoned for treasonous acts.

"You're rather nonchalant that you might be harboring a suspected spy in your household," he clipped out curtly.

In a tone pregnant with scorn, his mother stiffened and lifted her chin. "I'll remind you,

William, that we're sitting this very moment in a house that rightfully belongs to Trinity, though the King's soldiers have confiscated it and given it to your father in recompense for the destruction of our own property. And I might add this, so that you won't continue to exhibit such contempt for Trinity, she and Eldon were the first to take pity on Adrianna and me at the beginning of the war when zealots burned Trenton Hill out from under us. Not only did they face patriot censure for harboring us but they protected us from harm."

She paused, her regard set uncompromisingly on his face. "I will show her the same courtesy, whether it meets with your approval or not. Furthermore, I'll inform you in no uncertain terms that I've no use for masked Tory riders who use their loyalty to King George to viciously attack their former friends and neighbors, as happens in these parts nearly every night of late."

"Then I will be equally blunt, Mother." William chose his words with utmost care. "Your remarks could very well be construed as traitorous. Perhaps you should guard your tongue when speaking against allies of the Crown."

His mother did not back down from her convictions. "Eldon Kingston and his family have been friends of my heart since many years before you were born, William. I'm pleased to say it's not a flaw of my character to forget my past associations." She gave him a significant look, the meaning of which he was able to read only too well. "Nor could I, or would I, ever forget my pride in my colonial heritage."

William felt her rebuke with the impact of a balled fist to the stomach, though she had couched the blow quietly, with her usual silken civility. Supremely irritated that he had allowed himself on his first day home to become embroiled in arguments with both his mother and his sister, he pushed himself to his feet and sought out the brandy decanter kept behind a glass door in a cabinet alcove.

Concentrating on pouring the cognac into his snifter, a goodly portion to calm his anger, he decided that—considering the disloyal undercurrents threading through their previous discourse—his father was absolutely inspired to order his wife and daughter back to England where they belonged. He was faintly surprised at himself for thinking such, for it was rare indeed of late for William to agree with his father on any subject. But the way Victoria and Adrianna came across at the moment, it was only a matter of time before they were openly aligned with the Americans.

He shouldn't be so surprised, because, as his mother had openly admitted, she was, after all, Victoria Ballantine Remington, a Charlestonian, and distinctly proud of it. For generations her family had cut a fortune from the Carolina swamps, and William's father had married her strictly for those same financial considerations.

And indeed the Duke of Thorpe had gained much wealth from his American heiress—the immense profits from Ballantine indigo and tobacco had refurbished the ancient walls of their massive ancestral edifice known as Thorpe Hall where it lay nestled in vast deer parks fifty miles north of London, as well as funding the acquisition of the magnificent town house near Hyde Park and a second London abode where William himself kept his residence.

Stepping across the plush gold and navy blue carpet, he paused in the threshold to enjoy the faint breeze. He'd forgotten how damnably hot and humid South Carolina could be in the summertime. In front of him, the grassy lawn spread out into the distance for a good three hundred yards to where the raised levee edged the first watery field of rice. Beyond those crop-filled lakes lay the sea where palmetto palms lined wide sandy beaches.

The view brought back memories of the days when he and Stephen used to come here from Trenton Hill to play. They'd been very little then, and Trinity had followed them around and pestered them relentlessly. Trinity's older cousin, Geoffrey, had been William's best friend for the first decade of their lives, and William still thought of him fondly, though they hadn't seen each other in years. William had heard that Geoffrey, too, had become a rebel, but he hoped to God his old friend would come to his senses and pledge loyalty to the Crown before it was too late.

His relaxed stance revealed nothing to the ladies in the room behind him. But within his stoic calm, he was becoming more and more angry with Trinity, and the longer she made him wait, the more incensed he became. The whole affair was a difficult business at best, and all he wanted was for the farce to be over and done with. And as rapidly and painlessly as possible so he could get back to England and wed Caroline, who was infinitely more suitable as his duchess than Trinity Kingston ever had been.

Bloody Zeus, his father would succumb to apoplexy at the mere hint of Trinity's collusion with the enemy. Under no circumstances could such intelligence get out among his father's cronies in Parliament. His father was openly and outspokenly—despite his Carolinian wife—a staunch anti-American hawk, and had carefully hidden any kinship with Eldon Kingston. If any of his political enemies learned the truth, the newspapers would have a heyday with his credibility.

"There," Adrianna said from where she now stood at the gallery balustrade, after having stalked past William in a huff. "Trin's coming now, just as I told you she would."

Still cradling his glass, William moved to the smooth marble wall and watched three riders leave the distant levee and set out for the house. The road edging the lawn was a straight white strip against the green grass, paved with the crushed oyster shells so prevalent on thoroughfares in and around Charleston.

The last time he had laid eyes on his hellion bride, he'd been standing approximately in the same spot, and he could still remember the astonishment he'd felt when she'd guided her horse unerringly up the precarious marble stairs. He glanced at the graceful winding steps off to his right. If he hadn't been there, hadn't watched her accomplish the feat, he'd declare the tale a fabrication. As the riders reached the flagstones below in a clatter of shod hooves, he wondered if Trinity was still fool enough to do such a thing. Would she now? Brazenly? Just to annoy him?

"Come out here, Mother, Trinity's arrived," Adrianna called inside to Victoria. "Not to see William, of course, but because you bade her to make an appearance."

His sister was becoming more than adept at looking him in the eye while she boldly insulted him, William noted as their mother joined them on the pillared gallery. He caught a faint whiff of the bougainvillea climbing the balcony, mingled with the lemon verbena toilette water that was his mother's favorite perfume.

As she moved up beside him and her wide skirt brushed his pant leg, buried memories awoke and stirred in his mind, resurrected from days long past and nearly forgotten. He looked down at his mother, his affection dimmed considerably by many, many years of separation, and now complicated by conflicting loyalties. Victoria remained unaware of his tender thoughts as she stood, erect and dignified, watching the trio of approaching riders.

William suppressed a sigh and turned to refocus his attention on Trinity, perversely dreading to confront the girl but at the same time curious to see if she had changed from the wild thing she'd been when last they'd met.

Chapter Two

"It seems Trinity's dragged along a couple of admirers," William remarked several minutes later, placing his glass down atop the wall. He braced his palms on the balustrade, observing the military uniforms of the two men—the scarlet jackets and white trousers worn by His Majesty's officers. "A bit surprising, isn't it, that soldiers of the Crown would court a suspected rebel?"

"Actually, they're her guards, I'm afraid," Victoria revealed reluctantly. "The poor child cannot leave the house without one of them at her side. She finds it quite tiresome to be treated in such a way."

Trinity's wild streak was still a mile wide, William thought grimly, his jaw assuming a determined slant. His desire to rid himself of any association with her intensified tenfold. He would waste no time coddling her. He would tell her what he expected her to do, exactly how she must do it, then insist the deed be accomplished with all due haste.

His eyes latched on the slim young woman

below as she expertly reined in her prancing mount. He leaned forward so he could see her better. She sat the magnificent Arabian mare and controlled the sleek, slender-legged animal easily as it sidestepped excitedly along the flagstones. She raised her head suddenly and peered up at those awaiting her on the balcony.

William felt a small ripple course through him as her eyes captured him boldly, completely unintimidated by his presence. He stared back at her, realizing at once that Trinity Kingston was no longer the skinny, pigtailed tomboy he remembered. Now, she was lovely, all tawny and golden—skin, hair, eyes—but it was the recklessness in her gaze that rocked him. There was a challenge there, not difficult at all to read, and he was suddenly fearful that she did mean to spur the Arabian up the steps again. The sensation was so strong, he was half-surprised when she merely glanced away as if to her mind William rated no consideration whatsoever.

Instead she sat in the saddle with the regal bearing of an Egyptian queen being barged down the Nile while her two English jailors leaped to the ground in an unspoken competition to assist her from her mount. As she unhooked her knee and placed both palms atop the shoulders of the man who won that honor, William noted with surprise that Trinity had at least conformed to one convention. She sat the horse as a lady would, upon a sidesaddle.

"Trin's really incredibly beautiful, don't you

agree, William?" his sister taunted in a ha-ha-see-
what-you-gave-up-you-silly-fool voice.

William ground his teeth in annoyance but decided to ignore Adrianna, watching instead the
obviously besotted pair of Englishmen jockey for
Trinity's attention. On the ground now, she curtsied gracefully to first one beaming officer and
then the other, deigning not another glance in
William's direction. As she moved to the stairs,
the two soldiers gave William a respectful salute,
then retreated, leading the horses in the direction
of the stableyard.

Trailing one gloved hand along the marble
sidewall, Trinity held her head high, and he took
a moment to absorb everything about her. She
had changed so much; he could hardly believe
this paragon of maidenly beauty was Trinity
Kingston. She wore a velvet habit, a long skirt
and a short matching jacket, both a warm burnished golden color that matched her eyes. The
bodice was laced tightly as was the current fashion, and revealed enough slender curves to engender a masculine response in William that he
definitely did not want. Could not tolerate. Even
so, he had to remind himself not to stare like
some farm boy eyeballing an empress.

"Forgive me, Victoria." Trinity curtsied to his
mother, then flashed a quick, affectionate smile
at Adrianna. She continued to ignore William.
"We carried a picnic hamper to the beach. 'Twas
so enjoyable a day that we forgot the time."

She was a proud woman, very much so, and
the haughty tilt of her chin was a sure signal that

she allowed no one to look down their nose at her. She was not going to care for the news that William had brought to her, not one bit. As she tugged off her cream-colored leather gloves, she continued to treat him as if he were entirely invisible.

Forced to address her directly to gain a response, he fought down his displeasure and said mildly, "Good afternoon, Trinity."

Trinity turned as if she had no idea he was anywhere within miles of the shady gallery. Her eyes were enormous in her heart-shaped face, and oh, so fine and clear. He had remembered their unusual color and how striking they'd been, but at the moment they glowed warm and deep. The color of honey. Honey flooded by a shaft of bright sunlight. Beautiful indeed, but as she focused her attention solely upon his face, he realized with an unpleasant plummet of spirit that those exquisite eyes held nothing for him but contempt—cold, undisguised, unapologetic.

"Milord." Her chin dipped in the barest acknowledgment possible, then she glanced away.

He wished he could see her hair better. Most of it was pinned neatly in a tight knot at her nape. A flat-crowned straw hat rested atop her head, shading her wind-flushed face and tied beneath her chin with a wide blue velvet ribbon. A knot of blue ribbons trailed gaily down her back and a red rosette was attached to the brim. He wondered if her hair was as red and frizzy as it had been when she was little. But no, it had changed, too, now much more blond, coppery in fact, not anything close to the carroty color he remembered.

"You do recognize me, don't you, Trinity?"

Perverse though it was, he wanted to force her to talk with him. Whoever would have thought that possible?

"Unfortunately, yes, I do," was her less-than-civil answer. She didn't look at him as she spoke but shared her regard with a smug Adrianna.

William stiffened, the realization hitting him full force that this lovely young woman was going to be no more docile and accommodating to his wishes than his sister would be. She was going to be difficult to deal with as she always had been, perhaps more so, since he'd openly rejected her. Be that the case or not, he would just have to force her to cooperate.

"I truly had hoped, Trinity, that you and I might put our past problems behind us and become friends." He smiled encouragingly and *was* encouraged until her unwavering golden gaze nailed him to the wall.

"Perhaps, milord," she murmured quietly, "it is easier for you to bear the distinction of being the man who jilted me before the whole of Charleston than 'tis for me to suffer the humiliation of your dishonorable acts."

Heavy, unnerving silence reigned until Victoria attempted to lessen the tension crackling between her son and the woman he had spurned.

"Let's all retire inside for tea," she suggested with quiet grace. "Maria's made her wonderful scones, and we can all become reacquainted while we partake of refreshment."

William was not so certain that anything, much less tea and biscuits, could ease the strain of distrust and betrayal that smothered the breath out of the family reunion, so cloying it seemed they'd all been covered by some thick, moldy old quilt, but he obediently followed the three ladies inside. He would have to put up with Trinity Kingston somehow, at least until she agreed to his bidding. And she would eventually have to do so. After all, he held immense power back in England, and in America, as well. That, in itself, should give her pause, should it not?

Why the devil did he have to come slinking back to Palmetto Point anyway? Trinity fumed inwardly, absolutely furious now that she'd actually seen him again. Mentally she scourged Lord William of Thorpe in phrases so profane that she'd never dream of uttering a syllable of them aloud. Hiding her agitation, she seated herself gracefully on the silk divan beside Victoria and concentrated on arranging her long velvet skirt around her ankles.

Shielding her feet from others' view was false modesty at best, since she cared not a whit who eyed her ankles, toes, or any other part of her. Out of respect for dear Victoria, however, she would maintain the proper decorum. Victoria wanted so for Trinity to act soft and demure, like a lady of quality should, like Adrianna did so prettily.

Intentionally, steadfastly, she kept her interest averted from the man who had treated her with such vile disrespect but such nonchalance was a hard emotion to affect. She hadn't seen the man in eight years, the last time when he was nineteen; she, twelve; but it was since then that he'd seen fit to embarrass, humiliate, and carve out her heart in front of everyone in South Carolina. No one would ever truly know how much she had suffered when he annulled their marriage.

When she was certain he'd turned to select a chair, she scrutinized his person, using the wide brim of her hat to shield her interest. He didn't seat himself, as it turned out, but remained standing behind the tufted velvet bench on which Adrianna now sat. Erect of bearing and relaxed in manner, his handsome face appeared as impassive as it was impressive. His hands were hidden behind his back now, clasped together, a habit of stance Trinity remembered from his last visit—a quintessential portrait of aristocratic arrogance.

As Victoria leaned forward to pour tea from the ornate silver urn, her every motion elegantly precise, Trinity tugged loose the ribbon fastened beneath her chin. Removing the smart straw bonnet she'd purchased from a millinery shop on Church Street—a style most popular now because, unbeknownst to the redcoats, the blue ribbons and scarlet cockade secretly signaled support for the patriot cause—she smoothed her hair at her temples, then captured a few wayward curls behind her ears.

Though more than aware that his mighty English lordship was contemplating each and every movement she made with his inscrutable, green-as-grass eyes, she couldn't help but consider what he might be thinking about her behind his perfect classical features. At the same time she was quite certain there could be no one walking the earth who thought him as handsome as he thought himself.

After her earlier and immensely self-satisfying renouncement of his character—and to his face, too, she recalled with a secret burst of inner pleasure—he'd said little else, just watched her, closely and silently, but she was finding it a bit difficult to keep up a pretense of ignoring him, of pretending that he wasn't in the least so tall and attractive, certainly not imposing by any means, and not able to outshine anyone and everyone in the room as he'd always been able to do since he was a boy and she had so desperately adored him.

Trinity brought herself up short, barely managing to stop a gasp of dismay. Her thoughts concerning William were so traitorous, so, well, unacceptable, *completely* unacceptable, that she shook her head, overwhelmingly disgusted with herself.

I should do well to remember the day I stood with the seamstress being fitted for my wedding dress, she thought in self-chastisement, a garment that had cost her father more than the new landau he had ordered from London for the wedding. Papa had come into her bedchamber that day, looking shockingly distraught, but that soon had turned to outrage, frightening her when he clutched his heart and collapsed into a chair. His other hand, however, held the true scandal, the coldly worded legal annulment.

If that were not insult enough, the letter had been addressed to Eldon Kingston, signed by the ducal firm of solicitors in London, with not even a mention of Trinity, not her name, not any manner of apology or explanation for such an egregious affront.

Even now, years later, her face burned like a bonfire from the sheer cruelty of the way William Remington had chosen to reject her. All of Charleston had learned within days that her bright future, her good fortune and the honor of becoming the future Duchess of Thorpe had been snatched away, all her dreams destroyed like a castle of sand before a crashing wave. Instantly she had become the object of gossip, ridicule, and, in her eyes the most awful and unacceptable of all, pity.

"Father's most eager for you and Adrianna to return to England," William remarked suddenly, his voice cutting through the gloomy silence. "His Grace has suffered a good bit of abuse from his cronies at his gentlemen's club with his wife and daughter residing on enemy territory."

Victoria paused in the act of presenting to Adrianna one of the small gilt-rimmed white teacups—Trinity's grandmother had received the entire set of china for a wedding present—and eyed her son with visible distaste. "I fear it does

His Grace little credit that he considers his political stature first and foremost over the safety and happiness of his own family members."

Trinity could not hide her pleasure at witnessing Victoria's rebuke of William. To her disappointment, William seemed unaffected.

"I meant no offense, Mother. To the contrary, actually. The truth is that Father's concerned for your welfare. He's begged you for years to make Thorpe Hall your permanent home, and now he's extremely eager for you to do so. He wishes your help in arranging the details of Adrianna's London debut."

"London debut? What London debut?" Adrianna's face had gone quite pale. She didn't bother to hide the extent of her alarm. "Tell me what you mean, William!"

Equally concerned, Trinity returned her attention to William's face. He was wearing a frown now, faint and fleeting, but it was no secret that Adrianna's demanding tone irked him.

"Well, I suppose you'll have to know sooner or later," he admitted, leaning down to pick up his cup and saucer. He stirred a spoonful of sugar into the tea while they all waited impatiently for his explanation. He finally looked up. "His Grace has ordered both of you back to England, and for good this time, I'm afraid. He intends to cut all Remington ties in the colonies now that the Americans are in rebellion. He's also decided that the time has come for Adrianna to become betrothed. He's making inquiries into the most suitable match for her."

"Most suitable match? What about me? Why wasn't I told about this before? And who is he considering, pray tell? Am I not even to be consulted?"

The angry, anguished questions bursting forth from his distressed sister floundered as Trinity absorbed the true ramifications of his calm pronouncement concerning her best friend's future. The thought of Victoria and Adrianna departing from Palmetto Point forever was intolerable to Trinity. Besides, Adrianna was crazy in love with Trinity's cousin, Geoffrey. She would never marry anyone else.

"Adrianna, please remember your duty." Her mother's reproof was kind, gentle, but firm. "You've known since childhood that your father would choose the appropriate man to be your husband."

"But it's different now, Mother! The war has changed everything. I don't want to go back to England. I'm an American, and this is my home. You know it's true. I don't want to marry some Englishman I've never met."

Adrianna's black eyes sparkled like wet obsidian as she forcibly restrained the tears threatening to spill over her bottom lashes. A more volatile emotion kindled inside Trinity and flared without much fanning into full-blown fury. "All of us here can attest to His Grace's skill in matchmaking, can we not? Did he not marry me off to His Lordship here in front of all our kith and kin? Perhaps you worry for naught, Adrianna, perhaps the groom he chooses will be as dishonorable as your brother and will forsake you while you ready yourself for the altar, as was done to me."

This time William reacted plainly, for all of them to see. His jaw went taut, his bronze skin grew a shade darker as blood rushed into his face, and Trinity took lovely, no, sublime pleasure in watching a spastic tic begin to jump in one lean cheek, little jerks at the base of his jawbone that did much to reveal his wrath. She leaned back, enjoying his rage to the hilt. Why, he was actually grinding his teeth now, she noted in unparalleled glee. No longer was he so unfeeling, so impervious to the verbal darts she threw at him. She smiled sweetly, but her expression faded quickly enough under his tightly uttered pronouncement.

"I wish a word alone with Trinity now, if you please, Mother."

If there was one thing Trinity never wanted, it was a forced private audience with William Remington. She had no trouble voicing her objection. "I assure you, milord, there'll never be a need for the two of us to spend time alone together. Not now, nor anytime in the future. Victoria's become the mother I never had, and Adrianna's closer to me than any sister could be. I've no secrets from them. State your business and be done with it for I've little inclination to make time for you during the remainder of your visit."

The frankness of her words came as a mighty shock for William. She could see the astonishment in his face, stamped there quite clearly for a brief instant. All emotion disappeared then, as if he'd taken a cloth and with one all-encompassing swipe wiped away any and all feelings like unwanted dust from a tabletop. His visage turned into a granite mask, his eyes as frosty as early winter dawn.

"So be it, Trinity, if you have no sensitivity concerning your privacy, I'll oblige you in that respect." In the stilted moment that ensued, Trinity realized by the very scorn dripping off his words that something absolutely awful was about to happen, but she had no inkling just how terrible it would be until William pierced her with his eyes and said, "The annulment signed by your father four years ago has somehow been misplaced. There is no document registered in the courts that negates our marriage vows. You are now, and always have been, my legal wife."

Trinity's jaw actually dropped. Hung open in less than ladylike fashion. Horrified, she gaped at him in mute astonishment. It was William's turn to taunt her with a smile, and he did so, a faint curve of his fine lips that bore not a whit of true mirth.

"No," she muttered, her voice quite low and husky and unlike herself. "I don't believe you."

"Believe me, my lady, I would not joke about something this important."

"Why, this is . . . this is . . ." She struggled desperately for words to describe her horror, groped for a phrase terrible enough to express her distress. "This is a travesty! A calamity! It's too dreadful even to contemplate! It's—"

"Yes, yes, all that, and more," William agreed, cutting off further protestations. "I can assure you I'm not particularly thrilled with this state of affairs, either."

His sarcasm chased away some of Trinity's initial shock. "Then you must do whatever is necessary to rid me of you. I will *not* accept you as a husband, do you understand?"

Something moved, deep inside William's eyes, like smoke caught inside a clear green bottle, an emotion she could not quite identify, so rigidly controlled was it. "That's precisely the reason I left a very pleasant life in London to travel here, milady, to inform you that I do have the means to rectify this unfortunate dilemma."

"Then you've brought the appropriate document for my signature, I trust?"

Several moments crawled past while the three women watched William in silence, their apprehension growing. "There is such a document, of course, one you must sign," he said, "but I fear it won't be binding unless you return to England and attend to the task, in person, before the bench of justice."

Trinity shot to her feet, trembling with outrage at the mere suggestion. "Never! Never, do you hear? I'll never set foot on British soil, not with Papa in one of your filthy English jails."

William remained unruffled by the outburst. "Then I suppose you'll have to grow accustomed to calling me husband."

"I'd rather be dead."

Her remark, melodramatic but quite obviously heartfelt, hung in the air like an attack flag. Unwilling husband and unwanted wife glared at each other, all hostilities unleashed, as raw as bare flesh opened by a saber slash.

Victoria lay a comforting hand on Trinity's arm. "Perhaps it would be best, my dear, if you do discuss this subject alone with William. Adrianna and I shall stroll beside the goldfish pond. Trinity, do join us there, after you and William have civilly worked this matter out to your mutual satisfaction."

Chagrined, to be sure, at the forced tête-à-tête, Trinity stonily observed the two ladies take their leave. She clasped her hands tightly together, to bolster her resolve. Though she'd prepared herself that he might return someday, forcing just this kind of audience alone with him, she found herself nervous, flustered, entrapped, and the burning in her cheeks told her that her face was probably aflame with a combination of those emotions. No, anger was all it really was, and that's exactly what she needed to sustain herself when dealing with such an arrogant, condescending man. Her chin came up, and with renewed courage, she leveled fiercely determined eyes upon his face.

William met her challenge with cool indifference. He moved to the gallery doors, closed them quietly. She watched him, aware of his masculine grace, his height, his muscular body. He was older, a great deal more mature than he'd been

the last time they'd met, but with the same good
looks and wavy auburn hair. He had the patrician look about him, high cheekbones and regal
stature, all witness to his impeccable lineage. He
was the epitome of a titled Englishman, everything she no longer wanted in a husband. Her
desire to end the marriage leaped in intensity.

"How have you been, Trinity?"

Under the circumstances, Trinity thought the
question completely ludicrous. How did he think
she'd been? And listen to him, he was trying to
sound so sincere, so caring, as if he gave a fig if
she lived or died. He hadn't inquired of her
health in the last four years, had he? He didn't
care now either, he just wanted her to do what he
wanted. Incensed, she took a deep, steadying
breath.

"I'm well enough, I suppose, considering my
county's occupied by Tarleton's bloody butchers,
all my property's been confiscated and given
over to your family while my father rots in an
English cell. Worst of all, though, I must say, the
most galling part of my plight by far, sir, is the
revelation I'm still wed to a man as arrogant and
unprincipled as you've proven yourself to be."

Obviously, he had hardened himself to her
abuse and therefore revealed no reaction to her
heated remark. "Mother informed me about your
misfortunes. Whether you believe me or not, I'm
truly sorry you've suffered so much."

She fixed a steady glare on him, once again
thinking how he, in his perfectly tailored charcoal coat and trousers, his spotless white stock

and inherited title, with more wealth and power than any single man should possess, he, more than anyone she knew, personified everything the patriots rebelled against, everything she now detested.

"You deserve an explanation as to my reasons for the annulment, I suspect. Father informed me he sent only the document to you without any personal letter . . ."

Trinity was quick to interject. "I assure you, sir, I expect nothing from you. I was as pleased to be rid of you as you were to cast me off." A lie, of course. She'd been hurt by the rejection, more than he could possibly comprehend. Completely, utterly devastated, as she endured the whispers and pointing fingers until the impending war dwarfed her personal affairs in the public sentiment. But his high and mighty lordship, the future Duke of Thorpe, had no need to know what she had suffered at his hands. Pride sent another falsehood spiraling out of her mouth. "Actually, there's another man in my life."

"Oh, God, you haven't eloped with anybody, have you?"

Lies engendered lies, her father had always told her. "Of course not. He fights with George Washington in the north, I'm proud to say."

"If you want to marry this man, then you'll have to agree to return to England with me."

Trinity frowned, nerves bringing her to her feet and into an agitated prowl about the perimeter of the room. He watched in unperturbed silence until she finally stopped in her tracks and stared speculatively at him. "'Tis only in English courts that your laws bear weight. Here in America, we go now by American statutes so I am free to wed whomever I wish."

A flash of irritation twisted across William's face. "Don't be a damned fool, Trinity. That's bigamy, and you know it. We were married by a priest in the eyes of God, if you'll recall."

Trinity glanced away. The idea of going to England with him was absolutely repugnant, even if Adrianna and Victoria went with them.

"There's another reason for you to cooperate," he began with a reluctant enough pitch to his voice that Trinity perked up and listened carefully. "Before I had any inkling that our marriage contract was still intact, I considered an engagement to another woman. She knows nothing of this . . . matter between the two of us, of course, but I won't be free to marry her until you and I have found a suitable resolution."

Trinity gazed scornfully at him but she was astute enough to detect the pendulum of power between them had swung over to her. If he wished to marry this lady of his, he had better meet Trinity's demands, any and everything she wanted. And there was only one thing she wanted more than anything else in the world.

"I'll accompany you to London on one condition."

William considered her with extreme wariness. "And what might that be?"

"My father's freedom."

William immediately shook his head. "Don't

be absurd. I don't even know where he's being held."

Again wills clashed. William broke the silence first.

"If I could manage to find your father, will you come to London? And cooperate fully?"

"Of course," she agreed, then pushed for more, all the while aware there was little now that he could risk refusing her. "But Papa must come with us."

"Be sensible, Trinity, I can't promise you something like that."

Trinity's heart trembled with disappointment but she held firm. Her father was in ill health and had been in prison already for nearly a year. The rebellion could drag on for many years to come. She had to get him out.

"Then, milord, for better or worse, you will remain married to me."

His face darkened, highly displeased to be sure, and she smiled in triumph, reveling in her newly acquired power over the man she most despised. Making William Remington grovel on his knees in her presence held an undeniable delicious appeal.

"I can only make inquiries as to his whereabouts."

"I want him freed, pardoned of all crimes, and taken to England with us, or you might as well be on your way back to London. I'm sure the lady you mentioned will understand that you'll never be able to marry her."

William considered, frowned, reconsidered,

then sighed with heavy resignation. Trinity recognized a sound of defeat when she heard it. She'd won! The most delightful sense of accomplishment settled over her.

"I'll exert my influence as best I can to attain his parole."

"See that you exert it well, milord, or expect to enjoy a long life chained to me, with no chance for any male heirs to carry on your holy Remington bloodline."

Trinity lifted her skirt and swept out of the room in a rustling swirl of velvet and fluttering petticoats, leaving her threat hanging over his head. Filled with newfound hope, she hurried for the gardens to console poor Adrianna. Her friend would be most distraught about the duke's plans to marry her off in London, and so would poor Geoffrey when he learned the news later that night when Trinity sneaked out of the house to ride courier for his patriot unit.

Chapter Three

The night, as black and sticky as pitch, seemed alive and moving, pregnant with the nocturnal screeching of cicadas and hoarse throbbing of bull frogs. As Trinity melted out onto the south gallery, a breeze swelled out of the muggy still air, a cool, refreshing kiss against her forehead and cheeks. Inside she felt warm, edgy, and excited by the danger facing her.

Garbed like a highwayman, she wore a black shirt and breeches, her bright hair stuffed securely under a dark man's cap. She paused momentarily, inhaling the very essence of the torrid Carolina night. Bougainvillea, scarlet, trumpet-shaped, heady in its sweetness, lush in its creeping splendor. It covered the banister like a living glove, and she paused where shadows lay in silvering moonlight like deep dark pools.

Lightning glimmered. Far, far out over the sea. A brewing storm, its celestial energy magnified by the hot, heavy atmosphere. Again, a mere flash of white, then darkness settled down around her like a weightless black cloak. Moisture hung in the air, invisible but almost tangible.

Before the morning light, the dark earth would be drenched, the swamp waters swollen, the rice paddies lapping their levees.

Long before dawn, God willing, she would have accomplished her mission and would lie abed. A tendril of hair escaped, tickling her cheek, and she absently tucked it back. Crouching behind thick fragrant vines, she watched the south sentry saunter past below, his boots clicking a steady cadence on the flagstones. She had been quite pleasantly surprised by the ineptitude of the redcoats. She'd not had a moment's trouble evading detection since early summer when the guards had been assigned to watch her.

When the time was right, she dissolved like a floating wraith into the slanted shadows thrown by the thick white pillars, darting from one to another until she reached the mimosa tree. Wide, leafy limbs welcomed her as if she were a ladybug cupped in a hand. She could have descended through the intersecting boughs blindfolded. The branch was sturdy, wide, and full of fragrance, and the lacy blossoms barely danced as she stealthily inched along it.

A mosquito brushed her temple, the whining drone reminding her to tuck the black lace scarf into the neckline of her shirt. She paused long enough to secure it with her father's black cravat. The biting flies would have taken over the rice paddies now that it was dark, hovering in great living clouds over the submerged crops. The swamp with its black mire and stench of decay would be even worse.

Without protection every inch of her exposed flesh would be attacked and bitten. At that thought she almost envied Adrianna, safely asleep in her net-draped tester bed. Though she had to admit she relished the pleasure of outwitting the British by coming and going beneath their very noses, almost at will. The climb to the ground, well practiced since the age of five, took only seconds. Heart pounding she made the mad, exhilarating dash to the cedar thicket where Enoch the stableboy had left Moonbeam saddled and ready to ride.

She patted the mare's neck, smoothing away the horse's unease with whispered assurances. She pressed her cheek briefly against the velvety muzzle. She checked the strap holding the black blanket over her white coat to keep it from glowing in the darkness, then placed the toe of her boot in the dangling stirrup. She swung up lightly into the saddle and settled comfortably astride, feeling free without having to endure the ridiculous confines of a sidesaddle.

The exploit she was about to undertake was not a childish prank but a crime punishable by the hangman's noose, she reminded herself and instantly became as sober as a vicar as she leaned forward and patted Moonbeam's neck, waiting for the right moment. Her father could be facing a noose. He would have already been executed, on the horrible gallows set up in Charleston, if not for Victoria's intervention in his behalf. She bit her lip, pain wringing her heart. Oh, bless him, where had they taken him? Was he still alive? Was he in some dank, awful hole that would aggravate his gout and make his foot swell? She had to do something, had to get him out, and she would.

Determinedly she shook her father's plight from her mind. She couldn't let herself think about him now, too much was at stake. Geoffrey was waiting for her at the charred ruins of Trenton Hill. He'd not be pleased when he heard the duke's plans for his daughter. She patted her breast pocket where she had tucked Adrianna's letter and found it securely in place.

Impatient now, she forced herself to remain motionless, surrounded by the nearly overpowering pungency of the cedars, waiting for the guard to turn the corner of the house. Finally, when he disappeared from sight, the sound of his boots fading in the distance, she rode slowly alongside the tiled goldfish pond to where it ended at the first garden terrace. She leaned low, urged Moonbeam into a gallop, and gave the sleek, swift animal her head. They galloped toward the first levee, across thick green grass that muffled the flying hooves to dull thuds.

Wasting no time now, she reached the raised bank and set off down it on the first leg of the serpentine route to the Remingtons' burned-out estate. Above her, a crescent moon floated in a starry sea, its faint white light periodically obliterated by wisps of scudding clouds pushed inland by the threatening storm like paper boats in a swift current. Enough silvery light remained, however, to throw into relief mounds of earth rising from the black water. The fields of rice looked like giant, ominous graves, she thought, then shivered as if it were some precursor of doom.

William Remington's face intruded into her thoughts, and she wished he could see her now. Riding courier alone, defying the English in the dead of night for the patriot army. He'd no doubt be unimpressed, affecting a haughty sneer and decreeing her a silly fool. Or perhaps he would flush underneath his dark tan as he had done when she had reminded him of his dishonor.

Frowning at the course of her thoughts, she reined the horse onto a westward embankment. Why did she continue to fret about him? He was nothing to her any longer, didn't mean a fig to her. She couldn't care less what he thought, did, or said. More important matters pressed her for consideration and concentration than some holier than thou Englishman. Let His Lordship sleep like a babe in his comfortable feather bed and dream of that other woman he now deemed good enough to be a duchess. She felt nothing but pity for the poor lady. Who was she anyway? she wondered. Probably a proper lady renowned for her great beauty and impeccable manners. A man like William Remington was unlikely to choose an unattractive bride.

Unless he coveted her for her dowry. That seemed a qualification most admired by Thorpe men, as in her own case, as well as Victoria's. She smiled evilly. What would the chosen bride think if she found out that William had been secretly wed to Trinity for years? A delightful vision flashed through her mind. She'd curtsy and introduce herself as William's wife, perhaps at some fancy London ball. How'd she love to see William's dark handsome face at such a moment!

Trinity spent the length of the next levee entertaining herself with delicious scenarios in which she effectively ruined William Remington's life before she reached the old Indian footpath that meandered through the mucky, low-lying ground and dark infested waters of the cypress swamp. A surefooted causeway was available to those initiated in its tricky bogs and sinkholes of quicksand, but it was a death trap to any witless English soldier bold enough or stupid enough to follow her.

Though the moon was now enshrouded, the wind whipping against her face, she felt no fear of getting lost. She'd ridden the treacherous twists and turns of the swamp paths countless times with Geoff, but more often of late without him. Though dangerous in the extreme, the route had always been the quickest to Trenton Hill and the pleasant afternoons she'd spent there with Adrianna. The rebellion had taken all that away from them, every simple pleasure they'd enjoyed.

Had they not all been true Englishmen and -women, obedient to English laws? If only the King had listened to American grievances, all talk of revolution could have been squashed without a drop of blood shed. Yet George had stubbornly pressed his heel upon their freedom until the Continental Congress had no choice but to declare tyranny. Since that moment their peaceful, comfortable world had been turned upside down, with neighbors accusing neighbors, and committing terrible acts of vengeance and cruelty.

At the stroke of a patriot pen, Victoria and Adrianna had been branded as the enemy—a good family that had resided in Fulton County for countless generations, who had attended the same village fairs, donated food and coin to the same Episcopal charities, hosted parties, danced at balls, attended weddings and funerals. The Remingtons had been good neighbors, fine honest Carolinians, yet once word of the Declaration of Independence had reached Charleston, the entire town had gone crazy, dividing themselves into enemy factions, as surely as oil poured into a water ewer. And anyone claiming kin to the Duke of Thorpe became the worst enemy of all.

The very night the word had come through, there commenced all manner of looting and burning in Charleston, hideous disgraceful crimes against humanity, cruelties against the most defenseless of their citizens, the women and children. Her father, bless his stalwart heart, had protected the Remington women, though he had not been able to save their magnificent home from the torch. And what reward did he sustain? Arrest and ruin when the British retook the city.

The Tories rose in a wrathful fury against their former neighbors in a fashion totally incomprehensible to Trinity's mind. How could they forget the past as if it had not happened? Forget the fact that they were all colonists, all friends? She wondered if the day would ever come when they would again sit together on the town green and gaze out over the harbor, watch children play or gather together in their churches at Christmastide as they had in the days when she was growing up.

A cutting sense of helplessness wounded her heart, and she willed herself to fight off despair. Early on she had accepted that she, one woman, had little recourse over what was to be. Now her plight was even more dire. She had no choice but to leave Palmetto Point with William Remington, a repugnant duty indeed, but a worthy sacrifice if it would earn her father's freedom.

Twisting the reins firmly around her gloved fingers, she kept Moonbeam firmly on course, grateful when the moon sailed into view long enough to find the twist in the overgrown path that would lead her across the last half of the swamp waters. She recalled riding this trail only to catch a glimpse of William, back when she considered him to be her own true love. She had thought him so very wonderful in those days though he'd been little more than a boy. His smile had been a treasure she had hungered for, then cherished, willing to do just about anything to garner another. She could remember how she had shivered all the way down to her toes with each flash of his white smile and warm green eyes.

Oh, he still had that pleasant smile, she

thought with a sneering curl of upper lip, he'd donned it easily enough earlier that afternoon, but no longer did it hold her so enthralled. No longer was she his awestricken marionette tangled in her own strings. Suddenly she realized that her thoughts had been on little else besides him since he'd returned, and she fiercely berated herself.

You, dear Trinity, are a fool indeed. Why do you dwell on the odious man when he has already thrown you aside for some other woman? One he considers a better match? Not a tender man, he, but one with gall enough to reveal such plans to her, face-to-face, telling her that she was no longer good enough to bear his name, as if she had no feelings. No, William Remington did not think much of her, nor she of him, but he could spring her father from prison, and that was all she wanted from him.

It took a quarter of an hour longer to wind her way through the miasma of the foul-smelling swamp with its hungry, attacking swarms of mosquitoes. When she finally reached the far side, she leaned forward as Moonbeam lurched up onto firmer turf at the south end of the thick forest tracts surrounding the outbuildings of the ruined plantation.

The vast lengths that had been miles of tobacco fields now stood flat and silent, the burnt rubble of hundreds and hundreds of cash crops, a senseless waste of hard labor and resources that made her angry every time she saw it. 'Twas like burning money, and she had to blink back tears when she saw the lovely old Georgian manor, where it lay charred and crumbling, only its six graceful chimneys and a small portion of its former grandeur still standing, like macabre sentinels against a lightning-lit sky.

She drew up underneath an old elm, the limbs of which nearly swept the ground and would hide her from view. She waited astride, not daring to dismount until she picked out the tiny pinpoint of flame flickering somewhere under the standing part of the rear portico. Geoffrey always awaited her in the shelter of the interior, and the lantern signal gave her the all-clear to join him there.

Ever cautious, she tied the mare in a well-hidden thicket, then crept through the waist-high weeds of the side lawn, where they had played games as children. It was not until her footsteps crunched on the fallen debris underneath the colonnade that Geoffrey made himself known, stepping into view down the length of the corridor and raising the partially covered candle to bring her to him.

The sight of her beloved cousin calmed her considerably, and she felt better about the tenuous state of affairs. He'd always had that effect on her, especially since her father had been captured. Geoffrey was the only kin she had left to cling to; she couldn't bear it if anything happened to him.

"You're late. Dammit, Trin, you know how I worry when you don't come when you're supposed to." He spoke very low, curtly, the anger revealed in his voice giving her some pause. She hesitated near the blackened ribs that used to be Victoria's lovely grand staircase. Part of the roof was still intact high above, and Trinity could see a spangle of stars through a gap where one beam had fallen, seemingly millions of glowing pinpricks among a swirling mass of encroaching rain clouds. Somehow the sight filled her with sadness. She lowered her eyes and vowed not to notice the sky again.

"Well, what kept you?" Geoffrey demanded impatiently, setting down the candle lantern and turning expectantly to her. He was annoyed, to be sure, but she couldn't quite summon up an answering anger because he looked so drawn and tired. He had been wounded two fortnights past in a skirmish with the redcoats, a deep saber slash across his left shoulder. He still wore a sling.

"I got here as soon as I could." She paused, watching him rake his fingers through his thick blond hair, too long now that he rode with the roaming patriot band.

"You look too pale, Geoffrey. Is your arm bothering you again?"

"Aye, it aches, the comin' rain, I reckon, is the reason for it. I've been dodging redcoat patrols this whole day through. They've put more soldiers on us, riding all the roads this side of Bacon's Inn. We've hardly a place left to ride except in the swamps."

"There's good reason for their swelling numbers," she told him, still reluctant to reveal her tidings. She had no good news to soften the bad, and his foul mood was about to grow very much worse. Since the war had begun, he made little effort to hide his temper.

"Lord William's come home. He arrived today."

Geoffrey jerked his face toward her. "Will's here? Good God, I figured we'd never set eyes on him again, not with Uncle Eldon in an English jail cell."

Trinity took a deep breath. "I truly hate to have to tell you this, Geoff, but he's come here to collect Adrianna and Victoria." She paused when her voice caught sorrowfully, then forged on, bracing herself for his reaction. "His Grace, the duke, has decided Adrianna's to marry a titled Englishman."

The expression that overrode his features was so naked with pain that Trinity had no need to be told how he was affected by such news. She felt she had to say something, had to comfort him some way. She couldn't bear to watch him wrestle with such palpable agony, twisting his face, deadening his blue eyes.

"She didn't know anything about it, Geoff. She doesn't want to go. She wants to stay here with you. Here, she's sent you a letter."

Geoffrey took the folded parchment then turned away from her, bracing his good hand on the wall. She waited, feeling awful inside, while he composed himself.

"She has no future with me anyway," he finally got out, his voice quietly resigned. "I've nothing to offer her, not with a price on my head."

"She doesn't care about that, and you know it. She's a patriot herself and supports everything you do. She's told you that, I know she has."

"Well, I care. I won't subject a woman of her quality to a life in a hovel."

His pride, she thought. A flaw that must be in their Kingston blood, but at the moment his seemed even stronger than hers.

"There's more," she said. "I have to go with them."

"Go with them? Why?" He'd turned back, frowning.

"The annulment Will and his father arranged was never finalized. I'm still legally tied to him. Unfortunately."

Geoffrey stared at her, as flabbergasted as she had been when Will had told her the shocking truth.

"How in the devil could that have happened? They told us it was all over!"

"Will said the document never reached England, but I don't care about that. He said he'd get Father released if I came with him and signed the papers."

"Can you trust him?"

"He'd better do exactly that, or he'll never get rid of me."

Geoffrey almost smiled but could not seem to manage it. He was always so serious now, not like before the war when he was gay and light-hearted, always making Adrianna and Trinity laugh. Now he looked ten years older, and exhausted.

"I suppose it's better if you spend the rest of the war in England. At least you and Adrianna will be safe there. But I've got to see her before she goes. Tell her, will you, Trin. Tell her I'll come to her."

"I fear we'll leave for Charleston soon."

"I'll come into the city, if need be. Tell her I'll get a message to her somehow."

Trinity nodded agreement but before she could speak the sound of a footfall crunched outside in the hallway. Geoffrey pulled his weapon from his holster but before he could douse the candle lantern, William Remington stepped out into the dim light. His flintlock pistol was trained dead center on Geoffrey's heart.

Chapter Four

"Don't shoot, Geoff. I'm not here to make trouble."

With slow, steady movements, so as not to make Geoffrey nervous with the trigger, William raised his own weapon until the barrel lay against his shoulder, muzzle upward, then raised his left hand in a gesture of surrender. Not reassured quite yet by the dangerous look on his old friend's face, he stood waiting, defenseless. A quick glance aside at Trinity told him, by the angry look on her face, that William was lucky that she wasn't the one holding the pistol.

"How did you find us? Did you bring the redcoats?"

William ignored Trinity, his attention glued on Geoffrey. "I'm alone, I swear it."

Riveted, they stared at each other, and William found it hard to believe that they had come to this—a deadly standoff between best friends from their youth, two men who'd pricked thumbs together and pledged loyalty as blood brothers. Geoffrey did not look good—tired, older than he was, almost haggard. Will's eyes lowered to the sling on Geoff's wounded arm, then jerked back to Geoff's face when the other man slowly lowered his guard. As Trinity's patriot cousin jabbed his gun back into his waistband, Will released a breath and holstered his own weapon.

"You can't trust him, Geoff! He could be lying, probably is, knowing him. What if it's a trap to capture us? The soldiers could be hiding outside to nab us." Trinity moved past Will, peering out into the darkness where she feared the King's guard waited to arrest them.

"I've no reason to do that, dammit," Will growled aside to her, increasingly put out with her constant hostility and distrust.

"Then why are you here? What do you want?"

"I'm here because I want to see Geoff. I had a gut feeling Trin would come to you so I kept watch on her bedchamber, and did the job a helluva lot better than my fellow countrymen did."

"I don't believe you. No one could have followed me here. I was too careful."

Will cocked a mocking brow. "Not as careful as you boast, apparently. You're damn lucky I'm the one who followed you or you might be nursing a bullet hole about now."

"All the better for you," she snapped. "'Twould end your annulment woes if I were dead and shrouded in the crypt."

William ignored that, let her glower impale him, and turned again to Geoffrey. "Trinity endangers her life every time she rides out at night by herself. I ran across an English patrol not a mile from here. If they'd seen her, they wouldn't have cared if she were a woman or a man. And couldn't have told the difference anyhow, with her in that garb."

Geoffrey said nothing.

"I've no fight with you, Geoff. How could I? I just wanted to see you, to talk. I swear to God."

Silence descended. One beat, two beats. Geoffrey seemed extremely wary, and not particularly pleased to see his old friend again. The two men stood facing each other, foes now in philosophy, in politics, but that was the very subject William wished to address. For once, Trinity had sense enough to remain quiet but she moved closer to her cousin, standing shoulder to shoulder with him, close, a united front against their enemy. William felt a current of sorrow flow through him.

"Why'd you come here, Will? What do you really want?" Geoff watched him closely, awaiting his answer. Will was keenly aware of how he kept his hand at rest on the carved ivory handle of his pistol.

William stood still, unthreatening. "We leave for Charleston in the morning so I had no choice but to seek you out tonight. Can you put the rebel quarrel behind you long enough to greet an old friend?" He stretched out his arm, right hand extended.

For a moment he wasn't sure Geoffrey would accept the overture, but then he took a step forward and their hands locked together firmly.

Their eyes held, and a bit of the distrust, the many years of separation, drifted away.

"God, I can't believe it's been so long." William grinned, unable to help himself out of the sheer pleasure of seeing his boyhood chum again. At that, Geoffrey let down, too, a smile tugging the corners of his mouth. Even so the grin was begrudging. It broke the ice, however, and they embraced, slapping each other on the back as they used to do when Will journeyed home from England, as if no time had passed, no bloody war waged around them. Over his friend's shoulder, William saw that Trinity had gone absolutely livid.

"I didn't expect I'd ever see you again, Will." Geoffrey sank down beside a charred sideboard that had been dragged into the middle of the chamber, and William found a rickety chair and sat across from him.

The tin-punched candle lantern burned between them, coloring the small chamber with shadows that darted as if strummed by the fingers of wind whipping through the damaged ceiling beams.

Stony-faced, Trinity took a stance behind Geoffrey where she could lay a supportive hand on his shoulder. And where she could glare at Will, Will surmised when her fine amber eyes never wavered from his face, every nuance of her expression and body emanating disgust, perhaps even hatred. *She must truly loathe me*, he thought, suddenly understanding with no small surprise. He had wronged her, and she hadn't forgotten it.

Her eyes veritably burned into him, like deadly pools of golden lava.

"What do you want from me, Will?"

Geoffrey's question was direct, straightforward in the way Geoff had always had, even as a boy. With a difficulty Will didn't quite fathom, he had to pull his attention off Trinity's flushed face. She looked even more beautiful angry than she did otherwise, which he wouldn't have thought possible. He shocked himself by admitting that he was attracted to her. Mightily so. Unfortunately so. He concentrated all his attention on Geoff and leaned forward in earnest entreaty. A lot rode upon what he had to say. He just hoped Geoff would listen to reason.

"I want to help you, Geoff. I can offer you a pardon for what you've done so far against the Crown, one that'll give you a chance to swear allegiance to King George. I've got important connections in London that'll back me on this parole. We need good men like you on our side when we put down the rebellion. Throw in with us now and I can offer you just about anything you want. There'll be wealth and power for Carolinians who supported England, perhaps even a royal governorship for you."

In the stillness that followed his offer, he heard Trinity's gasp of outrage, but he didn't look at her. Geoff's eyes glinted blue in the candle glow, searching Will's with unwavering, unreadable intensity.

"You insult my honor, Will, with that kind of

drivel. Surely you know I'd never turn my back on my country."

William did know it, of course, had from the beginning. He shook his head in frustration but he remained calm, desperate to make Geoffrey see the inevitability of the war's outcome.

"I meant you no insult. But think, man, Washington's ragtag force is barely able to march. How could you possibly expect them to over-come well-trained, well-equipped British foot soldiers? Geoff, our numbers alone are enough to overwhelm the patriot forces."

Geoffrey leaned back and propped a booted foot on his opposite knee. "True, every word you utter. But you've got to understand, old friend, we're fighting for what we believe in. For our liberty and freedom to govern ourselves. We'll never give up. Every single one of us, to a man, has vowed to fight to the death for our beliefs." He paused, appraised William for a long moment. "You were born here among us, Will. You grew up on American soil. You considered yourself one of us for a long time. How can you even think I'd forget what I fight for?"

"Because you don't stand a chance in hell to win." William kept his voice hushed but he spoke from his heart. "I don't want to see your life forfeited for a lost cause. We've been friends too long for me to sit back and watch you destroy yourself."

At that, Geoffrey was forced to smile. "You sell us short. We patriots might surprise you. We've a great deal of fight left in us—"

"For God's sake, Geoff, face the facts. Charleston is under British rule again; Savannah's been occupied for over a year. Cornwallis told me only days ago that he's gaining more and more strongholds all across the Carolinas, even inland along the rivers. Tell me what chance you have, Geoff." He paused, took a deep breath, frustrated at his inability to convince Geoff. "Within the year North Carolina and Virginia are doomed to fall, Washington's army will be cut in two and surrounded by royal troops. It's already over, Geoff, you just won't accept it."

Trinity spoke up at last, her words as clipped and precise as a tailor's stitches. "You conveniently forget that the French have come in on our side with their great fleet. The course of the war could very well change in a matter of days. It *will* change."

William stared at her, then looked back at her cousin.

"The French'll be defeated by the Royal Navy. They've not lifted a musket sight yet to help you win, and they won't. It's over, and both of you need to accept that and return to England with me. Now, before it's too late and you get yourselves hanged. You can ride out the conflict in London, Geoff, with Trinity and Eldon, if I can effect his release. Mother and Adrianna are returning there for good as well, because it's just too dangerous here for them any longer. Just look around you."

As an emphasizing gesture, he swung his arm wide, encompassing the charred, crumbling room in which they sat. "Think about what happened to Trenton Hill. 'Twasn't the King's men who set this place afire but your own side, patriots who torched my mother's house. American-born men terrorized my mother and sister, both of them helpless women, made homeless—"

Infuriated, Trinity leaned forward and braced both palms flat on the table. Her face was inches from William's, full of scorn.

"And what about the butcher Tarleton, milord? What about that bloody minion of George? He's murdered, raped, and ravaged more innocent civilians than I could ever name. He's the one who's the monster here, parading about in his fine scarlet jacket, enjoying his killing and maiming like a demon in the guise of a mortal man."

William sat stunned. He heard her pain, and more surprising the fear underlying it. He frowned. "Tarleton's committed atrocities here? He's known in London as an honorable officer, an officer who'll—"

"Tarleton's a murdering animal," Geoffrey interjected, placing a restraining hand on Trinity's arm. She drew back at once, but she was shaking with emotion. "I can only hope I'm the man who can fire the bullet that'll put an end to his miserable life," Geoffrey finished.

William sat unmoving. Tarleton was the least of his concerns. "There's no way I can convince you to turn?"

"Not so long as one British soldier stands armed upon American soil."

"I wish to God I could change your mind."

"And I, yours. I could ask from you the same favor, Will, with many of the same arguments. Join our fight for liberty. Your mother was born here in the colonies. She's an American to her core, as were all your maternal forebears. Their stalwart Ballantine blood flows through your veins just as the English bloodline of Thorpe. Are you not torn in your loyalties?"

The truth was that he was divided, that he did what he could in London and the halls of Parliament to soften the rhetoric against the American cause but that did not diminish his duty to the Crown.

"I am English, first and foremost, as you have always been until the Declaration of Independence."

"Then we're destined to remain enemies until we win freedom from oppression. When that day comes, when the United States is recognized by Britain, I'll welcome you back, my arms wide in friendship."

A sense of resignation settled over Will, sorrow, for only one of them would emerge the victor. Just as in their childhood games of soldiers and pirates, but this time the fight was real with lead bullets and razor-edged bayonets, and death the ultimate price for many.

"Only time then, and the will of God, can determine our future."

"Aye. God's will be done."

Geoffrey's comment effectively ended all discussion; both knew no further persuasion would make a difference.

Regret came flooding through William at the finality of it, dark and heavy and defeating. His oldest friend, possibly the best he'd ever had, was doomed, and there was not a damned thing he could do about it.

"There is something I think you must know." Geoffrey's eyes captured him again, their blue depths serious, tormented. He paused, sighed, then spoke quickly as if he forced himself. "I bear great affection for your sister. I had every intention of asking her hand in marriage when the fighting was over."

William thought that he surely must have misunderstood him.

"Adrianna?" he said stupidly but at the same time felt the ramifications of Geoffrey's avowal.

"That can never be. His Grace has ordered her home to England for a betrothal."

"Aye. Trin told me of it this very night. And now I call upon your help, as an old friend. Intervene in my behalf with the duke. I assure you, Will, my intentions are honorable. I've hesitated to request her hand only because I cannot offer her a stable future at present. Once the war is won, I'll give her everything within my power. She deserves nothing less."

William knew that what his friend asked of him should be thoroughly, completely out of the question. He couldn't bring himself to relate as much to Geoffrey, who watched him calmly, only his eyes revealing his emotion. He was in love with Adrianna, all right, it was written all over his face.

"And Adrianna?" Will asked slowly, almost reluctant to hear the answer. "Does she share your regard?"

"She cried her eyes out all afternoon because you're taking her away," Trinity supplied, with more than enough feeling to get her opinion across. Her revelation pierced both men with discomfort, if for different reasons.

"And she swears she'll not go to England," she went on, placing defiant hands upon her hips. "She's vowed to run away and elope with Geoffrey."

William shot a look of concern at Geoffrey, relieved to see his friend appearing equally shocked at the idea.

"No, Trinity, there'll be no elopement between us. You must tell Adrianna that it's my wish that she go with Will. She'll be safe in London until the fight is over. Especially with Tarleton running amuck. All of you will be safer under Will's protection." He raised inquiring eyes to his friend.

"Of course. That's my intention in taking them."

"I'll come for Adrianna as soon as I can. Please speak to your father. He might listen to you. He must understand that she'll be miserable if she is forced to wed against her will."

"I haven't been on Father's good side in years," William answered, thinking that was an understatement of immense proportions. "But I can tell you that he'll never allow her to wed an American. He's furious over the rebellion, that's why he's cutting all his ties here in the Carolinas."

"Please, Will. Do what you can. Adrianna and I have no one else to turn to."

William could not bring himself to deny Geoffrey. He nodded. "I'll do whatever I can to delay the inevitable. But I cannot promise you a miracle. Father's always tried to run our lives, and he's hell-bent that she make a beneficial match for the family."

William was suddenly sickened at the lives being destroyed all around him. Like crackling cornstalks before the scythe, good honest men were being cut down, their women widowed, their children orphaned. Here in Carolina the war was not merely a topic discussed while sipping coffee in a London drawing room but torn flesh and spilled blood. Here he'd seen the true effect of the war.

The jingling of harnesses drifted to them in the quiet night. William shot to his feet in alarm, but Geoffrey rose more slowly.

"It's my men. I must go. We've a long ride ahead of us before dawn breaks."

The two men stood looking at each other. William was the first to speak, his voice gruffer than usual.

"Be careful, old friend. God willing, we'll meet again in better times."

Geoffrey gripped his hand. "Aye, now that I know that you'll take care of Adrianna and Trin, I'll rest with easier mind."

William nodded, watching as Geoffrey turned

to Trinity and drew her in against his chest. He held her tightly for one brief moment, kissed the top of her head, and then he was gone, disappearing into the shadows, leaving William and Trinity to stare after him.

Chapter Five

Trinity fought swiftly rising tears as she stared into the night where Geoffrey had disappeared. Emotion fluttered like a wounded sparrow inside her breast, and she felt as desperate and alone as a trapped bird would feel. For she knew only too well that she might never see him again. Her heart clutched and held, and she struggled anew to control herself.

"He'll be all right." William's voice was close behind her, as if he'd read her pain, or perhaps the devastated expression on her face. "He won't get caught. He's got too much to live for."

Trinity did not turn but kept her gaze trained on the darkness. Far off, through a broken window she could see what used to be the front lawn, once an emerald expanse where Victoria had planted so many lovely rosebushes, now as dead and parched as a grave.

"Did you mean what you said about helping Geoffrey and Adrianna?" she asked him, very low.

"You can't bring yourself to believe anything I say, can you?"

"This time I want to, but look at you, you're evading my question which makes me think I should not."

She turned slightly, intending to watch his face while he replied, to judge for herself if he lied or not. Will stood near the candle now. He put his hand to his head and carelessly smoothed back the thick auburn hair above his temple.

"All I can do is plead their case to my father. I have no say in Adrianna's future, that's for certain, so I wouldn't get my hopes up if I were you. My father's developed a complete aversion to anything remotely American. I don't suspect Adrianna's feelings for Geoff will sway him in the least. Frankly, he doesn't care what any of his children think."

Disappointed by his answer, she stood in silence, though she did believe he spoke the truth, at least in that instant. Another thought occurred to her, one that gave her some hope.

"Perhaps he'll prefer you to be unentangled from me more than he wishes Adrianna wedded to an Englishman."

Will's eyes caught hers. "Are you making another demand?"

Trinity made up her mind at once that she very well was. "Yes. I care about Geoffrey's and Adrianna's happiness. That's more than I expect you, or the duke, can say."

"You don't know me very well if you can say something like that."

"That's right, I don't know you very well, and what I do know, I don't like."

To her surprise he found her jab amusing. His manner changed, and he gave a slow, utterly wicked smile. She had heard of his reputation with women; had feared the tales when she had thought herself wed to him, afraid she could not measure up to sophisticated London beauties. Now she could care less.

"It seems that you hate me more than is called for. If you think so ill of me, you should be relieved that our marriage didn't go through. Imagine how horrible it would be if it had, Trinity. Why, we'd have long been back from our wedding journey, and we no doubt would have a couple of children by now. That would be a wretched fate indeed, would it not? Sharing my life, my bed?"

She gasped a little at the last, not expecting him to mention anything of an intimate nature, flushing hotly and hating herself for it. She'd often daydreamed about that very thing and wondered if they would have had a child together, if not for the war.

"Despite what you think of me," he said, rounding the table and coming closer. She stepped back in tandem, as if they performed a dance. "I do happen to care if Adrianna's happy. Geoff's a fine man. I'd like to see them together."

"Then I'll wait and see just how diligently you strive for that to happen. But, alas, it might cut into your philandering pastimes which would no doubt distress you considerably."

"You truly do despise me, don't you?"

"I'm afraid so." She smiled tightly, a goading, cynical curve of lips that did not touch her eyes.

"You seem mightily concerned with the women in my life. Perhaps you don't hate me as much as you think you do. Maybe you're curious as to what you've missed. I must say I've wondered about it."

"I try not to think about you at all. I've been very successful at it."

"Oh, for God's sake, Trin, let's try to put all this behind us. We were friends once. You tolerated me then."

I adored you then, she thought helplessly, chagrined that he'd even reminded her. He smiled at her silence, knowingly, and her heartbeat quickened. Was he right? Did she still harbor some affection? How could she, after what he'd done?

She turned away again and moved to the door. She should leave, right now. Conversation with him would serve no good purpose. So why did she hesitate? Why did she stay? She tensed as he came up close beside her again, too close. He followed her gaze out into the damaged entry hall, ghostly and surreal in the faint silvering moonlight. He braced a palm against the doorjamb. "It's sad to see Mother's place in ruins. I can't believe this is all that's left of Trenton Hill. God, it was so beautiful with the white woodwork and high ceilings. Mother must've been sick when she saw it burned." He turned his face down to her, his green eyes darkened to black by the deep shadows. "Was she here when it happened?"

Trinity nodded. "I wasn't, but Adrianna told

me that your mother fell to her knees out on the drive and wept while the cowards set it afire."

"I'm surprised that even this much is left standing."

Trinity wondered if his mournful manner was sincere, if he had any residual affection for the plantation where he'd been born. She doubted if there was much left. He had told them in no uncertain terms that he was an Englishman, first and foremost.

"Fortunately rain came before the house was completely destroyed," she told him, wondering again why she lingered, why she indulged his curiosity about the past. She should have left when Geoffrey had. "By the time Papa and I arrived, the fire was nearly out."

"Yet Mother still defends the patriots as heroes."

"She understands that both sides in the war have committed despicable acts."

Nothing further was said for a moment. "I'd like to see what's left of the place. Will you walk with me?"

"No," she answered sharply. "I have to get back."

"I daresay your guards won't notice you're gone," he said with enough mockery to make her want to smile. She did not let herself. "Please?" he added.

Again, that grin that had once melted her heart, she thought warily. He extended his hand to her as if he were about to lead her into a minuet. Even more dangerous, she almost placed her hand in his, until she remembered herself. She stood straighter, squared her shoulders, ignoring his overture with cold detachment. Even so, for one moment, one fleeting instant, a memory came back to her, of a day long ago when he'd reached out his hand to her and she had taken it. He'd taken her for a horseback ride that day, and she'd thought him the most wonderful boy she had ever met.

William made no comment but picked up the lantern. Together they passed out from under the staircase into the ruined grand foyer. Trinity followed him, all the while wondering why she did, but she, too, felt sorrow over the demise of the great estate. And tomorrow she would leave it and her own home behind. At the rear of the foyer, where the west wing turned in an ell, the walls stood partially intact. He stopped outside one of the rooms, and stepping around the fallen door frame, he moved into the center of the interior, holding up the lantern to light their way.

Trinity hadn't returned to Trenton Hill except at night since the day after the fire when the house still smoldered. She looked now at the overturned divan of blue-and-white striped damask, charred and damaged until it was hardly recognizable. Most everything else of value had been looted by intruders, some of Victoria's former neighbors whom she had visited and helped in times of need, patriots, but men so caught up in anger and vengeance against the British that they forgot her goodness and thought only of her husband's title. Life had surely become a tragedy.

"Father used to keep his desk about here." The deep timbre of Will's voice reverberated hollowly up into the reaches of the ceiling. The air still hung heavy with the smell of sodden ash. She remained where she was near the threshold, watching him go down on one knee. He set the candle lantern on the floor and sorted through a pile of rubble and dead leaves blown in through the open door. "What happened to the desk? I wonder."

"I don't know. Most of the furniture was stolen."

"I remember it being gigantic, or so it seemed to me when I was little. I used to hide under it when I'd disobeyed my nurse."

She could tell he was smiling at the memory though she could see only one side of his face. His silhouette stood out in front of the flame, dark against the yellow glow, perfect in its symmetry. She stared at him, wondering what kind of man he really was. Was he truly the rogue that she had heard tell of, a man who took pleasure in seducing women? What were his habits? His interests? Did he love this woman he was thinking of marrying instead of her? Or was it merely an arrangement, as Adrianna's was supposed to be?

"What a bloody waste," he said, rising again and looking around, his fists planted on his narrow hips.

"The people were caught up in a rage against England and all her aristocratic lords."

William straightened, turning toward her until his face was fully illuminated. He looked dark, dangerous now, in those fierce, flickering shadows.

"Like me?"

"Exactly like you."

"Do you hate England that much, too? Enough to burn down someone's home like this?"

"I hate the evils England inflicts on her subjects. I hate the way you who are powerful crush the rest of us under your foot."

"You're fooling yourself, Trin. The same thing happens here in the colonies, and always will."

"Perhaps, but a man can better himself here with hard work and determination. Poor or rich, we are now free men and women, with rights."

William was staring steadily at her, no doubt thinking her a foolish idealist.

"You look beautiful right now."

Trinity was startled, and horrified at the flood of pleasure she felt. She actually blushed, angry with herself, especially when he grinned. Still, she couldn't think of an appropriate reply. How ridiculous to let him render her speechless. She'd been courted before, often, had been told any number of times by young beaus that she was beautiful. She could bat her eyelashes at gentlemen, could flirt quite acceptably, though it now seemed to her that courting rites were extremely shallow, silly exercises.

"I don't want you to hate me, Trin."

Well, William was certainly full of surprises this evening. What must he be up to showering her with compliments? It occurred to her then that he might be trying to seduce her. A laughable concept. No, he would know better.

Suddenly Will moved, so quickly she froze in her tracks. He blew out the candle, and the room plunged into pure inky blackness. Then he grabbed her. When he clamped his hand over her mouth, she regained her senses and struggled furiously against his hold.

"Hold still, Trinity. I heard someone."

She obeyed that whispered command at once, and his hand slid off her mouth, but he kept her back pressed against him, his right arm clamped around her waist.

She did not move, listening for whatever had alerted his caution. He held her tightly, locked together in the oppressive darkness. She could smell the scent of him now, a masculine one, leather riding vest and pine-scented soap. She shut her eyes, feeling his arm tense around her when a shout suddenly echoed somewhere outside. A thick cockney accent. English. She struggled to free herself, her first impulse to flee toward the rear of the ruins.

William's grip on her was too tight; she could not budge. "You can't escape, it's too late. They'll have already surrounded the place." His mouth was pressing against her ear, his lips warm. "Trust me, I know a hiding place."

"Let me go!" she hissed. "I can outrun them if I can get to Moonbeam."

He ignored that, refusing to release her, veritably dragging her back down the corridor and into a nearby room. Their feet made scuffling sounds, easily detectable in the quiet, and Trinity was relieved when he brought her to a stop somewhere inside, her back pressed up against an interior wall. Click, click, a scrape, and then the entire wall seemed to disappear from behind her. Will pushed her backward, and followed her inside until they were enclosed in some tiny cubicle, pressed together chest to chest, hip to hip.

"Where are we?" Her whisper was strained, and her cheeks burned with the intimacy of their position. She quickly lay both her palms against his chest as a barrier between their bodies, though it be a frail one.

"Shhh."

Trinity listened and heard nothing but the sound of the rising wind, up high, somewhere above them.

"Tell me," she demanded breathlessly, squirming inside his arms.

"Father's secret cupboard. Stephen and I played here as boys. No one knows about it."

Trinity relaxed a bit but her heart thundered anew as the clomp of heavy boots filtered to them from the distance. Will's arms tightened around her, and his palm held the back of her head, pressing her face into his chest. More shouts pierced the night and thudding, crashing sounds as if the intruders were overturning anything they happened upon.

Trinity did not move, squeezed very tight against Will's long, hard body. She could hear his heartbeat, rather steady and unalarmed, in view of the precariousness of their situation, she thought as her own heart hammered and tripped out of control, surely loud enough for him to hear. She suddenly felt trapped, closed in, as if she couldn't breathe. "I've got to get out of here, Will, please!"

"Shhh." He lifted her up, until her cheek rested against the side of his face. "Not now. They'll search the outer room, too. Think about something else, anything."

Within minutes the heavy footfalls approached, went past them, echoing loudly. Another man followed. Another. William's mouth was on her temple now.

More soldiers were outside, at least a dozen she suspected, and she wondered if one of them was Tarleton, leading his band of curs. She listened for what they were saying but could not hear. Her pulse beat had calmed considerably now that she felt they wouldn't be discovered, and of all the ridiculous things, she felt like laughing at the sheer absurdity of their predicament.

What if the cupboard door was thrust open, she thought, and she and Will were found crammed into a hidden closet together. She was dressed all in black, already a suspected spy, and harbored in the arms of the heir to the mighty Duke of Thorpe. Will would be finished in London once that distasteful scandal hit, his reputation in tatters, his father's politics endlessly besmirched.

Sobered, she wondered why he would put

himself in such peril. He could have made himself known and left her to her fate, allowed her to make a run for it as she had wanted. Why would he wish to protect her? For a long time they stood entwined, the sounds growing distant now. She could feel his breath fanning the hair at her temple, the low rasp of his breathing as he moved his head just enough to nudge her head aside. She felt hot male lips on the side of her throat, and her body reacted with a thrill she could not control.

She stiffened, squirming slightly and shifting her head away from him, but her action only made it worse. His lips brushed hers, moved on, but then as she gasped first in shock, then outrage, he came back to her mouth. He was kissing her, and she struggled but he caught her head and angled it to suit him as his kisses deepened. She could not move, could not free herself, and her mind was reeling from the implication of what he was doing.

How long had she dreamed of such a kiss? From the time she had become a young woman, even beyond that, when she was a child looking upon him as her future husband. And he kissed well, very well indeed, molding his mouth to hers, becoming a part of her. She almost moaned with pleasure, then cut it off as she finally came to her senses. He was playing with her, in the worst way possible. Taking advantage of her, and anger such as she never could remember before rushed like a red geyser of flame through her blood. She twisted her head and pushed hard against his chest. She heard the back of his head hit the other side of the closet, her own ragged breathing loud between them. But that was all she heard, the soldiers were gone.

"How dare you do that to me," she ground out, so low and furious that the voice was not her own. "Let me out of here."

He was still for a moment or two, as if deciding what to do, then without a word, he slid back the panel. Fresh air hit them, and Trinity held still until she was sure no redcoat prowled nearby, then she fled, out of the cupboard, shivering as she picked her way through the deserted house, wanting only to get away from him.

Once outside, she paused only long enough to know she was safe to cross to the cedars, then she ran hard and melted into the night, humiliated, sick at heart for responding to his insulting overture, if only for a moment. What a fool he must think her, after her angry outburst condemning him! She found Moonbeam without trouble, leaped onto his back, and galloped for the swamp trails as if pursued by Satan himself.

Chapter Six

At certain times, such as that very moment when Trinity knelt in the lush flowerbeds of Victoria Remington's Charleston town house, her fingers buried deep in the rich black loam, she could almost believe the rebellion had never begun, that everything was as it once had been, peaceful, happy, quiet. The coveted illusion lasted as she lifted the big, flattened heads of the sweet williams, reds, pinks, and whites, all nestled together around her, their spicy clovelike fragrance filling the air. Then she heard the sharp clatter of redcoats marching a quick step down East Battery Street on just the other side of the garden wall.

Frowning, she troweled the soil harder, punching violently around the roots. She pressed the loosened dirt down firmly with her gloved fingers around a tuft of fragile white asters, all the while trying to ignore the sounds of the enemy's show of force so close at hand.

Heaving a deep sigh, she sat back on her heels and stared at the row of perky lavender cup-and-saucer blooms of Canterbury bells. Behind them, tall salvia thrust purple spikes upward, their backdrop the high tan stucco wall that separated the interior garden from the courtyard of the Portmont family next door.

A wide-brimmed straw bonnet shaded Trinity's head, casting lattice-lacy shadows over her face, but the day was growing ever warmer as the noon hour approached. The clomp of jackboots against cobbles continued to ring out in the quiet day as she pushed back the beribboned hat and let it dangle from its strings against her back. She raised her face to the bright sunlight, welcoming the heat upon her bare skin. If Victoria saw her, of course, she'd receive a scolding. How many times had she reminded both Trinity and Adrianna to protect their creamy skin from the darkening rays of the sun? In truth, Trinity worried more about the sprinkle of dark freckles she had detested so when she was a little girl.

For a moment, she just sat motionlessly. The digging tool forgotten in her lap, she shut her eyes, her thoughts wandering back into the past. If the Continental Congress had not declared war against the mother country, everything would have been so different. Trinity would have been living as Will's wife for four years. The lovely mansion with its pale yellow stucco walls and wide breezy piazzas would have become their home, and she would have long ago packed away the ivory silk wedding dress with its pearl-encrusted train that had swept out an entire six feet behind her.

They would have had their grown-up wedding just down the street at St. Michael's Episcopal church, and Will would have swept her into his arms and carried her across the piazzas and into the large royal blue and white bedchamber on the second floor. She thought then of the way he kissed her and flushed at the memory of how she had let him. But it made her wonder if she might have conceived a child on the wedding night they'd never had—a pretty little girl, perhaps with his green eyes, or a strapping son with the auburn curls inherited by so many Remingtons?

Embarrassed at her own traitorous thoughts, she opened her eyes and threw the spade to the ground. How could she allow herself even to think about the man? Obviously every evil rumor she had heard about him was true. Shunning her was not enough, it seemed. He had to try to seduce her three nights ago at Trenton Hill. He was a reprobate, accustomed to using women as he wished, had she not found that out for herself?

A blaze of hot color ran up beneath her cheekbones, her humiliation made worse by far when she spotted William standing at the railing of the second-story piazza. He'd been watching her and had the nerve to grin and shake a forefinger at her. His voice called out, low but loud enough to float clearly through the garden, now quiet with the British soldiers gone.

"Better put that bonnet back on, Trin. You'll burn that lovely little face of yours."

Trinity gave him a disgusted glare, the expres-

sion she had consistently used to rebuff him
since that night in the cupboard. She turned
away in a show of disdain, as if she thought him
beneath contempt.

After their encounter, which she regretted so
sharply the cut of it slashed her every time she
looked at him, she vowed she would never let
him affect her again. She would never be alone
with him, not even for a moment, and thus far,
she had managed that with admirable aplomb.
Not once had they found themselves together,
much less spoken a word of conversation. *Oh,
yes, but you're aware of him, aren't you, Trin?* she
mocked herself, keeping her eyes resolutely on
the task of pulling up a dandelion. *Even now,
you're wondering if he's still looking. And what he's
thinking, and if that brief kiss affected him the way it
did you. You're a fraud, that's what you are, you silly
woman!* "Hush up, just hush up," she muttered
furiously under her breath, angry that she
couldn't control her own mind because she
wanted desperately to glance up, to see if he was
descending the stairs to the flagstoned terrace
where the white iron tables and chairs were
arranged near the banyan tree. She did not look,
would not look, ashamed that she even wanted
to. She picked up the trowel and dug the ground
with renewed vengeance.

Several moments later when swift footsteps
came crunching toward her atop the crushed
oyster shells forming the path, she froze, then
gathered her haughty distaste around her like a
cloak before she looked up. As it turned out the

effort went unheeded since it was not Will's tall figure gaining on her, but his sister, who looked extremely excited, with flushed face and out of breath, her soft red and green paisley shawl floating from her hand as she hurried toward Trinity.

Behind her friend, Trinity could see that Will had disappeared from the porch. Good, she thought, looking back at Adrianna, whose dark eyes were as bright as if lit from within, like stars in the midnight sky. Trinity put down the trowel, deducing instantly that Adrianna had heard from Geoffrey. And high time it was, too, the poor girl had been beside herself for days.

"Geoffrey'll be here tonight!" Adrianna cried softly, but still too loud for Trinity's comfort, what with an almighty Lord of the Realm like Will lurking about. She stole a glance at the long porches, saw no one, but nevertheless cautioned Adrianna with lowered eyebrows and a warning forefinger against her lips. Adrianna lowered her pitch but not her euphoria. "Oh, Trin, I was terrified he wouldn't get to come before Will takes us aboardship. I couldn't bear not to say good-bye to him."

Once Trinity, too, had lived for each meeting with a man. Unfortunately it had been Will, but that was a long time ago when she'd been young and impressionable, yes, and stupid. Now she was smarter. He was attractive, she was still attracted to him, she could even admit that, but she wasn't naive anymore. And she didn't believe in happy, storybook endings anymore. Love didn't triumph over all like the poets liked to imply but she wouldn't preach her own disillusionment and spoil Adrianna's happiness. Geoffrey was in love with her. He would not hurt her the way Will had hurt Trinity.

"How did he contact you?" she asked in an undertone, reaching out with her shears to cut a tall, perfect salvia stalk for the dinner table bouquet. She pretended a casual manner, for the benefit of any Tory spy watching from behind closed shutters.

"He sent a slave boy to the rear door. The child pretended he'd brought a dozen eggs from his mistress, Mrs. Mary Foster, but he asked for me and then he gave me Geoff's message." Adrianna sat down on the bench beside Trinity and looked around cautiously. She lowered her voice to a mere whisper. "He said Geoff would come tonight after everyone's left for services at St. Michael's."

"But you'll be expected to go, too. What will you tell Will?"

"I shall pretend I'm ill, and you must pretend concern for me and volunteer to stay home as well. I'll say that some such dish I ate disagreed with me. Melanie's boiling mushrooms and rice for supper. I'll say they made me sick." She suddenly knelt and took hold of Trinity's gloved hands. "Oh, please, Trinity, I beg you. Please help me. You must. If Geoffrey doesn't come tonight, I won't ever see him again, I know I won't."

Adrianna looked so distraught that Trinity was

quick to reassure her before the girl burst into tears.

"All right, I'll stay, too, but you've got to let me tell the fibs. Everyone always knows when you're lying because you get all excited and look so guilty. And I must say that right now you look absolutely radiant with happiness, not the least bit ill."

"Oh, I love him so, Trinity, I love him so much I sometimes think I can't bear it. I want to run away with him. I could stay here and fight at his side. I could follow him and wash his clothes and live in the swamp with him. Other wives do that, I've heard about them."

"Geoffrey would never allow that, and well you know it. He wants to offer you everything you've always had."

"I don't care about those things! I only want to be with him!"

"Well, he cares. Now that he's convinced Will to at least put forth his case before His Grace, he's hoping he can marry you with your family's blessing. If not, then he might consider an elopement, but I know that's his last alternative."

"But why must I go all the way to England? What if something happens and my father forces me to wed another? What if Geoffrey needs me and I can't get to him?"

Adrianna's face paled and there was no need to elaborate further. Both women knew exactly what she referred to. What if Geoff was wounded? Or captured? Neither of them, though, wanted to dwell on their worst fears.

"I'm going upstairs now and get ready to see him. What should I wear, Trin? Would my good blue dress with the lace sleeves and yellow fichu be suitable? It's one of Geoff's favorites. He always compliments it."

"He always compliments everything you wear, but that'd be lovely. Remember, Adrianna, you're supposed to be sick with an ailing stomach," she hissed softly but Adrianna was already halfway to the house.

Trinity bent over the flowers again. She, too, was looking forward to Geoffrey's visit. She had not expected to see her cousin again. She bit her lip, trying not to think morbid thoughts but she knew full well that tonight could be the last time she'd ever get to see him.

"Listen to me now, Adrianna," Trinity said sharply, later that evening in Adrianna's bedchamber, "you've got to calm down or no one will believe us."

Adrianna whirled around from her vigil at the window, her face instantly contrite, but in fact, Trinity had to laugh because she looked so comical with her short champagne satin bed jacket hitched over her elegant blue silk frock.

"I can't help it! He'll be here soon!"

"I know. But before he comes, we've first got to get your mother and Will out of the house without alerting their suspicions. Now, jump up and down or chase around the room, or something, so your face'll be all flushed when I bring them up to see about you. I'm going down now but I'll knock twice before I come in, so make sure you're in bed. And, Adrianna, don't forget to tuck all traces of your gown beneath the coverlet."

Trinity left her best friend happily running back and forth beside the bed, her own heart beginning to race with excitement. Fortunately, she could maintain her expression with not a trace of such incriminating emotion. Adrianna, on the other hand, was as transparent as a piece of glass.

The family awaited them in the front reception room, at the bottom of the elegant, freestanding spiral stairs. Victoria sat reading her Bible on a velvet chair against the wainscoted plaster wall but William prowled restlessly back and forth the width of the room, as if very impatient. Taking a moment to adopt a suitably concerned mien, she wrinkled her brow with just the right dose of worry, careful enough, though, to avoid Will's keen gaze. He had a way of searching her face with his piercing green eyes that unsettled her more than most others, and he might be able to see through her pretense.

Slowly she descended the steps, and as she rounded the curve that brought her face-to-face with him, she could feel his gaze upon her, almost like a physical touch. She paused near the bottom just beneath the lifesize portrait of Adrianna's Grandfather Ballantine who'd built this house, but remained on the fourth step, determined that if William took the notion to visit

Adrianna in her room, she would beat him to the punch.

"I'm sorry, Victoria, but Adrianna's not feeling well at all. She's decided to stay home this evening, with your permission."

Victoria rose in concern. She came quickly to the newel post and gazed up at Trinity. "What's wrong? She has been rather wan and unlike herself lately. I was afraid she was catching something."

"Her stomach's cramping a bit, 'tis all. She thinks she might have had an aversion to the mushrooms."

"Oh, my, that's miserable indeed. Well, I suppose I should stay here, too, in case she worsens." She looked at Will. "Will, you'll carry my regrets to Mrs. Foster, won't you? She's invited us for coffee and cake after the service."

Victoria bunched her copper-colored skirt in both hands and raised them as if to climb the steps. "Mary's leaving the city tomorrow and I did want to visit with her before she sets sail."

"No, no, Victoria, you go on now and visit with Mrs. Foster," Trinity said magnanimously, smiling. "And do stay for as long as you like. I'll be happy to stay home with Adrianna." She was intensely aware that William had come to the bottom of the steps and stood behind his mother. She could feel his eyes burning holes in her.

"Why, how very sweet, Trinity, dear. But I must check in on Adrianna before I leave," Victoria said, starting up toward Trinity with William right on her heels.

Trinity sprang into action, whirling and heading up the steps. Not too fast, but quick enough to rap twice on Adrianna's door before they could join her. She waited an extra instant, then turned the brass handle. She breathed easier when they found Adrianna languishing under her satin-draped canopy, her right forearm thrown listlessly over her brow. Her face was impressively flushed.

After a minute of clucking concernedly and tucking loose bedclothing around her daughter, Victoria pressed the back of her hand to Adrianna's cheeks and brow, finally agreeing she was quite flushed and unwell. Black leatherbound prayer book in hand, she turned to William. "Perhaps I should remain here as well," William offered, effectively ruining all their gains, and with not a little suspicion coating his words, Trinity thought.

"That's quite unnecessary, milord, we will do quite fine here alone. 'Tis your mother who doesn't need to be out unescorted on the streets, not with so many scurrilous redcoats slinking about."

Will frowned at her, but of course he couldn't deny her argument. He seemed mightily reluctant as he followed his mother from the room.

"We did it!" Adrianna whispered, leaping from her bed and tearing loose the ribbons fastening the front of her bed jacket. After turning the key securely in the lock, Trinity joined Adriana at the window overlooking the street entrance.

Will was already assisting Victoria into their carriage, but he paused before he climbed in after her, glancing up at the windows. He almost caught them, but Trinity managed to pull Adrianna back in time.

The near miss did not dampen Adrianna's joy, and she flounced off to redo her coiffure at the mirror, but Trinity watched at the window until the driver turned the coach at the corner of Water Street. After Adrianna was satisfied that her long raven curls could not look any better, they headed together for the back gate where Geoffrey would meet them.

Half an hour passed, maybe more, it seemed like a week to Trinity, but it was not until darkness had fallen when a low knock sounded from the alleyside. Smiling, Trinity pulled open the gate, and Adrianna threw herself into her cousin's arms. Trying not to stare, not to give in to the jealousy pricking her, Trinity pretended she didn't see the way Geoffrey kissed her, and the way Adrianna clung to him as if she were a drowning woman.

"Is there anyone in the house?" he asked finally, pulling Trinity against him with his other arm. She hugged him, so pleased to find him safe and with them again.

"No. Victoria and Will have gone to St. Michael's. The servants have retired to their quarters."

"Then come, let's go up to the roof. There's going to be a show tonight that no true Charlestonian will want to miss."

By the time they'd climbed the narrow third-story stairs to the covered widow's walk that formed the perimeter of the roof cupola, Geoffrey had filled them in on the patriots' plan to blow up a munitions ship in the harbor.

"There she is, see her? The large frigate lying farthest from the beach. She'll go up like a sky rocket before the hour's out."

"But how?" Trinity asked excitedly. "Will the patriots attack her?"

"The redcoats've been loading gunpowder aboard her all week long. Much of it's still stacked on the deck. A few flaming arrows ought to send her sky-high. Townsfolk are waiting to see this all over the city."

Trinity moved quickly to the iron railing and leaned far forward so that she could look out over the dark waters of the harbor. A half-moon hung in the darkness of the sky with a million stars aglitter all around it.

"Oh, we'll have a grand view from here!" she murmured, glancing over toward Church Street where Mrs. Foster had her mansion.

"I wish Victoria were here so she could see it, too," Adrianna whispered.

"Oh, she'll see it all right. That's the primary reason Mrs. Foster decided to have the party on her seaside piazza."

Trinity and Adrianna laughed, delightedly, but their enjoyment was short-lived because the clatter of a carriage turning into their gate rang on the stones below.

They ran to the portion of the walkway overlooking the courtyard, and Trinity gasped in dismay when she saw William alight. He was alone.

"Oh, no, Will's come back, and we haven't had time to even talk," Adrianna cried, grabbing Geoffrey's hand.

"He can't find Geoffrey here," Trinity said at once. "He may not let him go again." She made her decision at once, without hesitation. "I'll go down and distract him. Maybe I can think of a way to get him out of the house. Wait here until you see us leave."

Trinity rushed down the narrow stairs to the second floor, then flew down the hall and around the curve of the staircase where she could head off William before he left the foyer, with no clear idea whatsoever of what she could do to keep him away from Adrianna and Geoffrey, only knowing that somehow she had to do it.

Chapter Seven

Leaving the coach at the curb, William Remington ran up the steps and paused on the front stoop to pat down his pockets in search of his key. Why the bloody hell he'd come home so early, he couldn't begin to explain. Or didn't want to admit, he added with a wry twist of his mouth. One thing was for certain, however, he'd had no burning desire to visit Mrs. Mary Brewton Foster's house with his mother.

A hotbed aswarm with patriot sentiment, that abode was, and he'd rather lie down in a nest of pit vipers than subject himself to the carefully civil yet highly contemptuous acceptance of his presence displayed by most of his mother's friends. If he'd had any sense about him, he'd have joined the British officers he'd seen loitering, tankards in hand, outside Johnson's Tavern. A couple had been crewmen from his own ship, and swilling rum and enjoying their company was more than enticing at the moment. Even the attentions of a comely and accommodating barmaid might help him get another, less acceptable woman off his mind.

Scowling, he mumbled a curse when the key continued to evade him, wishing now he had gone out drinking, a pastime a good deal more attractive than watching his sister cry because he was taking her to England, and the rest of the time suffering Trinity Kingston's icicle glances. A memory came unbidden, one that plagued him often of late, when the lady hadn't been so cold, when her mouth trembled softly beneath his just long enough for him to know she found him every bit as interesting as he did her. Was that ever a mistake, kissing her, and dammit to blazes, where was the bloody key?

The truth was, of course, that he was more than suspicious of everything the two young women did. Staying home alone, out of the blue, didn't sit quite right with him, although he could readily admit Adrianna had certainly appeared to be caught up in a nervous frenzy since he'd announced the duke's intention to betrothe her to an Englishman.

A woman's prerogative, to be sure, especially considering her affection for Geoffrey. That marriage did not have a chance in hell; his father wouldn't even consider it, was Will's best guess. Still, he'd try to encourage him in that respect, as he'd promised Geoffrey. Now his little sister was abed, ill, or so she said, and he wondered if she wasn't using the evening to rendezvous with Geoffrey somewhere. Then, of course, and more infuriating, there was Trinity.

He finally found the key and got it into the lock. His unwanted wife had been dominating most of his waking thoughts, something he felt foolish even admitting to himself. He'd even caught himself spying on her from the library window when she was working in the garden. Today he'd even walked outside and called to her. Like some damn fool adolescent, he berated himself, thrusting open the door.

Inside he found a single lamp burning on the round marble table gracing the center of the foyer. Though the hour was relatively early, the rooms off to both sides were dark and deserted. He removed his black tricorne and gloves and laid them on the polished marble, then drew up in surprise when he realized Trinity had miraculously appeared at the foot of the steps. He'd neither seen nor heard how she'd gotten there, but she was breathing fast as if she'd dashed there in a hurry.

"Hello, Will." Then she graced him with something completely unexpected. An absolutely dazzling smile, the kind she usually bestowed on others but never on him. Perversely, he was pleased but at the same time still wary of her motives.

"Good evening, Trinity."

Repocketing the key he glanced up at the top of the stairs that lay in dark shadows.

"How is Adrianna feeling?"

"Oh, she's very much better. In fact, she's sleeping quite peacefully at the moment. I convinced her to take a small dose of laudanum to help her rest. She's very worried about what you're going to do about her, but I'm sure you've noticed that."

"Yes."

Trinity still wore the gown she'd had on earlier that evening, a deep rose satin gathered by a tightly laced pale pink stomacher. While he stood silently, waiting for her to continue, she took a dark blue shawl edged with long black silk fringe from over her arm and, seemingly quite unconcerned by his presence, gracefully fashioned the wrap around her shoulders.

"You've no call for concern, I assure you. If we don't disturb her, I'm certain she'll feel herself again in the morning."

He watched her pick up a black bonnet with pink ribbons, then blithely move past him to situate herself in front of the tall gilt mirror beside the front door. His eyes dropped appreciatively to her tiny waist and slim hips as she adjusted the hat to best advantage, remembering with an unsettling burst of clarity how that slim little body had felt pressed against him.

"Pardon my intrusion, Trinity, but you're not preparing yourself for an outing, I hope."

She finished tying the ribbons into a jaunty bow beneath her chin, then turned at once, all wide-eyed innocence. "Why, yes. I feel I must have a spot of fresh air after so long in the sick room. I've grown used to a late night stroll when the town lies sleeping."

"Or perhaps a night ride with a courier pouch strapped to your saddle."

Evidently offended, she moved as if to step

around him. He blocked her path. "I don't think a walk is wise for a young woman alone at this time of night."

"If you'll excuse me, sir, I don't believe I need your permission to leave this house."

William smiled tightly. "I couldn't in good conscience allow you to endanger yourself in such a way."

"I intend only a short walk down to the church and back."

"Not by yourself."

She observed him thoughtfully, then startled him with another pleasant smile and as gracious a capitulation as he'd ever heard.

"Then perhaps you'd agree to escort me. I'd appreciate your company."

William inclined his head, fully expecting that she might very well be drawing him into an ambush by a gang of her patriot cronies. He would not put it past her, but he was curious to find out, and more importantly, he was armed.

"I'd be honored."

"You're most kind."

All very stilted and polite, and now he knew for sure that she was up to no good. Increasingly, he was eager to find out what she had in store for him. Something about Trinity made him want to sharpen his wits and duel with her. Who knew, perhaps they'd end up in each other's arms again. He couldn't say he'd mind that.

"It's certainly a pleasant night to be out, is it not?" Trinity remarked as they descended to the street and set off side by side north toward St. Michael's.

"Have you truly been out alone at night since we've come to town?" he asked, wondering momentarily about her lack of propriety, then laughing at himself for having such thoughts. A stroll down Charleston streets was tame behavior indeed for Trinity Kingston.

"I'm quite capable of taking care of myself, as you are aware. Thanks to you and your King, I no longer have a father here to protect me."

Will was not immune to her dig, for subtle it was not. He chose to ignore it, determined to carve out a better relationship with the woman. Quite inexplicably, or perhaps not so, he found himself wanting to get to know her better. A dangerous pursuit under the circumstances, and with a woman as appealing as she was.

"Have you had word yet of my father?" she asked suddenly, glancing sidelong at him as they passed beneath a lamplight set at the intersection of East Battery and Water streets. The small flame cast a dim circle of yellow over her, causing her hair to gleam like molten gold. Though she usually spoke with great bravado, this mention of her father revealed her anxiety.

"Afraid not. Cornwallis is looking into the matter for me. We should know something soon."

Once again they walked along in silence, not touching, the hollow click of their footsteps loud in the quiet night. They passed a few other pedestrians but most of the houses they passed were bright with warm lamplight in the windows and the sounds of music or conversation floating off the wide breezy porches. Many families had only recently returned from evening church, and far-off in the night, the distant tramp of soldiers brought back the city's occupation.

They actually took a stab at chat—Trinity's thoughts upon the crystal-clear quality of the starry sky; William remarked upon the sweet fragrance of bougainvillea hanging in lush, splendorous festoons along the tops of the bricked walls of Meeting Street. All manner of inconsequential topics flowed between them, but at least they were talking together without shooting stinging barbs meant to inflict pain. Though he knew full well the hostility was still there, at the moment it was hidden under her lovely smile, subdued for some reason known only to Trinity. Perhaps only in order to gain an escort for a cool night walk. She did seem somewhat nervous, a trait he hadn't noticed in her before, as she continually seemed to glance out over the harbor.

When they reached the edge of St. Michael's churchyard, there came the cry of a baby from some nearby window but the infant's fussing soon faded, and the street lay silent again as they paused at the front of the church with its soaring steeple and four-faced clock. The sanctuary candles were still lit from the sermon earlier that evening, the tall windowpanes rising in elongated yellow squares that slanted rays of light into the walled cemetery.

"My mother's buried here," Trinity suddenly

said, her voice quiet. "Would you mind if we stopped there for a moment?"

"No, of course not." William was surprised for he'd never heard her discuss her mother. He remembered that Trinity had been a mere infant when she passed away.

Trinity led the way through the dark shadows to where a large mausoleum stood, its shiny white marble aglow against the night sky. Twin angels in flowing alabaster robes guarded each corner, their magnificent wings folded, their palms pressed together in prayerful repose. He watched as she knelt and rearranged the bouquet of roses gracing the bronze vase.

"I brought these earlier today from Victoria's garden. You see, I promised Papa I'd bring a bouquet every time I visited the city, since he no longer can."

This time there was no blame in her words, only sadness, and he wanted her to understand that he was not immune to her pain. "I'm sorry about your father, Trinity. I hope you'll believe that. I wish none of this had ever happened."

Trinity looked up at him, seemingly surprised. Her voice was hushed.

"Mother died when I was only a toddler. I look at her portrait sometimes and wonder what kind of person she was. Papa says she was stubborn at times, but mostly she was the sweetest, most loving woman he'd ever known."

She fiddled with the large red roses as she spoke but little difference was made in the arrangement, and he knew she merely wanted to touch them.

She sighed audibly, and William couldn't help but feel a pang of compassion for her. She'd never known a mother's love, and now she faced the world alone. She needed a protector, a husband, but even he had abandoned her. Suddenly she straightened and tilted her head up to the sky. "I do believe this is the most beautiful night I've ever seen, don't you think so, Will? Just look up at all those stars."

He had to smile at her innocence. He'd never seen her look as lovely as she did there under the starlight.

"I'd like to show you something," she said to him, "something truly breathtaking. Would you like to see it?"

He was already seeing it, he thought, full of admiration for the woman who would have been his true wife if circumstances had been different. And now he knew it would not have been an unhappy match for him, perhaps, but now the union was completely impossible. He had to remember that. She was not his wife, not his betrothed; she was nothing to him and never could be.

"What would that be?" He sobered when he realized he was smiling down at her like a besotted beau, but still it would behoove him to get along with her if he wanted her to sign the annulment.

"Then you'll come? It'll only take a moment."

She actually reached out and took him by the hand, all sweetness and womanly grace in rustling pink silk and soft, fragrant hands, and he followed her, like a lamb to the slaughter, he could not help but conclude.

Smiling, happier than he'd seen her for a time, she led him inside the vestibule at the front of the church. The vicar still stood at the altar with a handful of the choir members, and Trinity pressed her forefinger against her lips to silence Will. She opened a door in an alcove and revealed narrow steps leading up into the darkness.

By the first turn in the stairs, William realized she was taking him up into the bell tower. After a short climb, they exited into the fresh air where cool sea breezes whispered in Trinity's silk skirt and billowed them out in a gentle wave. She laughed, holding the fabric down with maidenly modesty, then seated herself gracefully on a bench beside the door.

"There. Is this not the most glorious view you've ever seen?"

William glanced out over the harbor, where he could faintly make out the dark hulking shadows of ships, their mast lanterns twinkling against the black water. Stars spangled the ebony sky and seemed to stretch out to infinity.

"Aye, 'tis lovely," he agreed, leaning a shoulder against the wall. "Is this a place you come often?"

"When I visit the city, I always come up here. But tonight is special."

"Special? Why?"

"You'll see."

Aha, she was hiding a secret from him. Intrigued, he watched her remove her hat, lay it aside, then absently finger the curls escaping the loose knot atop her head.

"It's always so cool up this high," she said softly. "Especially at night."

"Have you always been allowed to traipse around the city unescorted?" he had to ask, finding it incomprehensible that any man would allow such behavior in a female member of his family, especially one so beautiful.

"Yes. Father trusts me. Besides, what safer place for me to be than atop a church bell tower? And this night I even have a gentleman to protect me," she teased him.

Visions of her other nocturnal visits with other gentlemen immediately entered William's mind. How many suitors had Trinity brought up to this private roost to stargaze? Who were they? And had they had more on their mind than astronomy? Incredibly, he had to force himself not to demand answers from her as if he truly was her husband.

This young woman sitting before him was not his wife, he reminded himself again, not even his betrothed. He shouldn't be here alone with her now, or any other time.

"I'm surprised that you're not out hobnobbing with Tarleton and his cronies," she remarked suddenly. "Adrianna told me that you knew him in England."

"It's true I knew him there, though not particularly well," he answered with some care, alert to the harder edge to her tone.

"Did your mother tell you that Tarleton banished poor Mrs. Foster from Charleston?"

Mary Brewton Foster was the friend Victoria now visited, but his mother had made no mention of Mary's disfavor in British circles.

"No, she didn't. Why don't you enlighten me?"

"She offended Tarleton and in revenge he ordered her to leave the city. She departs tomorrow, that's the reason for tonight's soiree. She wished to bid farewell to all her loyal friends and neighbors."

William looked askance at her, more than skeptical.

"What could Mrs. Foster have done that could be so offensive that Banastre Tarleton would force her out of Charleston?"

"'Twas a remark she made after Tarleton's men were soundly beaten back by our brave Americans under Will Washington at the Battle of the Cowpens. He comes from here in Charleston, you know. Tarleton announced to Mrs. Foster that he'd like to meet this Washington fellow and she merely told him that he should have looked behind him at Cowpens."

William had to laugh, well imagining how that remark would have pricked the young British officer's pride. Tarleton was known to be a notorious snob, even on the best of days.

"He is nothing less than a monster, you know," Trinity went on calmly. "We have begun to call him Butcher Tarleton, and that is a far better designation than he deserves."

William opened his mouth to answer but his words were robbed from him as a terrible booming rolled inward from off the sea, rattling windowpanes in the church below. Trinity jumped to her feet and ran to the rail. He grabbed her arm, his first thought that they were under attack, but she was laughing, out loud, a pleased, joyous sound.

"There, my lord Thorpe, I give you your surprise," she cried out, whirling to see his reaction.

In the wink of an eye, her gentleness, her sweet manner, had disintegrated, obviously false from the beginning. Astounded that the patriots would attack the British-held city, but fearing just that, he turned slowly to peer down over the harbor. With solemn eyes he watched the great streaks of fire shoot up into the night sky, one after another, a furnace of flames already enveloping the great towering hull of an English frigate.

One explosion after another shook the night, sending reverberating vibrations rolling out over the waterfront like waves of angry thunder. And between each blast of gunpowder, each new geyser of sparks and flames, he could hear the distant clapping and cheering from the citizens of the occupied city. He turned to look at Trinity, and in her face, he saw sheer pleasure at the conflagration, and he realized just how filled she was with American pride, and he was glad he was taking her away from the horrors of war.

Chapter Eight

The patriot attack on the H.M.S. *Wellington* did not go unavenged by Cornwallis. Dire consequences descended upon the city of Charleston like the plague of locusts over biblical Egypt. The King's troops flooded the streets along the harbor and spread throughout the night into the outlying districts.

By the first golden crown of dawn, well nigh a hundred suspected traitors were rounded up, interrogated, and to the horror of every true libertarian, nearly a dozen were hanged by the neck until dead on a hastily constructed scaffold in front of the Old Exchange and Provost Prison on East Bay Street. In the days that followed the executions, front stoops and porch railings were defiantly draped with festoons of black crepe as the funerals of the patriot martyrs commenced.

Several of the executed men were well known to Victoria and Trinity alike, but one of the deceased was Waltham Coates, the eldest son of Victoria's dearest friend—a personable young gentleman who was close in age to both Adrianna and Trinity, and his death was taken particularly hard by the ladies of the Remington town house.

Though uncomfortable himself with the harshness of Cornwallis's retaliation, William felt obliged to forbid anyone in his household to attend the funeral. He did not know young Coates himself but was certain that the British command would observe and note the mourners for possible ties to the treason.

Thank God his mother had enough consideration for her husband's title to obey him. Both she and Adrianna accepted his order without argument, but Trinity of course was not nearly so cooperative. On the day of the funeral, while William was calling upon Cornwallis in the house on King Street that he'd commandeered from Rebecca Motte and her daughters, Trinity slipped away through the rear alley and was gone before anyone could prevent it.

Now William found himself in the untenable position of chasing her down before she got herself in more trouble. He'd heard the memorial services had become a forum for the expression of patriot outrage that could be adopted by the entire populace. The most courageous, or most reckless, as was more befitting in Trinity's case, would attend, and once they made themselves known, the British would surveil them from that moment forward, as well as everyone else in their families.

William strung together a whole litany of foul words under his breath, then increased his step down the cobblestones of Broad Street. He avoided looking at the gallows where Tarleton, already so blatantly detested in the city, had seen fit to leave several corpses dangling from the gibbet. Left out in the sun for two days now, they were a macabre reminder of England's might.

More and more often, and completely against his better judgment, William was beginning to see why his mother and all Carolinians were losing any loyalty they'd previously shown toward the mother country. Tarleton was a damned fool to incite patriot fervor in such a way, and William was genuinely shocked that Cornwallis would allow such brutality and had told him so. William himself was English through and through and proud of it, with an English title and property and loyalties to match, but these colonials were Englishmen, too. They were his family, his friends, and his maternal ancestors.

Many of those he watched persecuted by the occupying forces were innocent of any wrongdoing, other than a fierce love and loyalty to husbands, sons, lovers, and country. Now that he'd positioned himself smack-dab in the middle of the conflict, he could see firsthand the dire effects of the fighting, especially upon his gracious mother. She loved the Carolinas more than anything else, with the sole exception of her children.

Then there was Trinity. What in God's name was he going to do with her? She was impossibly impulsive, no, foolhardy would be a better word, dangerously so, and fearless. And lovely, and intriguing, he thought against his will, remember-

ing the way she'd looked bathed in moonlight
that night so high up in the bell tower. All that
aside, however, she was a frustrating, maddening woman, and if he didn't do something, if she
wasn't careful, she was going to be very dead,
very soon.

His primary concern now, of course, had to be
just to get her out of Charleston before something did happen to her. Unfortunately, she was
his responsibility now, at least until he got her
back to England where she'd be safe from harm.
Then the annulment could be reinstated, and he
could wash his hands of her constant trouble-
making. Now the time was at hand for their departure. He'd finally found out where Eldon
Kingston had been incarcerated, and that, if
nothing else, was enough to make Trinity do his
bidding. If she didn't first end up dangling from
a noose.

By the time he reached the white edifice of St.
Michael's, the interior was completely full and
overflowing into the churchyard. People dressed
completely in black hovered in groups among
the headstones, and more milled outside the
iron-spiked fence along the planked sidewalk.
He searched among the mourners for a glimpse
of Trinity, did not see her, but he eyed the soldiers in red coats and crossed white bandoliers
who lined the opposite side of the street, mus-
kets at the ready in an overt show of force. He
nodded to the nearest soldier of the Crown, an
adjutant of Tarleton's whom William had met before, then found his way through the pressing

crowd up the steps and into the foyer of the church.

The services had already begun. Friends of the deceased American hero sat shoulder to shoulder in the long mahogany pews, many weeping openly into black handkerchiefs, and William scanned the place, row by row, for a glow of soft red-gold hair, thinking the vibrant hue would show up immediately among the somber shades of gray, black, and dark blue. His search did not find her and he entertained the hope that she had shown a modicum of good sense for a change and not shown up. Then he saw her.

Hell, he should have known she wouldn't do herself or him the favor of blending in with the other grieving members of the funeral party. Oh, no, she had to make a spectacle of herself by planting her pretty little bottom next to the clergyman himself. At the very front of the sanctuary, where she couldn't be missed. He set his jaw even harder, absolutely furious with her as he edged inside and stood against the wall behind the last pew. He bowed his head when the pastor began the opening prayer.

Afterward, those in the audience ahemed, shifted restlessly, and sighed from their places in the pews. Many women still snuffled and sobbed into their palms. Nearly everyone in Charleston was in attendance, or at least it seemed so, he thought, glancing around the room. To his surprise, there were even a few members of well-known Tory families who'd previously welcomed the British invasion with open arms, but now sat in hard-faced support of their patriot neighbors. Apparently even their commitment to George could not condone the extreme cruelty of the Tarleton reprisal. No wonder the war had dragged on year after year. Every time the English committed such an act, they gave birth to more American martyrs and intensified patriot zeal to fight against injustice.

He watched the first man rise to eulogize Coates. Will recognized him as Brigham Watter, and noticed the man was careful to control his rage against the enemy, though his voice trembled slightly with it, and his frustration and pain were readily apparent in the sober lines of his face. Still, he held himself tightly in restraint, and spoke of young Coates in a deep-felt, hoarse voice.

Friend after friend, one family member after another, spoke of the young man's virtue in hushed, stricken tones. William listened and watched from where he leaned his back against the wall but his attention strayed more and more often to Trinity's place on the velvet bench behind the lectern. She looked absolutely gorgeous, of course, even in jet-black crepe, but then, when did she not?

Trinity, too, seemed to reflect the melancholy mood pervading the church, a sadness that was almost a tangible cloud one could reach out and touch. She sat motionlessly, subdued in a way William had rarely seen in her, her hands folded primly atop her lap. It was very strange to see her thus, so silent, without the animation and sparkle he'd grown accustomed to.

Since he had arrived in South Carolina, he had found her so full of life, all fire and passion, so much so that his own life had begun to feel bleak and predictable. In truth, she mesmerized him, like a dancing point of light in a darkened room, one that enthralled a man, captured his entire attention, and blinded him to everything else.

His gaze circuiting the church again, he wondered if any of the gentlemen present watched her as William did, or perhaps a better question, how many did so? Had some of them courted Trinity in the preceding year when she was still wed to William but thought herself a free woman? It was a true miracle she had not wed another man, he decided, but forgot those thoughts when Trinity suddenly rose gracefully and moved to the lectern.

God's mercy, she was going to immortalize Coates, too, and he had no doubt that she would not mince words, nor be so circumspect as the speakers before her. God only knew what words of treason would spill from her mouth. Mentally bracing himself for whatever catastrophe was about to happen, he prayed she'd contain herself enough not to get arrested. There was a limit to how many times he'd be able to save her fool neck.

As the rustling murmurs in the church grew quiet, everyone waiting, she began to sing. William stood stock-still, flabbergasted, as her velvet-coated voice rose up to resonate within the large room, a low smooth alto, hauntingly beautiful.

"Amazing Grace" flowed into the air with the calming effect of a slow and peaceful river, and she sang the words of the lovely old hymn in a way he had never heard before. Her face was so much a portrait in perfection, but even that dimmed beneath the crystal-clear waterfall of notes filling the chamber and touching the entire congregation with its sweetness. He'd never heard a better voice, not even in the most prestigious of opera houses. Trinity could earn a fine living on the stage, he realized, and with her fiery beauty, she'd be an overnight sensation.

As the last notes faded, people shifted, clothes rustled, coughs were muffled, then the eight men who were to act as pallbearers rose. They lifted Coates's casket with utmost reverence, and the family moved out behind them while others in attendance followed toward the gravesite in the cemetery. Trapped at the back of the church, William quickly lost sight of Trinity but managed to weave his way to one of the windows where he could see the people gathered among the graves. There, he saw her again, but only a brief glimpse before she disappeared into the crowd moving slowly toward the Coates crypt in a far corner of the property.

Trinity had seemed in no hurry, apparently preparing to witness the burial, and he felt no need to pursue her in haste so he resigned himself to wait with those around him until the church cleared.

Almost immediately upon stepping out into the warm sunshine, however, he glimpsed her again, and detected she was inching away from the crowd ringing the graveside service. When she glanced around, in a manner that seemed decidedly furtive to his eyes, he wasn't surprised when she ducked out of sight behind a tall marble obelisk. William knew then, with sinking heart, that she was up to mischief. Why else would she sneak away using the crowd and confusion in the cemetery to conceal her departure? Why, indeed? Unless she'd seen him and wished to elude him?

Careful to avoid being noticed, he wended a path through the rows of graves until he, too, was half-concealed by the marble bulk of larger crypts with towering granite angels. He cut behind one of them to an adjacent path that was well shaded by tall hedges, knowing instinctively she'd have chosen the path best suited to hide her flight. He struck out between gravesites to try to cut her off, becoming more and more irritated he had to chase her around. Dammit, he'd spent half his time since arriving in America doing just that.

When he came out ahead of the point on the curve of the path where he thought he'd intercept her, she had been too swift for him. He barely caught a glimpse of the tail of her black skirt as she rounded the corner off to his right. And a fair clip away. Damn the woman! He increased his pace, then muttered another furious curse when he reached that spot and found no trace of her.

Scanning the surrounding paths fanning out all around him, he tried to think where she could have disappeared to, when it suddenly occurred to him, if his memory was not faulty, that the Kingston family crypt that she had pointed out to him the night of the attack would be somewhere nearby.

After several moments searching the tombs, he found the tall rectangular marble crypt with its trio of praying angels. Four curved steps led up to the small building and a black wrought-iron gate, and the roses Trinity had arranged so artfully still graced the attached vase. Furious at himself for coming up with another dead end, he frowned, already turning back to rejoin the funeral procession, when he hesitated and looked up at the gate again. Almost as an afterthought, he climbed the steps and put his hand on the secured gate. The barred grate moved easily. She'd gone inside, he knew it as well as he knew his own name. Slowly, not sure what to expect, he opened the gate and turned the brass knob on the wooden door closing off the interior.

Without a sound, he nudged the inner door ajar with a finger. Sunlight flowed around him like liquid fire filling up the dark tomb, a smoky, slanted shaft of light that caught Trinity redhanded in whatever dirty trick she was up to. She spun to face him, the sun turning her hair into a golden red halo. Her face was at first appalled, then rapidly entertained him with a wealth of flitting expressions from shock to horror to guardedness. To her credit, she was not a smooth liar; her excuses came, quick and nervous, and a good deal more lame than usual.

"What are you doing here? Will you give me no privacy whatsoever? Not even at Mother's grave?"

So she meant to turn the tables of guilt, he thought, slightly startled when she rushed at him, as if to press past him and outside in a haughty, offended huff, but he ended her flight quickly enough. Grabbing her elbow, he stopped her in her tracks.

"Let go of me!"

He'd never heard her so furious, and she twisted her arm sharply against his tight grip. He held on, keeping her in place at his side as he peered into the gloom behind her. Kingston forebears had been interred in marble crypts stacked against each side with each name displayed upon a polished brass plaque. Still suspicious, he took a step inside, taking Trinity along, who did not hesitate to make her annoyance with him known.

Then he stopped. Two men were huddled together, pressed into a corner, patriot soldiers both, dressed in filthy tattered blue uniforms. A bloody bandage covered one's forehead; the other had gauze wrapped around his legs. But William stared at the one propped against the wall, the one who held a pistol trained on William's chest. Only a few seconds passed, however, before he lowered it, as if too weak to hold the weight. He let it clatter down against the stone floor, and his head lolled to one side.

"Please don't give them up to Tarleton."

Trinity moved quickly, placing herself as an unlikely barrier between him and the wounded men.

"They're friends of mine, Will, and they're hurt, terribly hurt. Tarleton'll hang them like he did the others."

William looked down into her face, then back at the two enemy soldiers. The bandage around the man's head was so saturated with blood that it dripped down his cheek and into his open shirt. The other seemed only half-conscious where he lay prone on the floor.

William hesitated. He was not sure what to do, though he well knew what he ought to do. He was shocked out of his dilemma when Trinity suddenly grabbed both his hands. He tensed for attack but she only sank to her knees in a pool of black silk at his feet. "I'm begging you, Will. Let them go, please. I'll do whatever you say, I swear. They're being picked up tonight. I arranged it myself. They're no threat to you now. Look at them. They can't even walk."

William had no doubt about the truthfulness of that statement. He was more affected by the tears welling up and glittering in Trinity's eyes. If he let them go, he'd be every bit as guilty as she, an accomplice to treasonable acts, in essence a rebel sympathizer. It was his duty to deliver them to Tarleton and Cornwallis. Trinity's tears were dripping off her lashes now, rolling down the soft curve of her cheek. "Please, Will, they won't fight again for months, neither of them. I swear I won't fight you anymore; I'll do anything you ask of me if you'll just spare them."

Her amber eyes beseeched him, full of fear for her friends, and he fought an internal battle between duty and compassion. He thought of his father and how appalled he would be that his son even wavered in this decision, but then again Will had stopped trying to please his father years ago. He stared down at Trinity, a vision of the gallows at the Old Exchange House coming to mind, as she pressed the back of his hand against her tear-damp cheek. It was her muffled sob that did him in.

"There are redcoats all over the place. Don't show yourself, or these men, until well after dark, or you'll be caught. Do you understand me, Trin? If that happens, you'll probably hang, too, and there'll be nothing I can do to help you."

Trinity nodded eagerly, a smile showing through the tears, but she was terribly relieved and her gratitude showed in her face as he helped her to her feet.

"Thank you, Will. I'll never forget this, never."

The soft look on her face came close to touching his heart but he tried to block that response, frowning blackly down at her, angry at her for putting him in such a dangerous strait, and even more furious at himself for allowing her traitorous activities.

"Just lock the goddamn gate this time," he told her through gritted teeth before he stepped out-

side and left her to her fate. He paused on the
steps, waiting to make sure he heard the metallic
scrape of the key inside the lock. As soon as the
door was secured, he hastily retraced his steps
toward the funeral service, all the while cursing
himself for being the biggest fool who ever
walked British soil. God help him if she did get
caught. Hell, she'd probably turn him in as a co-
conspirator. Somehow, down deep, he knew that
Trinity wouldn't get caught, in fact, would do
whatever necessary to get her friends to a safe
haven. He just hoped she didn't get hurt in the
process. That was one thing for which he'd never
forgive himself.

Chapter Nine

The tall case clock in the front foyer with its carved rosettes and swinging brass pendulum had long ago sent out the tinkling chimes of the midnight hour when Trinity opened the front door of the piazza without a whisper of sound, then tiptoed with the stealth of a mouse across the long deserted porch. Everyone was asleep, of course, and she noted with a sigh of relief that the drawing rooms and dining parlor windows were squares of black against the white stucco walls. She had lingered at the church, knowing full well she had to sneak back in the dead of night. She did not intend to confront William head-on, at least not when she was so exhausted.

Truthfully, she was slightly surprised he wasn't awake and crouching to pounce on her like a vulture with folded wings. Unfortunately, she owed him a debt now, one that dwarfed anything else in her life. Chagrined, her smooth brow puckered and she muttered a few choice remarks concerning him under her breath. Detesting him as a horrible, despicable devil had gradually become a way of life for her; almost like a gaily wrapped present she gave to herself each morning when she woke up.

Since he'd come home, she'd had a fine time pricking him with the most incredibly rude insults at each and every turn of conversation. What immense satisfaction she'd derived from it, and now that delightful pastime would be taken from her. He had done her a great service. She was grateful to him, though she wished she wasn't. From now on, she'd have to be much more accommodating and respectful to his wishes, drat it all.

Pausing at the parlor door, she slipped out of her black slippers and crept like a specter through the immense dining room, feeling like a child lost in a palace as she negotiated her way behind the twenty-six chairs and long table. She stole up the shadowy staircase, avoiding the third step from the top, one that she had learned was prone to creak. She stopped and looked down the upstairs corridor to where William had taken his father's old bedchamber. A good distance down the hall from her own, and quite dark and quiet.

Smiling, smugly impressed by her own cleverness, she ducked into her room and turned the key. She gave a low, pleased laugh as she leaned her back against the door. However, her high spirits quickly flagged. Sheer fatigue overtook her, and she headed straight for her own canopied bed, not bothering to light a candle, falling facedown upon the soft feather ticking with a sigh of pleasure. Enveloped in the soft quilts and private sanctuary of her familiar things, she knew she was safe.

Her eyes popped open when she heard a fluttering, rustling sound, a scrape. Then she smelled the tobacco, and she lunged up, bracing herself on her forearms as a candle flared. On the far side of the bed, not a yard-span away, William sprawled carelessly in her yellow-sprigged desk chair, drawn up close beside the bed. He had his boots propped on the side rail. Wide-eyed, openmouthed, she stared at him until she remembered herself. He leaned back, an indolent grin on his face, the newly lit cheroot held idly between two fingers. A bottle of brandy and two glasses sat on the graceful white bedside table beside him. His eyes locked unflinchingly with hers, he lifted a glass with his left hand, drained it to the bottom, then bent forward to refill it. To the top.

"You've no right to come into my bedchamber. 'Tis private," she finally managed in a breathy accusation, genuinely outraged by such a scandalous intrusion.

" 'Tis true, it's your private chamber, but then again, this is my house, and I go where I please in it."

Trinity frowned uncertainly, but William suddenly gave a low and pleasant rumble of a laugh that she had not heard often.

Why, perhaps he's already in his cups, she thought with some hope. Now that would be a sight to see, but no, she couldn't imagine him allowing such a thing—he was too self-controlled and imperious to succumb to inebriation.

"You do look a bit ashy-faced, Trin. Didn't you expect me to welcome you home? Not that I expected you to make it back. I feared we'd find you in some ditch tomorrow with a gaping bullet hole between your eyes."

"No such luck," she said, sitting up on her knees, her full skirts mushrooming around her. "I'm quite well with no extra holes in my person, so you can get along now out of my bedchamber and back to your own." She paused, again rather amazed that he would have done something so improper, and with his mother in residence at that. "You'd best hope Victoria doesn't find out about this. She'll be appalled at such behavior from a man of your breeding."

"If we're talking about propriety, Trinity, my dear, I will say to you that there's not a proper bone in your body, and never has been. You've flouted good manners since you were knee-high."

Trinity was almost tempted to smile. She quickly stopped herself. Instead she bunched her billowing skirt and swung her legs over his side of the bed until she sat facing him. Suddenly an incredible thrill of dark excitement coursed through her. There he sat in her bedchamber in the middle of the night, blatantly ignoring what anyone might say if they should find them. She had thought him too well schooled and well-bred to do such a thing.

She realized he'd shed his satin frock coat and

unwrapped the black silk necktie. The ends lay loose around his neck, and his waistcoat was unbuttoned and hanging open. The linen shirt he wore beneath was untied at the throat, and for the first time since she'd known him, he appeared informal, totally relaxed and at ease, sitting there with his dark skin and green eyes, smoking and drinking, and looking completely, deliciously, wickedly decadent. She laughed nervously as a silvery shiver raced up her spine.

He didn't spare her a smile.

"Well? Did you manage to save your friends?" he shifted in the chair, one that seemed much too slender for his large body, and propped one boot atop his opposite knee. He absently swirled the amber liquid pooled in the bottom of his glass, never taking his eyes off her.

"Thanks to you, they're safely on their way back to Will Washington's encampment." She shot a quick glance at the brandy bottle and arched a brow. "Aren't you going to offer me a drink?"

William stared at her in silence, and then she watched his fine lips curve in that slow, irresistible grin that had melted Trinity for more years than she could remember. "So much for your maidenly outrage about my compromising your sensibilities, eh? Now you're quite willing to share a drink with the enemy who has intruded upon the unsullied sanctuary of your bedroom?"

"Only so that I might toast the gentleman who saved two brave men," she said primly.

Neither spoke then, and Trinity watched without comment as he filled her glass with more spirits than he should, indeed nearly to the brim. He picked it up, leaned forward, and placed it carefully in her hand. She was not unaware of the way his fingers encircled hers, for several beats longer than necessary. His smile was full of challenges.

Trinity had never been one to ignore a gauntlet tossed at her feet. "Could it be, milord, that you have never before seen a lady partake of spirits?"

"Let's just say I'm curious to see if you toss it back like a drunken buccaneer."

"Then I'm afraid, sir, you're in for a disappointment," she replied, imbibing with the smallest of sips but nonetheless welcoming the bracing fire that slipped down her throat and hit the floor of her belly in a warm caress.

"Well, not exactly a pirate's swill, but no harsh fit of coughing, either, so I suppose you've more experience than I thought with a brandy decanter."

"My watering eyes proves you wrong, I fear," she answered, her throat still burning. She partook again, to bolster her courage, all the while studying his face from over the rim. "The truth is that I need a bracing libation to help me express my gratitude."

"Sounds intriguing. I'm listening."

She was struck suddenly that the light mood of their banter, the grudging smiles they were sharing, very much resembled a flirtation. Now that was a pastime she'd never dreamed of enjoying with William Remington, not that she was enjoying it. She wasn't, not in the least. But she had harbored fantasies of them together alone, when she was reaching adulthood and thought of him as her husband.

Dashing such thoughts from her head, she focused on less frivolous subjects, and gazed directly into his eyes. When she spoke, it came indeed straight from her heart.

"It was a brave thing you did today. Helping us. I was certain that you'd turn the three of us over to Butcher Tarleton."

"I should have, it's true."

"You had every right, every reason to do so."

"True, again."

She paused an instant, waiting for him to explain. He didn't, so she succumbed to her curiosity. "Why didn't you then?"

William leaned forward, close enough for her to smell the brandy and a faint tinge of his shaving soap. He did not smile but answered with grave sobriety.

"I didn't turn you in because I've seen too bloody many gallow shows with shackled patriots since I came back here. I'm not of a mind to cause another funeral, or listen to another mother weep."

Trinity leaned back, bracing her open palms on the bed behind her. She contemplated him, long and hard.

"Am I to assume then, despite all evidence to the contrary, that a human heart beats inside that brawny chest of yours?"

He cocked his head and arched one dark brow,

and the flickering candlelight darkened the hollows of his eyes. "So you think me brawny, do you?"

She had not expected that response, and for some reason, a hot, humiliating blush rose swiftly up her throat, into her cheeks. How bizarre, truly, that they were here alone, talking together in civil tones, after the things she'd said to him, and he to her. He seemed a completely different person now. A strange emotion fluttered inside her heart, down deep where she had banished the affection she had once held for him.

Struck silent by her own emotional confusion, she watched William settle back into his chair, wondering if he felt anything similar. Probably not, she decided as he took a long drag on his cigar, his eyes narrow and watchful.

"Maybe I let those men go today because I want a truce between us. Maybe I've found I like you more than I thought, perhaps even admire your courage, although I find it misguided most of the time. For some inexplicable reason I've found I don't like the fact that you hate my guts. I might deserve it, hell, I do deserve it for jilting you the way I did. But that's in the past. One thing's for certain, Trin, I don't want to see you get shot, or end up standing with a noose around your neck, and that is precisely what's going to happen if you continue to risk that lovely little neck of yours, time and again, the way you've been doing since before I got here."

By the time he had finished that most extraordinary speech, Trinity was too overwhelmed by the things he said to respond, for he'd uttered them with a soft sincerity and a genuineness she couldn't fault.

This time she tipped her glass back and took a great gulp to steady her nerves. She coughed hard as tears welled up.

William chuckled, a deep masculine sound, then he tossed back his drink and set the glass aside. He took her empty glass from her hands, then caught them and held them tightly. His hands felt warm, the fingers long and tanned, strong. No, she thought, a bit wildly, no, no, no, this cannot happen. This is dangerous, this softness toward him she was beginning to feel. She couldn't let it happen, couldn't fall into his web like some poor unsuspecting moth, pulling and fighting to free itself. She'd been there before, and she would not, would *not* let it happen again.

Frightened at the intensity of her feelings, she got mad, no, furious, and she jerked her hands away from him. His fingers tightened and held them in place. Painfully, excruciatingly, she became aware of how big he was, how attractive and masculine, and all the things she had forced herself to forget in the past five years.

"I've found out where Eldon is."

William's revelation came at her out of the blue, making her gasp, then breathe erratically, and she searched his face, his eyes, for any nuance of bad news.

"He's alive, Will. He is, isn't he?" She got that much out in a whisper forced through stiff lips. She held her breath, terrified.

"Aye, he's alive and well, from what I understand, but Cornwallis had little else to tell me."

"Where is he? Tell me, please."

"They've taken him to Fort Saint Mark at St. Augustine."

"But that's so far! Isn't that on the Florida coast?" She shut her eyes as shock gave way to a wave of relief, but she opened them again at once. "You are taking me there, aren't you? I have to get him out. He's not well. Prison will kill him." She started to remind him that she wouldn't sign the annulment but found there was no need.

"You made it clear enough that was my part of the bargain," he answered. He stood up, towering over her. "But listen well, Trinity, no more midnight escapades, do you understand? No more breakneck courier rides through the swamp, no more ships blown to smithereens, no more hiding of wounded rebels, or the deal's off. Do we understand each other, Trinity?"

Trinity gave a swift nod, quite sure she'd not be in Charleston long enough to complete another mission for the patriot cause anyway. Now she wanted to sail. To Florida. Tonight, if she could have her way.

"Good girl. Now, just maybe I can get a decent night's sleep for a change. Rest well, Trinity."

He moved to leave her and was in the threshold before she could ask, "When will we leave?"

"Day after tomorrow, at high tide," he answered, then he was gone, leaving her sitting cross-legged on the bed, smiling at the thought of rescuing her father at last from his prison cell.

Chapter Ten

A bove the mast of the *Trevor*, the clouds
stretched to the far horizon, low, leaden,
mounded like bolls of dirty cotton, threatening
rain and gusty winds, but not so fierce, Captain
Joseph Parks readily assured William, as to prevent their impending hour of debarkation.
William hoped he was right as they stood together on the high deck of the forecastle and
gazed over the many rooftops and church spires
that hugged the wide curve of Charleston harbor.

As his old friend and long-time ship captain
for the Remington family took his leave to over-
see the crew hard at work on various tasks that
would put them asea, William stared across the
choppy, gray waves at the Old Exchange. The
scaffold still stood in place, like some giant skele-
tal remains against the pastel stucco buildings.

Not a whit of nostalgia, nor regret, did he feel
about leaving the land of his birth. He was glad
to leave the war-torn city behind. Unfortunately,
his mother and his sister did not share the same
pleasure over their departure. He glanced down

at them where they stood huddled together in tearful misery at midship rail.

At his insistence they had boarded the previous evening so there would be no excuse for them to delay and miss the morning tide. Even more importantly, he wanted Trinity on board, bodily, preferably in one piece, just in case she changed her mind and decided to melt back into the swamp bottoms to join her merry band of rebels. She'd given him her word not to, that was fact, but then, he knew better than anyone that she was every bit as wild and unruly as she'd always been. William wanted to trust her, but wasn't stupid enough to do so.

As he paced the length of the port rail, watching a couple of burly sailors winch up the immense iron anchor, he felt a helpless onslaught of sorrow about the course of the war. The devastating impact on both sides was horrible to behold, but especially for the Americans. Now that he'd seen the extent of their suffering with his own eyes, his perceptions had changed. He found himself wanting to support self-government in the Americas—which would be sheer blasphemy in his father's eyes. Adrian Remington was violently anti-French and anti-American, and he fought daily for harsher penalties against the rebellion. Will disagreed with his father on just about every subject. Why should this be different?

Around him he could hear the snap of canvas in the wind as the crew set the great white sheets and launched them upward with a rattle of lines into full sail. He scanned the decks. Trinity was nowhere to be seen. Her absence made him nervous, like everything else about her, he thought with mild irritation. For that very reason, he had escorted her aboard himself the night before and settled her into her cabin. Perhaps Victoria knew where she was. He joined the women and asked that very question.

His mother was still dabbing at her tears, her delicate black linen handkerchief damp in her hand. She was dressed from head to toe in black silk, as if she faced the death of a loved one rather than a comfortable voyage home to a magnificent ducal manor in England. As she no doubt intended, a twinge of guilt plagued William as she turned tear-shimmering eyes upon his face.

"As I said before, she told me she'd come topdeck when we set sail. I'm quite sure she'll be here shortly."

"Was she still in her cabin when she told you this?" William realized his tone had become more demanding but he was beginning to suspect something was amiss, and he'd find himself again the dupe of a well-planned female conspiracy. The three ladies were as thick as thieves, and as devious, he feared, and he remained the enemy. If Trinity had fled the coop, so to speak, he did not doubt his mother and sister had been the ones lowering her by rope into the shore boat.

"Perhaps I'll check on her. In case she isn't feeling well."

"Oh, she's quite well," Adrianna snapped

peevishly, revealing her unhappy state of mind. His sister had been impossible to reason with since she'd found out she had to go to England. "Maybe Trinity doesn't feel up to watching Charleston fade into the distance. I know I'm certainly not enjoying saying good-bye to everything and everyone I love!"

William elected to hold his tongue, having learned early on that it was wiser not to attempt argument with his little sister. No matter how rationally he spoke to her, or how well he set forth his views, regardless of subject, she either disregarded him or contradicted him with unnecessary vehemence and more than a little hostility. Surprisingly, he'd found Trinity easier to deal with. On the night of the funeral when they'd shared a nip of brandy he'd almost enjoyed her company. God's truth, he *had* enjoyed it. A lot more than he should have. Trinity Kingston was far less frivolous-minded than he'd thought, but that certainly didn't mean she wouldn't enjoy playing him for a fool as often as she could manage it.

By the time Captain Parks had the vessel safely through the harbor and skimming out toward open seas, William began to relax a bit. The frigate was long and sleek, quite luxurious actually for a seafaring vessel, though everything owned by the Duke of Thorpe was built to fit his station and wealth. Though his father rarely sailed the seas anymore, his personal ship was kept in good condition and ready to transport colonial rice and indigo back to London market squares.

More important, the ship was armed and secure against the pitiful, hastily incorporated American navy, as well as the ever-present French and Spanish privateers. With eight ten-pounders at both port and starboard, she was poised and ready to protect the duke and his guests.

William turned and let the wild sea winds whip through his hair, but after one last glance around the rail, he was unwilling to wait a moment longer for Trinity to appear. Fighting the swell and roll of the ship, he made his way below and down the gangway that led to the passenger quarters. The cabins were most comfortable, built with all the amenities and more spacious in size than most shipboard chambers.

His father had furnished most of the cabins with plush furniture and facings equal to those at Thorpe Hall and both their London town houses. There were six individual cabins placed side by side for the convenience of the servant staff. The three ladies would enjoy private quarters, and Eldon would have one as well, if William succeeded in negotiating his release.

Another chamber, larger than the others, was the ducal bedchamber that he would use, and the adjacent one, just as large, served as a private sitting room where the passengers could assemble for dining, cards, or conversation. Immense wealth and social privilege did have its advantages. Intentionally he had directed that Trinity be situated in the cabin next to his, for obvious reasons of security.

And perhaps for other reasons, ones he didn't particularly want to admit to himself, much less analyze. His mouth twisting with self-mockery, he tapped a knuckle on the door panel. Once, then again. Impatient now, he frowned, annoyed at the answering silence. He knocked more forcefully, waited a moment, then tried the door handle. Locked tight. A good sign. That was, if Trinity was inside.

"Trinity?" he said softly, nodding as one of the stewards passed by with a stack of clean white towels in his arms. "If you're in there, please let me in."

More silence, dammit. Then, after a long moment, her voice floated from just the other side of the door. "What do you want?"

"Open the door," he muttered in irritation. His female companions had given him nothing but trouble since he'd joined up with them, and he was growing tired of it.

His uncompromising tone apparently moved Trinity to comply, if halfheartedly. She took her time, but the door finally swung inward. She stood before him, effectively blocking him from entering.

"Well?" Her voice had adopted a demanding twinge. "The door's open. What do you want?"

"May I come in?"

She didn't seem particularly enthusiastic about the idea. "Why?"

"My, aren't we gracious today." His sarcasm

was cutting but she didn't seem to notice. Nor did she step back. "Funniest thing, Trin, I seem to remember you telling me something about being grateful, wasn't it? About how cooperative you were going to be. I suppose you forgot?"

Her elegantly arched brows dented together, the tiniest of frowns, but his chastisement apparently hit the mark because she gave a put-upon sigh. She stepped back. "I never forget my promises. Not that you'll let me."

William stepped inside the cabin and glanced around, not sure what he had expected to find. The narrow bunk was made up in blue velvet with yellow fringe, and her clothes were unpacked and stowed away, every article neat and in its place. The cabin had but one porthole, small and round, and it stood open, the navy blue, gold-tasseled curtain flapping and snapping on the brisk breeze. The salty sea tang filled the cabin, that and the sweet scent of roses, the perfume he'd found that Trinity favored.

"I'm curious. Why aren't you topdeck to watch our leave-taking? Victoria and Adrianna are both there."

"I prefer it down here alone. Why should you care where I am?" She was in a cantankerous mood, he decided when she gave him a surly glare. She sank down in her berth, clasped her hands tightly, her expression unchanged.

"Why do you want to stay down here alone?" he pressed, her defensiveness alerting him to the possibility of hidden motives.

"Why do you care why?" she snapped again, in a tone reminiscent of Adrianna's foul mood.

"Truthfully? I'm afraid you're up to something no good."

"Now why would you think that?"

He had to laugh at the sheer absurdity of the question, and after a beat, her lips curved, too. A smile for him, if a begrudging one.

"I'm not up to anything. You're overly suspicious is all. It's nothing like that."

"So what's it like then?"

Glancing toward the blowing curtains, she shrugged one shoulder, somehow a vulnerable motion.

"All right. If you must know, I'm a bit nervous, is all. I've never been on an ocean voyage before."

William couldn't hide his surprise. "Never? Not to England? Or even New York or Philadelphia?"

Trinity shook her head but her chin came up in that utterly enchanting way she had. "No, but so what? It's not a crime that I prefer to stay home at Palmetto Point. I like solid ground beneath my feet." She paused as the ship lurched in a trough and held on to the bunk with both hands. He saw it then for just a moment, a flash of fear in her eyes. "Besides that," she admitted defiantly, "I never learned how to swim so it's unnerving to me . . . with all this water around, and all."

Understanding now, William sat down beside her. She inched farther away, turning her head until he saw only her elegant profile and the creamy white flesh of her cheek.

"Is that right?"

"Yes. I don't like the water, if you must know." Proud to the end, he thought, but he said, "I can't fathom that Eldon taught you to ride like a warrior and shoot a pistol, and God knows what else you can do better than most men, yet didn't teach you to keep afloat in the water. And what about Geoff? We used to swim in the ocean when we were children, well before I left for England. You didn't do that?"

"Yes, I did, until I got caught in an undertow and almost drowned. Papa got me in time, but I haven't been back in the water since."

She tossed her head, facing him with fire in her eyes, daring him to make something of her fear.

He knew better than that. "I see. That's certainly understandable. You must have been very frightened."

She relaxed a little, he could see the stiffness leave her posture, but her eyes still searched his face, narrow and wary.

"Let me reassure you, Trin. The *Trevor* is as seaworthy a vessel as they come. His Grace spared no expense on his personal craft. You've nothing to worry about. Just don't hang out too far over the rail."

With that, he did manage to draw another tentative smile. She was glad of his reassurance, he could see the relief in her eyes. "You've no need to worry on that count. I plan to keep a safe distance from the water."

"Then come up and get some fresh air. You can hold on to my arm, if you like. You'll have to get used to being at sea sooner or later. We'll be aboard for weeks, and the waves are fairly calm at the moment."

"Yes, weeks," she repeated without a spot of enthusiasm. She heaved a sigh. "All right, let's go. Papa always encouraged me to embrace the things that frighten me most, so I'd conquer my fear of them. I suppose that means the ocean, too, as long as I don't have to get wet."

He stood up. "I salute your courage, milady."

With no further urging, Trinity rose and preceded him out of her cabin. Then to his further surprise, once they'd come out onto the deck, she deigned to take the arm he offered while they strolled down the deck toward the other two ladies. Perhaps, he thought, with Trinity aboard and being receptive to his attentions, the voyage wouldn't be so long and boring after all.

Chapter Eleven

"Are you certain I can't get you something, Victoria? Some nice hot chamomile tea, perhaps?"

In answer to Trinity's solicitousness, Victoria gave a muffled groan and flopped her head from side to side like a beached fish. Trinity winced with sympathy because the dear lady looked like one, too; she was absolutely green around the gills. The poor woman had lain abed for nearly two days now, since the *Trevor* had run into a tempest at sea the night after they'd set sail.

High winds and stormy weather had pummeled the ship, hitting them over and over in a rolling, plunging onslaught. Adrianna as well could not withstand the heaving decks and topsy-turvy conditions and collapsed on her bed, ill with the same nausea, and utterly miserable.

Trinity found, astonishing even herself, that she bore no ill effect from the tilting, heaving vessel. In truth she found the storm rather exciting in all its windblown glory because the ship plowed onward relentlessly with no sign of serious danger. Indeed, since the moment William had coaxed her out of her cabin that first morning, she'd grown to enjoy thoroughly the wind and water, and the gray-green waves with their caps of white that stretched to the horizon as far as her eye could see.

"Run along, child, truly," Victoria urged her, lifting her head with extreme effort. "You're very sweet, but there's nothing you can do for me. Oooh—" She stopped to moan and pressed a small linen towel against her mouth.

"Surely the storm will abate soon," Trinity murmured compassionately, patting Victoria's shoulder, then turned and grasped the sturdy brass rails affixed to the cabin's wall. She slowly dragged herself across the rocking floor, and it took her several minutes to get out the door. With effort she managed to shut it, then clung on for dear life as she endured the next plunge to bow.

Both hands locked on the gangway rail, she giggled as the bucking of the ship continued, almost as if it were a wild angry stallion determined to unseat her. At length she gave up the idea of negotiating the full length of the corridor to her own cabin, instead making her way toward the parlor cabin.

Inside, she found William there already, relaxing in the depths of a bolted-down wing chair at the dining table. He looked up, then laughed at her when the ship dove and plunged again, sending Trinity in a reckless sliding run the slant of the upended cabin. She caught herself on the arm of the chair directly opposite him and plopped herself down in its cushions, breathless to have finally made it.

"I must say that was quite an entertaining entrance, Trin. If I didn't know better, I'd like to think you ran in here just to amuse me."

Not so far off the mark, she admitted inside, but she kept that betraying sentiment to herself. After his kindness toward her sickly friends, she'd had little choice but to give him a second chance and ample opportunity to redeem himself. Besides, she'd decided she had much more to gain by cooperating with him than by holding a grudge against his past treatment of her. That part of their relationship was far over, after all, and as long as he remained civil and pleasant toward her needs, she might as well present a sunny disposition to him, too, whether it was a true one or not.

"I'm glad to see you've turned out to be such a good sailor."

"Yes," she agreed, more pleased about it than he was. "I'm finding I rather enjoy the sea, even this stormy one."

"What about Mother and Adrianna? They weren't faring so well the last time I looked in on them."

"They're still very sick, both of them."

"They won't get better until the storm subsides."

"When will that be? Does the captain know?"

"Not until morning, if that soon. Captain Parks thinks we'll run out of it eventually."

Trinity grabbed the edge of the table as the

ship rolled, starboard this time, rather amazed that her stomach could handle the uneven dips and plunges with so little effect. She had yet to feel even the hint of nausea.

Above the polished surface of the table, an oil lantern swayed and bobbed and threw bizarre dancing shadows over them, cavorting up the walls to the ceiling like playful squirrels. She could hear the rain now, ticking like a snare drum on the two small round windows behind William. He was watching her so intently that she fought the desire to squirm.

"It's surprising you're not terrified with all this going on, considering your father nearly let you drown."

"You make it sound like he did it on purpose."

He smiled. "He couldn't have been watching you very closely, if he let you endanger yourself that way."

"He was most certainly watching me. I begged to ride the waves to the beach like Geoffrey was doing, and he let me."

"If I recall correctly, Eldon let you do about anything you ever wanted, bar nothing."

Bristling with offense, she sent him a dark look. "Since when are you such an expert on fatherhood, Will? Papa was always a wonderful father. At least he spent time with me. Adrianna never even saw your father. He didn't seem to care much about any of you, if you ask me. I'll take my father over yours any day."

The minute the words left her lips, she was sorry she'd let her temper get the better of her because she saw the expression in his eyes. Very brief but very clear. She'd managed to hurt him—the coldly arrogant, aristocratic English lord.

"I'm sorry, Will. I shouldn't have said that."

But now his face was devoid of any emotion, the flash of vulnerability gone forever, or perhaps only well hidden under his handsome facial facade. In answer, he merely gave a casual shrug, as if the observation bore no importance to him.

"No need to apologize. In truth, I'd be the first to admit His Grace was not exactly an exemplary parent. Not to any of us, but especially not to me. Unfortunately, the two of us are like oil and water."

Well, well. Trinity had always assumed the reverse to be true. She said as much, and to her surprise William leaned back, seemingly more comfortable with the subject than she would have thought.

"Father preferred to use my school holidays expounding on my honor and duty as the next Duke of Thorpe. He's been preparing me since I was born. Stephen and Adrianna didn't have it so bad. They were the lucky ones. He ignored them for the most part."

Trinity barely remembered the younger Remington brother. He was slender, with blond hair, if she recalled, and tall like William, but always in his shadow. But back then, Trinity had idolized William to such a degree that she wouldn't have noticed if the sun fell from the sky and rolled across the lawn. "Where's Stephen now? No one ever mentions him, not even Victoria."

"He's in London most of the time. He breeds and races my father's Arabians. He rarely sees His Grace, unless he's summoned."

Trinity observed him for a long moment, for the first time truly curious about his past. She didn't know him at all, she realized, and never had. Though she'd had only one parent to raise her, from what he said, it sounded like he'd had none. "Did you miss your mother when His Grace took you away to school in England?"

"God, yes. I adored her, and poor Stephen was even younger than I at the time. His Grace didn't exactly take us under his wing."

"Why do you call him that? Isn't His Grace a bit formal?"

"That's what he's insisted upon since we were boys. As I mentioned, he won't win any medals for tender parenting. We rarely saw him anyway—only at Christmastide when we were allowed to visit Thorpe Hall. Sometimes he forgot to show up even then."

Hurt no longer revealed itself in William's voice, or eyes, and he spoke quite matter-of-factly about his father. His openness surprised her. Trinity thought of her own Christmases at Palmetto Point with the great feast of roast turkey and oysters, and yam puddings, and lemon coconut cake and pecan pies. Her father always brought her a whole cartload of presents from the shops of Charleston.

"How awful for two little boys," she said with

true sympathy. "How in heaven's name did you bear it?"

William leaned his chin on his palm and smiled at her. "It wasn't as bad as it sounds. Stephen and I were always allowed to share a room at boarding school because of our father's rank. It made us close, and we've stayed that way." As he spoke, he retrieved a silver flask from his inside breast pocket. Uncapping it, he took a swig, then offered it to her, silently, but with a raised brow.

Trinity laughed at his challenge and she took the small flat container. She drank from the top, tipping her head back and upending it much the same way he had. It was whiskey, she found as her eyes teared up, strong and dark and mellow, and it burned like fire all the way down her gullet. The liquor was stronger than any she'd partaken of in the past, and she coughed as it heated her stomach.

William smiled. "I'll teach you to hold your liquor before we get to England. This is a good enough night to start, with the storm tossing the boat around like a palmetto leaf. A little liquid fortitude can't hurt us."

Trinity looked past him to where great torrents of rain sluiced down the porthole glass, blurry, in sliding waves.

"Do you think we've run into a hurricane?" she asked, unable to control a cold chill at the thought of being out upon the sea in one of the violent storms that sometimes swept in over the coast of Carolina and battered landward everything in its path.

"On the outer fringe, perhaps, though it's a bit early in the season. You probably know more about hurricanes than I do."

"The worst one hit Palmetto Point when I was little, about six, I think. I don't remember much, except that everyone was very frightened, especially my nursemaid, Nana Marie. The wind blew down the giant magnolia tree and it crashed into the side of the house and broke through the French doors of my bedroom. I can remember getting out on it the next morning and climbing almost to the ground before Nana Marie got me. I scared the daylights out of Papa."

"As I recall it, you did that quite regularly."

"How would you know that? You were only around me a few times."

"That's true enough, but you always make our meetings, well, shall we say, memorable? And if you don't believe me, I still have the scars to prove it." There was no condemnation in his words, and his grin utterly charmed her, as did the devilish glint in his green eyes.

"What're you talking about?" she demanded, smiling, too.

"You saw fit to sink your sharp little teeth in my hand. Deep enough to leave a scar after all these years."

Trinity gasped. "No! I don't believe you. What an outrageous thing for you to accuse me of! Papa says I was a little angel when I was little."

"Not even close. The opposite would be closer to the mark."

On the verge of being insulted if not for his teasing manner, Trinity bent forward and gazed down at the hand he held out for her examination.

"See for yourself how angelic you are. I remember it all too well. You hung on to my thumb like a dog on a ham bone."

Trinity's eyebrows knitted, and she picked up his hand and cradled it in hers, not believing him for a minute. "I don't see a scar."

"Right here"—he pointed it out—"on the heel of my hand. See, there, just below my thumb."

Trinity finally saw the thin white scar shaped like a tiny crescent. It showed quite clearly against the darkly tanned skin of his hand. Distinctly embarrassed, she realized it might very well have been made by the teeth of a little child. On the other hand, a dog could have made it, too.

"If I bit you that hard," she paused, capturing his eyes again, "I must have had a very good reason to do so."

"As a matter of fact, you had an excellent reason to take a hunk out of me. I gave you one hell of a hard pinch, and you retaliated forthwith with your dainty white teeth." He took another swig of whiskey.

"You're making every bit of this up, aren't you, just to annoy me and make me feel guilty?" she accused, bracing herself again as the ship tilted.

She pressed her palms flat on the table and found herself looking down at William.

"Now why would I wish to annoy you, Trin? You've been so sweet ever since I got home."

Trinity ignored his sarcasm. "Tell me more about it, if it's true. When did it happen? How old was I?"

"Oh, let me see," he said, placing a finger against his cheekbone as if he had to think. "About twelve, I guess, or thirteen, maybe."

They laughed together softly at the ridiculous picture that brought to mind. The ship wallowed starboard and Trinity now looked up at him again. "Be serious. Tell me the truth. If you know how. When was it?"

"All right, cross my heart and hope to die. The truth is"—he stopped as if to enhance the suspense, and Trinity found herself smiling at him again—"you gnawed on me in front of the altar while we were exchanging our wedding vows."

"Stop it! Tell me true!"

"That's it."

"No! I wouldn't have!"

"Oh, yes, you would. And you enjoyed it, too, believe me."

"No one's ever told me I did such a terrible thing."

"That's rather surprising since everyone for miles around was there to see it."

"I don't remember that day at all."

"You were only three at the time, or maybe four. I don't know." He shrugged. "But I was eleven years old, and I'll never forget it, not one embarrassing minute of it."

Mightily intrigued despite herself, Trinity just had to know more. "All right, say that it's true. Tell me what else happened."

He handed her the flask, and she drank again. The liquor was beginning to taste rather good now. She'd never felt so warm. "I'm sure nearly everybody wanted to forget that particular wedding."

"Why?" she demanded, but he was beguiling her in this new lighthearted, teasing mood. His teeth flashed often, looking very white and even in the flickering candlelight. She admitted readily that she liked this Will an awful lot better than the Will she had met just a few weeks ago.

"Do you really think you can listen to such a morbid tale?" he asked, straight-faced but the glints still glowed deep inside his eyes. "It's pretty bloody horrible."

"Oh, stop it. You're teasing me about all this, aren't you? Tell me everything that happened. The truth this time!"

Will feigned mock hurt but then treated her with a smile that was absolutely melting. She'd always thought it astounding how a mere smile could change a person's expression. With a man like William, who was so incredibly handsome anyway with his patrician bearing, this easy grin he was exhibiting made him seem warm, approachable, maybe even human. She hadn't really been sure he wasn't a monster through and through, and she'd bet a hatful of silver coins that Victoria and Adrianna had never seen him grinning and joking like this, either. It suddenly occurred to her to wonder if he might be a trifle tipsy and acting like a normal human being against his will. More likely, he had to be nice to her or he wouldn't get to marry his new lady friend.

"How long had you been drinking before I joined you?" she asked suspiciously.

"I daresay I can remain sober with the mere tad of whiskey this little flask holds," he said with a wry twist of lips. "I'm not sure about you though. You're being rather too friendly and agreeable to be completely yourself."

She marveled at the way they'd come to parallel conclusions about each other and watched him take a drink again, then recap the flask.

"Well, sir, I'm waiting. Did I bite the priest, too?"

"Oh, yes, three or four times. No one in the chapel escaped your toothsome anger."

"Stop it now," she said, chuckling, "I said to tell me the truth, or I'm leaving right now and going to bed."

William leaned back and observed her over his steepled fingers. "All right. First off, I remember that I wasn't exactly thrilled to have to marry some little crybaby brat like you." Trinity wasn't offended because she knew he was still bantering with her. "But, you, Trinity, my love, hated my guts, not to mention everything else about me."

She tried to ignore the endearment because

he'd used it lightly, probably said it constantly to women, but she still lowered her eyes, affected. The truth was, of course, that she hadn't hated him until he jilted her, oh, no, not at all; she'd loved him then and all through her childhood for almost as long as she could remember. But she didn't want to think about that. No, that was something she wanted to forget.

"Why did you pinch me?" she asked, to interrupt her own betraying thoughts.

"Believe it or not, you ran and jumped on me in front of our parents and everybody else in the chapel. You locked your arms around my neck until I couldn't breathe, but worse than that, you locked your legs around my waist."

Trinity's face flamed, her lips parted, and her skin grew hot as she visualized quite vividly that pose and the intimacy of it. She didn't know what to say.

"You were dressed in lots of ruffles, if I remember," he went on, "and a bonnet with lots of ribbons but it was hanging off because you were screaming and yelling and fighting with your father."

"Fighting with him! Why?"

"Eldon was trying his best to calm you down and make you behave, without an iota of success. You were as mad as a hornet trapped in a milk bottle."

Trinity pictured the scene, thinking it downright callous for parents to put little tots through such adult ceremonies. Look at all the trouble their fathers had caused both their families with such a farce.

"We were too little to be wed," she said, shaking her head. "Your father was much too greedy for Kingston property. Now everyone involved regrets that wedding. It's only caused grief for all of us."

"All the same it was binding. We're still legally wed, my dear, even now, at this very moment."

Her eyes found his quickly, and all hint of humor was gone from his face. She swallowed hard, somehow deeply affected by the way he was looking at her. "But only in name."

"Only in name," he agreed readily enough. "But I can't help wondering what would've happened if things had been different."

Trinity's heartbeat doubled, then tripled, and she suddenly recognized her own danger. The note of wistfulness in his voice had sent her heart dropping inside her breast, had rippled a chill up the outside of her spine. She hardened her heart and made sure her eyes were cold and unforgiving. "Oh, my, Lord William, have you forgotten? I'm an American, and that terrible sin cannot be overlooked. Not by the true English, not by the exalted future Duke of Thorpe, now can it, sir?"

William said nothing, went stony-faced, all the camaraderie gone. He stared silently at her until she could not bear the look on his face. She rose, suddenly anxious to escape his company. For they had somehow managed to forget their bitter differences, even if for a few minutes, but their past association bore too much pain and misery for that to last. They could never be anything to each other, not even friends.

"Sleep well, Trin," he said softly as she made her way across the tilting floor toward the door.

She didn't answer, couldn't, because she knew that she would not sleep well at all. She would lie in her tossing bunk and think about him, and wonder, as he had wondered a moment before, what it would have been like between them if their countries had not gone to war, if they were truly married, and shared a life as man and wife, shared the marriage bed with all the mysteries that went on in its feathery depths. She stopped outside the door and squeezed her eyes shut until she could summon her familiar defenses, shields of anger and resentment. Once they were in place, she felt better. She would never let herself soften toward him again.

Chapter Twelve

Unfortunately for Trinity, even worse for William's mother and sister, the inclement weather held fast, a relentless drizzle and wind-mangled waves that made Trinity's strolls around the foredeck decidedly less than comfortable. Late one afternoon after many days at sea, Trinity, thoroughly bored and equally restless, braved the cold, misty elements anyway, grasping firmly to the ropes that had been strung from mast to mast and rail to rail for use by crew members negotiating the slick, slippery planks. A quarter hour of the exertion of hand over hand groping along the cords did in her need of fresh air and sea spray. With her lightweight cloak drenched and clinging to her skirts, her hair pulled from its knot and ringleted in damp disarray despite the protection offered by her cowl hood, she retreated hastily belowdecks, in the hopes her dear friends might be up and about at last. No such luck. Both ladies still groaned and held their bellies and wailed, "When, oh, when, dear God, is the storm to end!" Certainly they were in no mood to appreciate her company.

Hesitating, she stood in the dim light of the gangway and stared at the door of the common room. She'd like indeed to take refuge there instead of closeting herself in her dismal, lonely cabin. At the same time she didn't relish time alone with William, in which she could be tempted into intimate conversation that was so dangerous to her heart. Unable to endure the idea of her own claustrophobic cell, however, she made the length of the corridor, opened the door, and, of course, found him sitting there, no doubt waiting for her to give in and join him again.

To his credit, he appeared exceedingly bored, flipping playing cards into the bowl of his overturned black tricorne. Still miffed slightly by the way their last gallant attempt to provide each other with civil company had ended, she barely glanced at him, acknowledging him by the barest and curtest of nods. She struggled out of her wet cape—he didn't lift a hand to assist her, didn't even offer—and slung it in surly manner onto the hook beside the door, showing the fit of pique that was overtaking her. She made her way, handhold by handhold, to the built-in bookcases along the adjacent wall.

Clutching the brass rail that secured the tomes in place, she perused their titles and authors, fingering the soft leather bindings and gilt-edged pages. Most were novels or histories she'd already read to occupy the many hours she'd spent attempting to avoid William's company. All she found left for her reading pleasure contained subjects dry enough to eclipse even her lonely shipboard existence. She sighed in defeat, then plopped down on the bench beside the bookshelf. William desisted with his flipping of the cards. He held an ace up between his forefinger and middle finger. "Wanna play?"

She should refuse, she thought, and in no uncertain terms. But he was smiling that smile again, the one she had trouble resisting, no matter how hard she tried. Her anger was melting away already, and she felt like a soft malleable little ball of wax that he could pick up and mold into any shape he wanted.

"Ah, poor Trinity. I know exactly what you're thinking. You're bored, you're fidgety, restless enough to spit, and you want to say yes, really badly, but your pride is kicking up a god-awful fight inside your head, telling you to stick up your nose and tell me to go jump over the rail, or something equally detrimental to my bodily well-being."

Trinity met his gaze with a steady regard of her own but inside he was laughing at her and she knew it. "My, Lord Thorpe, you do have extraordinary insight."

William laughed and gathered up the cards. She watched him shuffle them, expertly, slap, slap, slap until he shoved them across the table for the cut. "What would you say to a few hands of whist?"

Trinity hesitated, but then she was quite good at card games, and she'd never been one to walk away from the kind of dare he was dangling before her. "I suppose I'm bored enough to spend

time alone with you. There's certainly nothing
better to do on this horrible ship."

"You wound me," he murmured, a dramatic
hand upon his heart, without a whit of honesty,
at least none that she could detect.

As she crossed the floor, he leaped to his feet
and with grossly exaggerated courtesy bowed
deeply as she seated herself. She looked up at
him in surprise when he dropped a dry linen
towel into her lap.

"Your hair's dripping wet. Better dry it, or
you'll catch cold. I certainly wouldn't want that
to happen."

"Ha!" she jeered as she took the towel. "I'm
sure you've spent most of the last four years fretting over the state of my health."

William met her mockery with unruffled
aplomb. Smiling broadly, he sat down across
from her and watched her loosen her chignon
and let the damp hair fall around her shoulders.
She pulled it to one side where she could blot it
with the cloth as he nudged the deck closer to
her. She pushed it back with the heel of her hand.
"Be my guest. I, more than anyone else, I suspect, know how utterly untrustworthy you are."

"Ah, but that's all in the past. Now we can be
friends, can't we?" With a benign smile—there
was just no riling him this day—he shuffled the
cards, but never once looked down at them, his
eyes steadily on her face as she gently toweled
her hair dry, chagrined at how curly it became
when it was damp. He dealt swiftly and surely,
with obvious expertise as if he'd spent many

hours at the gaming tables. He'd had a great deal of practice but so had she.

"How about a wager? Just to make it interesting?"

"The game is quite interesting enough to me as it is, I assure you. Besides, what would a poor misguided rebel like myself have to offer a great man like you, with all your wealth and status. The great and future duke."

She'd meant the barb as a disrespectful jab at the high and mighty self-importance of the British peerage but he took it all wrong, and in a way she should have expected from a man.

"I would have to disagree with that analysis." His eyes roved over her face and caressed her unbound tresses before returning to her eyes. "You've more to offer me than just about any woman I've ever seen. Truth be told, you even tempt a disagreeable man like myself."

"Ah, yes, my lord, I'm so very tempting to you that you sailed the length of the Atlantic Ocean to throw me over for some new paramour you've set your sights upon." With each word her voice grew more bitter, revealing more than she wanted him to see. Again their gazes connected. She waited for him to deny it, to explain, but he said nothing. What could he say? She had stopped his playful flirtation cold in its tracks, pierced him with the truth, had gotten the last word, but while he seemed unabashed, she was the one who felt empty and depressed.

The game began with intense, methodical concentration, in total silence, neither player looking at the other. Only the constant spatter of rain, the haunting whistle of the wind, the creaking timbers of the hull. How ridiculous she was, Trinity thought, blithely sitting across from the man who'd so vilely wronged her. She was bored indeed to consider such entertainment.

She watched him as he studied his cards, his eyes focused downward, revealing black eyelashes that were absurdly long and thick. As he considered a card to select with great seriousness, she could not help but examine him. A lock of hair fell over his right eyebrow, dark and soft, and a niggling recollection was abruptly triggered inside her mind—a vision of the boy he'd once been so very long ago. His hair had always had a tendency to tumble down over his brow, even when he was little. She remembered that, and thought how strange memories were. Why would she remember that and so little else about their younger years?

She'd often thought about the first time she'd ever seen him, and wondered if that was when she'd begun to love him. She'd been so little then, seven or so, and her nurse, Nana Marie, had held her hand tightly, because Trinity was so terrified to meet him . . .

"Come 'long, *cher*, Lord William be waitin' on the pillared gallery. He is your husband mon, you know. You must be a proper little lady this whole day through."

Trinity listened to Nana Marie's soft voice but at seven years old, Trinity was very shy, and she didn't quite understand why her nanny was telling her such things. She did know that her house was filled with excitement about the husband mon coming to call on her, with all the servants bustling about dusting and stewing chickens in the kitchens for the huge feast they were giving for him. She'd heard the butler and cook when they were cutting the turnips and yams whispering about the "little mistress's husband," but they lowered their voices when they saw her so she didn't know what they thought of him.

In truth, she wasn't precisely sure what a husband mon was, and was certainly too afraid to ask. She hadn't even known she had one of them until yesterday. And she didn't want one, either. Whoever this Lord William of Thorpe was, he was making her papa wring his hands together and sputter about how the boy-husband was going to be a duke someday.

Her grip tightened around Nana Marie's long, thin fingers as they walked together the length of the wide carpeted corridor from her airy bedchamber to the upstairs drawing room where her father always entertained his most honored guests. The husband mon was already there. Waiting for her. Terror welled quickly, pressing through her until her breath got all painful inside her chest. She stopped, her amber eyes wide and fearful, and when Nana Marie looked down at her, she asked, her voice tiny and trembling, "What's a husband mon, anyway, Nana Marie? Is it something real bad? Will it hurt me?"

Nana Marie's narrow brown face reflected surprise, then she threw back her head and gave the lusty laugh that usually made Trinity giggle, too. This time Trinity was too frightened even to smile.

"Laws, no, *cher*, he just be the mon who you's going to live with when you gets old enough. Don't you worry none now, he ain't nothin' bad 'tall. And he won't hurt a hair on your pretty little head."

That revelation mollified Trinity a good deal but still her stomach was churning like the ocean at the far side of the rice levees. "I don't wanna go see him. I don't want any husband mon."

Nana Marie's amusement faded completely, her face growing serious as she crouched down until she could look into Trinity's eyes. She drew Trinity close against her, and comforted by her nurse's tenderness, Trinity lay her cheek gratefully on Nana Marie's soft bosom.

"Now, don't you fret, little one, you won't have to go off with milord for a long, long time. Why, not 'til you're all grown-up and as tall as me!"

Indeed, Trinity was very relieved then, but she still didn't want to come face-to-face with whoever it was waiting for her. She was glad when they entered the drawing room and found it empty, but then she heard Papa's voice outside on the pillared gallery. He was talking to Geoffrey, she realized, very glad her cousin was there, too. Geoffrey was her friend, and even though he was only twelve, he wouldn't let the husband mon hurt her. Still, she felt trembly and sick and scared as Nana Marie led her through the open French doors.

Eyes enormous, she looked around, panic rising, and hung behind Nana Marie's gray skirt until her father came rushing forward and took her by the hand.

"Trinity, dearest, come along now and meet young Will. He's been waiting for you all morning. My, how lovely you look in all those pink ruffles."

Trinity obeyed but she did not like the flounces sewn in rows across her long full skirt, and she didn't like the full satin sleeves and scratchy lace collar either. They were hot and uncomfortable. She wished she could have worn the cool plain linen frocks that Nana Marie made for her so she could run and play on the beach and not get scolded if she got sand in the hem or tore the ruffles off.

"Lord William's gone down to the flagstones. He and Geoff are readying their horses for a ride to the shore. He's quite taken with the horse I gave you for your birthday. Apparently, he's quite the equestrian now. He thinks the mare's magnificent."

The twin marble staircases that led down to the flagstones curved gracefully on either side of the pillared gallery on which they stood. The steps were broad and smooth, fashioned from polished white marble that gleamed in the sunlight. The stone balustrade stood almost as tall as Trinity's shoulder, and as she descended, she moved as slowly as if she marched behind a black-plumed funeral carriage. She stopped at the first sight of the husband mon.

Why, she realized with joy flooding her heart, he's a boy, too, mayhaps a few years older than Geoffrey! Much of the dread left her heart, but her reluctance to meet him did not. Geoffrey was talking to him, using his hands with great animation, waving his arms around, and laughing as if he wasn't afraid at all. So he was the one she would live with when she got tall. She watched him stroke the flank of the beautiful white horse that her papa had given her for her birthday.

Milord had thick wavy hair, a dark reddish brown like the chestnuts she and Nana Marie roasted in a long-handled pan on the kitchen hearth. He had it tied back in a queue like the one Geoffrey usually wore his yellow hair in, but he was dressed much more grandly than her cousin. In truth, his garb outmatched in splendor even her father's fine attire. All his clothes were cut from soft green velvet, and he wore a shirt of fine white silk with lots of lace around the cuffs. She wondered if all his fancy lace scratched him, too. When he turned and stared at her, she saw that his eyes were as green as his coat.

"By Jove, Trin, you've grown like a dandelion weed! Come here and let me look at you."

His grin was wide and friendly, with nice white teeth, and most of her trepidation faded. She walked toward him, pleased that he was just a boy and that he remembered her, even though she didn't remember him at all.

"The last time I saw you, you bit me. Real hard, too. Do you remember that, Trin?"

"No, milord," she answered, wondering if he was still angry about that. She had bitten Geoffrey once, on the arm, and he was so mad he wouldn't play with her for three days.

"You sank your teeth in deep enough to leave this scar at the bottom of my thumb. It's still there, see?"

Trinity examined with interest the tanned wrist he held out and detected the tiny crescent-shaped mark.

"I'm sorry, milord," she said, and it was the truth. She added quickly, "I haven't bitten anyone in a very long time. After all, I'm nearly eight now."

"Well, the truth is I gave you a frightful pinch that day so I probably deserved what I got. You were screaming like a banshee and I was trying to get you to stop."

"What's a banshee?"

"It's an evil spirit, everyone knows that," Geoffrey interjected from nearby, his voice highly impatient. "Now run along, will you, Trin? Will and I are going to ride down to the beach."

"Well, actually, Geoff, a banshee's a female spirit whose awful wail predicts a death in the family. There's a boy from Edinburgh in my school, you know where that is, don't you, it's in Scotland. He told me all about such folktales."

William stepped onto the mounting block as he finished the explanation, took hold of the pommel, and swung easily up into the ornate

gold-studded saddle. The white mare stood obediently while one of the attending grooms settled
milord's glossy black boots into the stirrups.
William took hold of the reins and smiled down
at Trinity.

"Your mare is truly a beautiful animal, Trin.
What's her name again?"

"Moonbeam, because she glows in the dark
when the moon comes up."

His lordship laughed. "I do hope you don't
mind if I ride her?"

Trinity liked this husband mon better and better. She shook her head. "Oh, no, milord. Papa
says I'm much too young to ride her, anyway."

"Too young? Nonsense. Father insisted I learn
to ride when I was barely three years old." He
glanced over her head to where Eldon Kingston
stood watching. "May I take Trinity on my horse
with me, Mr. Kingston? I will hold her quite securely in the saddle, I assure you, sir."

Her father looked mightily concerned, and less
than enthused, but he finally agreed. "All right
then, Your Lordship, but do hold on to her
tightly. She has not been upon a horse before this
day."

William nodded amiably as he stretched a
hand down to Trinity. "Come, step up onto the
block, and I'll give you your first lesson in horse-
manship."

Trinity did not hesitate, but took the hand with
the scar on it, excited that he talked to her as if
she wasn't a brat like Geoffrey always said. Her
cousin hated it when she tagged along after him

and his friends, and when she glanced at him, he didn't look happy now, either.

Lord William's fingers closed around her small hand and pulled her up into the saddle directly in front of him.

"What a pity you had the misfortune of being born a female, Trin," he told her as he guided the mare down the drive. "You'll never get to jump the hedges and gates like Geoff and I do. You'll have to wear all those full skirts, you know, and petticoats, and all manner of nonsense such as that. And you'll have to use a sidesaddle, for modesty's sake. It's really too bad that ladies don't get to jump because that's more fun than anything. I'll show you once we get to the levee gates."

A moment later he pulled back on the reins and expertly sidestepped the prancing mare to face back toward the house. Her father was still watching from the bottom of one of the twin curving staircases. He lifted his arm in a farewell to them, and Trinity waved back.

"Back in England my best friend is the most skilled equestrian in my school. He wins the steeplechase every time he rides it. I daresay he could even take your beautiful Moonbeam all the way up that winding stairs just behind your father, without even a stumble. Someday I intend to do the same, for I practice my riding every single day. Perhaps next time I come to visit you here, I will ride my horse up the steps and fetch you off the gallery for our ride."

Trinity watched her father mount the sweeping marble steps, her eyes huge and awestricken. The image of a horse trotting up the marbled steps seemed wondrous indeed. But then all her thoughts scattered as His Lordship kicked the mare into a flying gallop, and although William's arms encircled her tightly, Trinity's breath caught and she held on for dear life.

The coolness of the wind rushed against her face, flushing her cheeks to a rosy pink, and she could hear milord laughing behind her as they flew along the road toward the beach. In that moment she decided that she liked the new boy just fine, perhaps even better than she liked Geoffrey, and she'd liked her cousin a lot ever since she was born. In fact, now that she had met him, having a husband mon like milord wasn't going to be so bad after all. Not so bad at all . . .

When William glanced up from the cards he held splayed in his left hand, he found Trinity's pure amber eyes fixed on his face, but he knew at once that she did not see him. Caught up in what appeared to be the most pleasant of daydreams, obviously some memory so wonderful it brought a small smile into play about her lips, turning one corner of her mouth up in a gentle curve. She looked like a vision sitting there, lovely but with the most charming innocence, almost like a child. What an absolutely breathtaking woman she'd turned out to be, he thought with appreciation. But what on earth could be holding her in such a trance? Was she thinking about that patriot she'd mentioned once back at Palmetto Point? The soldier beau?

"Trin?" No response. He spoke louder. "Trinity?"

Trinity floated back to the present, her eyes refocusing on him. "My play? Forgive me. I was thinking about something."

"What?"

"You'd be surprised, if I told you."

"Probably. Tell me."

"I was thinking about you—and the first time we ever met. At least that I remember. Do you remember the day I'm talking about?"

William was surprised, but certainly not displeased to learn he'd been the cause of that enchanting little smile. On the other hand, he couldn't bring to mind any past childhood encounter with her where they hadn't either argued or actually come to blows.

"I'm fairly confident you're not talking about the day we were wed. You were too hysterical to remember much, I'd say."

"Yes, I know I was, you already told me that," she snapped impatiently, tossing down a card in play. "I'm glad I don't remember behaving that way."

"So don't hold me in suspense, Trin. When was the first time you remember laying eyes on me?"

"You came to visit me at Palmetto Point when you were about fourteen. Do you recollect? It was springtime."

"Vaguely, I suppose."

"Then you tell me what you remember."

"Why?"

"I'm just curious to see if we recall it the same, is all. Why are you always so suspicious?" She shrugged. "Oh, never mind, it doesn't matter. Forget it. It's your play."

But she wanted him to try to remember that day, Will could tell. He wracked his brain for appropriate memories. Why was it so important to her?

She waited and watched him, her fine golden eyes latched on his face, full of more warmth and friendliness than he'd seen in days. Desperately, he strove for the incident she was talking about. If he'd been fourteen, she'd been very little. Seven, maybe? Slowly, that long-ago day began to push its way back.

"Let's see. I do remember you let me ride your horse that day. Down to the beach. And Geoff was with us, too, wasn't he?"

She nodded, her expression becoming what looked to him, well, almost happy. He plumbed his mind deeper, and more images flooded up from the past. "And you came with us. You rode in the saddle in front of me, didn't you? And you wore pink ruffles. Lots of them."

"I thought you were wonderful." Her eyes gleamed with the affection she'd felt then, but she remembered herself quite quickly and added sternly, "But that was a long time ago. Before I knew any better."

"I thought you showed a lot of courage to gallop with me. I expected you to cry and be afraid but you never did. When did you start hating me?"

"The next time we met. And you hated me, too. You called me names when I rode my horse up the steps."

"I didn't hate you. I just couldn't understand why you'd endanger such a magnificent horse like you did. Riding her up those slick marble steps was foolish."

The open expression on her face seemed to close up, as hard as a white river clam. He had touched a sore spot in her, he realized, but it was far too late to remedy it.

"It's your fault I did it, you know," she admitted a moment later, sounding defensive.

"My fault? I didn't even know you were going to do it. But it was truly spectacular, I will admit. I'm not sure anyone else could've done it without killing themselves."

She looked pleased but then she sobered and concentrated on the card she was turning over and over on the table before her. She suddenly came to her feet and moved away from the table. She stood a few feet away, her back to him. He watched her warily. With Trinity you never quite knew what to expect.

"I did it . . . well, I guess the reason I did it was to impress you." Her voice was low as if she was mortified to be baring such a secret. "You told me the day you and Geoff took me to the beach that you intended to ride up those steps someday, you mentioned some friend of yours who was a good rider, I forget his name now. So I did it the next time you came home from England. I hoped you'd like me as much as I liked you."

Oh, God, he'd hurt her that day. Terribly, too, if she'd never forgotten it. Vividly, he saw himself through her eyes and realized how young and brash he'd been. He'd humiliated her in front of everyone, including her beloved father. Even now, years later, she held her shoulders stiff and unnatural with her face averted. Her head was bowed, and he wanted to comfort her. He moved across the room and placed his hands lightly on her shoulders. Her muscles tensed even harder beneath his palms and he worked them with his fingers, softly massaging the tightness away.

"I'm sorry if I hurt you that day, Trin," he whispered. He found his lips were suddenly against the top of her soft hair. He shut his eyes, savoring the sweet scent of roses. "I shouldn't have embarrassed you. Who knows, maybe I was just jealous because you tried it, and I didn't."

She had relaxed now beneath his touch, and she sighed audibly as if she'd waited a long time to hear him say such words. When she turned around and tilted her face up to look at him, the candle shimmered on the tears in her eyes, turning them into golden pools. God help him, he wanted to kiss her, just about as badly as he had ever wanted anything in his entire, livelong life. He was going to kiss her, now, without waiting a moment longer. He lowered his head close enough to feel her breath against his mouth.

"Trin . . ."

Then he found her lips, found them as petal soft as they looked, parted for him, moistly waiting, eager for him to take more, for his tongue to delve deeper into her mouth. She wanted him to do just that, he could feel it in the way she quivered, the way she pressed against him ever so lightly, but God help him, she couldn't want it any more than he did. He took hold of her upper arms and tried to think straight. He was an experienced man, he knew women well, and Trinity wanted a deeper kiss, he knew it instinctively, her breasts were heaving, brushing the front of his shirt.

He should not, should *not*, he said over and over but he didn't listen to himself, and he bent her back against his arm, losing himself to the moment, to her, to the sweet taste of her mouth, to the silk of her hair now grasped tightly in both his hands.

After a few blissful moments he felt her move, felt her hands between them, palms flat against his chest. When she shoved him back he wasn't prepared for it, and he stumbled a step or two. He stared into her eyes and saw the awful emotions swirling in those vivid depths—shock, anger, pain—then she was gone in a rustle of silk and petticoats and lingering essence of roses, leaving the door standing wide open behind her. Oh, God, would he never, ever learn? What had he been thinking? What had he done? What had they done?

Chapter Thirteen

Stupid, stupid, stupid . . . how in God's name could she have been such a stupid, mooning, sentimental fool! Trinity flipped over on her stomach and covered her head with her pillow, then a moment later switched to her side and stared morosely at the mahogany-paneled wall. Her eyes simply ached with the need to cry. She'd slept fitfully throughout the night, for only a few minutes at a time, or at least it seemed that way.

When she had dozed off, she'd endured one dream after another, all about Will, about the way he held her and kissed her. Oh, Lord, how could she have let him do that? No, she couldn't blame him when she had pressed up against him like some . . . some loose harlot. She'd thrown herself at him! He probably felt sorry for her and that's why he'd kissed her! Face aflame with unmitigated mortification, Trinity buried her head again in the soft silk of her pillow, moaning and groaning.

After all her fine words, her righteous indignation, after protestations of hatred, disgust, disdain, she'd clung to him like some awful, needy, lovelorn waif! Oh, how absurdly humiliating! How he must be laughing at her, comparing her to all the other women with whom he'd dallied and played the lover. She'd rather stay cooped up inside her cabin for the entire duration of the voyage than to face him again! Why had Victoria and Adrianna gotten sick and left her to fall helplessly into his clutches?

She could never again allow herself to be alone with him, not for a single minute! He was too dangerous, and she'd found out in the worst way possible that she still had a weakness where he was concerned. A physical attraction was all it was, of course. He was too handsome and suave and adept at the arts of seduction for her to be immune to him. Oh, he was good at that all right! But she'd held admiration for other men, more than one, and she hadn't acted so disgustingly wanton with them.

Oh, mercy, what had she done? She'd had no intention of sharing any kind of intimacy with him—he'd just caught her in a weak moment, when she'd grown all soft and nostalgic with romantic thoughts of their childhoods and the good times before the war had started, before he'd decided he didn't want her anymore.

Shutting her eyes she forced herself to relax, clear the anxieties out of her mind, and finally did manage to doze, out of sheer exhaustion. But the sleep was light and disturbed and left her feeling even more groggy and unsettled when well into the early morning hours she awoke abruptly at some unfamiliar sound.

Squinting, she pushed herself up onto her elbows. She could hear footsteps running outside her cabin door, several men, it sounded like, then a masculine shout followed by more commotion. Fearful that the storm had worsened, perhaps even disabled the ship, she climbed quickly out of the bunk. The floor still swayed against the heaving waves but was no more violent than it had been earlier that evening. The gentle tick of rain on porthole glass filled the quiet cabin. Certainly not the unleashed fury of a hurricane. But something was wrong. What could it be?

It dawned on her that perhaps Victoria or Adrianna had gotten worse. The idea was enough to compel her to action, and she thrust her arm into her warm velvet wrap and belted it tightly at her waist. At the door, she grabbed a woolen shawl and threw it around her shoulders. Shivering, she checked the other cabins and found both women sleeping peacefully in the calmer weather.

Puzzled greatly, she made her way up the gangway steps and outside. Once topdeck she ran into riotous turmoil with more shouts, and sailors hurrying this way and that. Most ran toward the starboard bow, however, and she followed behind them, lifting her shawl overhead to protect against the misty drizzle. Most of the crewmen gathered around a lantern near the rail, but she couldn't see what they were doing so she pushed through the perimeter of the crowd.

"What's happened?" she asked one of the nearby sailors.

"There's been a shipwreck, mum. Nearby, it seems. We've been pickin' up signs of the wreckage since ten bells, and they've only just now fished a woman out of the drink. She'd been afloat, clinging atop a capsized longboat."

"A woman? Where is she?" Trinity asked, trying to peer over his shoulder. When she heard a thin wailing cry above the patter of rain on the deck, she first thought it was the wind but pushed toward the light to see what was happening.

The first person she saw was Will. He knelt near the woman, who lay outstretched upon her back. The ship's doctor, a man by the name of Schneider who had tended Victoria and her daughter, was working over her under light thrown by the lantern being held up by a cabin boy. The cries started up again, pitiful, weak little mewling sounds.

When William caught sight of Trinity, he came to his feet, and that's when she saw that he held a baby. She gasped in shock, then was appalled by the way he was holding the poor child, out in front of him with both hands under its arms, facing him, as if he held a teeth-snapping, snarling badger rather than a tiny squirming infant.

Trinity moved forward at once and took the child from him, cradling the kicking, fussing baby in her arms. Its clothes were soaked through, as was the blanket it was wrapped inside. The child was shivering with cold, and she immediately stripped off its sodden quilt and enveloped it inside the warm folds of her shawl. She felt its face and found the skin cold and clammy, which frightened her, but the terrified cries abated as soon as she snuggled it up against her shoulder.

"Oh, Will. What about the mother? Is she going to be all right?"

William looked at her, bareheaded and coatless, as if he'd run topdeck in a rush, his dark hair plastered over his brow. "I don't know. She's barely breathing but she stayed afloat out there long enough to save her baby."

"Are there others? Was her husband with them?"

He shook his head. "We haven't found anybody else, not yet. We're still looking."

Trinity clutched the babe closer, gazing down at the poor woman lying so pale and ghostly in the dim lantern light.

"I'll take him down to my cabin where it's warm," she told Will, then rushed off without awaiting an answer, uttering a silent prayer for the poor woman who struggled for life.

By the time she returned to her quarters, the baby was squirming around in her arms, and his cries became increasingly more strident as she carefully laid him down on the bunk and began to strip off the damp white gown. A little boy, she thought, a beautiful little boy with light brown curly hair and big blue eyes.

"Don't cry, my little precious one," she cooed softly, blinking back a hot rush of tears. "Don't you worry now. I'll take good care of you. Everything's going to be all right. You're safe now."

The sky was the color of burnt charcoal lined at the east horizon with a band of glittering pewter where the sun struggled to rise and kill the night. The ship was still bucking periodically under the lift of swells and scattered squalls. Dead on his feet, Will finally was able to make his way belowdecks. Massaging the back of his neck, he trod past his mother's and sister's cabins in the dim, narrow corridor. Both of them were doing better, according to Schneider, but still too weak to be up and about.

The half-drowned young mother they'd fished from the sea did not fare so well. She was racked by fever and chills, only partially conscious. She called endlessly for her baby in hoarse, heartbreaking sobs, and they'd covered her with warm blankets and could only pray she would recover.

As he neared Trinity's door, he heard the baby's muffled cries. He stopped just outside. Unsure what to do, he ran both his hands straight back through his wet hair. The loud yells went on for a minute or two, angry and shrill, and still he hesitated. Trinity wouldn't want him inside her cabin, that was for damn sure, not after what he'd pulled earlier. But he didn't want to think about that. He thrust the memory of her warm, eager mouth out of his mind, a difficult task at best. He glanced at his mother's cabin just down the hall. Victoria was much too sick to help, or he'd go to her for assistance. She'd certainly know how to quiet an infant. Apparently Trinity was having trouble doing so.

Fists planted on his hips, he gazed longingly down the hall where his own warm bunk awaited him. The baby screamed louder. Sighing, he tapped on Trinity's door. No answer. Impatient now, he turned the knob and stuck his head inside. Trinity was walking the floor, a tiny white bundle held up against her shoulder. She had on a nightgown, white with full sleeves and a high, ribbon-laced neckline, long enough to swish and flutter against her legs. Her hair hung loose, lying like a shawl of flame down her back. Within a second or so, she became aware of his presence. She whirled on him, and with distinct surprise, he watched relief flood into her worried face.

"Oh, Will, I'm so glad you're here! I've done everything I can think of for him. I've rocked him and sung to him, and changed him into warm clothes. Something's wrong, because he won't stop crying."

She looked distraught, upset about the baby, yet all he could think about as he moved across the cabin was how beautiful she looked with her hair long and flowing free and the way the sweet essence of roses seemed to permeate the very air around her. A fragrance unique to Trinity. He'd recognize her by that alone, even if they stood in a pitch-black room.

He watched her shift the child from her shoulder to the crook of her left arm. Sobbing, hiccuping, the infant's face was flushed beet-red, his eyes shiny with tears. William reached out and touched its forehead with the back of his fingers to see if he'd caught the fever. The skin was warm but not with the dry heat of fever that parched and dehydrated the skin.

"I haven't been around little babies much, I'm afraid," Trinity admitted softly, bouncing it lightly on her arm but that only caused the baby boy to give a shriek. "Have you?" she asked hopefully, but by her expression he knew that she feared he hadn't. She was right.

"To be exact, never."

"I wish Victoria could help us." Trinity's words were wistful, paralleling his own earlier thoughts. "I started to lay him down once but I didn't for fear the waves would throw him to the floor."

"Well, that's a problem I can fix," he said, relieved there was finally a task he could deal with. He headed quickly for one of the built-in cabinets beside the door. He retrieved a hemp hammock stowed there and quickly strung it between hooks bolted to the ceiling beams for that purpose. He tugged on each end to make sure the sling was secure, then took a quilt from the same cabinet. He fashioned the blanket into the hammock until he'd formed a soft, padded cradle.

"Maybe if we put him in this, the boat'll rock him to sleep."

Trinity brightened with the suggestion and hastened to try out his idea. She quickly tucked the kicking infant securely inside the plaid quilt.

They moved closer and stared down at the baby, but rather than becoming calm, his fit gained momentum, his tiny round face turning purple with rage.

"Oh, no, I can't bear to see him cry so hard! I've got to take him out!" She wasted no time in that pursuit, snatching the child out of the makeshift cradle. That seemed to work for a few minutes as the baby settled down until he obviously came to the conclusion that Trinity was not his mother, after all. The new wave of wails reverberated off the low ceiling and into Will's brain like vocal needles. Will and Trinity stared helplessly at each other, both at a complete loss.

"Maybe he's hungry?" Will didn't sound sure.

"I fed him almost a full saucer of broth earlier and even a little juice from an orange. He did quiet then, for a moment, but not for long." She, too, was beginning to crumble, and Will could hear the desperation quavering in her voice.

"He's not wet?"

"No. I used one of my linen towels for a diaper. And I've been walking him back and forth ever since then . . ."

A sheen of moisture began to glow inside her eyes, but when she mentioned walking the baby, a memory came floating up out of the dark ocean of William's past. He'd seen another yelling, angry baby once, years and years ago, and he remembered the way the father had calmed it.

"Give him to me. I've got an idea."

Trinity gratefully handed over the baby, and he took the child awkwardly, marveling at how

tiny it was. Afraid he'd drop it on its head, or
something, he realized that before that night he'd
never held a child in his life, much less an infant.
God, he hadn't had any experience with any children, not even older ones. Somehow he got the
wriggling lad turned around where he could sit
on Will's right hand. He leaned it back against
him with his left hand cradling the front of its little chest. He rocked him gently side to side. The
baby still cried. Will rested his chin on the top of
the baby's head the way he remembered the
other man doing, and feeling like the biggest
idiot who'd ever lived, he began to hum a low
rendition of a rather bawdy drinking song he
hoped Trinity didn't know the words to.

After a moment or two of jerking his arms and
fussing, the child finally grew still. Rather
amazed himself, Will grinned triumphantly at
Trinity, where she had perched anxiously on the
edge of her bunk. She stared at him, as if awed
by his accomplishment, and more confident now,
he continued to hum and sway back and forth
with the baby. Still watching Trinity, he was re-
warded for his trouble with a slow, but absolutely radiant smile. So blindingly tender did
her eyes lay upon him that he forgot to hum for a
moment but remembered soon enough as the
baby squirmed and complained.

He resumed his song without delay, walking
slowly around the cabin until the baby lay quiet.
He moved to where Trinity sat on the bunk and
raised his eyebrows in silent question.

"He's fast asleep," she breathed out in wonder.

William basked under her admiration, for rare it was indeed for him to impress Trinity Kingston.

Trinity was whispering now. "Do you think we can put him in the little hammock without waking him up?"

"Hell if I know."

"Well, let's try, unless you intend to hum to him all night long."

He acknowledged her teasing with a negative shake of his head, then watched as she carefully took the baby into her arms. He held the hammock open while she tucked the exhausted infant into the downy folds. They both leaned over the sling, holding their breaths as the net cradle began to rock gently to the calming rhythm of the waves. The baby slept on in peaceful oblivion. They shared self-satisfied smiles.

Trinity reached out and took William's hand, then led him to the far side of the cabin where she spoke in hushed tones.

"Where on earth did you learn to do that? You were wonderful with him."

"Actually," he admitted in the same undertone, aware of the way her eyes shone warm and golden in the candlelight, "I saw your father do it once when you were a little baby, even smaller than this one. We were at a summer picnic at Palmetto Point, and the women were out on the gallery with the children, while all the men smoked inside the study. I never forgot it because I'd never seen a father leave the gentlemen like that and take a baby from the arms of its nurse."

"Really? Are you telling me the truth?" she asked, tilting her head to one side with an openly suspicious look.

"Gospel. I was just a boy, and I watched him do it. Eldon said the low pitch of a masculine voice would calm a cranky baby faster than anything. He held you just that way, with your head under his chin."

"And did I stop crying?"

William nodded, surprised to see her eyes filling up with tears again, even more shocked when she came up against his chest and caught him around the waist with both arms. "I miss him so much, Will," she managed to get out, but her voice was clogged, and she wept unashamedly into the front of his shirt. Will held her and comforted her, but inside his chest, he felt new and dangerous responses, his heart warming toward her, burgeoning with newfound feelings he should not be feeling.

But Trinity felt so good pressed against him, so soft and sweet, and so charming in her heretofore unrevealed vulnerability. Though he'd hold her and stroke her silken, golden red hair, and comfort her for as long as she needed him, tomorrow he'd have to harden himself again and remember there could never be anything between them. Tomorrow he would put her aside and remember his duty to family and King.

Chapter Fourteen

The day was clear, the sky a vast, brilliant dome of delft blue. Not a wisp of cloud marred the vista, and to Trinity, the Atlantic now seemed an entirely different ocean; in truth, a completely different world, as calm, beautiful, serene as a seascape painting. Enjoying the restful view stretching far away to the horizon, she gripped the wood rail, lifting her face to the bright sun. The warmth poured down over her skin like a gentle caress.

A rare pleasure indeed, and one forbidden her since she was scarcely out of childhood. All her life she'd been reminded daily to shield her fair complexion from such darkening rays. But today it felt too good to heed those warnings. She felt free and alive, and in that moment she envied the males of the world who seemed to have so few restrictions about how they led their lives.

"Where's your bonnet, dear? You know full well how you're prone to freckle, even more than Adrianna is." Victoria's voice had come from just behind Trinity's place at the side rail. Surprised to hear her friend was up and well enough to tool around the deck, Trinity turned and gave her a welcoming embrace. She pushed away and held the older woman at arm's length, studying her face and finding it still pale and wan, a shadow of her prior robust health.

"You must be awfully much better," she said with a smile, happy to have female company once more. "How do you feel?"

"A bit wobbly on my feet, I must say, but now the sea's so calm, I'm quite sure the worst is over."

"What about Adrianna?"

"Oh, that poor dear's still weak as a lamb, and can't hold down a morsel. We've had a bad time of it but mercy be praised that you've weathered the storm so well."

"Will says I'm a natural-born sailor."

Trinity cast a sidelong glance at William where he stood beside Captain Parks a good distance away in the stern. The smile that turned up the corners of her mouth came unbidden, and when he saw her looking and waved a friendly greeting, she found it difficult to pull her eyes away.

"Why, Trinity, I swan, have you and Will declared a truce? I never would've thought you'd think him anything other than a villain." Victoria didn't hedge her words or her insight.

Guilt attacked Trinity like a swarm of wasps, and her pleasure at Will's friendly overture melted away. "Why do you say that?"

Victoria's dark eyes caught Trinity's gaze, searching and appraising in that disturbing way she had. "By the look on your face. I rarely remember you smiling his way in the past."

"Actually I will admit that he's been most kind since we left Charleston."

"Indeed? Will?"

"Yes, and to everyone, really. Especially the Spanish survivors."

Victoria observed her son with some interest. "There's a change in him, I agree. He visited my cabin earlier this morning and told me both the mother and child will survive quite well. I understand the lady was dreadfully ill at first."

Trinity nodded. "We feared she would succumb to exposure in the first days, but now she's able to take care of her baby again. Will speaks fluent Spanish, did you know that? He's found out she's got distant kinfolk in St. Augustine, and we're hoping they'll take her in. Captain Parks feels certain that her husband was drowned. It's all very sad."

Victoria nodded. "I feel lucky this vessel rode out the tempest in one piece. We could've easily shared that poor lady's hardships instead of merely being blown a bit off course."

"Will feels they must have encountered hurricane winds but that we somehow managed to skirt the worst of it."

While Victoria listened to her, she gazed thoughtfully at her oldest son. William smiled and acknowledged them again, and Trinity felt the first wave of heat rise into her cheeks. Victoria noticed, too.

"Forgive me, Trinity, darling, but I feel I must

warn you about becoming too enamored of Will. He's my firstborn child, and of course I love him with all my heart, and as you well know, he is handsome and can be incredibly charming, but please remember that he's nearly thirty now, and no doubt vastly experienced with women. What I'm trying to remind you, dear, is that you and Will are no longer wed, nor even betrothed. He's told you himself, and quite bluntly, that he intends to offer marriage to another young lady."

Trinity stiffened, flooded with acute embarrassment to hear such humiliating words spoken aloud. It struck her almost like a physical slap across the face but she tried to laugh, as if she thought Victoria's concerns absurd. Of course, they were absurd, she thought with a stab of irony, she just no longer wanted them to be.

"I haven't forgotten the way Will treated me, Victoria, and I shan't. You mustn't worry yourself on my account. I've only come to the conclusion after spending more time with him that he's not quite the ogre I once thought. How could he be? You raised him, did you not? He would have to have some inherent virtues."

Her flattery and bright smile did not initiate a similar response from Will's mother. Her expression remained somber, almost pitying, as she studied her son. "Alas, but I only had him with me for eleven short years. His father raised him by different standards, I fear. Adrian is, and always has been, a cold, heartless man. Unfortunately he endeavored to teach our sons to think in like manner."

Trinity's lips parted slightly, never before having heard Victoria utter an ill word against anyone, much less her husband, the Duke of Thorpe. She glanced down at Will again, wondering if his childhood truly had been so cold and sterile as his mother feared.

Though she knew Victoria only meant to caution her, instead, the idea of William being a lonely, unloved boy made her heart ache for him. He'd said as much himself about his youth though, had he not? She remembered with a poignant smile how gently he'd held the baby and hummed him to sleep. He was not completely without feeling, she knew that now. And she knew, against her will, her better judgment, and every barrier that she put up against him, that she still did care for him.

What an utter idiot she was! She had to end it now, before all those old feelings became strong again. She'd been in love with him once, and how easy it would be for her to fall into his trap again. Especially now, when the hatred of him she had nurtured for so long was beginning to crumble. Yes, of course, that's what she would have to do. And she wouldn't forget herself again.

Within three days the coast of Florida loomed in dark green mounds against the horizon like a bracelet of emerald stones. Trinity once more occupied her favorite spot at the starboard bow, where the offshore winds cooled her face and billowed her petticoats. Her gaze was fixed relent-

lessly on the shore where her father was being
held prisoner. Somewhere on that distant strand,
he wasted away in a cell, perhaps ill, perhaps
abused by his jailers.

Biting her bottom lip, she tried to erase that
image from her mind and replace it with more
pleasant ones. She'd see him soon, after all, and
get him out of prison, and feel his arms around
her in the giant bear hug he always gave to her.
She missed him terribly, just as she'd told Will
that night in her cabin, more than she could have
ever possibly imagined. He'd always been there
for her, the only family in her life, whenever she
needed him, always, until the night the British
had dragged him away in chains.

"It won't be long now, Trin."

Trinity stiffened with dread. William stood
right beside her, so close to her that their elbows
touched. Since her conversation with Victoria
she'd spent her time fortifying her resolve
against any kind of friendship with him. Her admiration for Will was growing in perilous leaps
and bounds. Mercy be, a few kind words from
him, a mesmerizing smile or two, and her dislike
and distrust had slid away like an otter off a
bank. The sight of him holding the baby had
done her in, and now she felt weak-kneed and
quivery because he was so near. She had been as-
siduously avoiding him the last few days, but
she had made her plans for rebuffing him. The
time had come. She took a deep breath.

"Come now, Trin. I know good and well you

recognize me. I'm the one who rescued you from the crying baby, remember?"

Her first mistake was to look up into his face. His green eyes, so warm on hers, glinted with humor, and that grin again, melting her. She was instantly disarmed and hated herself for it. Her own smile came unbidden, slow and sweet.

"The captain says we'll be landing in a couple of hours," he told her but his eyes had latched on to her mouth now. Affected, she quickly lowered her eyes.

"I've found out from Elena that there's a house near the fort owned by a Spaniard by the name of Gonzalez. He might quarter us while we're ashore. You'll be comfortable there while I go up to the Castillo and arrange Eldon's release."

Trinity swiveled her regard to the shoreline, searching until she picked out the massive dark walls of the old Spanish fortress. Now under the control of the British, it rose like some medieval dragon against the sky. "I prefer to go to the prison with you."

"Sorry, Trinity, that's out of the question. It'll be better if I see the commandant of the prison alone."

"I'm going." Mouth firmly resolute, she stared at him, watched him shake his head.

"I can't let you do that, and that's final."

"Please, Will," she whispered, relenting enough to add, "you know how much it means to me."

The humility of her supplication caught him by surprise, and he frowned. Hesitating, he planted his fists on his hips, his arms holding his blue linen frock coat open at the waist. His auburn hair was tied back with a black ribbon but shorter strands blew around his face. When he looked back at her, she knew she'd won the argument before he uttered a single word.

"All right, dammit, I guess you can tag along. But you're to do everything I tell you, is that understood? And for Christ's sake, don't rile the guards with patriot rhetoric, or you just might find yourself looking through bars with your father."

Though he'd used profanity and certainly wasn't hiding his annoyance, she smiled, unimpressed with Will's angry scowl. "Thank you, Will. I'll do whatever you say. I promise."

"I'll believe that when I see it," he muttered under his breath, but she could tell he wasn't really angry when he left her and proceeded aft to join the captain. Heart lighter than it had been in some time, she latched her gaze on the coastline once again, barely able to contain her eagerness, wishing she could fill the sails and propel them faster to shore.

As it turned out, however, it took nearly four hours to reach landfall, and the sun lay on the ocean surface behind them like a red ball of fire. The shore boat was launched without much delay, and trembling with nerves, Trinity settled into the front seat between Victoria and Adrianna. Will sat in the stern, and in the middle of the small craft, the Spanish woman, Elena, sat alone with her baby, whose name Trinity had

learned was Juan. Elena smiled and nodded at
Trinity, for Will had told her how Trinity had
cared for the boy, but her eyes were as dark and
sorrowful as the black shawl she wore as a man-
tilla.

Eight crewmen, burly and hulking, with gigantic upper arms that seemed as big as hams,
bent into their oars and propelled the craft with
deep, long strokes toward shore. Trinity leaned
forward where she could see the tiny whitewashed huts fringing the wide curve of tan
beach. The sand was a lighter shade than they'd
known in South Carolina, and there were many
more palm trees, taller and more majestic than
the palmettos she was used to.

"William says the fort's called the Castillo de
San Marcos by the Spaniards, but after the British
captured it, they renamed it Fort Saint Mark."
Adrianna had lowered her voice so as not to be
overheard, but her voice was strong, and she was
almost her normal self again though a good ten
pounds lighter than before her illness.

Trinity glanced at the British warships anchored in a calm inlet where they were protected
by the guns of the fort.

"Geoff says they stage their attacks on both
Georgia and the Carolinas from here," Trinity
whispered, speaking close to Adrianna's ear.
"Keep your eyes and ears open and try to find
out as much as you can about the garrison and
what ships have come and gone of late."

The idea of helping the patriot cause with such
information excited Trinity. She strained her eyes

to try to read the name on the nearest ship, a well-armed frigate with cannon bristling out of the gunports. In one sense, it made her feel good to think she could still help Geoff and the Continental Army, but in another way, one that was harder to understand, she felt she betrayed herself as well. She had considered herself a British subject for all her years, in every aspect of her existence. Spain and France had always been avowed enemies, but now her loyalties had been turned upside down since Spain and France had come into the war on the side of the Americans.

"Lower your voices, if you please," Victoria warned softly. "From this point on, there will be many around us who will look upon our views as treason. You must not forget where you are."

Trinity immediately took heed, but she wondered if Victoria alluded to her son as well. For it was in Will's direction that Victoria glanced, and Trinity knew then that his mother did consider him the enemy. Trinity felt a wave of sympathy flood through her because she knew Victoria was right. Will shouldn't be trusted; he'd been kind to her aboard the ship for one reason, and one reason alone. He wanted her signature on the annulment documents so he could be free to wed another. He'd kissed her because he'd been bored and thought her an easy conquest, no doubt. She absolutely had to scorch his real motives into her brain.

Instead she thought of the way he'd comforted her, the burning need when his mouth found her own. She swallowed hard, fighting the shiver the memory brought back. If his own mother could hold herself aloof and cautious around Will, then so could Trinity. She forced herself not to look at him again but focused her attention on the tall round turrets jutting from the four corners of the Castillo de San Marcos. She saw the bars on the windows and that helped more than anything to harden her heart. William was English, just like the men who had locked her father away behind those iron bars.

When she saw her father, he would make her feel better about the roiling turmoil torturing her heart. A scald of tears hit her, and she closed her eyes tightly. *Oh, Papa, please be safe and well. If you're not, I cannot bear it.*

Chapter Fifteen

Although William had sent a note to the commandant of Fort Saint Mark immediately upon landing, the officer in charge did not deign to reply until early the following morning. Despite the delay, which Trinity did not accept well—he'd almost had to restrain her bodily before he could convince her that her father's best interests would not be served by storming the prison and making demands of his jailors—William himself was encouraged.

He'd had no idea until their arrival, of course, but it turned out that he was well acquainted with the British commander. Hadringham was an old friend of the Remington family, both socially and professionally. Will knew him to be a fair man, a dedicated soldier, but a man, nevertheless, obsessed with quelling the American rebellion. Hadringham would not be thrilled with the idea of releasing a rebel incarcerated for treason.

As Elena had told him, Gonzalez had been able to accommodate them, and they'd taken lodgings in his modest two-story house just south of the fort. Made of coquina, the ground-floor rooms were spacious enough, considering the remoteness of the settlement, with floors made from a local concrete of mortar and crushed oyster shells he'd learned was called tabby.

Above the spot where he now stood near the fireplace, great hand-hewn cedar beams stretched across the ceiling. The hearth was huge, and the breakfast cooking in its smoky reaches smelled of pork and coffee and freshly baked bread. An old woman and a young girl named Larita bustled around a long planked table flanking the fire, putting down plates and cutlery with clicks and rattles while they conversed in a rapid-fire patter of Spanish about their guests and the fine gowns and lacy shawls they wore. He smiled when Larita likened Trinity's hair to the copper pans hanging on a rack above the hearth.

Trinity had not come downstairs yet but the hour was very early. He glanced at the narrow stone steps leading up to the sleeping quarters. The beds had been comfortable, feather mattresses and bed linens that were clean enough to suit him, but he'd not slept well, unused to the heavy humidity of the southern seacoast.

Lifting the thick white mug the old woman had fetched for him, he drank down a draft of extremely strong black coffee, and savored the rich, aromatic brew as it warmed his empty stomach. He moved to another window where he could see the morning sun struggling to extricate itself from a dark blue sea amid a glorious crown of golden spikes. It was going to be another beautiful day, sunny, calm, all remnants of the hurricane washed away. Perhaps today, if God was listening to Trinity's prayers, they'd find Eldon Kingston as hale and hearty as he'd been the night his daughter had kissed him good-bye.

The click of footsteps descending the stairs caught his attention, and he turned and watched Trinity move quickly across the taproom toward him. She was dressed to impress, all in royal blue and black lace, and she succeeded admirably. She looked lovely, breathtaking, but had he not found her so since he'd first laid eyes upon her again at Palmetto Point?

Will knew full well that he was in an exceedingly dangerous situation as he regarded with a smile the lovely young woman in rustling silk who smelled like heaven. He should step away from her, forget the magnetic pull tugging at him. He should leave her be, ignore her, do nothing else to encourage her . . . but he was more and more unwilling to do that. The truth was, as god-awful hard as it was to admit, that he liked her, might even go so far as to say he admired her. She had shown courage, determination, but most of all a fiery spirit absent in most of the simpering ladies of society that he'd known in London. Including Lady Caroline Rappaport, whom his father wished him to take as his wife.

Today, however, would entail a different kind of test for Trinity; facing her father's fate would not be pleasant for her, nor easy. When she smiled up at Will she seemed very anxious, her fine amber eyes were worried, weary from lack of rest.

"I didn't sleep a wink," were her first words, verifying his observation. "Oh, Will, what if they won't let me see him?"

"They will. I'll see to it." At that moment he would have promised her the moon.

The concerned furrow etching her brow softened and smoothed away, just the result he'd wanted to elicit, yet one he shouldn't enjoy quite so much. Trust, that's what was in her face now. A response to him he wouldn't have bet a farthing on a mere week ago.

"Would you care for something to eat?" he offered, gesturing toward the table. "They've quite a selection of morning fare prepared for us."

Trinity negated the idea with a quick shake of her head, as if the thought of ingesting food was absolutely repugnant.

"All right then, let's go. The only means of transport I could find was a market wagon."

Trinity wasted no time, lifting her full skirt and preceding him hurriedly through the portal and out onto the sandy, rutted street. The wagon looked a hundred years old, and he'd paid an extra shilling to the ancient blacksmith to drive them. The old man already sat atop the driver's seat, and Will assisted Trinity up beside him, then climbed up himself for the short ride up the hill to the fortress. The wagon lurched under Will's weight, then squeaked and squealed as the wheels began to turn.

Will tried to relax, hoping he looked more at ease than he actually felt, especially when Trinity squirmed and fidgeted, twisting her black silk purse between her fingers as if she meant to kill it. She sat perched on the edge of the board seat, gazing forward, her eyes riveted on the massive white coquina walls of the Castillo de San Marcos, as if she hoped to catch a glimpse of her father in one of the barred cells.

The closer they came to the fortress, the more agitated she became, and he finally could not watch without at least attempting to calm her nerves. Without speaking he reached over and laid a steadying palm over her clasped hands. She was trembling.

"Easy, sweet. It's going to be all right. We're almost there."

She still looked straight ahead but did not try to extricate her hands from his. "I'm just so afraid for him, Will. It's been over a year since I've seen him, and we've never even been apart before. He wasn't well then, you know about his gout . . ."

William wondered how it would have been to have such a closeness with a parent. Often, even when he was but a lad, two years or more had gone by without him speaking with his father. Even longer than that with his mother, years and years sometimes. He and Trinity had been brought up under very different circumstances, yet here they sat together, married and unmarried, friends and enemies. He could not ignore the supreme irony that they both still trod the path upon which their fathers had placed them when they were mere children.

To get her mind off the coming audience, he began to speak of other things, the lush vegetation and creeping scarlet flowers on the low coquina walls and wooden fence posts lining the road. Not surprisingly, he had little success in that endeavor, and fell into silence watching the lacy shadows of morning sunshine that burned down through the fringed palm fronds and danced upon her gleaming golden red hair.

The massive wooden gates of the ancient Spanish fort came into sight at last, heavily guarded by soldiers wearing the familiar scarlet coats of His Majesty's army, but when they were told that Lord Remington of Thorpe had arrived, they hastened to admit him. They passed through the great walls that looked to be at least twelve feet thick, made of the coquina so prevalent in Florida, some sort of natural aggregate of seashells embedded in lime mortar. As the wagon lurched through the outer gates, a cool darkness enveloped them, blocking the warm sun as if they'd driven from day into evening. Other soldiers stacked tall pyramids of cannonballs near one of the lethal twenty-pounders facing out over the sea.

The old driver silently guided the horse across the interior courtyard and rolled to a stop at the base of narrow stone stairs that climbed up to a higher level where a small wooden building had been constructed against one side of the towering stone wall.

As Will assisted Trinity to the ground, he looked upward and found Lord Hadringham already halfway down the steps to greet them. Thomas was much older than Will, actually more his father's friend, around fiftyish though he looked younger. Rather squat in build, he was broad through the shoulders, his body resembling a sturdy bulldog, with the slightly hanging jowls to match. He descended toward them, a wide, welcoming grin on his face, his hand outstretched. But despite his warmth, he still held himself in the erect posture of a man long accustomed to the strictures of military service.

"Egad, William, but it's been ages since we've crossed paths. God help me, if I can even remember when 'twas. I daresay, it's good to see someone from home."

As they locked hands and shook warmly, Will had to admit he was glad to see the brash adjutant general again, and even though he was more a crony to His Grace, William remembered more than a handful of enjoyable nights of cards and cognac in the gentlemen's club on Rutherford Street.

"It's got to be at least six years, I suspect," William answered.

"At the very least," Hadringham agreed, continually nodding his head. "And most of that time I've sat here rotting in this godforsaken hellhole. The better part of four years, it's been. I can't tell you how I long for the sight of Kent's cool green grass. Here all we have is black biting flies that'll drive a man to Bedlam."

"Aye. Happily, I'm on my way home to Thorpe."

"And His Grace? Is he well? I saw him last in the halls of Parliament, giving the doves a mouthful." He laughed at the memory.

"He's probably still doing the same."

"And his heart ailment? Is he well?"

"Aye, though he suffers attacks now and again. He was hale and hearty when I left him in London."

"Good, fine news, indeed," Hadringham answered, but he was looking at Trinity now, as if he'd become aware of her for the first time. She still stood below them, beside the dray, uncharacteristically reticent, at least for Trinity Kingston. But that meant she was heeding his warning to let him handle the commander of the fort.

"And who, pray tell, is that glorious creature you've brought to visit me? God, man, surely you've not taken a wife? You, the smoothest talker who ever wooed the ladies of London?"

Hadringham didn't know how close to the truth he was, Will thought with droll, unamused humor.

"As I put forth in my note, Mistress Kingston's here to visit her father."

"Eldon Kingston, you mean? Then the lady hails from the American colonies?"

"Yes, from Charleston. Actually the Kingstons are old friends of my father."

His arched eyebrows, shot with gray, puckered

with distaste. "Rebels now. Kingston's here for treasonous acts against the King."

"I'm aware of his crime. Nevertheless, Trinity is his only daughter, only kin, actually. She's quite concerned about his health, you understand, and most anxious to see him. I told her I'd do what I can to help alleviate her worry."

Hadringham nodded, then his expression lightened. "How about a spot of port first? The best out of Lisbon and a half-dozen crates to use up. Compliments of a Spanish galleon run aground just south of here."

William glanced aside at Trinity, who looked ready to run them both through with the saber sheathed at Hadringham's belt. He lowered his voice.

"The poor lady's not seen her father for well nigh over a year, Thomas. How about us enjoying that drink afterward? I'd be most grateful. Extremely so."

Their eyes met for a long moment, an unspoken flash of understanding passing between them. Bribes were alive and well in the ranks of the British army, William thought, wondering how much the visit would end up costing him.

"Bring her along then. We can reach some mutually satisfying understanding, I have no doubt."

Descending to Trinity, Will took her elbow and spoke softly to her as he led her up the steps toward Hadringham. "Be polite now. Thomas looks harmless enough but I know that he's got a hair-trigger temper. I've seen him go off like a rocket for no good reason other than a foul mood."

"I'll remember to grovel and bat my eyelashes like a proper lady," she answered in the same hushed tone, but despite her show of bravado, she still sounded shaky.

"Mistress Kingston, please allow me to introduce Lord Thomas Hadringham, adjutant general of the force garrisoned here at Fort Saint Mark."

"How do you do, milord." Trinity greeted him with an absolutely dazzling smile, one that affected the sought-after response from the heretofore less-than-impressed officer. His eyes moved over her in a lustful leer.

"Oh, the pleasure is mine, mistress. 'Tis rare indeed for this wretched fort to be graced by a lady so fair."

"You are very kind." Trinity dipped into a graceful curtsy, and Will watched Hadringham's eyes measure the modesty of her décolletage. An unwarranted streak of annoyance burned through him, or perhaps it was more akin to jealousy. Whatever it was, he summoned up the good sense to ignore it.

Beaming down at Trinity, Hadringham offered his hand and, as if she were indeed Will's duchess, led her up the stairs and into the cool gray depths of the fortress. The chill air felt good after the oppressive heat but there was a dank smell of mold and mildew, of misery, and Will wondered how many prisoners had drawn their last breaths behind the dark, pocked, and pitted walls.

"Are there men in all these cells?" Trinity asked, subdued as she was led ever downward into the bowels of the edifice.

"We've less than a hundred prisoners here at the moment," Hadringham informed them in a loud, pompous voice, one that sent resonant, echoing reverberations down the subterranean vaults through which they walked. "Most of the rebels are transported to prison ships anchored in New York harbor. Here we keep those of a more political bent, rich planters and others who forget their loyalty and betray the Crown."

Trinity's face froze into a waxen, ashy-hued mask, then blanched even whiter as they descended deeper into dungeons of the old castillo. She was wise enough to hold her tongue, thank God, but her eyes revealed shadows of fear, and she peered uneasily into the tiny barred grates of each chained door they passed.

After a long, bone-chilling walk through dark, increasingly narrower stone corridors, during which time Will cursed himself soundly for allowing Trinity to accompany him to such a place, Hadringham finally halted and removed a ring of keys on the hook beside the cell. As he unlocked the heavy wooden door, Trinity rose onto her tiptoes and gripped the bars, trying to peer through the dusky light hiding the interior.

"Papa? Papa, are you in there?" Her whisper was hoarse, distressed.

The door stuck fast as if it had not often been

used, and Will put his shoulder to it and shoved it open enough for Trinity to enter. Trinity pushed past him but drew up just inside, unable to see through the gloom blanketing the windowless cell. William lifted one of the hanging lanterns from its hook in the corridor and moved into the cell with it. A murmur came to them followed by a raspy cough, and he was able to pick out the narrow shelf carved from the far wall. The tiny cubicle stank of musty straw and human excrement.

"Oh, my God. Papa, what have they done to you?" Trinity was sobbing, already on her knees at Eldon's side. She wept inconsolably, and Will understood why when he saw the shriveled, emaciated creature who lay atop the cold slab that acted as his bed.

William winced, hardly recognizing Eldon Kingston, his most vivid memory of him, the plump and affable, smiling father who'd hummed the lullaby to his baby daughter that day so long ago.

"Trinity? Child?"

Eldon's voice was tremulous, weak, and hesitant but gained strength as Trinity held his hand in hers. "God help me, am I dreaming you again?"

"No, no, Papa, it's me. Will's here, too. We've come to get you out. Can you hear me? Oh, Papa, you look so ill. You can walk, can't you? You've got to, we've got to get you out of here!"

"Now not so fast, Mistress Kingston."

Hadringham stepped forward to intervene. "I've no orders concerning his release."

Will saw the terrified look on Trinity's face, and then she looked at him, raw, naked pleading in her eyes. He turned to Hadringham and drew him aside.

"Eldon Kingston's a personal friend of mine, Hadringham. His Grace would look kindly upon you if you showed us a bit of compassion."

The British officer hesitated. "He's an enemy of the King. I can't just let him go."

Now came the negotiation. "Release him into my custody, and I guarantee you'll be paid most handsomely. His Grace has personally requested him brought to England. He'll be appropriately dealt with there, rest assured. And I'll vouch for him while he's in my custody. You'll be relieved of any and all responsibility."

Again their gazes locked, and Will knew he'd get no agreement, verbal or otherwise, until he offered a sum. Greed veritably glowed inside Thomas's deepset dark eyes.

"I've not the authority to give the prisoner a pardon." Thomas lowered his voice again. "I've often longed, however, to retire my commission and return to Kent for good. I've missed my wife and children these years abroad."

"And what figure would make that possible?" Will found it hard to restrain the contempt he felt.

"Twenty thousand pounds." Hadringham searched his face eagerly.

Will didn't make him wait. "Done."

Obviously surprised by Will's easy acquiescence, not to mention generosity, Thomas seemed shocked, quickly followed by a smile of unveiled elation.

"So, that settled, I'd appreciate your summoning a pair of guards to assist Mr. Kingston to the wagon."

Hadringham hurried from the cell, rubbing his palms together as if he were already counting coin. Will moved to Trinity's side, but even while he whispered the good news, a cloud of foreboding darkened the moment, for as he looked down upon Eldon Kingston's pale, frail body wracked with deep, harsh coughing, he was not at all sure Trinity's father would survive the night, much less the long voyage back to England.

Chapter Sixteen

Will's concern for Trinity's father had not diminished by the time they got the poor old man off the shore boat, aboard ship, and into his berth. Eldon Kingston appeared dangerously weak, his eyes—which William remembered as sparkling bright blue—were glazed and listless, his limbs hanging slack at his sides as if he had not the strength to support them. He lay abed, unspeaking, unable to reassure the three very distraught ladies, who together clucked over him with a great deal of tucking of bedclothes, plumping of pillows, and wringing of hands.

Standing some distance away from the fretting women, Will watched Dr. Schneider lift Eldon's right arm, a pitiful sight with its parchment-thin flesh clinging to bone. The physician felt the patient's pulse, and Will realized that he was handling Eldon carefully as if he felt his bones might snap. He heard Trinity gasp when the doctor raised the blanket and revealed Eldon's grotesquely swollen, gouted foot.

Long, tense minutes later, it was with a great

deal of relief that Will heard the doctor give a favorable prognosis to Trinity.

"I know he looks terrible, but the truth is, I believe he'll recover just fine. He's malnourished, of course, and weak, but all he needs is bed rest and proper diet to sustain his recuperation."

"Are you quite sure, Doctor? He looks so ill, so pale, and he's been coughing."

"Aye. He has a cough but that'll fade now that he's in a nice warm bed. I've given him a heavy dose of laudanum to help him sleep, and intend to continue it for the next few days. That way, his body will have time to get stronger when he awakens. Then he'll get better."

"Do you think I should sit with him through the night? In case anything changes?"

"No, there's really no need for that. Actually, it'd be better if you got some rest as well. He'll need you more in the next few days. You'll disturb his rest if you hover too close. I assure you that I'll come in and check on him periodically."

For almost an hour after the doctor had given those instructions, both Victoria and Adrianna remained with Trinity at her bedside vigil, but as Eldon continued to sleep peacefully, eventually even they pleaded exhaustion. Insisting that Trinity call them if Eldon's condition changed, they retired to their cabins. Still, Trinity leaned close, bathing her father's forehead and cheeks and murmuring softly close to his ear, despite the fact that he slept. Even when he was awake, he'd exhibited no sign of recognition since he'd first croaked her name when she'd come into his cell.

Fully aware that he should leave the room, Will found himself lingering. He leaned back against the wall beside the door, uninvited, and all but ignored, but glad at least the ship was under sail again. An hour before, the anchor had been winched, and hopefully they would have no more problems on the voyage. Enough of those awaited them in England, of course, larger, more serious problems.

Sighing, he stood up. He had no business hanging around waiting. For what? He ought to go to his own cabin, should have some time ago. He ought to get the sleep he'd been robbed of so he could think straight. And so should Trinity, just like the doctor said. What he bloody well needed was to forget all about Trinity, he amended, and her father, once and for all. As soon as he got to England, the annulment could be signed and his life would go on. That's right, he should go on to bed and let them have the privacy they no doubt wanted.

Half an hour later he found himself still on the bench, thoroughly cursing his growing obsession with the woman who would have been his wife. Maybe that was it; his whole predicament in a nutshell. Trinity was untouchable. Completely, inexorably out of his reach. There was no way they could ever be together, even if they wanted to, and of course, he didn't want to, and neither did she. God, any kind of relationship between them would be impossible under the circumstances, even friendship, an absurd, undeniable disaster.

But now as she wept softly, her cheek lying

upon the mattress beside Eldon's hand, his heart twisted, and it took every ounce of his self-control not to go to her, not to take her in his arms and comfort her. To kiss away her tears. That idea brought on other, less compassionate thoughts, and he found himself fantasizing of tugging loose her bodice and burying his face in her breasts, of making love to her, slowly, thoroughly, for hours on end. The images, as unacceptable as they were unavoidable, welled inside his mind, taunting him, haunting him, making him crazy.

Frowning blackly, furious with himself, he forced his eyes away from her. Within moments, however, he was looking at her again, admiring her hair, aware of just how soft it felt between his fingers, like floating gossamer. Golden red as a Caribbean sunset. Like a damned adolescent who'd not yet had a woman, he longed to bury his hands in it, loosen it from pins and combs and drag her mouth up so that he could taste her lips, her tongue.

She was too desirable for her own good, and he was plagued by thoughts of what would have happened if she'd reached sixteen before the damn Continental Congress declared war. Perhaps if they'd met then, as adults, as they had now, they would have already been husband and wife, happy with each other. He'd been much too eager, it now seemed, to rid himself of the wild, unruly redheaded pest he'd known. In doing so, he just might've made the biggest mistake of his life, one that could not be undone.

Will was jerked from his dark brooding when

Trinity moved suddenly, lurching out of her chair. He rose more slowly, not sure what was happening as she whirled toward him, toward the door. She froze when she saw him, as if she'd been oblivious to his presence. The lantern hung from its ceiling chain, suspended just above her, bathing her face and hair in a dim circle of flickering candlelight, turning her golden, but he could see her pain, the intense suffering in every line of her face. Tears of grief glistened but he was surprised when she lashed out at him in anger.

"What are you doing here? Haven't you done enough to us?"

Shocked by the sheer unexpectedness of her attack, he didn't reply. He stepped aside as she fled past him and out of the room. He stood unmoving for another moment and heard the sound of her door slamming down the gangway. She was distraught, of course, but why wouldn't she be? What she needed was rest, and time alone to gather her ragged emotions. He'd go to bed and leave her to work through her misery, that would be the best thing for both of them.

Instead, he walked down the corridor and stood outside her door, cursing himself a blue streak all the way. Damn, damn, damn, he thought, tapping and entering without asking permission.

Trinity was not pleased to see him.

"Why can't you leave me alone?" she demanded tearfully—a bloody good question, Will thought, and he sure as hell didn't have a suitable answer.

"Do you have to torment me like this?" she cried in anguish. "Do you enjoy it so much?"

With that, he closed the door. "I merely wanted to make sure you were all right. Anyone could see how upset you were a minute ago."

"And that surprised you? Do you really expect me to be pleased to find my father more dead than alive? Your British friends nearly starved him to death! Well, I hate them for what they've done to him. And I hate you, too! I hate you because . . . because . . . you had to ruin everything, didn't you? You had to come back after so long and make me care about you again. You had to be kind and help me get my father out . . ."

Her trembling accusations lost their steam, dwindled and died in emotion-clogged silence.

"He's going to be just fine, Trin. Dr. Schneider assured you of that. You've got to believe him. Once Eldon gets enough rest he'll look and feel better, you'll see. You've just got to have a little faith. You're exhausted yourself."

Her eyes welled up and glittered with tears, then to his complete astonishment, she was in his arms, holding on to him and sobbing hopelessly. He put his arms around her and shut his eyes as she bared her soul to him in low, tortured despair.

"I thought I didn't love you anymore, I truly did. I thought I could hate you for everything you'd done, for being an English lord and not wanting me anymore. I tried so hard, but every time I pushed you away, you came back with words of kindness that touched my heart until I didn't want to push you away anymore. You brought Papa back to me, and now, look at you, here you are again, holding me and comforting me when I need someone, as if you care about me, when I know you don't, and never have."

She raised her face, tearstained and flushed, the distress and bewilderment she felt readily apparent, and the words came unbidden from his heart, words he should never think, much less utter aloud.

"I do care about you. How can you possibly not know it?"

They stared at each other, neither able to speak until Trinity's teeth caught at her quivering lower lip, and she whispered, pain hoarsening her voice. "Oh, Will, what's to become of us?"

Will pulled her against his chest, gripped by the import of what she'd asked, what they were doing by being together alone, tempted with intimacies that never could be anything more. He kissed the top of her hair, and it felt softly fragrant beneath his lips. All his good intentions, all his grand ideals of duty to his father's wishes, to his rank, began to slip away, slide out of his grasp. His arms tightened around her, and when her palms slid up the front of his shirt to clasp tightly around his neck, he heard himself groan, a welling of torment from deep within his chest.

They gave way to their true feelings and clung to each other, lips finding each other and forging together like two heated brands. He lost all ability to reason, to remain rational enough to push her away and force himself to leave. She was pressing herself intimately against him, the feel of her body indescribably intense to a man as starved for her as he was. He felt his body react, grow hard with desire, and he gave into that flaming need, cupping his hands under her hips and raising her up tight against his loins. He found her mouth, eagerly, no longer capable of thought as she opened her lips and admitted his tongue, then moaned inarticulately, the weak murmur of surrender inflaming him more.

Breathless, hearts throbbing, they clung to each other, chests heaving when he bent her over his arm, his fingers tangled in her hair, disrupting the loosely wrapped knot until the small combs gave way and pins scattered and made plinking sounds against the planked floor.

With a soft brush of rose scent, her long tresses swept down over her back and shoulders in a satiny cascade. He knotted a fist in that silken texture, never having wanted anything, anyone, as much as he wanted her. He lifted her bodily, kept her locked against him as he backed her toward the bed. He sat down, kept her on his lap, and she relaxed, her arms tight around his neck. Their hunger was unabated, in truth growing more desperate as Trinity's fingers caught in his hair.

Will couldn't capture his jumbled thoughts, could only feel her body, the warmth and softness of it, the way she opened her lips for his pleasure. Low sounds rumbled inside his throat, and he spread his hands across her shoulders, catching the sheer lace fabric of the fichu draped around her shoulders and tugging it away. He felt the silk fabric slide under his palm, then he was touching the smooth flesh where her breast curved.

He slipped his fingers inside her bodice, cupping the full swell, and she made a low cry as the nipple grew taut beneath his palm. He rolled the sensitive nub between his fingertips, felt her shivering response. She was arching herself against him, long lashes covering her eyes, her teeth catching her full lower lip. The sight of her lying there beneath him, his to take at will, took his breath away. He needed no further encouragement. He turned her onto her back, and tore away the laces binding the front of her gown until naked fragrant skin was exposed to him.

He lay his face against that delectable soft flesh. He closed his lips around the hard nipple, suckling, pulling at it until she cried out and writhed with ecstasy, both hands curled over his shoulders, her nails digging into his back. He turned his head to the other breast, savoring the feel, the smell, the essence of her.

Trinity cried out again, clutching his head and holding his face against her body, and he struggled to control his own blinding need long enough to remember that she was still young, most likely still a virgin, at the least very inexperienced. He had to bring things back under control. He stopped, turning his head until his cheek rested against the trembling softness of her breast.

"God help me, Trin," he managed, his voice muffled, unnatural. "I'm not made of stone. Stop me now, if you don't want this as much as I do."

"I do . . . I do want you, I always have, for as long as I can remember, I've wanted you to hold me and kiss me like this . . ." Her murmurs were all he needed, and he muffled any further words with his mouth, and she clung to him as he practically ripped away the thin barriers that kept them apart. Bared to the waist Trinity gazed up at him, eyes dark with passion, and Will rose to his knees and jerked his shirt over his head. He came down full-length atop her, squeezing his eyes shut at the feel of her breasts flattened against the muscles of his chest.

Hardly able to breathe now, he got his arm under her back and jerked her up tight against him. Her hair flowed over his arm, and he found the hem of her skirt and pushed it out of his way, sliding his hand up the inside of her leg, his fingertips frantically working loose the ribbons of her pantalets and pulling them off her. She cried out when he found and slid a finger deep into the soft core of her womanhood.

Trinity arched and threw her arms over her head, twisting and biting a knuckle as he caressed her there, very gently, coming onto his knees again and pushing aside swaths of silk and lace until he could see her fully. He dragged the rest of her clothes over her hips until she lay nude before him, then sat on his heels, looking down at her firm, lithe body, every bit as beautiful as he had imagined in his endless, vivid dreams of the past weeks. She was warm, golden perfection, and he continued his gentle probing of her body until she was moist and ready for him.

When she reached up to him, stretching her arms in eager welcome, he was no longer sure he could stop even if he wanted to. He jerked open his breeches and tore them off while Trinity lay on her back, watching him. He parted her legs and lay down atop her, her hands coming up to knead his waist. He forced himself to move slowly despite the way she was arching up to meet him, and at last came down into her, gently, slowly, eliciting low groans of pleasure from both of them when he was finally able to fully possess her. She pressed up against him enticing him, and he could wait no longer.

Will thrust himself inside her, jaw clenched, never in his life having felt such intense pleasure. He'd wanted her so damn long, since the first day he'd seen her again, and now, now, she was his at last, she was writhing underneath him, wanting him, her slender white legs around his own hips, and God, oh, God help him he loved her, he did. How had such a thing happened, how could he have let it? But even that bewildering thought was thrust away, forgotten, as he exploded into her, wracked by the sheer intensity of his pleasure, bracing himself on his hands as he shuddered over and over again with unbelievable waves of blinding ecstasy, then slowly collapsed atop her, and felt her shudder with her own climax as she clutched him tightly to her.

They lay as one, hearts thundering but beating as one, and drifted slowly back to reality and to the sheer magnitude, the sheer folly, of what they'd done.

Chapter Seventeen

Once the passion had cooled and they lay quietly entwined, Trinity knew full well that she should feel regret, even remorse, for what had transpired between Will and her. She nestled close against him, molded against long lean muscles, so hard and masculine and unlike her own. Her cheek rested on his shoulder, and she didn't want to move, not even an inch; she wanted to lie still and listen to the strong, resonant beat of his heart. She wanted to be a part of him.

All she could bring herself to feel was satisfaction with their closeness because she'd felt all along it was there, waiting for them to find it. She closed her eyes. Yes, she was sated, sated and happy, and she wasn't ashamed of what had passed between them, not at all. How wicked of her, she thought with a vague sense of surprise but still could find nothing to dampen her pleasure. They were both grown adults and they had been ruled and dictated to by too many people since they'd been cast together in wedlock. For once they'd done what they wanted to, right or wrong.

More important, Will wanted her; she had thrilled to the eagerness he'd shown, the joy he took in exploring her body, and most of all, the pleasure she'd been able to give him. He'd told her he wanted her, needed her, and she knew he spoke the truth. Even if only for a few stolen moments, she was glad they'd been unafraid to show each other their true feelings. She expelled a long-drawn breath, a deep sigh hinting of the sorrow at the separation that would surely come.

Will stirred, sliding his open palm down the curved hollow of her spine to rest on her naked hip. She shivered at his touch and snuggled deeper into the shelter of his arm.

"Cold?" he murmured, very low.

As he drew the soft quilted blanket up over her shoulders, she whispered, "Not anymore."

For a few minutes they merely held each other, then Will spoke softly, his fingers idly caressing the top of her bare thigh. "I'm sorry if I hurt you. You've not been with a man. I should've been more gentle."

Trinity smiled as she drew tiny circles with her forefinger on the hard surface of his chest. "It doesn't matter. I thought it was wonderful."

"Well, it matters to me."

She leaned her head back enough to look up into his face. "I've no regrets, Will. I'm the one who wanted you to hold me. I wanted you to make love to me, and I'm not sorry it happened."

He turned onto his side, then spoke when their faces lay very close.

"I know. I'm not either. But we shouldn't have done this."

"Yes, I suppose it was a terrible mistake . . . under the circumstances," she agreed, her breath catching when his mouth sought her lips, nuzzling them apart in a gently seeking kiss.

God help her, he made her tremble, he took away all sense of reality and set her adrift on some dark blue uncharted ocean where she knew nothing but him, craved nothing but his hands and mouth and murmurs of love.

"It's wrong," he murmured again, his mouth moving to the deep hollow of her collarbone, his lips hot against her skin.

She lolled her head aside so he could have better access in his endeavor and agreed, "Yes, yes, it was, it's scandalous for us to be lying here like this."

"We can't let it happen again." His words stopped as he took her breast into his mouth.

"Never, ever again," she agreed until a deep gasp tore from her throat as his lips closed over her nipple. He moved atop her, inching down where he could suckle each breast in turn, and she could only moan until his mouth found hers again. Their breathing quickened, his tongue invading her lips in an erotic, openmouthed dance of fire. Her thoughts spun away as she joined him in the kisses that only grew more desperate, more deliciously maddening as he slid his fingers in her hair and held her head steady, and she did the same, grasping fistfuls of his hair at the temples, enthralled, transformed by what he could make her feel, how unbelievably close she felt to him.

She never expected the act of physical love to be so overwhelming, so overpowering that she fell a willing captive to his every whim, every need and pleasure.

"Oh, God help us, this is crazy." Was that her voice? So shaky and rough.

"I ought to get up right now and leave before it's too late." Will's voice; words muttered against her open mouth, words she did not answer. She thought only of Will, her legal husband who was not her husband, as he tore his lips from hers, lifting himself on one elbow and staring deep into her eyes. Oh, God, he was so beautiful, a magnificent example of masculine grace, like Apollo come down to earth to astonish mere mortals. She felt him exploring her body, slowly, expertly, his hand spread open as he trailed his fingers down her breast, cupping it, kneading her nipples with his thumb and forefinger until they rose, hard with her desire, her flesh tingling with tension and need.

Her heart had gone out of control, in a cadence that made her chest heave. Will smiled when she wet dry lips with her tongue. She spoke somehow, her voice raspy and unnatural.

"We can't let this change things between us." She stopped as his face pressed into the flat of her belly.

"We'll have to forget any of this ever happened . . . oh, oh, Will, Will . . ."

His head was moving lower now, his fingers

exploring the most sensitive part of her—she squeezed her eyes tight and actually quivered with pleasure from what he was doing to her. Slowly, gently, deliberately turning her body to fire and her mind to nothing but feeling, excruciating pleasure, pure and sweet, almost painful in its intensity. Somewhere, down deep in the wavering blur of subconscious thought, she realized he was well versed in the art of pleasing women, where to touch her with fingers and lips and tongue. No doubt he had been with many others, but still she didn't care. She wanted him to be the one who taught her how to love a man, she wanted him to touch her and let her touch him, to revel in each exquisite moment of how it could be between them if they could remain wed, how it should have been if fate hadn't seen fit to keep them apart.

He explored her, her body now so attuned and sensitive that she quivered uncontrollably, the soft feathery caresses robbing her of any rational thoughts, until she strained, body and mind, for something, some release from the torture of waiting. Then it came in blinding white fire, a spasm that hit her like a bolt of lightning, shocking her body rigid. She let out a long, breathless groan, her clenched fingers clutching his broad shoulders. She relaxed as the supreme enjoyment faded slightly but then another wave of pleasure hit her, then another, over and over, great, wonderful, lovely waves of release.

When her climaxes finally faded, she collapsed weakly, unable to move, unable to think, unable to comprehend the wonder of the experience. When she could breathe once again, she opened her eyes, a dreamy smile still hovering on her lips. Will was grinning down at her, looking devilishly pleased with himself, the side of his head propped upon his palm.

"You liked that, I take it?"

Still so breathless that she had to draw in air in order to find words, she tried to give voice to her emotion.

"That was, well, I must say . . . very . . . no, most, extraordinary." A husky sigh punctuated her satisfaction, then she added, "You're truly quite . . . skilled . . . in all sorts of things, aren't you?"

Will laughed, very low, a sound sensuous enough to send another chill rippling her bare flesh.

"Ah, my love, there is so much more that I can teach you. Pleasures you've never even dreamed of."

Trinity wasn't sure she could believe that.

"More than what just happened? Surely not. I don't think I could bear anything more than that."

Will smiled at her innocence but as their eyes held, his expression faded into seriousness, and she knew he was realizing how completely hopeless a situation they had created for themselves. A future together for them was impossible. They both knew it well. What had happened, though sweet, though wonderful, would not change the facts of their relationship. They'd been foolish, and Trinity knew she was being even more foolish, because she didn't want this night to end, not now, not ever.

"Stay here with me tonight, Will." The words seemed to tumble out of their own accord, and she could not stay her hand as it reached out and cupped the lean contour of his jaw. "Let's stay together just this one time, just for this one night, let's pretend everything's all right, that we can be together." After her words faded, she felt so incredibly vulnerable, in a way she didn't like at all because she knew, she knew he should not, could not. She looked down, studying the dark tangle of hair upon his chest and added, quite low, "Then we must never be together again, not like this. Promise me, Will? That you won't pursue me, that you'll leave me be, and never tempt me again. I couldn't bear that, I simply couldn't. Not now that Papa's here with us."

She raised her eyes, sad, hopeless, and his green eyes looked as dark and troubled as her heart felt. He nodded but did not speak, his lips lowering to brush her mouth, so utterly gentle and tender that emotions surged and burned like a flame kindled at the base of her throat. Her eyes swam with tears as she admitted to herself that she did love him, always had, she feared, and she shut her eyes, and held them closed and tried not to think about a future without him. *Enjoy the moment*, she told herself, *because it's the last one you'll ever have with him.*

She met his kisses with total abandon, and soon the pleasure did overcome the pain filling her heart, but the sorrow remained there still, a deep black void that she feared could never be filled.

A fortnight after they had sailed away from the coast of Florida, Eldon Kingston was able to sit up on the edge of his built-in bunk. He emitted a short, painful grunt but managed to push himself upright. Gritting his teeth, he persevered, hardening his resolve to walk. He was tired of being waited upon, of lying abed. He was a free man again, and despite the complicating sway of the floor beneath his feet, by God, he was going to get around on his own! He was a great deal stronger already, thanks to dear Trinity, as well as Victoria and her daughter. All had pampered him with tender care, but enough was enough. The time had come for him to resume his life.

With one hand clutched tightly to the bulwark beam, he steadied his stance and waited for the ship to gain even keel before he reached out and grasped the ivory-headed wooden cane that Trinity had secured for him in a deep cubbyhole near his bunk. The moment he put the walking stick against the floor, his equilibrium settled down a good bit, and he felt quite secure in attempting the short walk to the portal. He took a moment to cinch the belt of the fine crimson velvet dressing gown—one lent to him by William Remington—then slowly, with cautious step and favoring his good foot, made his way across the tiny cabin.

Next door, he could hear the others at dinner and decided that compartment, a mere four feet down the corridor, was an admirable goal. Once outside, however, he leaned heavily on his cane and looked down the gangway where the door seemed to stretch to at least a hundred feet away.

Taking his time, grasping the cane with his right hand and steadying himself with his left palm against the wall, he proceeded carefully, stopping only once in order to cough, cursing the congestion that still lay heavily inside his chest. The illness lingered despite the warm and soothing poultices Victoria had prepared for him with her own hands. She was indeed a good woman, one of his oldest and dearest friends. Thank God, she had taken Trinity in and sheltered her from the bloody red-coated curs.

By the time he reached the next portal, he felt exhausted and paused while he sucked in several breaths before finding enough wherewithal to open the door. Inside the three women and Will were seated around the dining table but once they'd turned and seen him, all four came to their feet in alarm. Trinity got to him first, of course, her face full of concern.

"Papa! What are you thinking of?"

She hovered about him in a pleasant rustle of silk and cloud of floral fragrance that reminded him of her mother. He smiled, his love for her burgeoning up inside his chest, so strongly felt that tears burned the back of his eyes. Before his incarceration he'd been able to control his feelings but now emotional turmoil affected him deeply. He could not speak.

Trinity took his arm and Will was there to assist him. Suddenly Eldon felt weak, dwarfed by Will's six-foot frame, and he found himself glad to lean upon the powerful arm of the young English lord.

"Now, don't fuss over me so, Trinity, it's high time I'm up and around. Besides, I'm tired of staring at the ceiling and twiddling my thumbs." He thought of the cramped, dank cell and the endless hours he'd spent there, and a coil of nausea formed in the pit of his stomach. He choked it down but the images persisted, crowding up unwanted, endless dark days and darker, pitch-black nights, the shuffling click of rats' claws and swarming vermin in the filthy straw. Tears stung, embarrassing him.

To his relief, Will seemed to sense his distress. "You're looking fit to me, and I, for one, am glad to have the company of another gentleman."

Grateful for Will's welcome, he allowed Trinity to help him into one of the armed wing-backed chairs.

"You're looking so much better of late," Victoria remarked from where she sat on his right. She patted the back of his hand. "Your color's quite good now, you know. What you need, I daresay, is some fresh air."

"Yes, I do believe Mother's right. I'd be happy to walk along the deck with you, Mr. Kingston. Would you like me to pour you some brandy? 'Twould steady your nerves a bit." That kind offer came from Adrianna, such a sweet girl, grown up so much, and as beautiful and kind as her mother. It was little wonder that Geoffrey doted on her the way he did.

"Here's a plate for you, Eldon." Victoria rose and fetched a serving from the buffet. Her dark eyes glowed with pleasure at finding him on his feet again.

"Thank you, my dear, but please carry on as you were. Your fare grows cold. Do not worry yourselves with me."

Still, Trinity filled his plate with the broasted fish and boiled potatoes and turnips, then hovered near his side, anticipating his every wish.

The dinner hour continued with the low murmur of conversation amid the rattle of china dishes and clink of silver cutlery. He felt more relaxed than he had in a good long time, finally able to believe that he was actually safe from the British noose, or at least while he was under the protection of a man as powerful as the future Duke of Thorpe.

Grateful for the man's generous intervention in his behalf, though unexpected since the war still raged, he glanced at Will, who had remained quite amiable though rather quiet where he sat at the head of the table. He found with some surprise that the handsome young lord was watching Trinity with not a little intensity. Enough, in fact, to give Eldon pause. The expression on Will's face told Eldon a great deal, especially the way Will quickly averted his attention to study the contents of his wineglass whenever Trinity shot him one of several surreptitious, sidelong glances.

There was no question about the look on her face, either. Unless he was greatly mistaken, she looked at Will with pure, undisguised longing. Eldon's heart sank like a rock in a well. Oh, God help them all, what had transpired between the two young people since he'd languished in jail?

Fortunately, Victoria didn't seem to notice Trinity's and Will's awareness of each other, and the meal continued in good cheer with that lovely lady filling him in on the progress of the rebellion since he'd been carted off to prison. From what he could gather, the outlook sounded rather grim, yet the three women did not seem unduly demoralized.

In fact, they seemed quite certain the Americans would prevail, and openly discussed their hopes for a speedy conclusion, despite the daunting presence of an English lord at the table with them. In any case Eldon could not work up much outrage. The war was pretty much over for him, at least until he regained his strength again. And his freedom. He was still only under parole, and that, with many conditions.

"Eldon, we had planned a stroll after dinner to enjoy the night air," Victoria was telling him as a young chubby-cheeked cabin boy cleared away the dishes. "Do you think you're up to a short walk?"

"Yes, Papa, do come. We'll hold on to your arms and help you along."

"No, no, I thank you, but I'm not quite up to that yet. But please don't let me stop you."

"Oh, no, I won't think of leaving you all alone. I'll stay here and keep you company," Trinity insisted.

Eldon shook his head. "No, daughter, go along with you now. Truth to tell, I'd prefer to enjoy a cigar here with Will, if he's of a mind for my company at the moment."

"I'd be pleased, sir."

Trinity appeared more than reluctant to leave the two of them alone together, but at Victoria's urging, she finally did take her leave. Eldon leaned back in his chair and watched William retrieve a carved wooden box from a hinged cabinet. He sat down in the chair opposite Eldon, selected a pair of square-tipped cheroots, clipped the ends, then lit them off the candle set down in a recessed nook on the table.

Eldon took a deep drag, inhaled, enjoying the mellow taste and aroma of yet another pleasure that had been so long denied him. He exhaled and watched the curling blue smoke rise in wisps toward the ceiling beams. He observed as William puffed his own smoke to flame, then leaned back to savor it.

"I must tell you first off, Will, how immensely grateful I am for everything you've done. Both for me and for Trinity." Eldon held his gaze steady upon the younger man's face. "I'm afraid I owe you a great debt, one it's doubtful I can ever repay."

"You owe me nothing. It was my part of a bargain made between Trinity and myself. Has she mentioned it to you?"

"Aye. 'Tis a mess Adrian and I got the two of you into. Thanks be to God, there's a remedy available to right the wrongs we've done you."

William partook of his glass of brandy. "This bloody, unnecessary war has caused many tragedies."

"It's fortunate, indeed, that neither you nor Trinity saw fit to wed another before the mistake concerning the annulment was discovered."

"Especially in her case. She's very beautiful. Any man would be lucky to have her as his wife."

"She's had a good many offers, God knows that to be true, but none ever appealed to her. As you probably remember, I'm quite the indulgent parent. I could not bear to make her unhappy, so she was never wed."

"I realize now how much she was hurt by the way we broke off the engagement. Please know that I had no idea my father would give her no advance warning. I was in Italy at the time." Will seemed genuinely regretful as he continued. "You probably recall that His Grace always does things in his own way. He only asked me if I preferred to end the marriage, and at that time I had no desire to marry Trinity, or anyone else."

"At that time?" Eldon watched William's handsome features darken with an inexplicable flush. "Have you changed your feelings about Trinity?"

"We both know that the war makes it impossible for me to wed an American. But I will say that I've come to look upon your daughter with a great deal of admiration."

"I thought as much. I watched you tonight, and I watched Trinity. And I watched you watch Trinity."

"My father wishes me to wed Lady Caroline Rappaport as soon as I return to London. But I've not made the decision to do so, at least not yet."

"Isn't she a goddaughter to the King?"

"Yes, I believe so."

"I understand then why Adrian wishes you betrothed to her. 'Twould be a lucrative political alliance."

"Yes."

They smoked in virtual silence after that exchange, but Eldon knew somehow there was much more between his daughter and the man who sat opposite him. His heart ached because he feared no good could come of the newfound friendship that had sprung up between them, only more heartbreak and humiliation for them both, but especially for Trinity.

Chapter Eighteen

Three weeks and hundreds of nautical miles later, the *Trevor* met landfall at Ipswich in the dead of the midnight hour. The bile-black, starless dome over the sea fit William's dark, hostile mood. He had just suffered through the most hellish weeks of his entire life, long days and endless nights of fierce sexual frustration, and the annoying, grating, maddening sense of helplessness known by a grown man caught in the trap between duty versus personal desire.

The family name, his inheritance of one of the most cherished, coveted titles in England, was the one thing he'd been bred to respect, to look forward to claiming, and now it felt like a damned millstone around his neck, dragging him down, drowning him. He cursed himself for letting things proceed so far with Trinity. A bloody fool he was to allow his lust for Trinity to override his principles.

Sleeping with her, that had been his primary undoing. He had thought he could bed her and walk away. He'd done it before with other women. Their intimacy had been a mutual decision; he'd certainly not forced himself on her, so he wouldn't blame himself entirely for what had happened. Yet in another way, the mistake was acutely his, because he'd thought of nothing else since he'd held her in his embrace. One night, but one he could not forget.

Clamping his jaw, he glanced at Trinity where she stood on the dock, just underneath a flaming tar-soaked torch. She was fussing over her father—who in Will's mind had recovered in admirable fashion, considering the incredibly harsh conditions through which he'd suffered—while Victoria oversaw Adrianna and the loading of their trunks aboard a coach that would transport them all to Thorpe Hall in the countryside.

Trinity had kept to her word, unfortunately, and had consistently avoided him, barely acknowledging his presence while being icily polite and civil. And she was doing the right thing, of course. She knew it, and so did he. Why prolong their friendship—or more aptly now, their love affair—when any bond between them was doomed from the start?

He supposed she could become his mistress, there was always that option. Many men of his station kept women, God knew his father always had, but Will dismissed such a thought at once. Trinity would never agree to that, never. And he didn't want her to become a woman like that, either. He wanted more. More than he could have. His own feelings about her were in turmoil, and he was sickened to be having doubts about his own future.

He'd set sail from this very spot only a few months ago, his days full of personal pleasures and in damn good shape, his life planned out in precise fashion acceptable to him. What in God's name had happened to him?

In his heart the answer loomed, concrete and unshakable, the long, dark shadow of the truth falling over his mind like that of a gigantic stone monolith. Still, he didn't want to deal with it, not yet. He needed time alone, away from Trinity's intoxicating presence so he could think straight again. Maybe then he could find reason in the scheme of things and bring some kind of order back into his life.

For that reason he'd decided to return to his father's residence in London by himself while the others traveled on by carriage to Thorpe. The idea had been heartily welcomed by Victoria who had made it clear she wanted to be settled into her old home and rested from the journey before facing her intimidating, estranged husband after so many years of separation.

More important, William had need to blunt his father's shock once he found out his old friend turned enemy, Eldon Kingston, a known rebel traitor, was visiting Thorpe Hall, an honored house guest of his own duchess. His Grace would not be pleased. And that was a gargantuan understatement. He'd be furious.

After he'd bid his family good-bye—Trinity barely glanced at him as she climbed into the coach and turned her face away—Will watched the carriage roll down the cobbled street, then he

turned quickly, anxious to return to the ship, trying not to feel the sense of loneliness that was already plaguing him. They would sail on to
London, a voyage that would end by the next
evening. Once aboard the *Trevor* again after having given the order to sail, he retired to his cabin
and surprisingly passed a restful night, considering the tasks facing him.

By twilight the next evening they had proceeded up the Thames River to the Hole of London, and he was dressed and packed to
disembark, and extremely eager to get home. He
left Captain Parks to take care of the landing as
well as to supervise the unloading of the rice and
indigo packed inside the hold, and summoned a
hired hack to take him to his father's mansion
near Hyde Park.

It was an hour after dark by the time he arrived
there, and he cursed his bad luck and his father's
habit of hosting gala events in the white ballroom. Lights blazed from every tall window of
the three-story, red-bricked edifice. The last thing
he wanted the moment he returned was to have
to greet and converse with dozens of friends and
acquaintances, but he had little choice now. He
was tired and only wanted a private word with
his father.

As he climbed the gray granite steps to the
half-moon-shaped front portico, he realized with
full impact the supreme irony of his own predicament. Trinity. He already missed her, dammit.
Jutting his chin he forced her face out of his head
and thrust open the front door, daring to hope he

just might evade most of the guests whom he assumed would be in the ballroom at the rear of the house. Instead, he blundered smack-dab into his brother, Stephen, and, far worse than that, Lady Caroline Rappaport, the young woman his father was hell-bent on him marrying.

"God's mercy, Will! Where the devil did you come from? I had no idea you'd returned from the colonies!"

Stephen strode toward him, his face reflecting genuine surprise and pleasure, and Will pumped the hand he offered, then embraced him warmly, glad to see his younger brother again, despite the ill timing.

"Well, it's about time you came back!" Stephen said, stepping back. "We thought you'd have been here nigh a month back."

"We ran into stormy seas," Will answered laconically, and nodded politely to Lady Caroline, who smiled and simpered like the young, inexperienced child she was. Pretty at seventeen, in her own way, with silver-blond curls and innocent brown eyes, she resembled a porcelain doll that he remembered Adrianna playing with as a little girl. She had none of the fire and excitement Trinity exhibited so effortlessly. Caroline would make an eminently suitable wife, true, one he could be proud of, goddaughter of the King, for Christ's sake. Thank God, it was not too late for him to disentangle himself from any more talk of their engagement.

His own thoughts startled him, and as he bent

his head to kiss the backs of her fingers, he tried
to hide the discomfiture he felt.

"Welcome home, Lord Remington," she murmured shyly. "His Grace will be most happy to
hear you've arrived. I understand that he's quite
anxious to speak with you about your travels."

"I was told by our man at the docks that he's
here this evening. Is that true?"

Stephen nodded. "That's right. I believe he's retired to the billiard room with his favorite cronies.
You know how he is—always talking politics."

"Then I'll go find him straightaway. I've a lot to
tell him."

"Did Mother come along with you as Father
wished? And Adrianna? Is she well?" Stephen
asked, looking past him as if expecting to see the
ladies appear in the threshold any moment, but
when he looked back at Will with upraised eyebrows, Will knew he was also questioning him
about Trinity.

"I thought it best to send the ladies on to
Thorpe. Mother was ill during the voyage, and I
knew she'd be more comfortable in the country."

"I see." Stephen eyed him speculatively, well
aware of the mess surrounding Will's long-ago
marriage, but he asked no more questions.

Will turned to Lady Caroline and bowed. "I
must ask your pardon for the moment. It's imper-
ative that I speak with His Grace. I'll look forward to seeing you again soon."

"Perhaps we'll have the pleasure of your presence at Diamonant soon. My father enjoys your
company immensely, as you well know."

"And I, his. I'll look forward to such a visit," he lied, on both counts, certainly not wanting to confront her father until he decided for sure what to do about Trinity. He bowed again, then escaped with relief down the wide central hallway to the winding staircase.

His father's study was on the second floor at the front of the house and adjoined the spacious reaches of the billiards parlor, which was one of his father's few passions outside of political intrigue. He took a deep breath before entering, never eager to confront the Duke of Thorpe. More and more of late, father and son had begun to spar with open antagonism, and on just about any subject that arose.

Rapping lightly on the door, he waited for permission to enter. When a voice called from within, he opened the door and found his father, cue in hand, participating in a game of billiards with Sir Robert Bynton and Lord Ian Restforth. Both gentlemen were of noble birth, the highest caliber, had worn Eton blue, were school chums from Oxford, rich from bountiful holdings in and around London, and had titles nearly as distinguished as Thorpe. Nearly, but of course, not quite. Both Bynton and Restforth greeted him with warmth. His father was more reserved. Cool and aloof, as usual.

"I see you've finally made it back," His Grace said, turning away to insert his custom-made ivory cue in the brass wall rack. He wore a white wig to hide his balding pate that Will knew pricked his vanity now that he was in his fifties.

His eyes were intense when he finally did place them on his son. "Did your journey go well?"

Will nodded. "Aye, well enough, but for the storm we encountered on the return voyage. But I'm afraid I do need to discuss an important business issue with you. Perhaps you'll grant me a short audience? Inside your study, perhaps?"

"I'm sure it can wait until morning, William. As you can clearly see, I'm in the middle of a game." A dismissal, albeit a polite one, but still insulting.

Will was not to be put off. He wanted this over and done with, the sooner, the better.

"It's most urgent, or I assure you I would not disturb you."

Adrian frowned, stroking his great curving white mustache, irked to be pressed on the subject, quite obviously put out by Will's insistence, but he acquiesced with a nod, never one to air family difficulties in front of outsiders.

" Very well. Gentlemen, carry on with your game, if you will. I'll return momentarily."

"So," Adrian said a moment later, shutting the door to his study with a quiet click. "Did you accomplish what you set out to do? Are you free to wed Lady Caroline? She's downstairs, by the by. You'd do well to spend some time in her company, you know." He eyed Will's dark traveling attire. "You've evening wear in your chamber in the east wing. I do hope you'll take time to change into something more suitable."

"Mother and Adrianna are well, Your Grace, in case you've any interest in them whatsoever."

His Grace frowned darkly but Will did not retract the sarcasm. He gazed dispassionately at Adrian, having long ago lost respect for the man his father had become.

Adrian walked around his long desk and sat down. "They are well, I gather, or you'd have informed me they were not."

"Yes. Both are probably settled at Thorpe by now. If you've a mind to care about their whereabouts."

Adrian showed little reaction to Will's goading. "In time, I suppose, I'll pay them a visit there. I'm a busy man." He paused, leaning back and folding his arms across his trim waist. "Tell me the status of Trinity Kingston? Did she agree to return to England?"

"She did."

"Excellent. Our solicitors will draw up the papers immediately."

"She insisted on certain conditions."

"Conditions, you say! By the devil, what's that bloody chit up to now?"

Will felt his teeth come together, hard and tight, flexing the muscles of his cheek, never failing to be amazed at just how much he disliked his own father. "She's no chit, I assure you. In fact, she's turned into quite a lovely young woman. And a damn bit more intelligent than we ever gave her credit for."

His father presented him with a narrow-eyed gaze of speculation. "It appears your opinion of the Kingston girl's undergone a radical metamorphosis since you agreed to allow me to overturn the wedding. 'An ugly, spoiled brat' were the words I believe you used to describe her just before you set sail for Florence."

"I didn't care one way or the other then. I wasn't ready to be married. As for Trinity, she's changed very much, all for the better. And so has Adrianna. She has made it clear to me that she has no desire to wed . . ."

"Adrianna will do exactly as I tell her to do." His father cut him off with an offhanded wave.

"As I was saying," Will continued tightly. "She prefers to marry a man of her own choosing, and Mother agrees that she should do so."

"Oh, she does, does she? And who is this man, pray tell me?"

"Geoffrey Kingston. He has courted her for several years . . ."

"That's completely out of the question, of course. She's to wed an Englishman. By God, there'll be no more American alliances with Thorpe."

His face had grown scarlet with anger, and he placed both palms flat on the desktop. "Now tell me what conditions Trinity Kingston is attempting to force upon me? How dare she try to impose her will on the Duke of Thorpe!"

Will leaned back in his chair, beginning to enjoy a perverse pleasure in annoying his father to such a degree.

"For one thing, she insisted that I arrange a parole for her father, as well as his release from prison—"

Adrian's palms slapped the top of the desk,

258 Linda Ladd

then did so a second time, as the normal color of his face deepened to a mottled purple. "Why, the gall of that little bitch! How dare she try to tell me what to do!"

Adrian was sputtering in outrage, and Will waited patiently for the tirade to end, then calmly informed his father, "And I agreed to do so. I sailed with her to St. Augustine on the east coast of Florida and had Eldon released into my custody. He's at Thorpe Hall as we speak, with Mother and the other ladies."

Before the revelation had faded, Adrian was on his feet. "Have you taken leave of your senses? What do you mean allowing that damnable traitor to darken my door?"

William merely shrugged. "You wanted Trinity to cooperate, did you not? That's the only way she would do so. Besides, Eldon didn't deserve to languish in prison. He only stood up for what he believed in."

"Have you gone mad, William? Listen to what you're saying, for God's sake! Next, you'll tell me you want your vows with this Trinity woman to remain intact!"

"Perhaps I do," Will agreed calmly. "And perhaps not. I'm not sure what I want at present."

"I forbid it!" Adrian yelled, obviously forgetting about his friends in the next room, now as irate as Will had ever seen him. Will said nothing, unruffled by his father's outburst.

"By God, I've worked for months now on the betrothal negotiations with Diamonant. You will not deny me that alliance. Do you hear me, you ungrateful whelp."

Will stood up and stared across the desk at his father. "Now you listen to me, Adrian. I'll marry who I want, when I want. Neither you nor anyone else is going to make that decision for me. Is that clear?"

Adrian puffed as if he could not draw breath and placed his hand over his heart as if about to succumb. A trick that was quite familiar to Will. Adrian had often used palpitations of his weak heart to control his sons' behavior but this night the ruse wasn't going to work.

"God help us, William, have you forgotten your duty to the Thorpe name?"

"I've forgotten nothing. But I'll not be controlled like some goddamn puppet, not by you or this bloody title that's beginning to feel more and more like an iron yoke."

His father was so enraged now that he was trembling all over, his mouth hanging slack. William rose and moved toward the door. He paused and looked back.

"If you'd like to see your wife and daughter, I'll be entertaining them at Thorpe Hall, along with Mr. Kingston and his daughter. You're most welcome to join us there, if you can find the time."

He left without awaiting an answer, pleased to be done with the distasteful confrontation, but determined from that moment forth he would make his own decisions, according to his own conscience, and his father could be damned.

Chapter Nineteen

If Adrianna did not desist her horrendous, discordant pounding upon the harpsichord keys within the next five minutes, Trinity feared she'd have no choice but to flee screaming from the vaulted music chamber. Wincing as her friend hit another cacophonous note, she shifted where she sat alone on a camel-backed sofa of soft claret velvet, endeavoring to control nerves jangled raw from almost an hour of the auditory abuse.

Even Monsieur Stefan, the duke's own composer, had escaped a quarter of an hour past and, unfortunately for the rest of them, bid Adrianna to continue practicing for a full hour at the least. Thank goodness that Trinity, too, was not being groomed for a London season, or she would have had to spend many hours each day with various masters learning the art and science of snaring a husband.

Endeavoring to tune out the painfully halting renditions of one tinkling racket after another, she lifted her gaze far above where great murals spread out across the graceful arched ceiling like a pastel dreamscape of clouds filled with chubbylimbed, red-cheeked cherubs trailing long streams of garlands of pink and white roses. The tiny angels flitted about the plaster cornices or knelt in adoration of the Virgin Mary, amid other worshipers of the baby Jesus she held cradled in her arms—shepherds clutching hooked crooks, saints reading Scripture from long, unfurled parchments, beggars, soldiers, and beautiful goldenhaired angels glowing in their flowing diaphanous robes of silver and white.

In the center of the room, just above the ivory-topped table where Victoria and Eldon sat over a game of chess, a graceful gold-armed chandelier hung suspended with hundreds of crystal teardrops glistening in the sunlight. Victoria had told her that the magnificent treasure was obtained by William's great-great-grandfather from a magnificent palace of a Venetian doge. Afternoon sunshine flooded through the tall French doors of the circular room, all of which stood undraped and identical, like rows of guardsmen around the walls of a castle turret.

Trinity sighed and wished she were back home in South Carolina, on the shady gallery of Palmetto Point where she'd always been the most happy. She'd felt she belonged there until Will had come back and turned her life topsy-turvy. She picked at the gold braid edging the sofa cushion beside her, annoyed with herself for letting thoughts of him seep back into her mind.

Had she not dwelled on him enough the past weeks? Had she not thought of him daily? Hourly? Dreamed of him throughout all the restless nights under the velvet crown canopy of her bed here at Thorpe Hall? It was impossible, their relationship. She had known it from the beginning, and she'd made a terrible mistake to lie in his arms as if she truly were his wife. To let him hold her and make love to her. If she'd known how sweet it would be between them, how gentle and loving he would be, or the way he could send flames racing over her flesh with the mere stroke of his fingertips . . .

A quiver pebbled her flesh at that thought. She shut her eyes, startled by the sheer force of her feelings for him. Lord help her, she must forget him. She absolutely must. There was no conceivable way for them to be together. He had made that clear, and she had known it even before he had. She bolstered her resolve to forget him by thinking about what he was doing at the moment. He was in London, for sure, no doubt waiting to get his hands on the document of annulment that would sever their relationship forever. And it was for the best that he did so, it truly was. He would wed the other woman, the suitable one that his father thought worthy of his title, and he would bring her here to this beautiful, magical place where their children would run through the wide marble halls and make comical faces in the gilt-framed mirrors and their happy laughter would echo and ring up into the high frescoed ceilings. She swallowed hard, her stomach clenching with emotion. It should have been her. It should have been their sons and daughters.

Biting her lip to control the sharp stab of tears, she gazed across the room, through the open white double doors where an elderly maid in a gray gown and white linen apron and mobcap bent to polish the bottom shelf of a gleaming oak commode set underneath a painting of a hump-backed bridge covered with snow. The room in which she labored was one of the many private family withdrawing rooms; the old woman one of dozens of servants employed by His Grace to keep the gigantic household running smoothly. Many of them had worked for the Remingtons for generation upon generation, Victoria had told her so.

Only a week ago they had arrived and walked with Victoria through the ornate rooms, looking around in hushed awe, while the mistress, so long absent from England, greeted the household staff as if she'd only stepped out for a buggy jaunt into the nearby village of Thorpe. She had taken over the reins effortlessly, planning the meals, directing the chores, and her people had welcomed her home happily, no doubt remembering with pleasure the kind woman she was and the compassion she brought to a house more often empty than not. It was quite apparent that Adrian Remington and his sons preferred the excitement of city life to the quiet of the countryside.

Trinity was pleased, though, that her father had settled in nicely and thus far had been treated with the utmost respect by everyone he encountered—no doubt a strict directive from dear Victoria—but even so, Trinity was grateful. She glanced at her father again and found him watching her. When he smiled and blew her a kiss, a familiar gesture from her childhood, her heart shivered with love and relief. They had been very lucky that he had recovered so quickly. She had been terrified when she had seen him lying in the filthy straw in his prison cell. Will had saved his life. She could never let herself forget that.

Trinity lowered her eyes to her lap and toyed absently with the yellow tassels edging her full sleeve. She shouldn't allow herself to think about him, and certainly not with the warm glow of love she was feeling at the moment. She missed him so, no, it was stronger than that. She longed for him. To gaze upon him, to touch him, even casually as she had aboardship after their vow to remain apart.

Warmth surged into her face, pinkening her skin, and she took a deep breath to fight it, but the memories were there and would always be there. The two of them, entwined tightly on the narrow bunk, his mouth closing over the tip of her breast with such devastating expertise, his hands exploring her, the way his hard, calloused palms felt cupping her breast.

Appalled at her body's reaction to that thought, she dared not glance up, hoping no one watched her and suspected her wanton thoughts. Wicked, they were, and she should be ashamed of herself since they were not wed but merely lovers for a short time. Still, the memories were wonderful, and they were all she had left. Why did the two of them have to get caught up in such a complicated mess? Why couldn't they have just married as they were supposed to have and been together? Why did things have to go so wrong?

She had thought when the voyage was over, when she was not in close proximity to him, she could go on. She had vowed to think of the war and what she must do to help assure the future of their fledgling republic. But she had not been able to do so, not while fighting the roiling needs and regrets inside her. She felt helplessly adrift on a long dark river in the dead of midnight. She was frightened that she would never be happy again, not truly so.

Trying to get a grip on herself, she forced herself to wonder about the course of the war, about Geoffrey and the Continental soldiers fighting for their freedom, but it was difficult here, so far away from any city or newspaper in the peaceful surroundings of wooded deer parks, lazy meandering streams, and emerald pastures. Tidings were not easily had, and when rumors did surface among the servants, there was little proof of authenticity. But even here in this idyllic English countryside, they had already found Englishmen who supported their fight, some quite high in rank, friends of Victoria who had called upon her since they had returned to Thorpe Hall. And many more pro-American allies, according to them, resided in London.

She wondered if Will knew who they were. He

was torn by his dual allegiance; he had intimated that to her. What had he been doing these eight days he had been gone? Pressuring the courts for the annulment? Wooing his new fiancée? Lady Caroline Rappaport. Trinity wondered if she was as elegant as her name. If she lived in London and what she looked like. She would be pretty, no doubt. A man like Will, so tall and handsome himself, well connected and rich, with a dukedom to offer his bride, no less; he would settle for no one but the most beautiful and sophisticated woman, a lady of impeccable lineage to become his duchess and mistress of Thorpe.

Unlike herself, Trinity thought, who was so undeniably unsuitable, an enemy, an American, a commoner. Distressed by the idea, she sighed, then was even more upset that she tortured herself in such a way. The agitation brought her to her feet, abruptly, with enough fidgety energy to cause her father and Victoria to glance in her direction. Adrianna labored on her jangling Bach concerto without pause, and Trinity strolled to a window. Maybe a breath of fresh air would settle her churning stomach, a malady that had plagued her every morning upon waking of late, no doubt from the stress of living in Will's house.

She turned the handle and pushed the door ajar, breathing deeply as a gentle breeze wafted from the side lawn, cool and fresh and scented with pine. She had been pleasantly surprised by the beauty of England; she had expected to detest the country and everything in it as much as she hated its reigning monarch and his tyranny over the colonists. Instead, of course, she had found it lovely with its lush green grass and trees and the neatly tilled fields edged with hedgerows and low stone walls that rode the cresting hills like a low-leaning equestrienne.

On their way to Thorpe, they had passed through quaint hamlets with roofs made of rushes and whitewashed houses nestled in vales dotted with sheep, all so beautifully peaceful and idyllic. Then she'd gotten her first glimpse of Thorpe Hall, high upon its rising hill, white granite walls rising against the azure sky, shining in the sun like the fairy-tale castles Nana Marie had told her of. She had thought of Palmetto Point and the other Carolinian plantations, quite pleasing and grand in their own right, but nothing compared to the sheer magnificence of the Remington estate.

Suddenly, behind her, Adrianna's fingers stilled on the keys, and Trinity sighed with relief. Her shoulders went rigid, however, when the girl's voice floated out with a cry of delight.

"Will! Wherever did you come from?"

Slowly, practically paralyzed with dread, but eager beyond belief to see him again, she turned and watched with an embarrassing flood of pleasure as he strode across the floor toward them. Somehow she found that she had moved forth to meet him, though she did not want to and forced herself to stop behind the sofa. She was making a complete fool out of herself, she thought. *Why can't I show a little pride?*

Adrianna jumped up and ran to welcome him,

taking him by the hand and pulling him with her. Trinity gripped the back of the sofa when he finally looked at her. He looked superb, of course, but when did he not? Like the future duke he was, like the owner of this enormously rich household. He wore a suit she had not seen before, pearl gray in hue, a richer fabric than he had worn aboardship, with a black waistcoat stitched with strands of silver. A plain white linen neckcloth was folded at his throat, blinding white against his skin, now bronzed deeply from the long sea voyage. He looked tired, she thought, perhaps he suffered the same strain she had battled for the last week. Then he smiled at her, and she melted inside.

"Mother," he greeted Victoria first, bending forward and pressing a kiss to her cheek, "I understand from Homestead that you've settled in quite well."

"Very well," she answered, and Trinity could tell Victoria was pleased by Will's gesture of affection. "I found that I have missed Thorpe and all the staff even more than I expected." She paused and studied his face. "And did you find His Grace in good health, pray tell?"

"Well enough. He's in residence at Hyde Park for the winter. I told him he should join us here once you had rested sufficiently from the journey."

"I see." Victoria understood, as did they all, that her husband would make no eager trip into the countryside to welcome her home. Anger caught hold of Trinity. How dare he treat his own wife in such a cavalier, disrespectful fashion!

Their conversation was interrupted as tea was presented by a stocky maid with flaxen hair caught in a tight bun. Several tendrils had come loose and hung against her face as she placed the teapot and cups before Victoria, and everyone stood silently waiting until she curtsied self-consciously and gratefully took her leave.

"Please sit down, Will. We'll talk while I pour," Victoria suggested to her son.

William remained standing, however, his gaze inexorably fixed upon Trinity, and she stared back at him helplessly, a hopeless feeling clutching her heart. Oh, Lord, it would be torture now that he was back, close enough to touch, if she could, always watching her. She had to talk to Victoria, find some way to avoid him, or she couldn't bear it.

William, on the other hand, seemed to share none of her emotional turmoil, and Trinity's deep disappointment trembled inside her breast because that could only mean he cared nothing about her. Now that he was home in England, he would think only of his familial duty. And why wouldn't he? He'd been groomed from the day he was born to do that very thing.

"Actually," he said suddenly, breaking the uncomfortable silence that had descended like a weighty cloud of gloom over the tea-takers as Victoria picked up and filled a cup, then handed it across the table to Eldon, "I've need of a word with Eldon, if he doesn't object."

The annulment's final, was Trinity's first conjecture, and her heart plummeted like the *Trevor's* anchor. She'd not yet given up, had hoped perhaps some miracle would happen to allow them to be together. But, if it was over, if Will had brought the annulment, then she wanted to sign it quickly and put as much distance as humanly possible between Will and her. She never wanted to see him again, she thought, lifting her chin, and she would accept her fate as agreeably as he seemed to have done.

"Of course, milord," her father answered at once, nervously adjusting his newly acquired spectacles. "Shall we retire somewhere where we can speak in private."

"That won't be necessary." Will turned and looked straight at Trinity. "Simply put, sir, I've come here today to humbly request your permission to court your daughter."

The white teacup rattled in its saucer as Eldon clattered it down upon the tabletop. Adrianna gasped, quite audibly, and Victoria snapped her head sideways to see if she had understood her son correctly. Trinity, on the other hand, could only stare back at him. Her lips still parted from the shock of his calm pronouncement, she found herself unable to say a word.

The corners of Will's mouth lifted faintly, as if he were amused by their responses. Trinity was frowning now, not sure she could believe her ears when her father finally found his voice.

"Well, I say, Will . . . you've quite startled me with this . . . surprising development, to be sure . . ." He paused, unable to garner his thoughts, glancing at Victoria whose smile was so radiant that he could have no doubt she was more than pleased by her son's good judgment.

"And your father?" she asked Will pointedly. "I assume you received His Grace's blessing upon this matter?"

"I've decided that His Grace will no longer have a hand in my personal decisions." William was matter-of-fact, indeed, quite blithe under the circumstances. He turned again to Trinity. "Now, if you don't object, Eldon, I'd like to forgo tea and escort Trinity on a walk in the garden. We have much to discuss, I daresay."

Joy began to rise, from somewhere deep inside Trinity's soul, as if a great blossom was unfolding inside her, the tightly furled bud spreading and spreading until it was manifested in a smile so radiant that even she could feel its warmth. Will outstretched his arm, offering her his hand, and she took it eagerly, twining her fingers with his longer ones, still so pleased, so overwhelmed her throat seemed clogged by sheer emotion.

"Why, of course, I suppose a stroll would be acceptable, that is, if Trinity wishes to join you . . ." Her father was still not far above stuttering, openly nonplussed by the unexpected developments, but Adrianna was not one to hide her feelings. She laughed out loud and clapped her hands with delight.

"At last, brother, you've begun to show a bit of sense. And very good taste, I might add," she called after them, but neither answered as

William quickly led Trinity away from their smiling kinfolk. Just outside he stopped and glanced around, frowning when he found two young chambermaids, hardly out of their teens, squeezing soapy water from their rags as they cleaned the mirrored panes decorating a French door. He turned abruptly, taking the opposite direction toward the back of the house, pulling Trinity along beside him by the hand, and in such an urgent manner that she laughed softly at his haste to be alone, but so full of joy that he could not help but hear it.

"Where are we going, Will?" she whispered, glancing back over her shoulder at the girls, who were still watching with interest as he nearly dragged her down the hall away from them.

"I want to be alone with you," he answered in the same low tones, taking her around another corner into a wide, empty corridor that stretched out like a broad thoroughfare in a different direction. He proceeded along at a swift clip that sent Trinity nearly running to keep up, then pulled open a door and thrust her inside.

Trinity stood behind him, looking around her at the inside of the large linen closet to which he had brought her. Long rows of shelves lined two of the walls, wide, deep drawers filled with neatly stacked, ironed, snowy bed sheets. She watched Will take the key from the keyhole, shut the door, then lock it from inside. He turned to face her. They stared at each other for one instant, then she was in his arms, lifted off her feet and held captive against the solid wall of his chest. She sighed with innate, inexpressible, un-paralleled joy.

"I've missed you," he said, then his lips found hers, hot and eager and possessive, causing her head to loll back as she welcomed the kiss, positive that she must still be abed and in the throes of some wonderful, impossible dream.

"Oh, God, I wanted to do this for so long." His lips were on her mouth as he backed with her to the long bench and sat down, still holding her atop his lap. "I've missed you," he said again. He looked into her eyes, then kissed her some more, his next words muffled against her lips. "I've missed this even more."

Trinity felt breathlessly alive, her body responding to his touch, the hard eagerness of his body, but she had to know, had to ask. "But how? How can we do this? What about the annulment . . . has it been struck down?" Her voice faltered weakly as his hand brushed aside the gauzy length of her fichu and slid underneath the lace edging of her bodice. He found bare skin, and she trembled and caught the sides of his face between her hands as he lowered his mouth to the hollow of her arched throat.

"Damn the annulment. I want you with me, and I mean to have you."

Their lips came together again, tentatively, then parted only to come back in a desperation both felt, a pure need to touch each other. Their mouths forged together, tongues meeting and retreating in a sensual dance, and Trinity lost all inhibitions, only able to think that he was back, he wanted her as she wanted him. They were going to be together after all, and she didn't care what else happened. This was all she wanted. He was all she wanted.

When the door handle rattled, it took a second for the sound to penetrate their passion. Will lifted his head, but Trinity brought his mouth quickly back down to hers. The kiss was long, deep with pent-up desire, then he turned her and was pressing her back onto the long bench, his fingers at work on the buttons and ties securing her bodice. The ribbons gave and his cheek lay against her bare flesh, his warm lips closing over one erect nipple. She gave a low cry of pleasure.

"Will, Will, we can't do this," she managed, somehow gathering enough reason to realize that, but she could not bring herself to push him away. She put her hands on his head and forced him to look at her. "This isn't right. We can't. Father's here, and your mother."

"We're married as far as I'm concerned, and always have been." He stared down at her, breathing as hard as she, but she was shocked that he had come to that conclusion. There was so much more to it, so many obstacles to overcome. "We're at war, Will, we're enemies. You know that. Your father won't allow me to remain your wife. He's powerful, he'll think of a way to stop us . . ."

He sat on his heels beside her, caressing her cheek. "I'm a grown man, Trinity. I've made my own decisions for a long time now, and if my father doesn't like it, he can be damned." Again the knob rattled, followed by a loud rapping. Trinity quickly grabbed her gown up across her naked breasts, and Will swore softly beneath his breath when the sound of the head butler's voice came from the other side, loud and authoritative.

"Who is in there, I say?" Homestead demanded, shaking the door handle again. "Come out at once, do you hear?"

Trinity covered her mouth with her palm, the whole situation now so ludicrous that it was amusing. She giggled softly, and William grinned down at her, but the prim butler would not be ignored.

"Come out, I say, unless you wish me to have this door removed from its hinges followed by the termination of your employment. I will not tolerate such blatant behavior of those upon my staff. Do you hear me in there?"

William grimaced but left Trinity to straighten her gown as he moved back to the door. "I hear you loud and clear, Homestead. Now, if you please, go away and stop that infernal rapping."

Dead silence followed, and Trinity could visualize the stunned expression on the proper little man's face. A muffled female giggle could be heard, no doubt the chambermaid who first found the linen closet occupied by intruders.

"Yes, my lord." Homestead's voice was subdued now, but the tone was recognizable. He was scandalized, and for good reason, Trinity knew, feeling a rush of heated color flood her cheeks. Low sounds commenced as he shooed the girl away. Will turned back to her.

"Now where were we?" he said, very low, his eyes pinning her where she sat.

Trinity couldn't help but return his smile, shivering in anticipation as he came back, shrugging off his coat and throwing it over one of the shelves. He knelt before her, and she began to unfasten the buttons of his black silk waistcoat as he tugged loose the ribbons she had just retied on the front of her bodice.

"This is quite improper," she whispered as she helped him shrug out of the garment. "We should be ashamed of ourselves. We'll cause a scandal and I'll be branded a tart."

"You'll be branded the Duchess of Thorpe," he said, serious now, his fingertips trailing down the fragile line of her jaw.

The Duchess of Thorpe, Trinity thought, but she truly could not believe that would ever be. She didn't want to think about that impossibility now. She only wanted to think about him.

"I'm afraid, Will."

He lifted his brows and looked deeply into her eyes. He must have seen the worry lurking there because he pulled her close against his chest and held her. He cupped the back of her head in his palm. "Don't be. No one is going to hurt you. No one is going to separate us, I promise you that."

Trinity wanted to believe him, but she knew Adrian Remington, knew what immense power he wielded over other people, especially his family members. She could not be sure he wouldn't destroy them. Will's next words sent that dread evaporating for he murmured the words she had wanted to hear for so long.

"I love you. I want you to be my wife and live here with me. And you will. You are. Trust me, Trin."

His face was earnest, and she knew he meant what he said, and then she was lost. She could no more deny him anything he asked than she could get up and walk out of his life, as perhaps she should. Her lashes drifted down and she met his lips, in a kiss so gentle, so absolutely tender, that for the first time, she knew that what they now did bore no shame. She was his wife, and she had been since she was four years old. He was her true husband. Their love was meant to be. God had heard her prayers, after all.

Chapter Twenty

"Will! Tell me where we're going!"

"Just hold on to my hand. We're almost there."

Trinity gripped his fingers tightly, glad for his palm holding on to her elbow as he led her up a seemingly endless flight of steps. She could feel the coolness of the stone surrounding them, the chill of the narrow steps beneath her slippers. They climbed and climbed through the dusty air and lingering musty smell reminiscent of old, disused chambers. At last they reached the top platform and Will let her go. She placed a hand on the cold wall to steady herself, and heard what sounded like him pushing open a less than cooperative door.

Then brightness peaked around the edges of the silk scarf he'd bound around her eyes and a blast of crisp autumn air hit her face. She breathed deeply, smiling, as he took her hand again.

"All right, you ready?"

"Yes, out of breath, but ready."

He laughed as he unknotted the blindfold, then pulled it away. Trinity opened her eyes, squinting against the glare, then stared wonderingly out over the stone wall in front of her.

"Well, what do you think?"

"I think it's the most beautiful thing I've ever seen." She breathed the words, moving forward to rest her palms flat atop the waist-high wall. It was then she realized where they were, in the highest of the two square towers rising above the enormous roofs of Thorpe Hall. She had looked up at them often, wondering at their purpose but now it seemed apparent they had been, and probably still were, watch towers.

"Will, I don't think I've ever been so high above the ground." Warily, she looked over the precipice at the lawns stretching out five or six stories below. "But the view is extraordinary." She turned and realized that the catwalk was built to encircle the tower, giving a view in every direction.

"This was used to watch for enemies in the old days. Once Thorpe was besieged by Cromwell's soldiers for nearly a year. The Remingtons held firm. You can see for twenty miles in every direction."

Trinity looked at Will, having heard the pride permeating his voice. He loved Thorpe Hall, she realized, though he spent little time there. He spoke casually of his inheritance and title, but she could see clearly at that moment how proud he was of his Thorpe forebears. He stood leaning his back against the interior wall, watching her, and she knew he was enjoying her unabashed awe of the surroundings.

"You like it up here, don't you?"

"Aye, it's one of my favorite places on the estate. Stephen and I used to come up here when we were boys."

"Wasn't that a bit dangerous?"

"Perhaps. We played knights and shot play arrows down on any hapless gardener or scullery maid unfortunate enough to happen by. We vanquished Moorish invaders more times than I can tell you."

"Geoff and I defeated Blackbeard on the ocean levees," she said, a flicker of pain running like heat lightning through her. She missed Geoff and feared for his safety.

"And I played that with you a time or two," he reminded her.

"I worry about Geoff. I wish I knew if he was all right," she said wistfully, voicing aloud her concern to Will for the first time since they'd reached England.

"Geoffrey can take care of himself, as you well know," Will told her, but he could give her no true assurances. They both knew her cousin could be lying dead in some swampy field or dangling from a redcoat gallows. And here she stood, in the autumn sunlight of the oppressor's country, being courted by Will, Geoffrey's avowed enemy. Shame burned her face, and depression settled like a cloud of ashes over her spirits. She turned back to look out over the countryside. She was the traitor, not her father, not Will.

As far as she could see the fields and forest tracts wore a wondrous cloak of late autumn finery, the leaves a breathtaking mosaic of bright colors painting the countryside in a way Trinity was unused to. For miles around the leafy canopies were scarlet and yellow and gold, spreading out for miles like a giant patchwork quilt of many colors. She set her eyes on the sky spreading over the land like a vast parasol, as azure blue as the dress she wore. In the distance she could see the River Redling that meandered lazily through the vast deer parks of the Thorpe estate.

"What do you think, love? Is this not a beautiful day?"

Will had come up behind her and slid his hands around her waist. Pleased at his endearments that had come more frequently since he'd asked permission to court her, she smiled and leaned her head back against his chest, wishing to take succor from his affection. As she had grown accustomed to the feel of him, the masculine scent of his leather vest, the faint aroma of the tobacco he favored, the unique essence of his body, his skin, all brought her joy. She closed her eyes as his mouth brushed the top of her head. She put her hands over his, not wanting him to move away.

"It's lovely."

"See the kirk there in the distance? By the stand of oak trees where the river winds out of sight? His Grace gives out alms to the poor there on Christmas morning, then he returns to the great hall to give candy and presents to all our people. Someday you and I will do that. It's a tradition that's been honored by the duke and duchess for generations."

Trinity looked at the tiny spire rising gracefully

against the sky. But, as it always did, mention of his father brought up the fear lurking within her breast. She wondered if his vision of the future would ever come to be. And though she told herself it would, she was not at all convinced Adrian Remington would not stop their plans to honor their marriage.

"Have you any word from His Grace?" Hesitantly asking, she turned her head and looked at him, though almost afraid to hear the answer.

His gaze remained on the faraway trees. "He'll show up here to greet Mother someday, I suspect. It's barely been a month since I left London. I made my intentions clear enough. He's no doubt in the process of retreating from negotiations with the Earl of Diamonant."

"What if he doesn't?"

"He will." Will turned her around and smiled down into her face. "I told you not to worry, Trinity. He has no choice. We're married as long as we don't seek further recourse on the annulment contract."

"But he'll never accept me. I'm an American, and I cannot change my loyalties any more than he can."

"You won't have to change your loyalties. I understand how you feel, just as I understand how Mother feels. Father's too narrow-minded to see the reasons behind the rebellion."

"But I love Palmetto Point. I'm already homesick."

"It's dangerous there as long as the fighting continues. We'll visit there but I'll tolerate no ab-

sentee duchess such as my mother was. I want
you here with me."

Trinity allowed him to draw her into his embrace again, comforted by his words. In truth, and
despite her longing for Geoffrey and the palms of
her plantation home, she had no desire to leave
Will's side to go there. She wanted them to be together, to honor their vows made so long ago, but
she could not sustain the confidence in the outcome that he had. He must have sensed her fears
because he drew her down on a stone ledge built
against the inner wall.

"Come now, Trin, stop worrying so much. I
want you to be happy while we're here."

"I am happy. I just don't know how long this
can last. I guess . . . I guess I don't really feel married yet. I expected a church wedding, you know,
with Papa giving me away, and lots of girlish
dreams, such as that." She smiled a little but she
felt sad, robbed.

"We did have all that. You just don't remember
it. Unfortunately, I do." He grinned and held up
his hand and displayed the scar there.

She had to laugh but she immediately grew serious again. "There'll have to be an announcement
of some kind, won't there? I can't just show up as
your wife, can I?"

When he didn't meet her eyes, she knew he had
some reservations himself. He was not an evasive
man, and that's what he was being at the moment.
He was not as confident as he appeared.

"In time we'll be able to do that, I promise you.
But not for a while. As I said, His Grace has need

to end the marriage negotiations with Diamonant before anyone can get wind that I've been married to you all along. The Rappaports are important people, cousins to George. We cannot insult them openly. My father will have to find a diplomatic way to end the talks, then I will present you in society as my wife. Until then we'll introduce you as a friend of Adrianna's who has accompanied her to Thorpe. No one will know any different."

"But will His Grace do so? Victoria tries to hide it but I know she fears he'll try to force you to his bidding."

"You forget, sweet, that he cannot perform a wedding without the presence of the groom. I assure you I won't be there if such a wedding is held. Now come, let's have a boat ride upon the river. We'll have Cook prepare us a picnic lunch."

Trinity smiled and allowed him to lead her by the hand down the curving stone stairs but in her heart she still trembled. What if it all came tumbling down around them somehow? So many obstacles had been thrown in their path, from the very beginning. It did not seem that fate smiled upon their union, but even so, she could not deny herself the joy of being with Will, of loving him to distraction.

She blushed delicately, ashamed yet breathlessly excited over the way she felt about him. Would they make love later today, perhaps somewhere along the rippling water, in a private bower hidden from the world? She shivered in anticipation. She loved him, and that was the only thing that really seemed to matter to her anymore. She

wanted to enjoy being with him, cherish every
minute of every day they spent together because
deep inside, and despite Will's reassurances to the
contrary, she feared it could not last.

"Trinity, dear, could you join us for a moment?"

Trinity turned quickly from where she was hurrying down the hall toward the side portico, surprised to find Victoria standing in the doorway of
a rarely used parlor. She smiled and turned back,
though she was eager to join Will for their picnic
on the river.

"Well, I'm supposed to meet Will at the boat
dock. He's taking me rowing. I just ran upstairs to
get my shawl."

"We won't detain you long. It's rather important."

"All right."

Trinity entered the room and looked around as
Victoria closed the door. Her father smiled at her
from a sofa by the window. Another man sat in a
wing-backed chair across from him. She had
never seen him before.

"Trinity, this is Jason Tucker. He's an old friend
of mine from London."

"How do you do?" she murmured as the man
stood and nodded politely.

"Please sit down, daughter," Eldon said, patting
the cushion beside him.

Trinity obeyed, slightly put out to be required to
participate in entertaining a man she did not
know. The reason, however, was revealed without
any waste of time.

"Jason's one of us," Victoria said, very low. "He's brought word of the war back home."

"What news do you bear?" she asked quickly. "Is there word from Geoff?"

"Aye, as a matter of fact. He's sent inquiry after you and Adrianna. He's been wounded . . ."

"No! Is he all right?"

"Yes. He suffered a musketball to his leg and will require some time to mend. Washington's thinking of dispatching him here to woo the American factions for monetary aid."

"He's coming here! How wonderful! Does Adrianna know yet?"

"No, not yet." Victoria hesitated. "Adrianna's my daughter, and I love her dearly, but she does have a tendency to let things slip. I feel she has no need to know until he makes it safely to London."

"But she's so worried about him," Trinity objected at once.

"I'll tell her that he's recovering but I cannot risk any slip of the tongue in front of William."

Will, thought Trinity with sinking heart, that meant she could not tell him either. Although she knew that was true, that he had to be considered a part of the enemy camp, it was hard now to exclude him. Uncomfortable at keeping secrets from him, she frowned.

"I know you've become very fond of Will, dear," Victoria was saying, "but you must remember our fight back home. Jason says the war is going well now. We've had considerable victories both north and south."

"Is the end of the war in sight?" she asked

breathlessly, unable to comprehend that it would ever be won. If the rebels did succeed, perhaps the barriers preventing her marriage to Will would also fall to the wayside. Filled with more hope than she'd had in a long time, she listened as Jason spoke about what had been happening in the months they'd been gone.

"In mid-September the French fleet drove a British naval force from Chesapeake Bay, and word has it that Cornwallis is planning a march north. We all feel that the tide of the war has definitely changed."

"But we still have not won?"

Eldon shook his head. "No, but things look much better for us. The French will make a big difference."

"You have many supporters in London, mostly Englishmen with ancestral roots in the colonies. We work diligently to promote your cause against the warmongers. I fear Victoria's husband is the worst hawk of all."

No one spoke for a moment, realizing the delicacy of Victoria's position. "He has made his loyalties quite clear through the years, and so have I," she said finally. "I plan to leave England for America once we travel to London and I can make the proper connections for our voyage."

Trinity gasped, stunned by her revelation. She had not expected Victoria to break so openly with the Duke of Thorpe. "But what about Father and me?"

"That's why we called you here, sweetheart," Eldon answered, taking her hand in his. "Jason and his friends are working on a plan to get me aboardship and out of England. And we want you to be ready to leave as well, at a moment's notice."

She stared at them, trying to hide her dismay. "But what about Will? You were placed in his custody. He gave his word that you wouldn't escape."

All three looked at her, and in a way that caused a hot flush to rise in her cheeks. Victoria finally spoke.

"I'm sorry, child, but this is war. A word from my husband to the King and Eldon could be sentenced to hang. You know that. We must affect his escape, and as soon as possible."

"But what about Will? He's been so kind to us . . . so good . . ."

Her questions faded away because they were pointless. She knew the answers already. Their marriage could not be, not with their divided loyalties. He could never leave England and his heritage, and she would never be accepted there as his wife. She would cause him nothing but scandal with her father branded as a traitor to the crown. She swallowed hard, felt the burn of tears.

"I'm sorry, Trinity." Her father pressed her fingers comfortingly, and she forced herself not to break down.

"It's just so unfair."

Across the room the door suddenly opened. William stepped inside, obviously surprised to see them gathered in such a grave tableau. Trinity immediately came to her feet, horrified that he had caught them in their clandestine meeting, but Victoria handled the intrusion with aplomb.

"Hello, Will, I'm sorry we've kept Trinity so long, but I wanted her to meet my old friend from London. You know Jason, do you not?"

"Yes," Will answered, striding across the floor with outstretched hand. He clasped Jason's in a firm handshake. "We've spent more than a few occasions across the gaming tables at various gentlemen's clubs."

"It's good to see you, Will," Jason said with an affection that could not have been faked. "We've missed you in London."

"We'll all be going there soon enough." He smiled at Trinity, and when the others followed suit, he winked and tossed his head toward the door. She immediately moved toward him.

"I'm sorry to have kept you waiting. We can go now, if I might be excused."

"Of course, dear, by all means," Eldon said. "Enjoy yourself."

Once outside, Will kissed her cheek, then entwined his hand with hers as they walked together toward the side entrance. She smiled and listened to him relate a story about Jason Tucker, but inside she had turned to stone. She would now have to lie to him, keep things from him, and in time she would have to leave him. She was not sure she could do any of it.

Chapter Twenty-one

Of all the seasons of the year at Thorpe Hall, Stephen Remington loved autumn the best. Most of the glory of the leaves had passed but still the landscape seemed to glow with inner light. He had entered the thick deer park shielding the east facade of the estate, but when he topped one of the rolling hills of the road he could see the bell tower like a huge square keep against the blue sky. He slowed his bay gelding to a canter and guided him up a small rise to a winding wooded path that would bring him out at the humpbacked bridge at the edge of the lawns.

Within minutes he sighted the picturesque crossing point where he and Will had loved to fish when they were boys. He gripped the reins in his gloved hands, smiling to think about those days. They hadn't had many good times here when young, not with their mother and sister back in Carolina. He glanced up at the house at the rounded portico but saw no sign of anyone. He was anxious to find Victoria and Adrianna, a lot more so than his father was, he thought with not a little regret.

But he'd endured a long ride from London, and he felt hot and dusty. He looked at the brook below, the gurgling, chuckling sounds of water over rocks enticing him like a siren's song. He'd wash away some of the grime, he decided, before his mother received him. He dismounted under the sweeping branches of a willow tree and was about to lead his mount down to the water when he caught sight of movement out of the corner of his eye.

A boat, one of the red punts his father kept at the dock behind Thorpe, was floating in the calm current midstream, above the bridge where there were no rapids. He frowned, wondering how a boat had gotten loose from its moorings, but then he saw that it was not empty. He narrowed his gaze as it floated slowly toward him and at that point he realized he'd come upon a pair of lovers. He grinned. His expression faded quickly enough when he recognized his older brother's dark auburn hair.

Will was leaning back against a pillow propped against the stern, between the oars as if he had been rowing at one time. A lady lay atop him, her billowing cherry-colored skirts nearly hiding him. Will was kissing her, kissing her thoroughly and with considerable enthusiasm, his arms tangled in the back of her hair, and Stephen's eyes widened as they floated past his position without an inkling of his presence.

Little wonder, their minds seemed to be on

other things, he thought, shaking his head and glancing around. There was little chance of anyone seeing them on this part of the river, and Will knew that, of course. Still, he had happened along, had he not? He watched the boat disappear into the shadows darkening the water under the curved spine of the bridge. So Homestead had been right. Will was openly courting the American, and not bothering to hide his pursuit of her. Homestead had said his behavior was scandalous, and for Will, it was. His brother was not one to shun propriety, much less float about in boats making love to women.

Stephen stood still as the boat meandered lazily out the other side toward the long gradual curve of the river that would land them eventually at the stone boathouse at the base of the gardens. He took the time to lead his horse to the bank, then splash water on his face and hands before he swung back into the saddle and galloped the road homeward.

As he came out at the long sweep of green grass he saw the boat was nearly to the dock now, Will holding the oars, the girl sitting primly in the bow, a parasol shielding her head. He laughed to himself, to think of Will acting the country swain. His brother was well known for his prowess with women but he'd not known any lady of late who could entice him to lose control enough to lie with her in the bottom of a boat. Will was not himself, that was for damn sure.

He walked his horse to the dock as Will

moored the craft and handed the girl out. It had to be Trinity Kingston, Stephen knew, but the beauty gazing up so adoringly at his elder brother did in no way resemble Stephen's memory of her. He thought of wild red hair, not the coppery curls slipping down her back. Will seemed about to take her in his arms again, but to his credit, he glanced around first. He saw Stephen, recognized him, then grinned and waved him over.

Stephen rode the rest of the way and dismounted. Will came forward to grab his hand, and the girl watched, a small smile playing at her lips. She was gorgeous, he would give Will that, more than gorgeous, breathtaking.

"Stephen, God, I'm glad you've come. Mother's been waiting and waiting for you to arrive."

"I was detained," he answered, thinking that it was more truthful that he'd been trying to calm down their father, who raged endlessly since Will had so blatantly defied him. The London servants were in a state of terror over his easily provoked wrath, and after Homestead had brought the latest news to His Grace's attention, all hell had broken loose. Stephen dreaded to tell Will just how bad it was.

"Come on, I want you to meet my wife."

Oh, God, it was worse than he thought, if Will was openly claiming the marriage vows. "Wife?" he repeated cautiously.

"That's right." Will caught his eyes. He lowered his voice. "You were at the wedding, if you'll remember."

"Will, you're asking for trouble. His Grace is already furious."

"I'll be with whomever I want. He knows that." He glanced at Trinity, and smiled. "Now come on, we're being rude."

"Trinity, Stephen's come to visit."

Trinity smiled up at him out of eyes that glowed almost gold. His breath caught, and he began to understand Will's insanity.

"Hello, Stephen. I haven't seen you in a very long time." Her eyes twinkled enchantingly. "You chased me and stole my hair ribbon the last time we met. Do you remember?"

Stephen recalled that she had been the one who'd ripped it off his hair, and he very nearly couldn't catch her to get it back. She had been an imp back then, and where the devil had all her freckles gone?

"Aye, 'twas long ago, those days were."

Will took her hand and kissed it, and she smiled up at him, and Stephen felt a little sick inside for what he had to tell them. Unfortunately, he was not able to put it off.

"What is the news in the city?" Will asked him, and he hesitated, not wanting to get into the subject in front of Trinity. She obviously sensed his reluctance.

"Well, I will leave you gentlemen for a proper visit," she said at once. "Victoria expects us all for tea at four, and I must change in time to be ready."

Will smiled and watched her leave, and again, regret pinched at Stephen. He cursed inwardly, wondering how his brother had gotten himself into such a godawful mess.

"So His Grace hasn't gotten used to the idea, I take it?"

"Hardly."

They began to walk toward the stables, Stephen pulling his horse behind him.

"Then he'll just have to try harder."

Stephen hesitated. "It's worse than you think, Will."

Will stopped and looked at him. "What do you mean?"

"You won't like it."

"I rarely like anything Father does. Let's have it."

Stephen wished he could put it off but that would serve no purpose. The whole mess needed to be resolved, and as soon as possible. On the other hand, at times Will's temper was even worse than their father's.

"I wish I didn't have to be the one to show you these," he began as he unstrapped the saddlebag, "but you have to know sooner or later."

Will was already frowning as he pulled out the folded newspapers. "Here. Open them to the society page."

"What's he done?" Will asked but then he found the news item. His face went white, then crimson as fury overtook him. "Goddammit, what was he thinking to announce my engagement to Caroline?"

"He was thinking that you were too besotted with Trinity to know your duty. He got a letter from Homestead alarming enough to make him take action to end your relationship with Trinity."

"Homestead wrote him? What about?"

"All sorts of interesting things. Trysts in linen closets, for example. Doesn't sound like you, brother. Father was enraged at the affront to propriety."

"I needed a minute's privacy, was all. Blamed nosy servants."

"He also said you were openly calling her your wife and had asked Eldon to court her, all of which I didn't believe until a moment ago."

"I want to marry her. I am married to her."

"Father's requested the justices to continue with the annulment proceedings."

"Well, it won't get anywhere without Trinity's signature, and you can damn well bet she's not going to sign it."

"Diamonant is a powerful man. Caroline's whole family is. If you end the betrothal with her, the scandal will rock London. She's one of George's favorites, you know. You'll be displeasing the King."

"And His Grace can take care of those repercussions since he put this whole bloody affair into motion."

Stephen heard Will's offhanded replies but the expression on his brother's face told him more. Will knew good and well that the situation was extremely perilous now. Offending a man like

Lord Rappaport would be dangerous. He might even insist on a duel to avenge the damage done to his daughter's name. And Trinity, poor Trinity would be cut by everyone they knew.

"We'll work it out," Will was saying now, his jaw set in granite. "I'm married to Trinity, and that's the way it'll stay. Now come on, we'll change and meet the women in the parlor. Mother's been watching for you every day since we got here."

Stephen walked along beside him, and though they discussed other things, both knew they were in very big trouble. Few people could best Adrian Remington when he was determined to have his way, and especially not his sons.

Victoria had decided to have tea outside on the flagstone terrace overlooking the river view, and Trinity hurried along one of the long downstairs corridors, her satin skirt rustling in the hushed hall. She passed no one in her flight, not a single servant, and she could not help but marvel, though she'd been in residence a long time now, how very immense was Thorpe Hall. She could wander through its halls and wings for days, the vast rooms a maze that any adventurous child would love. Perhaps their children would explore the canopied beds and hidden closets— hers and Will's.

When she reached the French doors that led out onto the open air terrace, she drew up and patted her skirts in order, and made sure none of her hair was protruding from the black snood she had placed over the heavy bun at her nape. She did want to make a better impression on Will's brother this time. She realized how disheveled she'd looked down at the riverbank, still so breathless from Will's kisses. Stephen had disapproved of her, she had seen it in his eyes, though he'd hidden it very quickly from both of them. Still she should try to win him over. She needed every kind of support to help promote her in His Grace's eyes.

Outside she found the entire party already assembled, even her father, around a wrought iron garden table. Upon her entrance Will rose at once and came to meet her, and she smiled, warm inside at his obvious eagerness to see her again. Sometimes when he was so good, when they were happy together, she let herself hope that it really could work out for them to stay together. If only they could persuade his father!

"I was ready to come find you," Will whispered, kissing her on the cheek, and she colored with pleasure, her smile wide and happy as he led her to the others.

Victoria had been perusing a newspaper, and Adrianna a different one, but she noticed how both women quickly put them aside. It was odd for them to be reading at the tea table, and Trinity looked at them questioningly as her father and Stephen rose politely while she was seated.

"Did Stephen bring word of the war in the London papers?" was her first question to Adrianna.

Her friend evaded her eyes and shook her

head, and Trinity knew instantly that something was being held back from her, if only by the severe silence that descended all around.

"What is it?" she said, then with more feeling as she realized that something must have happened to Geoffrey. "Is it Geoff? Papa? He's not hurt, is he?"

"No, my dear, of course not." Even Eldon seemed distracted, and her alarm grew. She turned to Will, and he smiled reassuringly but his eyes were somber.

"Please tell me what's amiss. I know something is wrong."

Everyone turned to look at Will. Trinity searched his face. "Will? What are you keeping from me?"

Will sighed and seated himself beside her. He took her hand and smiled but she knew him now. He was not as calm as he wished her to think. He was angry and trying to hide it.

"I didn't see the need to worry you," he said at length. "So I asked the others not to show you the newspapers. Truly, it's nothing to get upset about."

"You're upset. I can tell." She looked at Stephen, and he looked as if he pitied her. She frowned. "I'd like to know."

"All right, but please don't worry about all this. I'm going to take care of it." Will hesitated, then reached out and retrieved Adrianna's newspaper. He unfolded it and laid it before her. "It seems His Grace felt the need to announce my engagement to Lady Caroline Rappaport. I suppose he thought he'd force my hand, but all it's going to do is complicate matters."

Trinity looked down at the newsprint. *The Earl of Diamonant announces the forthcoming nuptials of his daughter, Lady Caroline Rappaport, to William Remington, Lord of Thorpe.* She read no further, fighting the sickening feeling congealing like grease in the pit of her stomach. She realized then that the duke was not to be thwarted in his designs. He would not rest until he had his own way.

Trinity looked into Will's eyes, and despite his smile, she saw that he was indeed quite worried. She knew then, deep in her heart, that they had been playing at a game where they could remain wed; they had blinded themselves to reality. What they faced held incredible odds against them. She swallowed down her hurt but the disappointment would not be banished. Tears stung. She stared down at the paper, garnering control of her emotions, then unable to, she rose, unwilling to display her distress in front of so many.

"Please excuse me . . ." she managed, then walked swiftly from the terrace, inside the house where she could absorb the pain of realization in privacy, at least.

William caught up to her halfway down the hall. He took her arm and turned her swiftly to face him.

"Don't!" she cried, distraught. "Why did you have to pursue me? Why did you have to make me care for you again? You knew it was impossible! You had to! Just go away, go to that other woman and leave me alone!"

"Is that what you want, Trin? Is it? You want me to forget about you and what we've had together the last few months?" He cupped her face in his hands, smoothed away her tears with his thumbs.

Trinity stared at him, unable to accept a future without him either. "No, no, I don't want that . . . but I know it can't be, I know it . . ."

"Don't say that. Trinity, now listen to me. I want you. I love you. Father can't make this decision for me. All this is going to do is delay our plans for a while, don't you see that? How can he force me to wed her when I am legally married to you? Even if he could force through our annulment, it doesn't mean a thing. I'll marry you all over again." He smiled. "This time in a cathedral with five hundred guests, and this time you won't even want to bite me."

Trinity could not answer his jest with a smile, her heart hurt too much. He gathered her into his chest and she held on to him, wanting so desperately to believe him.

"Don't worry. We can work this out. You're going to have to be patient until I do what's necessary. I've already decided that we'll go to London where I can work to negate this announcement. Trust me, sweetheart. We've been through too much to give up now."

Trinity nodded her head, wanting to believe him but somehow she knew better, knew it was hopeless. Adrian Remington was too powerful, too important a person for them to fight, even his son, his own heir, *especially* his son and heir.

Chapter Twenty-two

The procession of ducal-crested coaches, three in all, caused a sensation as it rolled down the streets of north London. Will was well aware of the spectacle as he rode a black stallion alongside the first carriage, in which Trinity sat with her father in one seat, and his own mother and sister across from them. Stephen rode beside Will, a new ally in his defiance of the duke. After a few days in Trinity's company, Stephen, too, knew her worth.

"There's the widow Lady Streeter looking out her drawing-room window," Stephen noted from his side. "The whole of society will soon be apprised of our arrival."

"Aye," Will answered tightly. "Let the contest begin."

"Trinity'll have a rough time, you know. May be cut by one and all."

"Not if I have a say in it."

Stephen shrugged but Will knew his job was cut out for him. Without his father's support, and with one whisper of the truth about Trinity and him, not only would Trinity be branded an outsider but Will would bring down ruin upon his own family name. That included Victoria and Adrianna, and any chance his sister had of success in London. He had to be careful, very careful in the way he handled the matter.

And his father had known that, of course, he thought with an angry twist of his mouth; he had known the announcement would end any thought of proclaiming Trinity as his wife, at least until Will could placate Caroline's family. The truth was it was much more difficult and complicated than he had let on to Trinity, but he didn't want to demoralize her. Now, however, she had been put into a terrible situation. He hoped to God that she could weather it. He hoped he could, too, without losing his temper and causing an even worse scandal.

Clamping his jaw, he was glad they had rounded the corner of Popling Street and his town house was in sight. In rights his mother and Adrianna should have gone to his father's imposing city estate but Victoria had shown her support of him, bless her, by insisting that she would stay with him and thereby be chaperone to Trinity, for Eldon had to remain in Will's custody or face imprisonment.

He had sent a courier ahead with the news of their arrival, and it had obviously generated excitement among the neighboring houses since he had been abroad for so long. His own staff stood lined up along the curbing to greet him, all people he could trust to be loyal to him, something he had made sure of when he had purchased his own dwelling, for he knew better than most how His Grace manipulated servants when he wanted information. The father and son relationship had deteriorated considerably in the last four years, but now it was on the verge of complete collapse.

As the conveyances stopped with a great clatter and jingling of harnesses, he dismounted and handed his reins to the boy who ran forward.

"Hello, Charlie," he said with a smile, glad to see his people again, especially his head butler and personal valet, Tibbett, who came forward and bowed deeply before him.

"Welcome home, milord. I've assembled the staff and all is ready for your guests."

"It's good to see you, Tibbett. Did you receive my correspondence on the matter?" He had told his butler which bedchamber he wished readied for each person, with Trinity's, of course, next to his own. Something he should definitely not have done, but he wasn't about to give up his private time with Trinity because their public demeanor would have to be unquestioningly proper. At least for the moment. Everyone probably already knew about her anyway, as Stephen had predicted.

"Yes, sir. All is ready. Many of your friends and acquaintances have already sent inquiries as to the time of your arrival. I must say you've invitations to nearly every house in the city."

"Excellent."

As he turned back to the coach, he dreaded the coming days. Trinity would not enjoy the balls and soirees where he would have to, at least, pretend to enjoy Caroline's company. But an insult to her family would not go unavenged, as Adrian well knew. If he wanted an eventual life in London with Trinity, they would have to play the games that society demanded. He hoped she would withstand it.

Stephen had already opened the door and assisted Victoria to the street. Adrianna descended next, and then Trinity. He had to smile when their eyes connected. She looked beautiful in a traveling suit the color of goldenrod that only made her shining hair more glorious. He wished he could go first to her and introduce her to his staff as the mistress of his house. He could not, however, so he merely nodded and took hold of his mother's arm.

"Tibbett, may I present my mother, the Duchess of Thorpe."

Tibbett bowed very low, his face solemn with the utmost respect. "My honor, Your Grace."

"And this is my sister, Lady Adrianna."

"How do you do, Tibbett." Adrianna greeted the man with her usual bright smile. The servants would have to get used to the Americans and their ideas of equality for all men.

"And this is Adrianna's friend, Mistress Trinity Kingston, and her father, Mr. Eldon Kingston. They will be my guests for the duration of their stay."

Tibbett bent low and murmured a courteous welcome, but Will noted that all his servants eyed Trinity with utmost interest, which gave him good cause to believe that his affections for her were quite well known indeed. And if they were aware of their relationship, damn near everyone in London would be. His predicament grew worse by the moment. Damn Adrian and his interference.

Once inside, they retired to their rooms to direct the unpacking of their trunks. After Stephen had ridden away to give word to his father of their arrival—to soften the blow, as his brother had put it—Will spent an hour or so inside his study with Tibbett, overseeing the business of his town house and tenant properties and other matters that needed his attention after so long an absence.

His thoughts, however, continually roamed upstairs on the third floor, where Trinity would be supervising the maid putting away her possessions. He found himself smiling, pleased she was safely settled in his house where he could protect her from the ugly gossip that was bound to circulate. His pleasant expression faded. And there would be plenty of that. His own overblown reputation as a rake would engender it, if nothing else did.

As soon as the stir in the house abated, when the carriages were driven to the bricked courtyard in the rear, unharnessed, and carefully backed into the coach house, he took the front stairs three at a time. Feeling like a sneaking thief in his own house, he nodded at the footman leaving his mother's room with her red leather trunk, lingered until he had disappeared on the stairs, then tapped lightly on Trinity's door. At her call of admittance, he stepped inside and locked the door behind him.

She was standing at the foot of the tester, on the dais that raised the bed, a gauzy lace fichu held in her hand.

"How do you like your new home?" he asked, walking toward her.

She came to meet him, and they laughed together like children in conspiracy. He raised her up against him, eagerly seeking her lips. After a long enjoyable mingling of tongues that set him astir in any number of ways, he drew her down on the maid's couch at the foot of her bed.

"You didn't answer my question."

"It's very grand, of course. I think it's lovely." She smiled, and he was inordinately, ridiculously pleased. By God, he feared she was slowly reducing him to a simpering fool.

"You'll be the mistress of it soon enough," he said, wanting to reassure her again. He pressed the palm of her hand against his lips.

"I find it all very exciting, really," she said huskily, "pretending that I'm but another guest to you. But I fear that if you come so openly into my bedchamber again, all will know that isn't true."

"No one can stop me from that pursuit. Though I'll be careful not to compromise your reputation."

She smiled slightly at his illogic, but then lowered her eyes to stare at her lap. He became wary. He expected some sort of misgiving from her but certainly not the one that came unwilling from her lips, with her fine golden eyes intent upon his face.

"Perhaps we shouldn't continue with our . . ." She paused, blushing pink, and he sensed she was having trouble saying it. ". . . our trysts, not here in your house . . . perhaps you should stay away for a time . . ."

"I think not."

"Will, please, I cannot do so any longer under the very noses of my father, and your mother. 'Tisn't right, or proper, or any of those things. We'll wait until you have first righted your father's wrongs concerning that . . . other lady."

She was right again, of course, but he could not imagine having her so close and not being able to be with her, not now that he'd made a lasting commitment. But neither did he wish to dishonor her.

"Are you sure that's what you want?" he murmured, his mouth nibbling at her dainty earlobe.

"Oooh, stop, Will. I know what you're trying to do, and it'll work." She laughed softly, and he did, too, as he sought out her lips. Her mouth opened beneath his, and her tongue touched his, and he leaned her back, enjoying the moment.

"Well, maybe one last time," she managed breathlessly, "after all, we are married, if only in secret."

Will smiled as he unlaced her bodice and revealed white satiny skin, determined as he bent his head to taste her fragrant breasts that he'd waste no time ending the ridiculous charade his father had set into motion. Not with a wife like Trinity awaiting him. But he would honor her request; from this day forward he would not touch her again, not until their marriage was publicly acknowledged, even if it killed him.

"You'd best let loose the head of that cane or you'll crush it."

The Duke of Thorpe lifted his eyes and pinned his traveling companion to the other seat. His young friend, and now bodyguard—since the French assassins had marked the duke as one of their primary targets—stared back, one boot propped on his knee, totally at ease under Adrian's glare. Rupert Rainville bore no fear of him, and why should he? He'd soon become the Earl of Edmonton, when his father finally succumbed to the last stages of consumption, and was ever a more dutiful son than Adrian's own firstborn who defied him at every turn. Even the thought of Will sent a surging flush into his pale cheeks.

"Thinking of dear Will, I take it."

"The bloody boy's taken leave of his senses." Adrian scowled out the window at the shops. Crowds bustled on the sidewalks, bundled against the chill in the air. "You do recall what I want you to do when we meet the chit, do you not?"

"Aye, my pleasure, sir, especially if she turns out to be the beauty our spies insist she is."

"Just win her over and be quick about it, though I suspect if Will has won her affections, he won't lose them easily. Most women faint if he bloody well glances at them."

"Will and I have had our competitions for the

fairer sex in the past, and true, he is usually far more effective than I at the art of courtship, but that's even more incentive for me to steal away his lady love, if that she is. I've trouble aplenty seeing Will settle down with one lady, even if she is a wife and the most gorgeous creature in Christendom. You yourself know the pleasant benefits of keeping a young mistress to tend to your baser needs, if I remember correctly."

"He'll settle down, blast it, and with Caroline Rappaport, if I have a breath left in my body. I'll not have another American duchess besmirching the family name." His color heightened further at the thought of Victoria's insult to him. She should be at his house this very moment, awaiting his wishes instead of living at Will's mansion. Rumors were flying through sitting rooms all through London, damn them all.

By the time he reached Will's street it was almost dark, and nearly all the windows were alight. A damnable waste of candles, he thought sourly, as the steps were lowered. He stepped down first but did not wait for Rainville. The footman bowed deeply, as did the man who opened the front door. Tibbett, was it? Whoever he was, Adrian did not intend to be announced.

"Where the devil is my son?"

"He's in the music room, Your Grace. They're gathered to listen to . . ."

Adrian heard no more but stalked to the back of his son's luxuriously appointed town house. A glance told him that Rainville was just behind him now, a huge grin on his face, no doubt enjoying immensely Will's fall in Adrian's regard. The two younger men did not enjoy an affable relationship. Will despised him.

The white double doors were closed and Adrian did not knock, but shoved them aside. The cozy little party inside instantly dissolved, the tinkling notes of the spinet coming to an abrupt stop. Everyone came to their feet. At least they remembered that part of their duty, he sneered inwardly. He glanced around for the girl who was causing so bloody much trouble.

Will was standing at the spinet behind the playing bench, and there she sat. All golden red hair and huge amber eyes. No wonder his son was smitten. Adrian had a penchant for redheads, too. His last mistress had had similar rich coppery tresses, though she owed the color more to the dye pot than to God's bounty. She stared at him, looking fearful, and he felt an inner pleasure. Perhaps she would be tractable, if he exerted enough pressure on her.

"Your Grace," came an unmistakable voice from the other side of the room. Victoria. His long-estranged wife. More bitterness came rising in his gullet. She had never deigned to obey his commands unless she wished to. He was half-surprised she did so now. "Welcome."

He turned on her, found her greatly changed. She sat on a settee with an embroidery hoop lying in her lap. Eldon Kingston sat beside her, a cozy tête-à-tête, with a convicted enemy of the King. Rage consumed him, feeding on itself like wildfire, and he gripped his cane again, taking a moment to gain control of his temper. Stephen rose from his chair and came forward, as did Will.

"If you'd forewarned us of your arrival, we would have had a suitable reception, Your Grace," said Will. "Please sit down and I'll order repast. Rainville." Will nodded his head at Adrian's companion but there was no warmth in his voice, nor welcome in his face.

Adrian sat down in a chair the man Tibbett brought for him and Adrian stared at his wife. "You've aged."

He'd meant to be insulting, as she had been to him by the affront of making him come to visit her, like some poor relative. He watched the color suffuse her cheeks, but then he saw her chin come up in the way he remembered.

"You haven't changed a whit, it seems," she replied in a tone that alerted everyone present to exactly what she thought of his remark. "I am pleased you decided to visit. Adrianna and I have been in England several months now."

Adrianna moved closer to stand behind her mother. At least she was a pretty little thing, he thought in relief. He shouldn't have trouble arranging her a lucrative match. He hoped to God she hadn't inherited her mother's willfulness.

Adrian braced his hand on his cane, noticing out of the corner of his eye the way Rainville was moving toward the spinet bench. Will turned and watched him until Adrian spoke, drawing his son's attention back to him. It wouldn't do to attack the American girl in front of Will. Adrian knew his son well enough to know how to raise his hackles. A truer course would be the one he and Rainville had decided upon. Ruin her character in Will's eyes, and let him know that she was not suitable material to be the Duchess of Thorpe. If there was anyone who could ruin a woman, it was Rainville, a scoundrel known far and wide for his less-than-admirable seductions and exploitation of innocent maidens.

"You were expected to come directly to my house like a dutiful wife." His voice razored the words but Victoria seemed not to feel his cut.

"I would have, Your Grace, indeed I wished to, until I learned that you would not receive my dear friends, Eldon and Trinity. I've never been one to turn my back on those I care about."

Again Adrian heard her rebuke, was angered by it, but not enough to forestall the plans he and Rainville had laid in place. He would pretend to overlook her disrespect, but he truly coveted the moment when he could throw Eldon Kingston, the simpering traitor, back into prison where he belonged, and his bloody daughter, too, if he could arrange it.

"Then perhaps Will's hospitality is the best solution for Eldon," he said, pleased he had the power to coerce them to his will. "But as for the rest of you, I expect you to be packed and ready to take residence at my house for the duration of this visit, and before dusk tomorrow. And that includes you, Mistress Kingston. I'll remind you, if I must, that I hold the power to have your father hauled off to Newgate if you think of disobeying me."

Victoria's dark eyes hardened but her face didn't change. He laughed bitterly inside. They all knew he could have Eldon executed if he wished.

"Of course, Your Grace," his wife said, but Will was frowning, and so was Stephen.

"Do you really think this is necessary?" Will said angrily.

"I do. I care what gossip abounds concerning my family, even if you do not. I have made my decision, and I won't discuss it further."

Not that he particularly wanted any of the women under his roof, but their presence at Will's house would add fuel to the fire of the brewing scandal surrounding his family. Damnation, he muttered inwardly, he had worked hard to build up his good reputation and kinship to the Crown. And his own flesh and blood was about to bring it all down around his ears.

Across the room, Rainville was smiling down at Trinity Kingston. She watched him warily. Will noticed and escorted her to a chair a good distance away from Adrian's seat. What'd he think? Adrian would strike out at her with his cane? He'd like to, he admitted.

"I also should advise you that I'll be hosting a ball next Saturday night. The Rappaports are coming, Will. The first public appearance for you and Lady Caroline since I announced your engagement." He watched Will's jaw stiffen, watched him struggle to contain his anger, but he wouldn't cause a wretched scene in front of his little love, or his mother, he was too well bred. That's why Adrian had chosen this method of confronting him. The marriage was inevitable; all that stood in the way was the bothersome little American chit.

"You haven't introduced us to your daughter, Eldon," he said then, only half able to hide his disgust at her presence. "Trinity, I believe." He looked at her. "We've all heard tales about you, all the way here in London."

"I warn you, Father," came Will's voice, cold, lethal.

Adrian's wrath doubled. How dare he warn him? The Duke of Thorpe. Didn't the lad know he could disinherit him with one swipe of the pen? He should do it without further ado. But he had groomed Will since boyhood. He wanted his firstborn to assume his title, as all the other Remingtons had done for centuries before him.

"You warn me?"

His tone was so icy that a deep silence invaded the chamber. At last, the object of all their problems looked straight at him.

"I am Trinity, Your Grace. I am honored by your visit. Your family has been most gracious to my father and me."

At least she had some breeding, and her charm was not overestimated. From what he understood Will was passing her off to London acquaintances as a dear friend of Adrianna's. Adrian knew better, if for no reason than the way Will looked at her.

"And pleased we are that you have come to London," Rainville said, his handsome face wreathed with a smile directed only at her.

Trinity nodded slightly in return but Rainville

went on. "And if you please, milady, I would be honored to escort you Saturday next. One so lovely should not attend a ball without a gentleman escort."

Trinity looked surprised but it was Will who intervened. "That won't be necessary, Rainville. We plan to attend the ball as a party."

"I am crushed," he said, a hand on his heart. "But there will be other days and other nights when I hope I'll be allowed to call. Once you're settled in His Grace's home."

Will looked furious, but could not forbid it without appearing the fool. The others sat in silence. Victoria's eyes stared unblinking at him, as if she could read his mind, see through all his crafty machinations.

"Then I will expect you tomorrow," Adrian said coldly, pleased by his success. The sooner the red-haired girl was out of Will's house, the sooner Rainville could get her in his clutches. It wouldn't take him long. He was a master at seduction.

For a time afterward, he endured a small amount of stilted chitchat, as well as Will's attentiveness to Trinity Kingston's every movement. But he also saw the first simmering of his jealousy and anger, a very good sign. Adrian would strip the American girl of her appeal in the eyes of his son, if he never lived to accomplish another thing. And he didn't care how low he had to stoop in order to do so. He'd leave her downfall to Rainville. He couldn't wait to enjoy the spectacle.

Chapter Twenty-three

His fists clenched, his face set in granite, Will ascended the wide marble steps of his father's house, irritated beyond belief that Adrian had manipulated him into having to seek out Trinity there instead of in his own home. He walked straight into the front foyer, without knocking, startling the maid affixing fresh candles into an ornate gold wall sconce beside the door. She curtsied quickly as he handed her his tricorne and gloves and tamped down the anger flaring in him. Things were not proceeding well, a fact he wanted to keep from Trinity. His father had wasted no effort embroiling him in the betrothal fiasco with the Rappaport family.

"Good morning, Evelyn. I'm here to see Mistress Kingston. Has she come downstairs yet?"

"Oh, yes, milord, long past. I believe she be walking in the garden."

"With my mother and sister?" he asked, glancing through a parlor to the French doors that led onto the high walled verandas overlooking the extensive gardens. All three women had made it quite clear to both Stephen and himself that they'd been miserable throughout the week they'd lived under the duke's roof, and by God, he was going to make sure his father wasn't mistreating them in any way.

"No, milord. Her Grace and Lady Adrianna accompanied His Grace to the Parliament Hall, not an hour past."

Well, finally a spot of good news, Will thought. He was hoping to visit with Trinity alone, a gross understatement of that desire. He hadn't been alone with her since she'd been forced to leave his house. "She's by herself then?"

"Oh, no, milord. I believe Lord Rainville is escortin' her. He came early to call."

William stiffened angrily but tried not to show it. "I understand Rainville's visited her often of late. Is that true?"

"Yes, milord. Near every day, and most evenings, too."

Furious now, Will strode through the parlor and out onto the high terrace, scanning the flagstone paths below for a glimpse of the couple. His father was doing everything he could to drive a wedge between him and Trinity, and Rainville was just his latest weapon. Will's dislike for Rupert was probably the reason His Grace had chosen him.

He finally found them, a fairly good distance away as they walked slowly side by side down one of the meandering paths. As they rounded a curve and proceeded out of his view, he took the stairs in a rush, aware he could cut them off on the far side of the tiled blue fountain. All the while he headed toward them, he cursed his father's meddling in his affairs, and was not exactly pleased that Trinity would agree to walk alone with as bloody a reprobate as Rupert Rainville. He'd told her what kind of man he was, had he not? She should have refused his company.

He found them sitting in the shade of an arched trellis thick with twisting ivy, having been drawn to them by the sound of Trinity's laughter. Enjoyment he didn't particularly appreciate. The two sat together on a low white marble bench, not touching, of course, but too close for Will's pleasure. Rainville saw him first, and grinned as Will approached, a challenging smirk that set Will's teeth on edge.

"Well, well, look who's come to join us," Rupert said, causing Trinity to turn around and look.

She smiled happily when she saw Will, and immediately stood up and hurried to meet him. His temper blunted a degree or two by the obvious pleasure she took in leaving her other suitor to greet him. He lifted her hand to his lips, but his gaze remained fixed on Rainville's face.

"I almost didn't find you, out here so far from the house." His tone was mild but Trinity obviously heard his displeasure loud and clear. Her welcoming expression faded slightly.

"I came out to enjoy the sunshine," she explained quickly, glancing back at her companion. "I happened to meet Lord Rainville, who was searching the gardens for His Grace."

Will raised an eyebrow as he guided Trinity to a bench that sat facing the other man. "Indeed?" He was surprised that Trinity hadn't seen right through Rainville's lie.

"Mistress Kingston informed me that I'd just missed his lordship," Rainville said smoothly. "I intend to join him at Parliament directly."

"Please, don't let us keep you."

So pointed was his dismissal that Rainville flushed slightly at the insult but his posture remained easy and relaxed. He did not move to rise. "What brings you here, Will?" he said tightly. "Is your lovely betrothed not available this morning? Everyone in London's talking about the attention you've been paying to her since you arrived."

Beside him, Will felt Trinity flinch and look down at her folded hands. "I do believe it's time you took your leave, Rupert. I need to discuss something with Trinity. Alone."

Rainville raised one of his thick curved brows in mock disapproval. "Do you think that's appropriate, Will? Now that you've publicly pledged yourself to another?"

"Get the hell out, before I throw you out."

Alarmed, Trinity put a hand on his forearm, but Will ignored her attempt to restrain his temper. He glared unblinkingly at his enemy, spoiling for a fight. It was long overdue between them.

"As you wish," Rainville finally said, rising but only to approach Trinity. He bowed formally from the waist. "Before I go I'll remind you, Mistress Kingston, that His Grace has designated me as your escort at the ball Saturday next. He wishes to spare you the embarrassment of being unescorted since Will, here, will be attending with Lady Caroline Rappaport."

"I said to get out, Rainville."

Rainville grinned, a cynical twist of lips, bent low once more to kiss Trinity's hand, a leisurely caress of her fingers that went on much too long for propriety. Will had to grind his teeth together to keep from ripping his face away from her.

"Good day, milady. I'll look forward with utmost eagerness to this weekend's festivities."

As he disappeared down the path toward the house, Trinity looked up at Will, and he could easily read the hurt revealed in those limpid golden depths.

"You're going to escort her?"

Cursing Rainville, and his father, Will sat down beside her and took her hand. He kissed her palm. He could smell the roses emanating from her, softly, fragrantly. He had missed her more than he could ever have expected. "It can't be helped. I've got to play along with them for the time being, or she'll be publicly humiliated. After the season's done and we've returned to Thorpe Hall, I can gradually work my way out of the betrothal."

"Then I suppose I must also go with Lord Rainville?"

Though she didn't seem a whit pleased by the idea, a jealous dart struck Will's heart. "You seemed to be enjoying his company when I came upon the two of you. I heard you laughing."

"He said something amusing."

"Don't be fooled by him. He's black to the core, and he's using you against me. He's Father's pawn, and nothing more."

"I'll have to go with him, if His Grace orders it. You heard him threaten Papa."

Will was silent because he knew that was true. He muttered a whole string of oaths to have been caught up in such a frustrating situation. They should have stayed at Thorpe Hall, and that's where he intended to take her, the minute the bloody ball was at an end.

"And our annulment? Has your father been able to force it through?"

"Not yet. You're still my wife, thank God."

Will smiled, but Trinity did not, could not, with eyes so filled with pain.

"I don't feel much like your wife these days," she whispered, laying her temple against his shoulder.

He gathered her in closer and rubbed his hand up and down her back. But he had little news that could give her cheer. Though days had passed, he'd made no headway whatsoever in getting himself out of the unwanted entanglement with the Rappaports. It would take time, of course, and a great deal of patience, and he didn't have either. But he and Trinity were going to have a life together, the devil be damned, if he had to trudge through hell and back to make it so.

A LOVE SO SPLENDID   323

"I wish we could stay out here, alone and hidden away from everyone." She didn't look at him but he could hear the longing in her voice. "Or just run away, far away, where no one knew us and we could be together."

Dreams he would gladly adopt if he could, thinking how very much easier it would be for both of them if he was not the one destined to inherit the title, and she certainly could not abandon her family. "I'm working it out, sweet. It's just going to take some time. At least we can see each other here, like this."

She raised her face and smiled tremulously. "Then let's make the best of it, shall we?"

He smiled and lowered his head toward her. Their lips met softly, lovingly, and he hungered for more, to hold her the way he wanted to, and he knew he would never give up. He'd do whatever it took, for however long it took, to acknowledge this woman he loved to all the world as his true wife, his beloved wife.

"I don't understand why Mother didn't come with us. You know how close she is to Madame Fortier."

Adrianna and Trinity rode in the duke's finest black carriage, one pulled by four high-stepping black horses, on their way to the most famous couturieres in London, a woman who was a true, dear friend of Victoria Remington.

"I don't know why unless she's still feeling poorly. She hasn't been herself since your father made us move into this house." Trinity's stomach tightened at the thought of that cruel man and the indignities he was forcing upon his family. She pitied poor Victoria to have been bound to such a devil for most of her life, and Adrianna's expression reflected much the same sentiment.

"He's my own father, yet I'm terrified of him." Adrianna whispered the admission as if fearing retribution if heard, though the bodyguard her father had insisted accompany her everywhere she went was perched outside on the seat with the liveried driver.

"I know." Trinity disliked him even more but she knew how unhappy Adrianna was and endeavored to revive her spirits, though her own lay in a bruised and battered heap at the bottom of her soul.

"But he has given Victoria free rein to purchase you a whole wardrobe of new gowns, anything you want, she says," she reminded Adrianna, without managing to muster any enthusiasm whatsoever in her voice.

"Only because he wants to marry me off in grand fashion."

"And Will."

Adrianna turned to her, openly apologetic. "Oh, Trin, I'm sorry. I'm always thinking of myself and Geoff, but I know how difficult it must be for you, with all the talk about Will and Lady Caroline. Do you think you can bear attending the ball and watching them together? I'm not sure I could do it if it were Geoff escorting her."

Trinity wasn't sure she could, especially if the

duke announced Will's engagement to the assemblage. No matter how many times she told herself to listen to Will and believe all his reassurances, she had more misgivings than hopes. And the duke was insisting that she come, no doubt because he knew the pain it would cause her. Her chin rose a fraction at that thought, and she found she wanted to thwart him, to show him what Americans were made of, but then her heart began its familiar tumble because no matter how many times Will told her that he could work things out for them, deep down, where she admitted the truth, she didn't believe he could.

When the well-polished, fine-sprung conveyance rolled to a stop before Madame Fortier's shop, they waited for the burly, dark-caped bodyguard to open the door and assist them to the street. The famous dressmaker had settled her establishment in a modest two-story house on a corner intersection among a thick grove of elm trees. From outside it appeared to be a regular residence, much like the others lining the street, but inside the foyer, they found the lower floor had been converted into viewing rooms for her customers while the owner had her private quarters upstairs.

Madame Rachel Fortier herself came forth to greet them at the door, a smallish woman with graying blond hair and prematurely wrinkled skin for a woman in her fifties. She smiled widely though, and looked quite beautiful when she did. She dipped a respectful curtsy.

"Welcome to my shop. I must say I am pleased

to make your acquaintances. Your mother and I went to the same school, but that was many years ago indeed. You resemble her, you know, Adrianna, the way she looked back then when we were both so young and innocent." She sighed wistfully, as if that were impossibly long ago.

"Yes, I've seen a miniature of the two of you together. I'm pleased you see a likeness as I think Mother is most beautiful."

"I'm sorry she couldn't come with you today, but please sit down here in the front parlor and allow me to present what I've chosen for both of you." She smiled at Trinity, and Trinity felt the lady must be mistaken. His Grace had offered no coin to purchase her a new gown.

"Actually, I'm only accompanying Adrianna for her fitting. I won't be purchasing any new gowns."

"Oh, yes, you will, my dear. Lord William has already sent orders that you're to have the best I have to offer. Anything and everything you want were his exact words, I believe. He said to spare no expense."

Though the woman's remarks were meant to be kind with no condemnation coloring their meaning, Trinity blushed to the roots of her hair. What must Victoria's friend be thinking? For a gentleman to send instructions like that? To purchase her a gown to wear to his betrothal ball where another woman would be announced as his bride-to-be? She was mortified, and determinedly, she vowed she would not attend. No, she wouldn't suffer that humiliation, she just couldn't. But Will was her husband, he loved her, her mind countered stubbornly as it always did, and he was trying to find a way out of his betrothal so that he could acknowledge their vows.

Dropping despondently into a chair, she watched one young model after another move into the parlor, turning and preening in gowns of every hue and fabric. A year or so ago, when she lived in Charleston, she had dreamed of coming to London and viewing the latest fashions, but now it seemed a distasteful chore. A glance at Adrianna told her that her friend wasn't any happier with their plight. With desultory enthusiasm, Adrianna was finally forced to select a lovely gown of ochre yellow satin with a creamy swath of ecru lace for a fichu.

"A wonderful choice," Madame Fortier complimented with an approving nod, "and now you must scoot upstairs to be fitted. My seamstresses will take your measurements in the last room on the right side of the hallway, my dear. I'm sure you'll have no trouble finding it."

Adrianna lifted her skirts, heaving an audible sigh, as she obediently crossed to the hall and climbed the steps. Madame Fortier watched her until she was out of sight, then turned to Trinity.

"And now for you, Trinity, dear." She gazed down at her, cocking her head to one side with an appraising eye. "What glorious hair you have, not red, nor gold, but a lovely shade in between. I believe an emerald gown would suit you to perfection."

Trinity nodded, thinking that was the color of Will's eyes, but she probably wouldn't be allowed near him anyway. He was escorting Caroline, would be at her side throughout the evening. And she would have to endure Rupert Rainville's leers and bold touches. She sighed as loud as Adrianna had, paying very little attention to Madame Fortier as she brought forth silver trays lined with gloves and feathered ornaments to adorn her hair, silk-fringed satin shawls, and lovely soft undergarments. She chose whatever the lady suggested without much interest. She just wished the ordeal was over.

"Trin! Come quickly now, the fitter is ready for you!"

At Adrianna's excited call, Trinity turned all the way around in her velvet chair, amazed at the change in her friend. Adrianna's face was flushed with happiness now, her eyes bright, and though shocked at the abrupt reversal in mood, Trinity was glad the other girl was taking some pleasure in her new wardrobe. Neither of them had much else to celebrate.

"Run along then," Madame Fortier told her, smiling kindly.

"You must find the dress very much to your liking, now that you've tried it on," she observed to Adrianna, trying to act happy, too, as she followed the smiling girl up the steps.

"Oh, yes, and you'll soon see why," Adrianna answered, laughing and pulling her along by her elbow as they traversed the upstairs corridor. It was very quiet on the second floor, seemingly deserted, but for the two of them, and she followed Adrianna into the fitting room. She stopped in her tracks, stunned, as Adrianna quietly shut the door behind her.

"Geoff!" Trinity cried, then ran the few steps that took her into his arms. She hugged him wordlessly, so glad to see him she could not speak at first, but then the questions came forth, spilling out excitely as she pulled away.

"How did you get here? It's too dangerous! Are you all right?"

Geoffrey smiled and drew Adrianna in against his side as he hugged Trinity again. "I'm all right. Victoria arranged everything. Madame Fortier was born in Charleston. She backs the patriots in the war so we have no need to fear her."

Trinity stared at him, unable to stop her ecstatic smile. Adrianna looked even more overjoyed. "I never dreamed you were up here," she began but he drew both young women to the sofa positioned at the foot of the bed.

"I know, but this is the safest way for us to meet. Remington's having you both watched night and day."

Trinity suddenly realized why they were there, what was about to happen. "Are you ready to leave for home?"

"Aye. And I'm taking all of you with me, even Victoria and Eldon."

Immediately Trinity was torn, pleasure rising at the thought of leaving England and the Duke of Thorpe's mansion, agony clawing her heart at the idea of leaving Will. "Victoria's coming with us?"

"She's no desire to remain here, now that the duke is openly opposing her. She wants Adrianna safely away before he forces her to wed some man she detests."

Adrianna was beaming, holding on to Geoffrey's hand as if he were her lifeline, and Trinity tried to think, tried to imagine abandoning Will, never seeing him again.

"I know how you feel about Will, Trin." Geoffrey's eyes searched her face. "And he means well by you, I know, but what he wants is impossible now, especially if Victoria and Adrianna return to America. The duke'll disown them, and it's only a matter of time before they decide to throw Eldon back in prison."

Trinity nodded, because she knew that every word he spoke was true, had lain awake long nights tormented with similar fears. All along she had known she would have to go back. She was an American; she would never be accepted by Will's set. She would bring Will nothing but scandal and disgrace. She had to go. She had to.

"When?" was all the response she could muster.

"The night of the betrothal ball. There will be hundreds of people wandering in and out of the mansion. No one will notice if the three of you slip away. I'll have a coach waiting that'll take us to a ship. We have many friends in London, Trinity, more than I ever could have imagined. We'll set sail on the first tide for Calais where I have business with the French war emissaries, then home to Charleston. His Grace won't have any idea where we are."

"What about Will? What shall I tell him?"

This time Geoff picked up her hand, squeezed her fingers. "You can't tell him anything, Trin. I think we can trust him, but he won't want to have a part in destroying his family this way. He's caught in the middle, too, Trin, just like Victoria and Adrianna. I know he probably thinks he can make everything work for the two of you, but he can't. He'll be the Duke of Thorpe someday. His future here in England is already set in stone. He has no choice in his loyalties."

Geoffrey was saying all the things that Trinity knew in her heart to be true, but that she'd thrust determinedly out of her mind. Tears welled and she chewed her lip, but she knew Geoffrey was right. She would have to leave England. God help her, she would have to leave Will. Forever.

Chapter Twenty-four

"God in heaven, you look exquisite in that gown."

At the sound of Will's appreciative voice behind her, utter, unmitigated dread filled Trinity from head to toe. She didn't move from where she stood at her bedchamber window watching the long line of coaches depositing magnificently adorned guests on the Remington driveway. She was fully dressed, ready to descend to the festivities, but she didn't want to go. She didn't want to see anyone, not even Will, especially not Will.

"Trin?" He was closer now. She shivered, long ripples of fear and pleasure to have him so close.

Slowly, reluctantly, she turned to face him. He stood only a couple of feet away, dressed formally, in evening attire made of dark green silk, the color of his eyes the color of her gown. His gaze held her, intensely, willing her mind to forget everything but him, to listen and believe him.

"You shouldn't be up here with me. Your father will be angry."

"The devil can take my father."

They stared at each other but she wondered

if he really meant that, or anything else he'd told her. How could he? He was as trapped and controlled by the circumstances of his birth as she was by her own.

"Are you about ready to come down?" His gaze wandered down the front of her gown, and she could see the pleasure he took in the exquisitely styled pearl-encrusted, shimmering satin. The gown was stunning, even rivaling the lovely wedding dress in which she had taken such pride so long ago. The thought of the past only made her heart take on more weight, filled her eyes with more sorrow, made her more certain they were living a lie, endeavoring to believe what they wanted, instead of what was true.

"I don't think I want to."

He moved closer, and of course, she weakened at the very nearness of him, the familiar scent of his skin, his body. She was lost to him, she realized helplessly, trying to fight the need to press herself up against him for comfort. To sob and tell him she didn't want to run away from him, but she had to, she had to! She was as trapped as he was, and she had never felt it more than she did at that moment.

"Please, Trinity. We all want you to come. Adrianna's been hovering near the stairs for half an hour. She has no friends here in London at all, and she needs you to stand beside her."

Not for long, Trinity knew but could not tell him, because Geoffrey would come for her soon, for all of them. Pain knifed her heart at the thought of leaving Will, of not being able to say good-bye. Will reached out and brought her tenderly into his arms, and all her anger and frustration spiraled away. She shut her eyes, but she wanted to cry, to weep and rend her clothing and ask why they could not be together.

"I know tonight will be hard for you, sweet. But I've got to go along with it for the time being. You know that I don't care about Caroline. You must know that, more than anyone. But there are ways of doing things here that I have to abide by. Father arranged this to hurt us but he can't make me do something I don't want to do. The only power he has over me is disinheritance and he's too proud to acknowledge such a major rift with his son. He'd rather scheme and plot to make me do what he wants. After tonight I can start to cool the relationship and then when the season's over, the engagement will be forgotten quietly, without humiliating anyone. All I'm asking for you is a little more patience."

Trinity had heard all those words before, of course, but she still didn't believe it could happen. The Duke of Thorpe was too powerful, too cunning. He would not stop trying just because Will opposed him. He would force everyone to do his bidding as he had done since they had arrived in London. She had believed William then, but now she knew that even he was no match for a man like Adrian Remington.

"Come, I'll walk with you. Where's your fan and bouquet?"

Trinity motioned to the candlelit dressing table, and William moved there and retrieved her things. She had to go; she really had no choice. She tried to take pleasure in the fact that Will had come for her, that he spared no effort in reassuring her, and she wished she could tell him about Geoffrey. She couldn't, though the need ate at her throat like some awful acid. She had never been so unhappy, even when William had rejected her before the war.

William held on to her elbow firmly, giving her some courage, but she knew he could not linger with her once they reached the grand event. He would spend the evening squiring the unknown Caroline, for appearances only, of course, he wanted her to understand, but still, she knew exactly how she would feel. She'd feel like his mistress, the woman with whom he dallied on the side. And she was, she told herself with not a little scorn, that's exactly what she was.

"Oh, Trin, I'm so glad you're here. I've been waiting for you before I go inside. There are so many people here, hundreds and hundreds."

Adrianna met them at the bottom of the steps, and Trinity glanced down the long central corridor toward the rear ballroom where she could hear soft music filtering out and echoing up into the vaulted domes. She swallowed down her disenchantment with the idea of joining the festivities, surrounded by the enemies of America and the announced bride of her husband.

"I'll seek you out as often as I can," William whispered softly into her ear, "but now I've got to go. You can do this, Trin. God knows, you've done things that took a lot more courage than facing these people."

Trinity wasn't sure he was right about that. She tried to nod but only came up with a strained little silly grimace that certainly could not pass muster as a smile. Will smiled encouragingly and kissed her hand, and his eyes were calm, assured. He really believed he could work things out, she realized, he really did. But he was used to getting his way, too. His station had made him confident that his wishes would be granted. This time, however, he was out of his league. His father was a mighty adversary.

"Let's go in together. Mother's already inside with His Grace. He insisted that she meet his guests at his side, for appearances. She did so, but she made sure that I didn't have to, bless her."

Adrianna took the arm that William had released, and they walked slowly together down the hall. Trinity watched Will turn and smile reassuringly at her before he disappeared into the milling crowd.

"Do you think Geoffrey will be able to come tonight? With all these people about?" Adrianna said, extremely low. "I hope he can make it. I cannot bear to live in this cold place another day."

Trinity hoped he did, too, and just as violently she hoped he did not. How could she leave Will? How? She loved him so much. She felt sick to even think about never seeing him again.

Inside a cotillion was advancing, with many

dancers participating; many more stood watching on the perimeter of a floor set with black and white squares of glossy marble. All of London society must be in attendance, she thought, searching for a glimpse of Will. She found him beside his parents, and for the first time she saw Lady Caroline Rappaport. She knew it was her instinctively, for the young woman stood between Will and His Grace. An elegantly attired gentleman and lady stood on the other side of Will. The Rappaport family, no doubt.

"That's Caroline," Adrianna verified a moment later. "I met her just after they arrived. She's pretty, but not nearly so striking as you are. Will was barely civil to her."

Trinity thought Caroline was much more than pretty. She, too, wore the perfumed white powder in her curled coiffure that all the rest of them did, but Rainville had delighted in telling Trinity that she had pale blond hair and brown eyes. She was smallish of stature, barely reaching Will's shoulder. They made a handsome couple. Again, anguish shot through her, and she averted her eyes as Victoria caught sight of them and signaled Adrianna to join them.

"Come with me, Trin."

"No, I cannot. Please don't ask me to."

"But I hate to leave you alone like this!"

"I'd rather be alone. I intend to leave soon anyway. I only came down because Will insisted."

"He wants you to see how little she means to him. He'll come to you as soon as it's seemly."

"Go along, Adrianna, before your father comes and gets you."

Trinity certainly didn't want to exchange words with the duke. Even now she knew he was watching her, no doubt pleased that he had managed to put his son at the side of the woman he had chosen for him to marry, for all to see and comment upon. She turned away, determined not to look at them again, not for the duration of the evening. She moved toward one of the open French doors, her face hot with roiling emotions. She would escape as soon as possible. She could not bear watching Will court another woman, one who looked up at him out of adoring eyes.

Across the room, William kept a close eye on what Trinity was doing. He knew she was miserable and suffering, but he was proud of her. She held her head high, and she looked beautiful, more beautiful than any other woman in the room, in the entire city. He wanted to go to her, had to force himself not to. Cursing inside, he bent to listen to some remark of Caroline's. She was a pleasant enough young woman. It was a shame his father had embroiled her in such a mess. Will had no wish to hurt her, but he'd be damned if he'd marry her to keep from doing so.

Lord Rappaport spoke of a weekend hunt coming up within the next fortnight and what game they intended to bag, and William answered with noncommittal interest. During the exchange, he lost sight of Trinity, and hastily scanned the crowd for her, hoping she had not already fled to her chamber. When he found her, he went rigid with annoyance.

Rupert Rainville stood at her side, bending down solicitously, holding her arm, touching her. Will's jaw hardened, if only because he loathed the man. Trinity was vulnerable tonight, needed someone to comfort her, and Rainville was cad enough to take full advantage of that need. His eyes narrowed as Rupert led Trinity out onto the dance floor. What was she thinking to let him do so? Or was she humiliated and showing Will how it felt to watch him with another woman?

"Will, you are coming to Father's hunt, aren't you? It's to be a grand occasion."

Lady Caroline's polite conversation filtered through the red veil of anger blurring his mind, and it took all his willpower to pull his eyes away from Trinity and her doting partner. Caroline was smiling sweetly up at him, seemingly the picture of innocence, but there was something else in her eyes, some emotion that looked like resignation. Did she know that he had no intention of going through with their engagement? Somehow he felt she did, and if not that, then knew he felt nothing for her, other than mild friendship.

"I'm not sure. My mother and sister are visiting, and I have need to escort them to a great many functions here in town."

"Father will be so disappointed. As will I."

"Forgive me, Lady Caroline."

She nodded, and he glanced again to the couple gliding in and out in the slow steps of the minuet. He'd never seen Trinity dance, but he should have known she'd be as graceful and lovely in that pursuit as she was in everything else. Each time Rainville touched her hand and led her through the steps, Will ground his teeth in frustration, wishing now that Trinity would retire to her room. He didn't trust Rainville's motives, not for a moment, especially since he was in open alliance with the duke.

"Is that Adrianna's friend?" Lady Caroline asked him, obviously noticing where his eyes were riveted. "The young American woman I've heard about?"

"She is," he answered, trying to hide his growing annoyance with Trinity. "Mistress Kingston is visiting our family."

"She's quite striking, isn't she? Perhaps you'll introduce us before the evening ends."

"Perhaps." Not a chance. Even now, he chafed with impatience, wanting to leave the reception line and join Trinity. Rainville was courting her so blatantly just to anger him, and it was working. Damn his eyes.

When the orchestra was suddenly silenced, William was at first glad because Rainville would have to get his hands off Trinity's person, but when he turned and saw that his father was the one who stood on the raised dais, he was immediately wary. For good reason, as it turned out.

"My lords and ladies," the Duke of Thorpe began in his gravelly voice. Slowly quiet began to fall over the assemblage until only the distant murmur of voices floated in from the refreshment tables in the adjoining antechamber. In the wake of the expectant hush, Adrian continued. "I am most pleased that you have paid us the compliment of joining our celebration in the coming nuptials of my son and heir, Lord William Remington, and the lovely and gracious Lady Caroline Rappaport. Let the happy couple come forward for our toast to a long and prosperous life together."

William clamped his jaw, absolutely furious, but he should have expected his father would pull some stunt to make things even more difficult. Will had no choice but to take Caroline's gloved hand and lead her through the separating crowd to his father's side. Inside he seethed and boiled with resentment, and he tried to glance at Trinity, knowing how terrible this spectacle would make her feel. All her doubts and fears would be bolstered and he would not be there to soothe her.

"My son, I cannot tell you how proud I am to have you stand here before God and our friends with such a beautiful and gracious lady as your betrothed wife."

Will's eyes met his father's, and their gazes clashed in cold, hard combat, not a whit of warmth between them. But in the end, he would win this duel of wits and social standing. After tonight, there was little more his father could do to come between Trinity and him. After this last humiliation, Will could start rectifying all his father's dirty tricks. The duke's eyes retreated first, falling upon poor little Caroline with a great deal more affection.

"And Lady Caroline. You will be a most welcome and cherished addition to our family. I cannot imagine a more suitable lady to follow my dear wife as the Duchess of Thorpe."

Lady Caroline blushed prettily as Adrian kissed both her hands, then put them into William's."

"A betrothal dance!" he cried, engendering a quick applause from onlookers. "Strike up the music!"

The conductor complied, and William had no choice but to smile and lead Caroline to the center of the ballroom. As they began the first steps, he sought out Trinity's place. She stood at Rainville's side, her face blanched as white as her powdered hair. Their eyes met, locked, and he saw her agony before she turned and fled toward the terrace. Rainville remained where he was for a beat, just long enough to give Will a smirk and a two-fingered mocking salute before he turned and strode outside in pursuit of her. Will wanted to kill him with his bare hands.

Chapter Twenty-five

At the sight of Will revolving around the dance floor with Lady Caroline in his arms, Trinity had had enough. She didn't want to see more, didn't intend to, and she pushed through the people with their glittering jewels and dazzling clothes straining to see the handsome couple in their tender moment, her only thought to escape outside where she could breathe again.

When she gained the doors, she rushed through them, almost shocked by the cold crisp air that hit her face as she left the overcrowded, heated ballroom. She stopped, sucking in deep, fortifying draughts, trying to calm herself, to put a halt to threatening tears. She should never have come down and stood there for them to humiliate her, never, and she shouldn't have come to England, shouldn't have believed Will's words of love, shouldn't have taken him into her bed, into her heart.

Another couple came out behind her, laughing in the secret, conspiratorial way lovers did, in the way she and Will had done so often during their stay at Thorpe Hall. In the beginning when she still had believed everything would work out for them. Wanting only to be by herself, she turned and hurried quickly across the stone portico to where a great flight of steps rose to the higher walled terraces. She lifted her skirts and nearly ran up the steps, panting by the time she reached the top. There she paused in the darkness to get her direction, then remembered that if she crossed this terrace, around the corner another flight of stairs descended again and would take her eventually back to her own private chamber.

Determined to gain that sanctuary, where she could cry if she wanted, or scream her head off, or throw everything that wasn't nailed down, or just lie there and stare at the ceiling in complete despair, she rushed across the dark, deserted gallery. The moon was half-full but the illumination was only dancing mosaics of silvery light filtering through the swift-moving clouds that lined the night sky like sand ripples on a beach. This part of the house was dark, no candles lit behind the tall mullioned windows, the great edifice rising over her like a malevolent gargoyle. She felt no fear though; she welcomed the darkness as she wanted no one to see her.

Almost reaching the staircase she sought, she heard the click of swift footsteps chasing her. She paused, her hand on the stone wall, wondering if it was Will. She hoped not. She couldn't resist him; she'd go back inside if he asked her. Would do just about anything for him, and she hated that. She hated how he had taken her will from her. He had become the center of her life. He had become her life. But she had no reason to worry. It wasn't Will who called her name.

"Trinity, wait!"

Though the voice was low, guarded, she knew it was Lord Rainville, and she truly had no desire to linger about in the darkness with a man like him. But she was not swift enough to evade him, and he caught her at the very top of the steps, bringing her up short with a hand on her arm.

"Whoa, now, not so fast. Where are you going?"

"I'm not feeling well. I'm going to my room to lie down." His fingers bit into her arm, and she attempted to pull away. He held her fast. "Please let me go."

Rainville laughed, softly, and in a way that sent a rash of chill bumps climbing up her spine. For the first time she was afraid. She looked behind her at the dark house, at their isolation, at the way his hand bit into her elbow so tightly. A panicky feeling began to rise and she forced herself to subdue it.

"I said to let me go."

"I heard what you said, luv, but I don't intend to do what you want." He laughed again, cruelly, and his fingers dug deeper into her flesh. "You know I ought to thank you, my dear. By running up here all alone in the dark, you've given me just the opportunity I've been waiting for."

Again she almost shuddered because he was leaning close now, whispering in a voice that sounded both pleased and threatening, and she felt cold all over, cold and very alone. "What do you want?" Her voice, too, had dwindled to a weak whisper, and she thought somewhere in her mind that she ought to scream.

"You have no idea what a problem you've become, do you, Trinity? It's a shame. You're quite a beauty in your own right with all that fiery hair, and that smile of yours, oh, what a delightful smile you have. Even I almost melt when you direct it on me. Unlike His Grace, I can understand why Will is so bewitched by you. I'd take you, too, if I had the time, right here in the dark, I'd pull up your skirts and pleasure myself on you, where nobody can see us, nobody can hear your cries."

Hairs prickled and waved on her spine like long grasses in the wind, and she jerked away, opening her mouth to scream. The sound was stifled when he jammed his palm over her mouth and gripped her head so hard the sides of her face ached. She tried to struggle but then he lifted her as if she weighed nothing and wrenched her in one violent jerk that put her back against his chest. One arm came around her waist like a thick-bodied snake and held her up until her feet hung in midair. She began to kick and fight, but both her arms were pinned beneath his forearm, and he walked closer to the steps with her, handling her easily, her satin skirts dragging the ground and fluttering against his knees. He talked to her the whole time, but very low, his lips hot and wet against her ear.

"His Grace has taken the most violent dislike of you, sweetheart. I hate it that it has to end this way. I suggested other solutions, I do want you to know that. I was the one who thought the announcement would be sufficient to make Will return to his duty, but, no, he had to be obstinate. God, he must love you to distraction. Few women can exert that kind of power over a man as strong as he is. You truly ought to be proud of yourself."

Trinity was screaming now, but the sounds were pitiful and muffled underneath his hand, and when he suddenly jerked his arm tight against her midriff, air gushed from her lungs and rendered her silent.

"There, that's much better. Think of this as the best thing for you. You're miserable watching him with Caroline. It'll only get worse, because Adrian wants it that way, and that's the way it's going to be. Especially now that I'm able to take care of you for good."

They were at the top of the steps now. Her feet were dangling in the air over the steep stairs, and she lay still, chest heaving in terror, afraid to struggle for fear he'd drop her.

"He told me to do whatever was necessary. He didn't care how or to what extreme measures I had to go. But here we are, an accident about to happen. Very convenient, as if it's meant to be. All I have to do is let go of you and down you go. Poor girl, they'll all say, she shouldn't have been out there in the dark like that. She should have gone through the house; she should have lit a candle. She tripped over that long skirt, no doubt. What a shame, she's such a beauty, and so young, oh, so very young, to die . . ."

Trinity renewed her fight, shaking her head back and forth. She managed to dislodge his hand though he held her body in a death lock.

"Please, please don't do this . . ."

"I have to," he whispered, very gently, almost soothingly, and the very cold-bloodedness of his manner engendered such bizarre horror that it seemed to freeze her blood.

"You see, I get the big prize. If I do you in, Adrian's promised to give me Adrianna. But, more importantly, Adrianna's dowry. She's a pretty enough little thing, though she lacks your fire, but she'll be tractable enough once I get her trained the way I like."

Trinity fought harder but he was coiling back, she could feel it in the way his muscles were flexing, he was getting ready to thrust her forward and off the landing. She groaned in blind terror, trying to grab hold of his coat, but couldn't because he had her pinned so tightly.

Then, somehow, she was going backward away from the steps, and she sobbed in relief, but he was still holding her, and it felt as if they were falling. They did fall, backward, and she landed on his chest, but his hands immediately let go of her, and she rolled away in a great tangle of silk and satin and rustling confusion, trying to scrabble away on her hands and knees. She saw the other person then, a mere shadow against the night, and she came to her feet, panting hard.

"Get up, you bastard," said the other man, oh, thank, God, it was Will, it was Will's voice, Trinity thought as he jerked Rainville up by his lapels. He pulled back his arm and hammered a fist hard into her tormentor's face and sent him reeling backward to the ground again. But Rainville wasn't down yet and he came up with a roar of fury, head down, butting Will in the gut and staggering him back toward the staircase. She could hear Will's breath knocked from him, and saw that Will held on to the back of Rainville's coat. They both fell, on their sides, grunting from the impact, and Trinity screamed and tried to scramble away as they rolled together on the edge of the drop-off.

It was so dark, she could barely tell who was on top, who was slamming the other in the face with the awful, dull-sounding thunks of fist against bone. She managed to collect her thoughts and, tripping once on her torn skirt, looked around frantically for some kind of weapon, anything she could hit Rainville with. There was nothing, but then there was a scream, long and fading, that trailed up the steps to her as a heavy male body bounced and rolled all the way to the bottom. A most final-sounding thud at the bottom, then the night was still, except for the hard rasping breaths of the man left at the top. He turned, and Trinity held her breath, terror for William filling her so completely that she could not breathe.

"Trinity! Where are you?"

Will, oh, thank God, thank God, she thought, running toward him in the darkness. She pressed herself against him, and he held her close. She clung to him as if she could never let go, and he, to her, until he could draw enough breath to speak coherently.

"Are you all right? Did he hurt you?"

Her wrists throbbed, her waist ached where he had squeezed her in a viselike grip, but she was all right, Will was all right. "I was so scared. He almost threw me off, for your father, Will! Your father told him to kill me if he had to."

She felt his entire body go rigid, his breath catch in his throat, then a couple of shouts rang out from somewhere on the lower terrace. Footsteps clicked on marble as someone began to run up the other staircase, and William suddenly thrust her out from him and held her at arm's length. His voice was low, unflinching in purpose.

"I want you to go now, and let me take care of this. I'll handle it. I don't want you involved at all. Go on, run." He gave her a small push. "The porch will take you to the next stairs, then go up to your room and wait for me. Nobody knows you're up here, and I don't intend for them to find out."

"No, I'll tell them what happened . . . I'll tell them he tried to murder me . . ."

"No, Trinity, you listen to me. Trust me, I know how to handle this. He might not be dead. Just go. I'll come to you as soon as I can."

As the sounds of the men came closer, Trinity turned and fled around the corner of the porch, her heart in her throat. There were more voices now, loud calls, but all behind her where William waited to fend off anyone who might try to pursue her flight. She stopped once and pressed herself behind a statue of Diana the huntress, and tried to control the thunder in her breast, the pulsating panic in her head. She was trembling all over, inside and out, but she forced herself on, entering the house through a darkened room and finally finding a servant staircase through which she could gain her chamber.

The bedchamber wing was empty, though she could hear the buzz coming from below, a great din of startled conversation as the news of Rainville's accident made its way through the ballroom. She lifted her skirts and ran the rest of the way, thrust open her door, and slammed it behind her.

Victoria whirled around from the middle of her room. Adrianna stood just behind her. "Trinity! Where have you been? We've been looking everywhere for you!"

Trinity threw herself into Victoria's arms, finally able to let loose with her sobs, if only at the sheer closeness she had come to death. "Rainville tried to kill me, tried to throw me down the steps . . ."

Victoria was horrified. "What? What are you saying?"

"He tried to kill me! Adrian told him to! He said he'd give Adrianna to him for his wife if he got rid of me!"

"No, no!" Adrianna cried in revulsion, coming forth to grab Trinity's hand. Trinity held on to her tightly, all the fright returning, threatening to overwhelm her.

Victoria stood aside, her face white, watching the two girls cry and cling to each other. When she spoke, her voice was calm in a strange, steady way that belied her agitated expression.

"Then it's for the best what I have planned. We're to leave tonight. I thought it best to flee at a later hour but there'll be great confusion at the moment with guests leaving and carriages coming around. We'll go now. Geoffrey's got us a coach waiting. We've got to go now if Adrian has stooped to such evil as this. There's no telling what he'd do next. We'd all be in danger here."

Trinity and Adrianna both raised tearstained faces, somehow shocked that she intended to up and leave at that very instant.

"Don't just stand there!" Victoria commanded sharply. "We haven't much time before someone notices our absence. Get your bags, quickly! The ship sails on the next tide, and we must be aboard."

"I can't just leave," Trinity began, realization dawning. "What about Will? What about us?"

Victoria turned to her, no, turned on her; her face, usually so kind and gentle, so understanding, now wreathed in anger. "Don't be a fool, Trinity. They tried to kill you tonight. Adrian wants you dead. Will was lucky to have gotten to you before you lay murdered on the ground. Adrian has all the power here. You have to come with us where you'll be safe."

"But Will, he saved my life, I can't just leave now, without a word . . . I love him, Victoria."

Victoria's face changed and she only looked sad, so sorrowful that tears glimmered in her eyes. "And I love him but he is caught here, by his duty, by his allegiance, he can't disentangle himself from Thorpe, no matter how much he wants to. I know you want to think differently, think that he'll give it all up, that he'll work it all out. He thinks that, he wants that, but making it happen is a whole different matter. Adrian will never stop. He'll do whatever it takes. For heaven's sake, Trinity, look what he's done to you already!"

Trinity stared at her, and the truth came rushing in like some kind of terrible oracle and she knew it was true. They could never fight Adrian's will here, not in England where he ruled with a power that nearly rivaled the King's. They had no chance for happiness here, and they never would.

"I hate him," she managed, a garbled, clogged growl of rage.

"I hate him, too."

Victoria's face had grown hard again, her eyes like flint and shining with emotion. "But he'll not run my life any longer. I will be an American now, completely, and so will you."

"But Will's not like him. He wants us to be together."

"If he wants that then he'll come to Charleston after you, and we'll make him understand why we had to escape this place. Oh, Trinity, darling, he knows already. Do you think he doesn't?

After this night? After you were almost sacri-
ficed in order to bring him into line? He'll be
glad you're safely out of here. Now come, we
only have a short time to get away before someone stops us."

Trinity stood very still, watching Victoria
sweep her dark woolen cloak around her. Adrianna did the same, and both women picked up
their bag and moved to the door. They stopped
and turned back, waiting wordlessly.

Unable to move, Trinity locked eyes with Victoria, a terrible battle raging inside her, and all
she could think, over and over again, was Will,
how could she leave him, how could she take
that chance, how could she? But what would life
be here? For their children if they were blessed
with them? Would they be in danger, too? The
idea was so haunting, so sickening that it forced
her mind to become crystal clear.

Without saying another word, she took her
own valise and a heavy cloak from the chifferobe
and followed the women out of the room, out of
England, and out of Will's life.

Chapter Twenty-six

In the hushed darkness of his private study Adrian Remington, the fourteenth Duke of Thorpe, one of the most powerful men of the realm, sat completely alone, a single candle flickering a meager light on the desk in front of him. Silent and still, his elbows rested on the desktop, his face buried in spread palms. How could everything have gone so wrong? God help him now.

Outside on the coach drive, two hours after Rainville's body had been found, he could still hear the low buzz of shocked guests, part of the anxious, never-ending mass exit. He felt absolutely sick inside, his chest so tight with deep aching that he found it laborious to breathe. He couldn't think about that, didn't care. All was lost. He was in ruin.

He lifted his head at the sound of the door opening, saw his eldest son on the threshold, and cringed at the expression so vivid upon his face. Fury was written there, plain, ugly, and he moved like some executioner down the length of the room—stone cold, trembling fury. Adrian set his shoulders, tensed up until the ache in his chest intensified, waiting for the explosion that was surely to come. He was not disappointed.

"Are you satisfied, Adrian? Are you happy? Let's see now, what have you accomplished this night with all your goddamn scheming and plotting and destroying. Rainville's dead, if you're wondering, but you probably don't care about him either. Not unless his death affects you, or your plans for your goddamn ambition. Oh, yes, we mustn't forget, Mother's fled this cursed house, and Adrianna, too, for good this time, if they've got any brains in their heads. And you'll be glad to hear that Trinity's gone with them. So you've lost your wife, your daughter, and last but not least, you've finally driven me away as well. I'm not your son anymore, not your heir, not anything to you."

"What are you talking about?" Adrian demanded gruffly, but he knew exactly what William meant, even before William answered. He knew by the terrible look in those green eyes, the disgust twisting his mouth, the utter, unbridled contempt that dripped like venom from every word his son uttered.

"Let me make it perfectly clear. There's going to be an inquest over Rainville's death. And surprise, I'm the primary suspect, not Trinity, as you no doubt hoped. And I intend to cooperate fully with the law, and after the truth comes out, I'm through with you. I want nothing else to do with you. I don't want your wealth. I don't want your power, or even the bloody title you've been dangling in front of me my entire life. I don't give a damn about any of it. What's more, your little game's over now. Tonight. Forever." He gave a tight smile that was more a grimace. "I'm going to tell it all, Father. Every sordid little detail that you've wanted to hide so badly, the secret that you even stooped to murder to gain your way . . ." He paused there and gave a small shake of his head as if he couldn't really believe it himself. "You were going to murder Trinity, weren't you? Without a second thought, and she, nothing but an innocent young woman, her only crime that she was the woman I loved. What have you become? What kind of evil devil are you?"

"You can't tell any of that," Adrian whispered thickly. "My reputation . . ." He faltered there, knowing himself how weak and guilty he sounded.

William gave a cold humorless laugh. "Your reputation is already dead. I'm telling Lord Rappaport that I'm married to Trinity and have been all along. He won't take so kindly to your making a fool out of Caroline, but I'm not protecting you anymore, Adrian, never again."

"I'll disinherit you!" Adrian roared, coming to his feet and sputtering with outrage.

"Do it, goddammit! I want nothing from you! Not even your name! God help Stephen if he stands beside you in this filthy affair!"

"You ingrate, you stupid boy, you . . ."

But William was already halfway to the door. He wasn't looking back, wasn't listening, and he walked out, through the door, leaving it standing wide open behind him. Adrian pounded the desk with both doubled fists, so angry he could barely think. He could feel the pulse in his temples, resonating like great clanging bells, could feel his heartbeat stuttering and skipping, almost stopping. Then the pain came, hit him at center chest like some awful mallet blow. He grabbed his breast, clutched his shirtfront. Sweat sprang up all over his body, wetting his face, his chest, arms, legs, and then another agony jolted him, a cold white flash of lightning. His knees crumpled, and he fell backward, overturning his chair as he fell in a sprawl. He landed hard on his shoulder, and still clutching his heart, he struggled to get air until his heart slowed, skipped a beat, then stopped completely.

Victoria smiled, with pleasure, of course, but more than that, with relief, as Adrianna and Geoffrey shared a most tender kiss as they finished repeating their vows. They stood in the quaint parlor of the rustic inn where Geoffrey had brought them nearly a month before after they'd landed in France. There was only family present, at least for the most part; she, Trinity, Eldon, but there were a few others watching the wedding, new friends they'd made here in the hotel. Though it was not in any form or fashion the wedding she had envisioned for her only daughter, she knew Adrianna was deliriously happy. What else could one ask for or want for such a dear child?

Adrianna gave a peal of happy laughter as she threw back her creamy short lace veil and ran to embrace her mother. Victoria held her and kissed both cheeks, but her own delight in her daughter's joyous day faded a good bit as Adrianna moved to embrace Trinity. She thrust the tiny bouquet of roses into her friend's hands, and though Trinity smiled and hugged her friend warmly, she could not keep up the pretense once Adrianna had rejoined Geoffrey and his shipboard friends at the dining-room table where the wedding cake was being served. Trinity turned and slipped away into the seaside garden.

Victoria sighed deeply, glancing one last time at the bride and groom, and finding them only interested in each other. She followed Trinity outside and found the poor child sitting on a bench at the end of the yard, her eyes fixed on the blue waters of the harbor. She was not weeping as Victoria had suspected she would be, but Victoria ached inside at the terrible melancholy revealed like an open wound upon her youthful features.

"Trinity, darling," she said with forced gaiety. "We miss you inside. Won't you come and have a piece of cake? It's covered with pecans and your favorite butter icing."

Trinity looked up and gave a wan smile but she looked as pale as a statue, her face a white oval against her bright coppery hair. Dark circles were underneath her eyes, and she hadn't felt well since they'd fled England. Victoria feared, however, that it was her tender heart that suffered more than her health.

"I cannot, Victoria. I'm truly sorry. I feel the need to sit here for a while."

Victoria seated herself beside her. She patted her hand, and although she had dreaded this moment, she realized it was time to reveal to Trinity what had happened in England. Trinity could feel no worse than she already did.

"I've gotten word from London. About Will."

Trinity's face jerked toward her, animation enlivening the dead look in her eyes, but the eager expression dwindled as she searched Victoria's serious eyes. "It's bad news?"

"Yes."

"How long have you known?"

"About a week. Geoffrey got hold of the London daily papers."

"Why haven't you told us before?"

"I wanted to wait until after the ceremony. Adrianna's been so happy, I couldn't bear to ruin her wedding day."

"Will's all right, isn't he?" Trinity looked absolutely terrified.

"Yes, but . . ." She sighed deeply, still coming to terms with what she was about to relate to Trinity. "My husband, Adrian. He's dead."

"Dead? When? How did it happen?"

"He had a heart attack the night we left. I pray to God that our departure didn't bring it on, but he's suffered with the ailment for many years. I suppose I'll have to live with my part in it." She wondered that she didn't feel any sense of loss for her husband of so many years, the father of her three children, but in truth, she'd lost him long ago, to his own ambition and greed, if she'd ever had him in the first place. "Apparently, the seizure was very quick, and then he was gone."

Trinity's face held on to the shock she felt but realization soon dawned. "That means that . . . that now Will is the Duke of Thorpe."

Victoria nodded. "Yes."

The two women stared at each other, both knowing this last revelation would dash Trinity's hopes that Will would take a ship to Calais to join them. Trinity's chest rose and fell, in a pitiful sigh of resignation.

"And Rainville? Did he recover?"

"No, he died the same night he fell. According to the reports, there was an inquest. They suspected Will to be involved in the beginning, but . . ." She paused again, afraid how the next news would affect the young woman at her side. "Will told them the truth, everything. About your marriage years ago, and his father's attempts at annulment. The scandal's knocked London to its knees, and Will's bearing the brunt of the gossip and condemnation."

Trinity shook her head. "He'll never forgive me for leaving him to that. Never."

"Once he gets things settled, he'll come for you. I saw the way he looks at you. He loves you, Trinity, I have no question on that count."

Victoria watched as Trinity's eyes began to shimmer, then a tear rolled slowly down one of her cheeks. She brushed it away with her fingertips. "I'm afraid he won't anymore, Victoria, not now."

"You must have faith in him, dear. There's still the war, you know. He can't know for sure where we are. You'll be together again, perhaps sooner than you think."

Trinity turned to her then, more tears falling, but she ignored them this time. She stared at Victoria for a long moment, then spoke, in a voice so low that Victoria had to lean closer.

"I think I am with child."

Oh, dear God, no, thought Victoria, then realized that if true, Trinity not only carried Will's child, but Victoria's own first grandchild. Trinity looked miserable and defeated as if she sat waiting for Victoria's words of condemnation. Victoria took both her hands and looked deep into Trinity's eyes.

"William will be pleased, I know, once he finds out."

"No, he won't, he won't be pleased at all. What if he doesn't come for us? What if he can't forget that I left him without a word, without even saying good-bye? I promised him I wouldn't, Victoria, I gave him my word."

"He will come," Victoria answered firmly, squeezing her hands reassuringly. "But if he should not, or cannot come to you for a time, then we will take care of you. You are my daughter-in-law, but I love you as much as I love Adrianna, my own daughter. You've been married to Will since you were a baby, and as far as I'm concerned you always will be."

Tears began to leak in earnest now, and when Trinity sobbed out loud, Victoria pulled her head onto her shoulder and held her tightly. She let the child weep against her and murmured reassuring words but she was afraid, too, afraid that their marriage would never be recognized, not now that Will had inherited and bore the responsibilities of a dukedom upon his shoulders. Well, whatever else happened, she vowed firmly inside her heart, she would stand beside Trinity, she and Adrianna, and Geoffrey and Eldon, but would that be enough for the poor suffering young woman who wept so brokenheartedly against her shoulder? No, she thought, not at the moment, but only time would tell. Sighing, she sat for a long time as William's wife wept her heart out.

Long months later Geoffrey Kingston rode through the streets of Charleston like an avenging angel, his breakneck speed making a great clatter upon the cobbles of East Battery Street as he raced toward the Remington town house. Most residents of Charleston were already abed or getting ready to retire, but he was pleased to see that most of the rooms of Victoria's home still blazed with lights.

He brought his horse to a skidding halt, leaping to the ground before it could stop, then left it sidestepping on the pavement, reins still dangling. He ran up the front steps and burst through the door.

"Adrianna! Victoria!" he yelled, his joy evident

in his face, his teeth white in a face mud-spattered from a wild, reckless ride through the swamps. No one answered or appeared, so he took the stairs three steps at a time, still yelling for his family.

In the upstairs hall, Adrianna came running toward him, a large white pitcher in her hands.

"Geoff! What is it? What's wrong?" she cried, then gasped as Geoffrey grabbed her arms and whirled her around, causing the warm water to slosh out all over both of them.

"The war's over! It's over, Adi! We've won it! We've beaten Cornwallis! He surrendered at Yorktown!"

Adrianna squealed with delight and he whirled her again, spilling more water, soaking their shoes but neither of them noticed.

"Is it true? Can it be?" Adrianna cried as several of the servants heard the commotion and appeared at the end of the hallway.

"Yes, we've defeated George! We're free! Free from tyranny!"

"Come then, come quickly, and tell Mother and Trinity," Adrianna said, smiling and giving the heavy pitcher over to him. "But we've a wonderful surprise, too. Trinity's had her baby tonight. A little girl."

"A girl!" Geoffrey cried in delight. "Is she all right? Is Trinity?"

"Yes, they're both fine, but come, we've got to tell them the news!"

Geoffrey followed her down the hall to Trinity's room, pulling his wife close for a kiss when she stopped to turn the handle. "I've missed you, sweetheart."

"And I've missed you," she whispered in return but both were too excited with their tidings to linger long without telling the others. She opened the door, and Geoffrey followed her inside.

Victoria was sitting at the side of the bed but she jumped up at the sight of him. "Geoff! I thought it was your voice, then decided it couldn't be. What're you doing here!"

Geoffrey moved forward eagerly, his smile so broad and pleased he knew he could not stop it. "I've come with good tidings. The war's at an end. We've won it, Victoria, we've won!"

He'd kept his voice low because he could see that Trinity slept, her hair like a flame against the pillows. A tiny bundle lay in the crook of her arm, and her chin was tucked on top of its head.

"No! No!" Victoria placed her hand on her breast, shaking her head in disbelief, but her eyes were bright with joy. "When? How?"

"Washington managed to bottle up Cornwallis and all his troops on the peninsula at Yorktown. Lafayette and the French navy blockaded them there, and they were done for! We're free! We're a free, independent country!"

Victoria sobbed, but she was smiling through her tears, and she fumbled for her handkerchief. Geoffrey saw Trinity stir, and he went down on his knees beside the bed, wanting to be the one to tell her. She'd been so unhappy since they'd left England behind. Finally they had news that would make her smile!

"Trin, Trin, are you awake?" he whispered, and she opened her eyes. She peered up at him, cradling her baby nearer.

"Did you see her?" she asked at once, her voice hoarse. She looked exhausted, with the purplish smudges underneath her eyes that had been there for months.

"Yes, she's beautiful. Are you all right?"

Trinity nodded. "I just wish, well . . ." She paused, and he watched her eyes fill. "You know what I wish."

He smiled and took her hand. "Trinity, I have wonderful news. We've won the war. It's over."

Trinity lay very still as he told them all the details, with both Victoria and Adrianna at his sides. By now most of the servants had heard and were standing around as well, and Trinity wept softly with happiness while her little daughter slept soundly in her arms, oblivious to all that was going on around her.

Once the story had been told, Geoffrey squeezed Trinity's hand. "You picked a good day to have her. And hey, what've you named her? Nobody's mentioned her name."

"I haven't yet," Trinity said, touching the soft wisps of dark curls atop the baby's head. "But now I know what I shall name her. I'll call her Liberty, in celebration of this day."

Adrianna clapped her hands in delight. "That's beautiful, Trinity. And now Will can come to get you. I know he will."

Geoffrey saw Victoria shoot her daughter a look of caution. He turned back to Trinity, and though she smiled and looked quickly down at little Liberty, he saw that hope still hovered in her eyes. Will bloody well better come to her and his daughter, he thought, or he'd make sure he did. Those were his thoughts, but outside he merely smiled reassuringly at Trinity, and pretended like he didn't notice the tears dampening her cheeks.

Chapter Twenty-seven

Some months after the war had ended, William stopped in front of his mother's town house in Charleston and looked up at the flag Victoria had draped from the upstairs balcony. The symbol of the United States of America, he thought, realizing he had not seen the new republic's flag. It was striking with its red and white stripes and circle of white stars. It fitted the newly born country and the people who had been willing to give their lives to win their freedom. He glanced down the street.

The British were long gone, upping their anchors and sailing away for good last December, a month after the Americans and Great Britain had signed their peace treaty in Paris. He'd wanted to come then, had wanted to come every day since, and every day before the war had ended. But he had had to deal with his father's funeral, with his own succession as duke, with the ugly scandals and the awful affair with Caroline's family.

It had taken more than a year to get his house in order and then they'd lost the war on top of everything else. And here he was, like the fool he'd always been where Trinity was concerned, but he wanted to see her again, had to see her to tell her what he'd done. He wondered now if he'd made the right decision. He had not heard from her since the day she'd fled from him without even a note of explanation. That pretty well told him that she preferred things to stay exactly as they were, but there was one small point to consider. They were still married. That's what he'd come to discuss with her, that's what they had to work out now.

Trinity might not even be here with Victoria, he realized, he had no idea where she was, what she was doing, or with whom. She could have met another man, married him, a patriot who shared her future in the fledgling United States. The thought rankled, hurt him, she still had that power over him, but he set his jaw and renewed his resolve. It was time to settle things with her, once and for all, for better or for worse. He climbed the steps, not unaware of the irony of that last phrase.

A maid opened the door for him and must have recognized him at once, by the way her face paled milk white. She sank into a deep curtsy. "Your Grace, we did not expect you," she murmured as he moved past her into the house. She looked out into the street as if expecting a great retinue of liveried servants to be following a man so great. He gave a bitter inward smile at that notion, then answered her unasked question.

"I'm traveling alone. Is my mother here?" *Is Trinity here?* he wanted to shout out, but he could not bring himself to whisper the words, for fear she was not.

"Yes, Your Grace. She's taking tea in the parlor. She will be mightily surprised to see you."

"I expect so," he answered, trailing after her as she led the way down the hall. "Is she alone?"

"Yes, Your Grace."

And indeed she was. He found her sitting in a chair, a cup of tea poised in her hand. But she came to her feet at once, rattling it down onto the table as she smiled broadly, clearly glad to see him.

"William! Why, mercy be, you've come at last. I had no idea."

"I thought I'd surprise you," he said, slightly startled at the obvious delight she was exhibiting.

"Well, you accomplished that, I tell you true. Please sit down. I'm just speechless at the sight of you."

William looked around, glancing through the open sliding doors into the next room, but saw no one.

"I should congratulate you on your succession. How do you find it now that you are a man of such high rank?"

"I find it tedious," he replied, able to be truthful for the first time in a long while. "Especially since I've spent most of my time tidying up Adrian's nasty schemes."

"I find it admirable that you sought to do so." Victoria hesitated as he sat down in a chair across from her and watched her pour him a cup of tea. "I must apologize for the way we left England. I felt I had no choice, given the danger we found ourselves in. I do hope you can forgive me."

William took the cup. Forgive her, he thought, he hadn't ever really blamed her. But he could blame Trinity, he could blame her for every damned hour of lonely despair he'd endured for months on end.

"I can't say I blamed you for wanting to get away. You never liked England, and Father wasn't exactly a loving husband."

"May he rest in peace," Victoria was gracious enough to add. They settled into a short, uncomfortable silence for a moment until Victoria spoke again. "How long do you plan to stay here, dear?"

"Not long. I have responsibilities in England now."

"Of course. And Stephen? Is he well?"

"Stephen's fine. He's calling on Caroline now, and believe it or not, her father is letting him court her."

"I take it by that that you've ended your association with her."

William studied her, wondering that she would even have to ask that question. He nodded. "As I'm sure you know, the whole sordid mess came out after you left. Every hideous detail. She was so humiliated and offended that she fled the country for a year's stay in southern Italy."

Victoria sipped her tea. Well, he thought,

wasn't she going to mention Trinity? Was she going to make him ask her?

"Is Adrianna about?" he asked pointedly.

"No. She and Geoffrey live at Palmetto Point now that the war's been won. They're out there now, I'm afraid. They'll be very sorry they weren't here to see you."

So that's where Trinity is, he thought, then tried to reply in a casual manner. "That's all right. I thought I'd pay the plantation a call before I sail again."

Victoria smiled. "They'll be most pleased to see you. They, too, felt awful leaving you alone to face so much scandal."

He nodded, then nearly choked on his tea at Victoria's next casually uttered remark.

"I do hope you'll take a moment to see Trinity before you go. She's taking the sun outside in the garden."

William felt his heart rise up, as if it were a balloon suddenly cut free, tried to grab hold of it, fearing his smile would reveal everything to his mother. Trinity had left him once, had made no attempt to contact him. He had no idea if she would be pleased to see him or not.

"Is she well?" he managed somehow, but his voice betrayed him, coming out all gruff and unnatural. Victoria's dark eyes glowed with something he could not identify.

"She's well."

Well, call her inside, dammit, he thought, but he couldn't bring himself to suggest it.

"I'm sure she'd be delighted to see you, Will. Why don't you go see if you can find her?"

William's pride rose like a cobra to guard his heart. No, he wouldn't do that. He had traveled the width of the Atlantic to see her, had he not? She could damn well be the one to walk inside and say hello to him. "All right. I think I will."

"I think that's a very good idea, Your Grace."

As he set down his cup and stood, Victoria smiled and reached for his hand. "I'm very glad to see you again, Will. I'm pleased you came to us."

William leaned down and kissed her forehead but he was anxious now to find Trinity, for better or worse. There it was again, a phrase designed to haunt him. He left his mother smiling after him and exited onto the side veranda that overlooked the garden. Once, an eternity ago, he had stood there before and watched Trinity dig in the aster beds. He had been attracted to her, even then, just after he had arrived in Charleston, but how could he have known all that would come after that fateful day?

He stopped at the banister, then froze when he finally saw her. She was on a bench near the same spot where she had handled the trowel so long ago. She sat motionlessly, hatless, the sun gleaming on her hair. His heart reacted, racing with excitement, with the purest pleasure he'd ever known, but he wondered how he would be received. If she would shun him again. Well, there was only one way to find out. He turned and headed for the staircase that would take him out to the garden.

Trinity sat still, enjoying the warmth of the sun. It was especially mild for April, and she was glad that spring had come with all its colors and flowers and long, sunny days. She seemed always to feel cold, especially inside her breast where her heart lay dead and unbeating like a block of ice. Only little Liberty could thaw her sadness and make her smile. She turned her head and looked at her child, at Will's child, where she crawled about on a patchwork quilt spread out in the shade of the grape arbor.

Libby sat inside a ring of her tiny toys, a red rag ball that her Grandpapa Eldon had made for her before he went back home to Palmetto Point the day before, a beautiful doll with a porcelain head that Victoria had found in the attic, one of Adrianna's old favorites. There was a wagon nearby, and a tiny infant chair that rocked upon runners, and a box full of toy soldiers that Will was purported to have loved best of all when he had occupied the same nursery.

Trinity fixed her attention back on her lap, her needles clicking busily as she concentrated on the shawl she was crocheting. She almost laughed at herself, thinking it was sad indeed that she had been reduced to enjoying needlework when she had despised such womanly pursuits for the vast majority of her days. But it kept her hands busy, helped to keep her from dwelling constantly on Will. She couldn't bear to think about him anymore. She would go insane, wondering, hoping, despairing that he would never see their beautiful little girl. That he didn't care.

She kept sighing, one after another, as she worked, over and over again, until she got angry at herself, and threw the lacy garment to the ground, needles still jutting out from the fragile netting. She wished she had Moonbeam here in the Charleston stables, where she could jump on her back and ride and ride until she was too tired to think.

"I see you still don't particularly enjoy needle-work."

No, it couldn't be, she thought. It sounded like Will's voice, but he was in England. How many times had she dreamed of hearing his voice like this? Or had thought she'd heard him call to her from a crowd at the marketplace or while passing a group of men on the street corner?

"Trinity?"

The low timbre was closer, and too vivid to be imagined, and she turned her head slowly, heart beating in hard thumps, half-afraid to look. And there he stood. On the path before her, in the flesh, looking as handsome as ever, as big and strong, and as beloved, dappled by sunlight dancing through palm fronds.

Somehow she realized that she was on her feet, staring at him, her voice robbed from her. She couldn't believe it. He was standing right there, in front of her. Liberty, she thought, he'd finally get to see his daughter. The baby was behind him, hidden in part by a hedge. William was unaware of her.

"I hope you don't mind my coming out here. Victoria suggested it."

What did he mean by that? she thought with horrible dread. Had he not come to Charleston to see her? Had he intended to leave again without speaking with her, if Victoria hadn't reminded him of her presence? Hurt hit her like a slosh of ice water, and she clasped her hands to stop their trembling.

"I think I would've been upset if you had not," she managed somehow, more calmly than she ever though possible. She sat down, no, her legs gave way. She strove to appear reposed when all she wanted was to run into his arms and press herself against him and tell him how much she had missed him, how sorry she was that she had run away and left him.

"May I sit down?"

"Please do," she invited, all very formal and polite, wondering how he could seem so unaffected when her heart was giddy with the joy of seeing him again. She chewed on her bottom lip to retain control, but she couldn't take her eyes off him. He looked good, so handsome, and healthy and sound that she could not govern the smile that took hold of her lips, nor the words that sprang from her heart. "I'm so glad to see you, Will."

"Truly?" he asked after a beat. "I'm surprised, considering the way you took off without a word of farewell."

So he was angry, she realized with plummeting heart, still, after all these months. Had he been angry enough to allow their annulment to go through? She had to know, had to.

"You're my husband. I've missed you. Desperately."

"Am I?"

So he had let their marriage be dissolved. She glanced away, at Libby, who had rolled onto her back and was playing with her bare toes. "In my heart you are," she said, very low, without looking at him. "You'll always be."

"Not enough to stand beside me, it seems."

Trinity was tired of their verbal fencing. "I had to go, Will, don't you see? If I had been there, everything would've been worse for you, for everyone. I was scared. They were trying to kill me."

William plunged a hand through the waves of his thick auburn hair, an agitated gesture, emotional. "You could have come back, once the war ended."

"I was afraid you didn't want me to."

He looked at her then, seemed nonplussed by her remark, and Trinity had had enough of talk. She had little pride left, not when it came to Will, and she could not bring herself to wait a moment longer. She had to touch him, she had to, or she'd surely die.

She stood up. He stood up. Their eyes locked, the intensity shaking them both, then she walked to him, knowing that the next few moments would determine if she'd ever truly be happy again. If he rejected her, if he pushed her away, or told her he had ended their marriage, she would wither away inside until her heart crumbled to ashes.

Trinity stopped first in front of him, then she put her arms around his waist and lay her head against his chest. She clung tightly to him, shutting her eyes, praying he still loved her. "I love you, Will. I've always loved you. Since I was a little girl."

He stood, rigid and solid, then his arms came around her, tight, tighter and tighter as he caught the back of her head with his palm. He pulled her onto her toes, and she could hear his heart thudding under her ear.

"Oh, God help me, but I've missed you," he muttered breathlessly, gruff, tortured. "God only knows how much."

Then he had her face cradled in his palms and he was kissing her, his mouth warm against hers, as wonderful and sweet as she remembered. But she had to know more, before she could tell him about the baby.

"Why did you come, Will? Are we still married? Do you still want me?"

Will drew her down on the bench beside him. "Yes, of course, we are. Do you think I'd seek an annulment? I was afraid you'd changed your mind as time went on and I heard nothing from you. If you still care about me, why didn't you write?"

Trinity lifted his hand to her lips and kissed his knuckles. "I wanted to make sure you hadn't married another. I knew you'd inherited. I knew you felt betrayed by what I'd done. I had to be sure that you still wanted me before I came to you, because . . ."

Will's eyes questioned her but she had no need to speak because Liberty chose that moment to make herself known. She sputtered angrily from her place on the blanket, then ended in a long wail that made Will jump. He came to his feet and swung around toward the wriggling child. His face blanched, and he turned shocked eyes back to Trinity. Heat burned behind her eyelids.

"Would you like to meet your daughter, Will? Her name's Liberty, but we usually call her Libby, and she's wanted to meet her father for ever so long."

Will seemed stunned, but he followed her as she moved across the patch of grass and picked up the little girl. Liberty quit fussing at once, and Trinity turned with her, proudly holding her up for Will to see.

"My God, she's beautiful." Will stared at her but very slowly a smile began to spread across his face. "She's got your hair."

"And your eyes."

Libby seemed to notice him for the first time, and shocked them both by stretching out chubby arms toward him. Will took her, hugged her close, too close it seemed, because the baby began to cry.

Will looked down at her, his face so wreathed with delight that Trinity's heart flew free. They were going to make it. She knew it in that moment, could see it as if she looked into a crystal ball. Despite the differences, despite the complications of his being an English duke, they would make it. They would have a happy life and raise Libby with all the love and warmth they felt for each other.

Will laughed when Libby grabbed his cravat and pulled it loose, and then he gathered Trinity to him with his other arm.

"I'll never forgive you for not telling me about her," he said, but then his lips found hers, and Trinity knew he would forgive her, that he already had, and she lost herself in the embrace she had dreamed about for so long, neither she nor Will aware of Libby's chortling laughter as they squeezed her tightly between them.

Epilogue

Trinity sat in the great carved chair on the dais of the ballroom of Thorpe Hall, watching the festivities. In the tradition of every Duke of Thorpe since Will's first ancestor assumed the title, William was at work in the pine-festooned hall, giving away huge wicker baskets of fruits and sweetcakes to the household staff.

All the maids, and butlers, gardeners, coachmen, footmen, even the shepherds and stable-boys, lined up before the gigantic hearth, so great in size that logs five feet in length burned on the iron grate. Everyone wore their best clothes, many having adorned themselves in the brand-new blue wool cloaks that she and her husband had brought from America for them.

Hundreds of candles in the hanging chandeliers only added a glow of warmth to the good spirits and happy expressions alive in the faces of each and all, and in that moment, she truly regretted that they lived more than half the year away from these good people, back in Charleston. But, she admitted, when she was at Trenton Hill, which Will had rebuilt for Victoria, she felt the same way about her beloved Carolinas.

Across the floor Libby was walking alongside her father, her beautiful heart-shaped face quite sober as she handed out the baskets in turn, nodding formally as each family bowed and wished her a happy Christmas. At times, however, the solemn ceremony was a little more than her feisty, five-year-old heart could contain and she'd dance forward and give hugs to some of her particularly beloved friends on the domestic staff.

She was a delightful child, beautiful, adorable with copper hair and Will's lovely emerald eyes. Will absolutely doted on her, so much so that Trinity often laughed at him about it, but then, who didn't spoil her? Libby certainly had her Grandpapa Eldon and Uncle Stephen twisted around her fingers. Right now, in fact, Stephen had her hoisted upon his shoulders so that she could reach a pretty bauble he'd placed upon the mantel for her.

As the music began again, drifting down through the vaulted hall from the musicians' balcony at the rear of the giant room, many of the servants began to dance. William came to her at once, and bowed deeply before her chair.

"My lady, may I have the pleasure?"

"Aye, Your Grace, indeed you may."

They both laughed together, and she felt Will squeeze her fingers as he led her out onto the floor. Many of his people cried their names with wishes of good fortune for the coming year, and Trinity again marveled at the difference Will had brought into the cold, austere mansion since his father's reign as Duke of Thorpe.

"Are you feeling all right?" Will whispered, moving his hand around to her belly.

"Aye, your son is quiet tonight, at least for a while."

Will smiled and drew her in closer, and she warmed to his closeness, wondering how they had ever taken so long to get together. Since those early separations they had never spent longer than a fortnight apart, and both of them vowed they never would. In truth, she felt neither could bear being away from Libby so long.

As if conjured by her mother's fond smile, that little angel appeared, pushing her way between them, holding on to Will's waist as she stepped atop his glossy black boots to join them in their dance. Trinity put her arms around her, and kissed the top of her head, then smiled when Will did the same to her.

"Merry Christmas, my love," he whispered.

"Merry Christmas, Your Grace," she whispered back, quite sure that no one had ever been blessed with a love so splendid as theirs, and then Will whirled them away, duchess and daughter, and soon to be son.